Books edited by Robert Silverberg

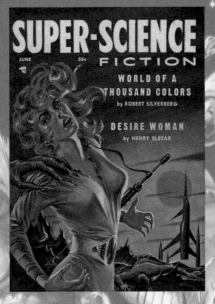

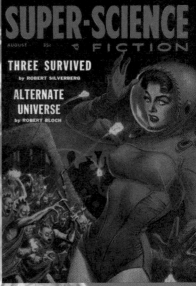

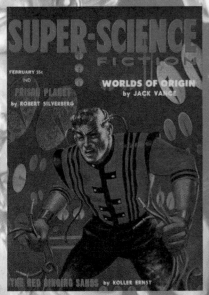

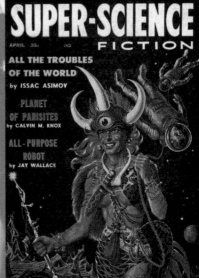

TALES FROM
SUPER-SCIENCE FICTION

Author Robert Silverberg and artist Ed Emshwiller circa 1957

TALES FROM
SUPER-SCIENCE
FICTION

Edited by
ROBERT SILVERBERG

Illustrations by
ED EMSHWILLER
FRANK KELLY FREAS
PAUL ORBAN
WILLIAM BOWMAN

HAFFNER PRESS
ROYAL OAK, MICHIGAN
2012

FIRST EDITION

PUBLISHER'S ACKNOWLEDGMENTS

The publisher wishes to thank the following contributors to the preparation of this book:

Gene Bundy, Debbie Lang, and the Special Collections staff at the Jack Williamson Science Fiction Library at Eastern New Mexico University.

Doug Ellis & Deb Fulton

Mark Steven Corrinet & Laura Brodian Freas

Carol Emshwiller

Bean & Leaf Cafe of Royal Oak, Zuma Coffee House of Birmingham, and Caribou Coffee of Royal Oak.

Rick Ollerman for proofreading the manuscript.

For
W.W. SCOTT
a cup of kindness yet, for auld lang syne

CONTENTS

INTRODUCTION
Robert Silverberg

The operative word was FUN. Take one easy-going old-timer of a pulp editor who thought science fiction was pretty silly stuff but knew how to slap a magazine together, two ambitious young writers who had rather more respect for the genre than he did but were willing to bang out space opera to order at high velocity to take care of the rent, and a publisher willing to pay quickly and well so long as his magazine came out on time every two months, and the result was a lot of fun, and even some profit, for all concerned.

It all started in the spring of 1956, when I was still a Columbia undergraduate, three months away from my degree, but already selling science-fiction stories about as fast as I could write them. I was living in a ramshackle residence hotel on West 114th St., just across Broadway from the Columbia campus—$10 a week for a room with shared kitchen privileges—and next door to me lived another young writer, a certain Harlan Ellison, who had come to New York in the winter of 1954-55, phoned me to let me know he was in town, went up to Columbia to see me, and decided to rent a room in the 114th St. place also.

His writing career had not taken off quite as suddenly or as spectacularly as mine had, for I had had a big assist from yet another writer living in that building—Randall Garrett, who, like Harlan, had turned up suddenly in New York looking for a place to live. Garrett took a room down the hall from me, and very quickly we fell into a busy and lucrative collaborative relationship. Under his aegis I met all the New York's s-f editors in the summer of 1955—John W. Campbell, Howard Browne, Robert W. Lowndes, Larry Shaw, and a couple of others—and began selling stories to all of them, some in collaboration with Garrett, some on my own.

Harlan had had a slower start; but by the early months of 1956 he, too, was off and running in the field. Just as I had been, he was an avid science-fiction reader who longed to have his own stories published in the magazines he had read in his teens, and very quickly Harlan joined me on Howard Browne's team of staffers at *Amazing* and placed material with several of the other editors.

He had discovered, though, that he also had a knack for writing hard-boiled crime stories—tales of juvenile-delinquent kid-gangs became a specialty of his—and in March or April of 1956 he began selling to two new magazines that published such material—*Trapped* and *Guilty*. They paid an extravagant two cents a word, big money in those days. It was twice as much as what most of the science-fiction magazines we were selling to then would pay, and $100 for a 5000-word story was a considerable bonanza when his room rent was $10 a week. Harlan went downtown to visit their editor, one W.W. Scott, at his office near Manhattan's Columbus Circle, and brought him a stack of crime stories that had proven not quite good enough for the reigning magazine of that field at the time, *Manhunt*. Scott bought them all. He seemed willing to buy as many stories as Harlan could bring in.

Harlan was kind enough to let me in on this bonanza, and, busy as I was turning out science fiction for all my regular markets, I started doing crime stories too. My records show the sale of "Get Out and Stay Out" to *Guilty* in June, 1956, right about the time I received my Columbia degree, and "Clinging Vine" to the companion magazine, *Trapped,* a couple of weeks later.

And then we both learned that W.W. Scott, acting, I think, on a suggestion from Harlan, had talked his publisher into bringing out a science-fiction magazine too, and would like us to write some stories for him. It would pay the same two-cents-a-word rate. Suddenly Harlan and I had the inside track on a lucrative new market.

The new magazine was going to be called *Super-Science Fiction*. Harlan and I both knew that there already had been a science-fiction magazine with a very similar title: *Super Science Stories,* which had appeared from 1940 to 1943 under the editorship of the very young Frederik Pohl, and, after a wartime hiatus, from 1949 to 1951, when it was again killed by wartime paper shortages, under Ejler Jakobssen, with Damon Knight as his assistant editor. I doubt that editor Scott was aware that another s-f magazine called *Super Science* had been in existence just five years before—only true fans like Harlan and me would have known that—and in any case he wouldn't have cared, since the predecessor magazine was out of business and, besides, it had not had quite the same title.

Scott—"Scottie," Harlan called him, though he preferred to be called "Bill"—was a short, cheerfully cantankerous old guy who would have fit right into a 1930s Hollywood movie about old-time newspapermen, which was what I think he had been before he drifted into magazine editing. His employer was a company called Crestwood Publishing Company, the main activity of which was producing slick men's magazines with names like *True Men* and *Man's Life.* Scottie was the one-man fiction-magazine department, with a tiny office of his own, a room just about big enough for a desk, a bookcase, and a shelf for holding recently submitted manuscripts. To us—and we both were barely past 21—he looked to be seventy or eighty years old, but probably he was 55 or thereabouts. His voice was a high-pitched cackle; he had a full set of top and bottom dentures, which he didn't always bother to wear; and I never saw him without his green eyeshade, which evidently he regarded as an essential part of the editorial costume. He freely admitted to us that he knew next to nothing about science fiction and cared even less, and invited us to bring him as much material as we could manage.

It was like being handed the key to Fort Knox. Two cents a word, for all the stories we could write! I brought him my first submission in late June—"Collecting Team," I called it, but Scottie turned out to be a compulsive title-changer, and when he published it as the lead story in the first issue of *Super-Science Fiction* he called it "Catch 'Em All Alive."

As you will see shortly, "Catch 'Em All Alive" tells the tale of a planetary exploration team from Earth that gets into trouble on an alien world. Scarcely an original theme—Stanley G. Weinbaum had dealt with it as far back as 1934, and so had many later writers, A.E. van Vogt's "Black Destroyer" of 1939 being a magnificent example of the type. My story was handled smoothly enough—it has been reprinted any number of times in textbooks for high-school-age readers—but its chief significance for *Super-Science Fiction* was that it impressed upon Scottie the excellence of the exploration-team plot, and no subsequent issue of the magazine was without one or two stories that were built on it, usually ending with a dark final twist. Seeing his fondness for the theme, I took care to keep him well supplied with such stories as the months went along.

In fact I took care to keep him well supplied with everything—month after month, story after story. I suppose I wrote nearly a third of the 120 stories the magazine published in the three years of its life: thirty-six of them. I also did batches of science fillers that Scottie asked me to write (at the same two cents a word!) to help him solve makeup problems by rounding off half-filled pages. They were little essays on space exploration, computer research, an interesting new drug called LSD, and anything else of the sort that happened to be making headlines just then. I would hand them in in batches, and he would make up pen-names for them as he used them—"Scott Nevets," "Steven Rory," "J. Foster Blake," and so forth. (Some assiduous Silverberg bibliographer really ought to include them in my roster of pseudonyms.)

The first issue of *Super-Science*, dated December 1956 and published in late September, was a reasonably strong one, considering that its editor knew next to nothing about science fiction and that two of its stories, mine and one by Harlan, were by wet-behind-the-ears kids and the rest had been drawn from the floating assortment of existing rejects currently circulating in the field. The Ellison story, marked by the intensity and tension that would be his narrative trademark in the years ahead, was called "Psycho at Mid-Point." The others in the issue were the work of two reliable old pros, R.R. Winterbotham and Milton Lesser, and one talented newcomer, Henry Slesar. Kelly Freas had done the cover. *Super-Science* was cheaply printed by an infamous lowest-bidder printer in Massachusetts, and its pages had an unmistakable printed-by-the-lowest-bidder look about them, but the covers were always bright and vivid, and were done by two of the best artists in the field—Ed Emsh for the second issue, Freas again for the third, and so on, Freas and Emsh, Emsh and Freas, for the whole run of eighteen issues.

And, as I said a few pages back, we were all having fun. Nobody took the work very seriously, but we were pros, and we all did a professional job. Those Freas and Emsh covers were lively, imaginative things. And Harlan and I, the core of Bill Scott's staff, quickly caught on to the kind of strong narrative and colorful prose that he preferred, and, powerfully motivated by the quick and relatively easy two cents a word, made the journey downtown from our Upper West Side apartments to his midtown office just about every month with something new for him.

The only issue I missed, I think, was the second one, February, 1957. I was too busy in the summer of 1956, graduating from college, getting married, and writing a three-part magazine serial in collaboration with Randall Garrett, to follow up immediately on my story for issue one, though I did turn in another batch of science fillers. Ellison had two stories in the second issue, though, one under the not very obscure pseudonym of "Ellis Hart," and the rest of the issue was drawn, once again, from the reject pool that such agents as Scott Meredith and Harry Altshuler kept constantly circulating to any new magazine. The third issue had one Ellison and one Silverberg story; the fourth, two of mine, one of his. And so it went, issue after issue. As I got into the swing of it, I began turning in longer stories. A 12,000-word story, the longest that the small magazine could hold—and from the fifth number on I was writing at least one of those for almost every issue—paid $240, more than the monthly rent on the handsome West End Avenue apartment that I had moved into after my marriage, and I could turn one out in two working days. Scottie never rejected anything I brought him, and I doubt that he turned down anything of Harlan's, either.

We were, of course, tremendously useful to him—we were eager, we were ambitious, we were jackrabbit fast, and we knew how to put together a competent science-fiction story. Scottie knew that whenever we turned up in his office, and one or the other of us was there practically every week, we would be bringing with us something publishable. Meanwhile, the three or four literary agents who specialized in s-f were trying to dump their ancient unsold material on Scottie, a fact of which he was, of course, quite aware.

You merely had to look at those bedraggled manu-

scripts to know that they had been making the rounds
for years. But on one memorable occasion the evidence
of that came right along with the story. That day I found
Scottie convulsed with laughter—it was a kind of hee-
hawing giggle—when I entered his office. He handed
me one of the gray folders in which Scott Meredith, my
own agent as well as the agent for dozens of other science-fiction writers, enclosed the manuscripts he submitted. I knew that that agency had a vast file of green index
cards on which Scott's first reader typed a brief summary
of the plot of every story the agency accepted for revision
and an evaluation of its chances for sale. (After the Meredith agency went out of business, a friend gave me the
huge drawer of green cards for my own stories. A typical
green-card comment on one of my earliest ones: "Rather
weak job about alien who comes to Earth to buy greatest
art treasures." It did sell, but only after four rejections, all
noted on the card.)

Why was Scottie laughing? Because this time, through
some grotesque mailroom error at the agency, the manuscript had been sent out with its green card clipped to
its cover. "Look at this!" Scottie cackled. "Been traveling
around since 1947! Rejected eighteen times! I've never
even *heard* of some of these magazines! Since 1947! *1947!*"
He couldn't get over it. He didn't buy the story, either, and
I guess it is still circulating in whatever afterworld there is
for stories that nobody ever wanted to buy.

Ellison and I, though, brought him fresh, new manuscripts all the time, making his life as an editor ever so
much easier, and he rewarded us with a constant stream
of acceptances. Some time in 1957, though, Harlan had

moved along to an army base, having been careless enough to let himself get drafted. (My draft exemption as a college student was still valid, and remained that way long enough for me to sidestep military service altogether.) So the job of filling the pages of *Super-Science Fiction, Trapped,* and *Guilty* devolved almost entirely on me. I rose valiantly to the occasion. For *Trapped* and *Guilty* I wrote bushels of crime stories ("Mobster on the Make," "Russian Roulette," "Murder for Money," etc., etc., etc.) and for *Super-Science Fiction* I did two or three stories an issue under a wide assortment of pseudonyms: Eric Rodman, Dan Malcolm, Calvin M. Knox, Richard F. Watson, Alex Merriman, and I know not how many others. A lot of them hewed close to what I had helped to define as the *Super-Science* formula, exploration-team stories or straightforward space opera: stories set on alien planets with vivid scenery, involving hard-bitten characters who sometimes arrived at bleak ends. I suspect I derived the manner and some of the content from the South Sea stories of Joseph Conrad and W. Somerset Maugham, both favorite writers of mine. At two cents a word for lots and lots of words I could support myself very nicely from that one market, and I did for three jolly years.

The non-Silverberg stories that *Super-Science Fiction* published were, by and large, stories that the top editors of the day, John W. Campbell, Horace Gold, and Anthony Boucher, had already seen and passed on. Scarcely anyone wrote new stories specifically for the magazine. One exception, though, was Isaac Asimov, who was in the process of leaving the academic world for full-time writing, and was revving up for high-volume story production.

Isaac contacted many of the lesser magazines of the day and offered to write new stories for them at a premium rate. Bill Scott was one of the editors he approached, and, since Isaac's name was familiar to him, he agreed to buy two stories from him at the premium price of four cents a word. Not his best work, actually, but they were authentic Asimov stories all the same. The other well-known writers of the day who appeared in the magazine—James E. Gunn, Robert Bloch, Jack Vance, and A. Bertram Chandler, for example—were there with stories that had traveled around to other markets first. But Scottie, though he knew next to nothing about science fiction, did know a good story from a bad one, and his editorial choices were, mainly, wise ones.

I suppose *Super-Science* was profitable enough to keep the Crestwood people happy for the first couple of years, since it was not a company known for coddling a money-losing operation. But by the summer of 1958 problems began to develop.

1958 was a bad year for all the science-fiction magazines. Their sales had been dropping ever since the peak year of 1953, when an all-time record 39 different titles were published (and helped to kill each other off by overcrowding the newsstands). By 1958 only six or seven were left. That was the year that the American News Company, the main magazine distributor, abruptly went out of business, taking with it a lot of magazines that it had been financing through advances against earnings. And the continued boom in paperback publishing was squeezing the surviving all-fiction magazines into a marginal existence.

Super-Science had independent distribution and was unaffected by the American News Company debacle, but the general recession of 1958 began to cut seriously into its sales. Against this gloomy background a sudden upsurge of fiction about monsters provided one commercial bright spot—one of those nitwit publishing phenomena, much like the vampire and zombie craze of fifty years later. In the late 1950s a magazine called *Famous Monsters of Filmland,* which specialized in photo-essays on classic Hollywood horror movies of the "Frankenstein" and "Wolf-Man" sort, had shot up overnight to a huge circulation. A couple of the science-fiction editors, desperately trying to find something that worked, experimented with converting their magazines to vehicles for horror fiction. Thus Larry Shaw's *Infinity* and *Science Fiction Adventures,* for which I had been a steady contributor, vanished and were replaced by two titles called *Monster Parade* and *Monsters and Things.* (I wrote for them too.) And over at *Super-Science Fiction,* Scottie concluded that the only way to save his magazine was to convert it to a book of monster stories also. He called me in and let me know that all material purchased thenceforth would have to have some monster angle in it. I didn't find that difficult, since most of the stories I was doing for him were space adventures featuring fearsome alien beings, and I would simply need to make the aliens a little bigger and more fearsome.

Strangely, Scottie didn't change the title of the magazine. This was odd, because the presence of "Science" in it wasn't something likely to appeal to horror fans. Instead he plastered the words *SPECIAL MONSTER ISSUE!* in big yellow letters above the name of the magazine on the April, 1959 issue, commissioned a painting that featured a

gigantic and notably hideous creature sweeping a couple
of space-suited humans up in its claws, and retitled every
story in inventory to give it a monster-oriented twist:
"The Huge and Hideous Beasts," for example, or "The
Abominable Creature." (His gift for the utterly flat-footed
title may have stood him in good stead here.)

The lead story for the issue was one that I had been
writing in July, 1958, just as the change in policy went
into effect. Evidently I found it necessary to restructure
the story midway through for the sake of monsterizing
it, because on my frayed and tattered carbon copy of the
manuscript I find a penciled note in my own hand-writ-
ing indicating a switch in the plot as of page 26: "They are
continuing along when they see a huge monster looming
ahead. They lie low, but the monster pursues them. They
hear it crackling along behind them. They trap it, but it
claws its way out of the trap and comes at them." Whatever non-monster denouement I might originally have had
in mind is lost forever in the mists of time.

I turned the story in with the title I had originally giv-
en it, "Five Against the Jungle," a nice old-fashioned pulp
title which of course was not right for the revamped *Super-Science,* so Scottie changed it to "Mournful Monster."
By so doing, he gave away, to some extent, the fact that it
wasn't really a horror story—that the monster, while ap-
propriately monstrous, was actually a sympathetic figure.
But so, after all, was Frankenstein's monster, and that didn't
harm the commercial appeal of the movie. The prime sub-
text of the whole monster genre, I decided, must really be
existential alienation.

Three of the five stories in *Super-Science Fiction's* glorious

SPECIAL MONSTER ISSUE! of April, 1959 were my work: "Mournful Monster," which was the lead novelet, "Vampires from Outer Space," the second lead, and a short called "A Cry for Help" bylined Eric Rodman. The other two stories in the issue were by writers no one had heard of before or has heard of since, because the s-f agents did not happen to have much of a pool of monster stories on hand to provide, and Scottie had to turn to some of the regular contributors to his crime pulps to fill the need.

That was the way it went for the rest of the magazine's life: I wrote most of the monster stories and unknown writers filled in around me. The June, 1959 number was the glamorous *SECOND MONSTER ISSUE!,* to which I contributed "The Day the Monsters Broke Loose" and "Beasts of Nightmare Horror," though other hands than mine were responsible for "Creatures of Green Slime" and "Terror of the Undead Corpses." August, 1959 was the gaudy *THIRD MONSTER ISSUE,* with no less than four pseudonymous Silverberg offerings ("Monsters That Once Were Men," "Planet of the Angry Giants," "The Horror in the Attic," and "Which was the Monster?"). Then Scottie stopped numbering them: the October, 1959 issue, with three more of mine, was labeled simply *WEIRD MONSTER ISSUE!* (They were "The Loathsome Beasts" as by Dan Malcolm, "The Insidious Invaders" by Eric Rodman, and "The Monsters Came by Night" by Charles D. Hammer. The Robert Silverberg byline was seen only once in the four monster issues.)

But the jig was up. The day I turned those three stories in, in March of 1959, Scottie sadly notified me that he would need no more science-fiction stories from me after that. Though *Trapped* and *Guilty* were going to continue appearing (for the time being), the publisher had decreed that *Super-Science* was done for.

I would miss it. It had supported me in grand style for three years, the income from it would be hard to replace. But also it had been tremendous fun writing those stories. During that period from the summer of 1956 through the winter of 1959, while turning out my 36 lighthearted excursions into super science, I had simultaneously been working in a more ambitious mode for such rather more sophisticated science-fiction publications as Anthony Boucher's *Fantasy & Science Fiction,* Horace Gold's *Galaxy,* and John W. Campbell's *Astounding Science Fiction,* for I did not want to be stereotyped as nothing more than a purveyor of pulp action fiction. But though as a reader I admired the work of such top-flight s-f writers as Theodore Sturgeon, Henry Kuttner, Fritz Leiber, Robert A. Heinlein, and Isaac Asimov, and yearned to be ranked among their number, I had always had a sneaky fondness for the pulpier side of science fiction as exemplified by such magazines as *Amazing Stories, Planet Stories,* and *Thrilling Wonder Stories.* And so when the chance came to write a slew of fast-paced action stories for W.W. Scott's *Super-Science Fiction,* I jumped for it eagerly.

Certainly I have no regrets over having written those reams and reams of space-adventure stories back in the 1950s. The more of them I wrote, the greater my technical facility as a writer became, something that would stand me in good stead later on. They provided me, also, with the economic stability that a young married man just out of college had to have.

It was fun while it lasted, all right. And what fun it has been now, fifty-odd years later, to prowl through the eighteen issues of that obscure magazine in an attempt to reconstruct a bit of that long-vanished era in science fiction!

Robert Silverberg
Oakland, California
April, 2010

The fauna on that new planet was amazing. It was just too good to be true. There had to be a catch somewhere for the happy zoological sci-entists—and there was.

Artwork by Frank Kelly Freas

CATCH 'EM ALL ALIVE
Robert Silverberg

I called this one "Collecting Team" when I delivered it to editor W.W. Scott in June, 1956, and I've reprinted it under that name in any number of anthologies. But Scottie called it "Catch 'Em All Alive." It was the first story in the first issue of Super-Science Fiction, *dated December, 1956, and it became the prototype for any number of exploration-team stories in that magazine, by myself and other writers, over the next three years.*

FROM FIFTY THOUSAND miles up, the situation looked promising. It was a middle-sized, brown-and-green, inviting-looking planet, with no sign of cities or any other such complications. Just a pleasant sort of place, the very sort we were looking for to redeem what had been a pretty futile expedition.

I turned to Clyde Holdreth, who was staring reflectively at the thermocouple.

"Well? What do you think?"

"Looks fine to me. Temperature's about seventy down there—nice and warm, and plenty of air. I think it's worth a try."

Lee Davison came strolling out from the storage hold,

I

smelling of animals, as usual. He was holding one of the blue monkeys we picked up on Alpheraz, and the little beast was crawling up his arm. "Have we found something, gentlemen?"

"We've found a planet," I said. "How's the storage space in the hold?"

"Don't worry about that. We've got room for a whole zoofull more, before we get filled up. It hasn't been a very fruitful trip."

"No," I agreed. "It hasn't. Well? Shall we go down and see what's to be seen?"

"Might as well," Holdreth said. "We can't go back to Earth with just a couple of blue monkeys and some ant-eaters, you know."

"I'm in favor of a landing too," said Davison. "You?"

I nodded. "I'll set up the charts, and you get your animals all comfortable for deceleration."

Davison disappeared back into the storage hold, while Holdreth scribbled furiously in the logbook, writing down the coordinates of the planet below, its general description, and so forth. Aside from being a collecting team for the zoological department of the Bureau of Interstellar Affairs, we also double as a survey ship, and the planet down below was listed as *unexplored*.

I glanced out at the mottled brown-and-green ball spinning slowly in the viewport, and felt the warning twinge of gloom that came to me every time we made a landing on a new and strange world. Repressing it, I started to figure out a landing orbit. From behind me came the furious chatter of the blue monkeys as Davison strapped them into their acceleration cradles, and under that the deep, unmusical honking of the Rigelian anteaters, bleating their displeasure noisily.

THE planet was inhabited, all right. We hadn't had the ship on the ground more than a minute before the local fauna began to congregate. We stood at the viewport and looked out in wonder.

"This is one of those things you dream about," Davison said, stroking his little beard nervously. "Look at them! There must be a thousand different species out there."

"I've never seen anything like it," said Holdreth.

I computed how much storage space we had left and how many of the thronging creatures outside we would be able to bring back with us. "How are we going to decide what to take and what to leave behind?"

"Does it matter?" Holdreth said gaily. "This is what you call an embarrassment of riches, I guess. We just grab the dozen most bizarre creatures and blast off—and save the rest for another trip. It's too bad we wasted all that time wandering around near Rigel."

"We *did* get the anteaters," Davison pointed out. They were his finds, and he was proud of them.

I smiled sourly. "Yeah. We got the anteaters there." The anteaters honked at that moment, loud and clear. "You know, that's one set of beasts I think I could do without."

"Bad attitude," Holdreth said. "Unprofessional."

"Whoever said I was a zoologist, anyway? I'm just a spaceship pilot, remember. And if I don't like the way those anteaters talk—and smell—I see no reason why I—"

"Say, look at that one," Davison said suddenly.

I glanced out the viewport and saw a new beast emerging from the thick-packed vegetation in the background. I've seen some fairly strange creatures since I was assigned to the zoological department, but this one took the grand prize.

It was about the size of a giraffe, moving on long, wobbly legs and with a tiny head up at the end of a preposterous neck. Only it had six legs and a bunch of writhing snakelike tentacles as well, and its eyes, great violet globes, stood out nakedly on the ends of two thick stalks. It must have been twenty feet high. It moved with exaggerated grace through the swarm of beasts surrounding our ship, pushed its way smoothly toward the vessel, and peered gravely in at the viewport. One purple eye stared directly at me, the other at Davison. Oddly, it seemed to me as if it were trying to tell us something.

"Big one, isn't it?" Davison said finally.

"I'll bet you'd like to bring one back, too."

"Maybe we can fit a young one aboard," Davison said. "If we can find a young one." He turned to Holdreth. "How's that air analysis coming? I'd like to get out there and start collecting. God, that's a crazy-looking beast!"

The animal outside had apparently finished its inspection of us, for it pulled its head away and, gathering its legs under itself, squatted near the ship. A small doglike creature with stiff spines running along its back began to bark at the big creature, which took no notice. The other animals, which came in all shapes and sizes, continued to mill around the ship, evidently very curious about the newcomer to their world. I could see Davison's eyes thirsty with the desire to take the whole kit and caboodle back to Earth with him. I knew what was running through his mind. He was dreaming of the umpteen thousand species of extraterrestrial wildlife roaming around out there, and to each one he was attaching a neat little tag: *Something-or-other davisoni.*

"The air's fine," Holdreth announced abruptly, looking up from his test-tubes. "Get your butterfly nets and let's see what we can catch."

THERE was something I didn't like about the place. It was just too good to be true, and I learned long ago that nothing ever is. There's always a catch someplace.

Only this seemed to be on the level. The planet was a bonanza for zoologists, and Davison and Holdreth were having the time of their lives, hipdeep in obliging specimens.

"I've never seen anything like it," Davison said for at least the fiftieth time, as he scooped up a small purplish squirrel-like creature and examined it curiously. The squirrel stared back, examining Davison just as curiously.

"Let's take some of these," Davison said. "I like them."

"Carry 'em on in, then," I said, shrugging. I didn't care which specimens they chose, so long as they filled up the storage hold quickly and let me blast off on schedule. I watched as Davison grabbed a pair of the squirrels and brought them into the ship.

Holdreth came over to me. He was carrying a sort of a dog with insect-faceted eyes and gleaming furless skin. "How's this one, Gus?"

"Fine," I said bleakly. "Wonderful."

He put the animal down—it didn't scamper away, just sat there smiling at us—and looked at me. He ran a hand through his fast-vanishing hair. "Listen, Gus, you've been gloomy all day. What's eating you?"

"I don't like this place," I said.

"Why? Just on general principles?"

"It's too *easy,* Clyde. Much too easy. These animals just flock around here waiting to be picked up."

Holdreth chuckled. "And you're used to a struggle, aren't you? You're just angry at us because we have it so simple here!"

"When I think of the trouble we went through just to get a pair of miserable vile-smelling anteaters, and—"

"Come off it, Gus. We'll load up in a hurry, if you like. But this place is a zoological goldmine!"

I shook my head. "I don't like it, Clyde. Not at all."

Holdreth laughed again and picked up his facet-eyed dog. "Say, know where I can find another of these, Gus?"

"Right over there," I said, pointing. "By that tree. With its tongue hanging out. It's just waiting to be carried away."

Holdreth looked and smiled. "What do you know about that!" He snared his specimen and carried both of them inside.

I walked away to survey the grounds. The planet was too flatly incredible for me to accept on face value, without at least a look-see, despite the blithe way my two companions were snapping up specimens.

For one thing, animals just don't exist this way—in big miscellaneous quantities, living all together happily. I hadn't noticed more than a few of each kind, and there must have been five hundred different species, each one stranger-looking than the next. Nature doesn't work that way.

For another, they all seemed to be on friendly terms with one another, though they acknowledged the unofficial leadership of the giraffe-like creature. Nature doesn't work that way, either. I hadn't seen one quarrel between the animals yet. That argued that they were all herbivores, which doesn't make sense ecologically.

I shrugged my shoulders and walked on.

HALF an hour later, I knew a little more about the geography of our bonanza. We were on either an immense island or a peninsula of some sort, because I could see a huge body of water bordering the land some ten miles off. Our vicinity was fairly flat, except for a good-sized hill from which I could see the terrain.

There was a thick, heavily-wooded jungle not too far from the ship. The forest spread out all the way toward the water in one direction, but ended abruptly in the other. We had brought the ship down right at the edge of the clearing. Apparently most of the animals we saw lived in the jungle.

On the other side of our clearing was a low, broad plain that seemed to trail away into a desert in the distance; I could see an uninviting stretch of barren sand that contrasted strangely with the fertile jungle to my left. There was a small lake to the side. It was, I saw, the sort of country likely to attract a varied fauna, since there seemed to be every sort of habitat within a small area.

And the fauna! Although I'm a zoologist only by osmosis, picking up both my interest and my knowledge second-hand from Holdreth and Davison, I couldn't help but be astonished by the wealth of strange animals. They came in all different shapes and sizes, colors and odors, and the only thing they all had in common was their friendliness. During the course of my afternoon's wanderings a hundred animals must have come marching boldly right up to me, given me the once-over, and walked away. This included half a dozen kinds that I hadn't seen before, plus one of the eye-stalked, intelligent-looking giraffes and a furless dog. Again the giraffe seemed to be trying to communicate.

I didn't like it. I didn't like it at all.

I returned to our clearing, and saw Holdreth and Davison still buzzing madly around, trying to cram as many animals as they could into our hold.

"How's it going?" I asked.

"Hold's all full," Davison said. "We're busy making our alternate selections now." I saw him carrying out Holdreth's two furless dogs and picking up instead a pair of eight-legged penguinish things that uncomplainingly allowed themselves to be carried in. Holdreth was frowning unhappily.

"What do you want *those* for, Lee? Those dog-like ones seem much more interesting, don't you think?"

"No," Davison said. "I'd rather bring along these two. They're curious beasts, aren't they? Look at the muscular network that connects the—"

"Hold it, fellows," I said. I peeked at the animal in Davison's hands. and glanced up. "This is a curious beast," I said. "It's got eight legs."

"You becoming a zoologist?" Holdreth asked, amused.

"No—but I am getting puzzled. Why should this one have eight legs, some of the others here six, and some of the others only four?"

They looked at me blankly, with the scorn of professionals.

"I mean, there ought to be some sort of logic to evolution here, shouldn't there? On Earth we've developed a four-legged pattern of animal life; on Mars they usually run to six legs. But have you ever seen an evolutionary hodgepodge like this place before?"

"There are stranger setups," Holdreth said. "The symbiotes on Sirius Three, the burrowers of Mizar—but you're right, Gus. This *is* a peculiar evolutionary dispersal. I think we ought to stay and investigate it fully."

Instantly I knew from the bright expression on Davison's face that I had blundered, had made things worse than ever. I decided to take a new tack.

"I don't agree," I said. "I think we ought to leave with what we've got, and come back with a larger expedition later."

Davison chuckled. "Come on, Gus, don't be silly! This is a chance of a lifetime for us—why should we call in the whole zoological department on it?"

I didn't want to tell them I was afraid of staying longer. I crossed my arms. "Lee, I'm the pilot of this ship, and you'll have to listen to me. The schedule calls for a brief stop-over here, and we have to leave. Don't tell me I'm being silly."

"But you are, man! You're standing blindly in the path of scientific investigation, of—"

"Listen to me, Lee. Our food is calculated on a pretty narrow margin, to allow you fellows more room for storage. And this is strictly a collecting team. There's no provision for extended stays on any one planet. Unless you want to wind up eating your own specimens, I suggest you allow us to get out of here."

They were silent for a moment. Then Holdreth said, "I guess we can't argue with that, Lee. Let's listen to Gus and go back now. There's plenty of time to investigate this place later."

"But—oh, all right," Davison said reluctantly. He picked up the eight-legged penguins. "Let me stash these things in the hold, and we can leave." He looked strangely at me, as if I had done something criminal.

As he started into the ship, I called to him.

"What is it, Gus?"

"Look here, Lee. I don't *want* to pull you away from here. It's simply a matter of food," I lied, masking my nebulous suspicions.

"I know how it is, Gus." He turned and entered the ship.

I stood there thinking about nothing at all for a moment, then went inside myself to begin setting up the blastoff orbit.

I got as far as calculating the fuel expenditure when I noticed something. Feedwires were dangling crazily down from the control cabinet. Somebody had wrecked our drive mechanism, but thoroughly.

FOR a long moment, I stared stiffly at the sabotaged drive. Then I turned and headed into the storage hold.

"Davison?"

"What is it, Gus?"

"Come out here a second, will you?"

I waited, and a few minutes later he appeared, frowning impatiently. "What, do you want, Gus? I'm busy and I—" His mouth dropped open. *"Look at the drive!"*

"You look at it," I snapped. "I'm sick. Go get Holdreth, on the double."

While he was gone I tinkered with the shattered mechanism. Once I had the cabinet panel off and could see the inside, I felt a little better; the drive wasn't damaged beyond repair, though it had been pretty well scrambled. Three or four days of hard work with a screwdriver and solderbeam might get the ship back into functioning order.

But that didn't make me any less angry. I heard Holdreth and Davison entering behind me, and I whirled to face them. "All right, you idiots. Which one of you did this?"

They opened their mouths in protesting squawks at the same instant. I listened to them for a while, then said, "One at a time!"

"If you're implying that one of us deliberately sabotaged the ship," Holdreth said, "I want you to know—"

"I'm not implying anything. But the way it looks to me, you two decided you'd like to stay here a while longer to continue your investigations, and figured the easiest way of getting me to agree was to wreck the drive." I glared hotly at them. "Well, I've got news for you. I can fix this, and I can fix it in a couple of days. So go on—get about your business! Get all the zoologizing you can in, while you still have time. I—"

Artwork by Frank Kelly Freas

Davison laid a hand gently on my arm. "Gus," he said quietly, *"we didn't do it.* Neither of us."

Suddenly all the anger drained out of me and was replaced by raw fear. I could see that Davison meant it.

"If you didn't do it, and Holdreth didn't do it, and *I* didn't do it—then who did?"

Davison shrugged.

"Maybe it's one of us who doesn't know he's doing it," I suggested. "Maybe—" I stopped. "Oh, that's nonsense. Hand me that tool-kit, will you, Lee?"

They left to tend to the animals, and I set to work on the repair job, dismissing all further speculations and suspicions from my mind, concentrating solely on joining Lead A to Input A and Transistor F to Potentiometer K, as indicated. It was slow, nerve-harrowing work, and by mealtime I had accomplished only the barest preliminaries. My fingers were starting to quiver from the strain of small-scale work, and I decided to give up the job for the day and get back to it tomorrow.

I slept uneasily, my nightmares punctuated by the moaning of the accursed anteaters and the occasional squeals, chuckles, bleats, and hisses of the various other creatures in the hold. It must have been four in the morning before I dropped off into a really sound sleep, and what was left of the night passed swiftly. The next thing I knew, hands were shaking me, and I was looking up into the pale, tense faces of Holdreth and Davison.

I pushed my sleep-stuck eyes open and blinked. "Huh? What's going on?"

Holdreth leaned down and shook me savagely. "Get up, Gus!"

I stuggled to my feet slowly. "Hell of a thing to do, wake a fellow up in the middle of the—"

I found myself being propelled from my cabin and led down the corridor to the control room. Wearily, I followed where Holdreth pointed, and then I woke up in a hurry.

The drive was battered again. Someone—or *something*—had completely undone my repair job of the night before.

IF there had been bickering among us, it stopped. This was past the category of a joke now; it couldn't be laughed off, and we found ourselves working together as a tight unit again, trying desperately to solve the puzzle before it was too late.

"Let's review the situation," Holdreth said, pacing nervously up and down the control cabin. "The drive has been sabotaged twice. None of us knows who did it, and on a conscious level each of us is convinced *he* didn't do it."

He paused. "That leaves us with two possibilities. Either, as Gus suggested, one of us is doing it unaware of it even himself, or someone else is doing it while we're not looking. Neither possibility is a very cheerful one."

"We can stay on guard, though," I said. "Here's what I propose: first, have one of us awake at all times—sleep in shifts, that is, with somebody guarding the drive until I get it fixed. Two—jettison all the animals aboard ship."

"What?"

"He's right," Davison said. "We don't know what we may have brought aboard. They don't seem to be intelligent, but we can't be sure. That purple-eyed baby giraffe, for instance—suppose he's been hypnotizing us into damaging the drive ourselves? How can we tell?"

"Oh, but—" Holdreth started to protest, then stopped and frowned soberly. "I suppose we'll have to admit the possibility," he said, obviously unhappy about the prospect of freeing our captives. "We'll empty out the hold, and you see if you can get the drive fixed. Maybe later we'll recapture them all, if nothing further develops."

We agreed to that, and Holdreth and Davison cleared the ship of its animal cargo while I set to work determinedly at the drive mechanism. By nightfall, I had managed to accomplish as much as I had the day before.

I sat up as watch the first shift, aboard the strangely quiet ship. I paced around the drive cabin, fighting the great temptation to doze off, and managed to last through until the time Holdreth arrived to relieve me.

Only—when he showed up, he gasped and pointed at the drive. It had been ripped apart a third time.

NOW we had no excuse, no explanation. The expedition had turned into a nightmare.

I could only protest that I had remained awake my entire spell on duty, and that I had seen no one and no thing approach the drive panel. But that was hardly a satisfactory explanation, since it either cast guilt on me as the saboteur or implied that some unseen external power was repeatedly wrecking the drive. Neither hypothesis made sense, at least to me.

By now we had spent four days on the planet, and food was getting to be a major problem. My carefully-budgeted flight schedule called for us to be two days out on our return journey to Earth by now, and we still were no closer to departure than we had been four days ago.

The animals continued to wander around outside, nosing up against the ship, examining it, almost fondling it, with those damned pseudo-giraffes staring soulfully at us always. The beasts were as friendly as ever, little knowing how the tension was growing within the hull. The three of us walked around like zombies, eyes bright and lips clamped. We were scared—all of us.

Something was keeping us from fixing the drive.

Something didn't want us to leave this planet.

I looked at the bland face of the purple-eyed giraffe staring through the viewport, and it stared mildly back at me. Around it was grouped the rest of the local fauna, the same incredible hodgepodge of improbable genera and species.

That night, the three of us stood guard in the control-room together. The drive was smashed anyway. The wires were soldered in so many places by now that the control panel was a mass of shining alloy, and I knew that a few more such sabotagings and it would be impossible to patch it together any more—if it wasn't so already.

The next night, I just didn't knock off. I continued soldering right on after dinner (and a pretty skimpy dinner it was, now that we were on close rations) and far on into the night.

By morning, it was as if I hadn't done a thing.

"I give up," I announced, surveying the damage. "I don't see any sense in ruining my nerves trying to fix a thing that won't stay fixed."

Holdreth nodded. He looked terribly pale. "We'll have to find some new approach."

"Yeah. Some new approach."

I yanked open the food closet and examined our stock. Even figuring in the synthetics we would have fed to the animals if we hadn't released them, we were low on food. We had overstayed even the safety margin. It would be a hungry trip back—if we ever did get back.

I clambered through the hatch and sprawled down on a big rock near the ship. One of the furless dogs came over and nuzzled in my shirt. Davison stepped to the hatch and called down to me.

"What are you doing out there, Gus?"

"Just getting a little fresh air. I'm sick of living aboard that ship." I scratched the dog behind his pointed ears, and looked around.

The animals had lost most of their curiosity about us, and didn't congregate the way they used to. They were meandering all over the plain, nibbling at little deposits of a white doughy substance. It precipitated every night. "Manna," we called it. All the animals seemed to live on it.

I folded my arms and leaned back.

WE were getting to look awfully lean by the eighth day. I wasn't even trying to fix the ship any more; the hunger was starting to get me. But I saw Davison puttering around with my solderbeam.

"What are you doing?"

"I'm going to repair the drive," he said. "You don't want to, but we can't just sit around, you know." His nose was deep in my repair guide, and he was fumbling with the release on the solderbeam.

"Gus?"

"Yeah?"

"I think it's time I told you something. I've been eating the manna for four days. It's good. It's nourishing stuff."

"You've been eating—the manna? Something that grows on an alien world? You crazy?"

"What else can we do? Starve?"

I smiled feebly, admitting that he was right. From somewhere in the back of the ship came the sounds of Holdreth moving around. Holdreth had taken this thing worse than any of us. He had a family back on Earth, and he was beginning to realize that he wasn't ever going to see them again.

"Why don't you get Holdreth?" Davison suggested. "Go out there and stuff yourselves with the manna. You've got to eat something."

"Yeah. What can I lose?" Moving like a mechanical man, I headed toward Holdreth's cabin. We would go out and eat the manna and cease being hungry, one way or another.

"Clyde?" I called. "Clyde?'"

I entered his cabin. He was sitting at his desk, shaking convulsively, staring at the two streams of blood that trickled in red spurts from his slashed wrists.

"Clyde!"

He made no protest as I dragged him toward the infirmary cabin and got tourniquets around his arms, cutting off the bleeding. He just stared dully ahead, sobbing.

I slapped him and he came around. He shook his head dizzily, as if he didn't know where he was.

"I—I—"

"Easy, Clyde. Everything's all right."

"It's *not* all right," he said hollowly. "I'm still alive. Why didn't you let me die? Why didn't you—"

WE HAD Holdreth straightened around by evening. Davison gathered as much manna as he could find, and we held a feast.

"I wish we had nerve enough to kill one of the local fauna," Davison said. "Then we'd have a feast—steaks and everything!"

"The bacteria," Holdreth pointed out quietly. "We don't dare."

"I know. But it's a thought."

"No more thoughts," I said sharply. "Tomorrow morning we start work on the drive panel again. Maybe with some food in our bellies we'll be able to keep awake and see what's happening here."

Holdreth smiled. "Good. I can't wait to get out of this ship and back to a normal existence. God, I just can't wait!"

"Let's get some sleep," I said. "Tomorrow we'll give it another try. We'll get back," I said with a confidence I didn't feel.

The following morning I rose early and got my toolkit. My head was clear, and I was trying to put the pieces together without much luck. I started toward the control cabin.

And stopped.

And looked out the viewport.

I went back and awoke Holdreth and Davison. "Take a look out the port," I said hoarsely.

They looked. They gaped.

"It looks just like my house," Holdreth said. "My house on Earth."

"With all the comforts of home inside, I'll bet." I walked forward uneasily and lowered myself through the hatch.

"Let's go look at it."

We approached it, while the animals frolicked around us. The big giraffe came near and shook its head gravely. The house stood in the middle of the clearing, small and neat and freshly-painted.

I saw it now. During the night, invisible hands had put it there. Had assembled and built a cozy little Earth-type house and dropped it next to our ship for us to live in.

"Just like my house," Holdreth repeated in wonderment.

"It should be," I said. "They grabbed the model from your mind, as soon as they found out we couldn't live on the ship indefinitely."

Holdreth and Davison asked as one, "What do you mean?"

"You mean you haven't figured this place out yet?" I licked my lips, getting myself used to the fact that I was going to spend the rest of my life here. "You mean you don't realize what this house is intended as?"

They shook their heads, baffled. I glanced around, from the house to the useless ship to the jungle to the plain to the little pond. It all made sense now.

"They want to keep us happy," I said. "They knew we weren't thriving aboard the ship, so they—they built us something a little more like home."

"They? The giraffes?"

"Forget the giraffes. They tried to warn us, but it's too late. They're intelligent beings, but they're prisoners just like us. I'm talking about the ones who run this place. The super-aliens who make us sabotage our own ship and not even know we're doing it, who stand some place up there and gape at us. The ones who dredged together this motley assortment of beasts from all over the galaxy. Now we've been collected too. This whole damned place is just a zoo—a zoo for aliens so far ahead of us we don't dare dream of what they're like."

I looked up at the shimmering blue-green sky, where invisible bars seemed to restrain us, and sank down dismally on the porch of our new home. I was resigned. There wasn't any sense in struggling against *them*.

I could see the neat little placard now:

EARTHMEN. Native Habitat, Sol III.

THE END

The young spaceman was a mixed-up kid. That was for sure! But then on the hideous planet of black death he found the right answer to his four-way confusion.

Artwork by Ed Emshwiller

WHO AM I?

Henry Slesar

Henry Slesar (1927-2002) broke into the science-fiction world in 1955 with a short piece in Imaginative Tales *and quickly followed it with dozens of other brief, ingenious stories for such magazines of the era as* Amazing Stories, Fantastic, Venture, *and* Fantastic Universe. *At the same time he published dozens of equally clever tales in mystery and detective-fiction magazines, and several novels, the first of which,* The Gray Flannel Shroud, *won the Mystery Writers of America's Edgar award in 1959.*

All of this was after-hours work, because the New York-born Slesar's daytime job was writing advertising copy at a large Madison Avenue ad agency. Before long he had left the pulp magazines behind and was selling stories to Playboy *and other slicks, doing scripts for television shows like* Alfred Hitchcock Presents, *and adapting a story of his into the 1965 movie* Two on a Guillotine. *He had also moved into writing television soap operas: from 1956 to 1984 he was head writer for the CBS production* The Edge of Night, *as well as being involved in such shows as* Somerset *and* Search for Tomorrow. *And somehow he also served for many years as head of his own advertising agency, Slesar & Kanzar.*

It was at the beginning of this busy career that Slesar wrote five stories for Super-Science Fiction, *four of them under his own name and one as "O.H. Leslie," that were published in each of the first four issues. "Who* am *I?", the first of them, from the December, 1956 issue, is typical of his fast-paced narrative style and lively plotting.*

CHAPTER I

THE GRAPPLING HOOK snaked out of the *Buccaneer.* Jake Fisher, the astrogator, followed it into space, murmuring into the communicator all the while. The things he said would have made a space-bum blush.

Gilwit, the pilot of the hoary vessel, was immunized to Fisher's invective. The vaccine had taken two years of partnership to become effective, but now he could listen to Fisher's voice all day and strain out everything but the pure, sweet thoughts.

"The guy's alive," Fisher said when he made contact with the space-sled. "It's a blankety-blank miracle!"

"Reel him in," said Gilwit. He could have done some fancy cursing himself. They had already lost four days in profitless trading with a planet of mute tripeds, whose intelligence level couldn't equal the dullest canine's back on earth. ("Look for eye-expression and digital dexterity in the species you contact. You'll find them helpful indices when you are judging intelligence," said the Space Trader's Handbook. "Phooey!" said Gilwit.) Now they would lose another precious few hours in rescuing some drifter in a space-sled.

Fisher's voice came over again. "The guy ain't got no spacesuit," he said. "I can't take him out."

"Come on back and pick one up," said Gilwit.

"No good." Fisher said something very dirty. "I can't get inside. This thing has no air-lock, and there ain't even room for two. We'll have to carry it alongside."

"Okay, so we'll carry it alongside!" Gilwit was annoyed.

"Then we might as well leave him here," said Fisher. "He's in bad shape. He won't make it to Tryon unless he gets medical care."

Gilwit exploded. "Well, what the hell can we do? This ain't no star-drive. This is a tank, Fisher!"

"Okay, then, you—" (here Fisher used a favorite expression). "We'll leave the guy to die. Maybe somebody will return the favor to you someday, you—" (He said the word again.)

"Well, what do you want from me?" pleaded the pilot. "I haven't got a solution. Have you?"

"We could land on Leo 3. That's the only idea I got."

"Leo 3?" Gilwit moaned. "You *really* want to blow our stake, don't you? Remember what happened *last* time we hit that sucker planet."

"Okay, wise guy. Don't forget who spent the night at the poker table. It wasn't me."

"Sure. You were with that blue-haired babe Margo—"

"For Pete's sake!" It was remarkable how much emotion Fisher could convey over the voice-deadening communicator. "There's a guy dyin' out here! Now let's decide what we want to do."

Gilwit reached to the panel and sent a magnetic current whistling through the grapple line.

"Hook up the sled," he said angrily. "We'll tow the guy to Leo." He added vehemently, "Then we blow outa there!"

WHEN the *Buccaneer* was moored at the New Monte Carlo Spaceport, the two traders and their "passenger" were welcomed by a smooth-faced man with the song of Ireland in his voice.

"Welcome to Leo, my friends," he said. "Before you go through Customs, I'd like to introduce myself. I'm Danny Trevelyan of the Vegas Club, and I'd like to help you."

"Stow it," said Fisher out of the side of his mouth. "We ain't here for none of your entertainment. We got a sick man to take care of."

The smooth-faced man wasn't to be put off so easily. "We have four of the galaxy's finest medical men in constant attendance at the Vegas Club."

Gilwit said: "What's the difference, Fish? The Vegas is as good as anyplace else."

"And I'll bet they kept the poker table warm for you," said Fisher. "Just like last time."

"Not this time, Fish. Remember? We haven't got a stake big enough to throw away. And besides, isn't that the place where that blue-haired babe—"

"Okay, okay," said Fisher roughly. "Let's not gab about it all day. We got to think about our boy here."

They both looked at their unconscious passenger. He was an ordinary-looking young man of about twenty-five, with pleasant, even features, and a brush of sandy-hair.

"He's a lucky lad," said Gilwit. "A million-to-one shot, spotting a space-sled out there." He turned to Danny Trevelyan. "How do you like *those* odds, gambler?"

Trevelyan smiled. "Here's my card," he said.

THE three men were quickly installed in a small, but luxuriously appointed room on the third floor of the Vegas Club. The rates were low, but the management wasn't giving anything away. They knew that the inviting rattle of dice belowstairs would soon make their investment worthwhile.

The traders placed the boy full-length on one of the beds. He lay there without stirring, but every now and then his lips would part and he would moan a word or two.

"What's he saying?" asked Fisher.

"Can't make it out. Think we should call one of those fancy doctors?"

"He don't look as bad as I thought," said Fisher. "Nothing wrong with him that a little snooze and a little booze won't cure. Besides, who knows what one of these gilt-edged pill experts will charge us?"

They found out, and were pleasantly surprised.

"I'm Dr. Stanton," the jovial-faced man said as he entered their door. "Mr. Trevelyan said you had a sick man with you." He went over to the bed briskly, and grinned up at their curious faces.

"There won't be any charge," he assured them. "All part of the service." He dropped his bag on the floor, and made a quick, routine examination of the boy.

"Nothing wrong," he said finally. "A little shock, a little space-fatigue. Nothing more. Who is he?"

"We don't know," said Fisher. "He was just floating around in a sled. We were on our way to Tryon—to the assay office."

The doctor packed up. "Let him rest," he told them. "Feed him, if you can. I'll drop by in the morning and look him over again."

"Thanks, doc."

Fisher showed the medical man out. When he came back to the bed, Gilwit had a surprised expression on his face.

"I just made out something he said."

"What was it?" said Fisher.

"He said . . . *Margo.*"

CHAPTER II

THE next morning, the boy was awake.

"What's your name?" asked Fisher.

The boy sat up in the bed and looked at the heavy-bearded faces of the space-traders.

"Joe," he said. "Joe Smith."

"Nice handle," said Gilwit. "What do you remember last?"

The boy raised his hands and looked at them curiously. Something about them must have startled him, because he jumped out of bed and went over to a mirror on the wall. He stared at himself, and rubbed the light blond bristle on his cheek.

"I don't know," he answered at last. "It's all hazy."

"You were out in space," said Gilwit. "In a sled, without a spacesuit. Do you remember that?"

"No."

The boy went back to the bed slowly. He sat down and rubbed his arms as if they were cold. Now, with his eyes opened, he looked different from the boy they had brought to the Club the night before. There was an odd intensity in his face, a brilliant light in his eyes and a set to his features that made him look—was it older?

"Can I get something to eat?"

"Sure," said Gilwit. "We can order up breakfast. What would you like?"

"Bacon," said the boy, moistening his lips. "Eggs, too. But lots of bacon."

Gilwit made the call to Room Service. But when the tray arrived, the boy looked at the plate in front of him and made a gesture of great disgust.

"Ugh! Bacon! I *hate* bacon!"

He pushed the plate away from him, and the two traders looked at each other.

AFTER breakfast, the three of them went out to see the sights of Leo, the Gambler's Planet.

There wasn't too much to see in the daylight. The facades of the three dozen "Clubs" that constituted the Main Street of New Monte Carlo looked pale and washed-out in the white sun that served Leo's system.

The boy looked about him curiously, but with no more curiosity than the two traders exhibited about him.

"You mean it's all a blank?" said Fisher. "Everything?"

"Not a blank," said the boy. "It's worse than that. It's

a kind of mental fog. I get a lot of confused impressions. Places. People."

"This joint is open," said Gilwit, pointing to a doorway that bore a sign: BARNUM BAR. They followed him inside.

"What kind of people?" Fisher insisted.

"I don't know. Just faces. I can't recognize them."

They were in a narrow bar, just outside the main gambling salon of the Vegas. The salon was deserted except for a lackadaisical domestic robot, wheeling softly around the upturned chairs. The bartender took their order, and they sat sipping cold green liquor from Tryon.

"So you got a hazy mind, eh, kid?" Fisher grinned at the boy. "Didn't get into some kind of jam, did you?"

"I don't think so," said the boy. "But I have an idea that *something* went wrong. It seems to me there was a spaceship—"

"There must have been," said Gilwit sharply. "Where else would you get the space-sled? Did you jump a ship, or did you crash?"

The boy moved his head from side to side. "I don't remember. A crash I think. But I don't remember any—any *impact.*"

"Well, drink up," said Fisher cheerfully. "These things will jog your memory. They got impact, all right." He winked at his partner, but Gilwit's gaze was elsewhere.

"Hey, look," he said.

The three men turned their eyes to the far end of the salon. Down the velvet-covered staircase came a shimmering white gown wrapped around a woman with bright, blue-dyed hair. They watched her hypnotically; there just wasn't any looking away.

"It's Margo," breathed Fisher.

She came towards them. Gilwit nodded to her, and Fisher greeted her with an enthusiastic hello. But the woman looked at the traders with only casual interest.

"Don't you remember me?" said Fisher, his face crimsoning under his heavy beard. "I was here last year. Me and my buddy."

"I'm sorry," Margo smiled. Her voice had as many blue tones as her hair. "I do meet a lot of people."

She looked at the boy. "Hi, there," she said coquettishly.

"Hello," said the boy. He looked impressed.

"What's your name?" she asked.

"Jim," said the boy. "Jim Mitchell."

Fisher nudged Gilwit in the ribs. "Kid learns fast," he said in a low voice.

THE Vegas Club hostess picked up the boy's drink and took a sip, looking at him over the edge of the glass. Then she put it down and went over to the wall. There was a jackpot machine in the corner. Her fingers trailed over it lightly. She turned and looked at the boy.

"Got some change, Jim?"

The boy flushed and slapped his pockets. "I—I guess I don't have any money." But he reached inside them anyway, and came out with a round, shining object. "I seem to have this," he said, looking at it.

"Wow!" said Fisher.

"Do you think it's valuable?" said the boy.

Gilwit snatched the object from his hand. He looked

at it closely, with the swift, perceptive examination of the experienced space-trader. He peered strangely at the boy.

"It's like a multi-colored diamond," he said. "Where'd you get it, kid?"

"Let me see that!" The blue-haired woman came over to Gilwit.

The pilot held it up to her. "Pretty bauble, eh?"

Suddenly, she swooped it out of his hands!

"Hey!" cried Fisher.

"You *pigs!*" Margo said. "You thieving *ghouls!*" She clutched the jewel to her breast.

"Hey, what's the big idea—!" Fisher reached for her arm, but she backed away from him. There was fury in her face.

"I know where you got this!" she rasped. "It was *his!*" She moved into the salon.

"Listen, lady—" Gilwit started after her. "Give it back to the kid."

"What did you do?" she said bitterly, looking at the boy. "Kill him for it? You couldn't get it away from him any other way. You space bums! You—" She used Fisher's favorite term of endearment.

Then Gilwit was on her. He held her wrists and bent her backwards. She tried to sink her white teeth into his arm, but he was too strong. She kicked at his shin, and the trader yelped but held on.

"Let go of me!" she screamed.

"Margo!" A door in the salon opened and Trevelyan came rushing out. Before he could reach the struggling pair, Gilwit had pried the gem loose from the woman's fingers.

"Anything wrong, gentlemen?" The Irishman was breathing heavily, but his manner remained urbane. Margo had composed herself, too, but she still stared at the boy with hatred.

"It's nothing, Dan," she said. "A misunderstanding."

"Honest, Miss," said the boy. "I don't know how—"

"Well!" Trevelyan flashed a wide smile. "If it isn't our sick friend. Feeling better, Mister—"

"Howard," said the boy, still looking anxiously at the blue-haired woman. "Gil Howard."

Fisher and Gilwit found their eyes meeting again.

IN their room that evening, the traders tried to make a decision.

"I say let's blow tonight," said Gilwit. "Before those wheels start spinning downstairs."

"Configurations off," said the astrogator. "Tomorrow would be better."

"Configuration, my eye. You just got a couple of hot Credits in your pocket, and you want to burn them up."

"Well, what about the kid?"

Gilwit swore. "What do you want to do? Adopt him? He'll shift for himself. He's got that rock, hasn't he? That's worth a small fortune."

The boy came over to them. "Look," he said. "You guys have been good to me. I don't want this thing." He took the gem out of his pocket. "Here—you take it."

Fisher eyed it hungrily. Then he waved his hand at the boy.

"Aw. I don't want your toys, sonny. We got plenty of stones in our ship."

"Sure," said the boy sourly. "Blind Man Rubies, silver dust, Rhinestone Wonders . . ."

Gilwit looked at him in surprise. "Hey, where'd you pick that up? That lingo? Were you a trader, kid?"

The boy looked confused. "No. I don't think so—"

There was a knock at the door. Fisher opened it, and frowned when he saw that it was Danny Trevelyan.

"Good evening, gentlemen!" He wore an impeccable white dinner jacket. The contrast to the grimy clothing of the traders was pointed.

Gilwit said: "What do you want, gambler?"

"I have an invitation. Ten thousand Credits, on the house."

"What?" said Fisher.

"For Mr. Howard," Trevelyan smiled, looking at the boy. "From Margo. She wants to make up for the—inconvenience she might have caused you this morning. It was all a terrible mistake."

Fisher whistled. "Ten thousand!" he said respectfully.

"Tell Margo that I accept her offer," said the boy smoothly. "I'll be down soon as I can get a change of clothing."

Gilwit looked at the boy in surprise. "Get him!" he said.

"I'll be happy to lend you some evening clothes," said Trevelyan. "I'll send them up."

He went out, with a mock salute to the traders. As the door shut, the boy went over to the mirror and began to comb his hair. There was a new cast to his young features now, and he looked like a man who knew very much what he wanted.

"Listen, kid," said Fisher, frowning at him. "I know this is all very new and exciting for you, but you gotta watch your step. These people aren't in the habit of giving something for nothing—"

"I can take care of myself."

"Then leave that bauble with us tonight," said Gilwit.

"No!"

"But you wanted to *give* it away a minute ago," wheedled Fisher.

"That was a minute ago. Now I want it."

Fisher came up to him, looking angry. "Look, buster. Don't go high-hat on us all of a sudden, just because some space-tramp—"

It happened so fast that Fisher didn't have time to blink. The boy's right hand dropped the comb and swept up from his hip, the hand closed in a white-knuckled fist. The blow landed square on the side of the rader's jaw, and he spun backwards. He collided with a chair and fell over it, sprawling on the floor. He looked up at the boy, more amazed than hurt.

"You little rat!" he said, mildly.

"Just watch what you say!" the boy said, shaking with his vehemence. "Just watch how you talk about her!"

Gilwit stepped forward. "Joe, listen—"

"Don't touch me!" The boy's face was knotted hard. "And don't call me Joe!"

Gilwit looked pained. "But, kid—"

"My name's Fritz!" the boy shouted. "Fritz Fredericks!"

"He's screwy!"

"And I'm warning you!" the boy said to him. "Don't ever talk that way about *my wife!*"

Then he turned on his heel and went into the bathroom.

CHAPTER III

AN hour later, the two traders had resolved their argument.

They shaved, changed into evening dress, and followed the boy downstairs. They had fairly well agreed that their "passenger" had been somehow deranged on his flying trip in the space-sled, and they were now "responsible" for him. Neither mentioned the fact that their pockets were stuffed with Credits as they came into the main gambling salon of the Vegas Club.

The place was crowded.

"There he is," said Fisher.

The boy was at the Astro-wheel, a game controlled by the incidence of cosmic rays striking an orbital rocket that circled Leo as an advertisement for the Vegas. This made the Wheel convincingly honest, but from the look on the boy's face, it didn't make it any easier to beat.

The pile of Credits had obviously diminished. His face was flushed, but grimly set. Margo was alongside him, leaning on his arm, her blue-dyed hair touching his shoulder.

"Forty-four," the Wheel operator said.

A muscle jumped in the boy's jaw, and the traders deduced that he had lost again. They saw Margo say something in his ear. He made a short reply and shoved a stack of bills on the betting counter. The Wheel spun again.

"Number Twelve!"

The boy had lost again. They watched Margo argue with him, but he seemed to pay no heed. He pushed the remaining stack of bills onto the counter. A small crowd gathered to watch this last-ditch effort.

"Thirteen!" the operator said.

The boy was cleaned. Fisher cursed softly.

Margo steered the boy over to their table.

"Hello, gentlemen," she said pleasantly. "I hope you have better luck tonight than your friend here."

"I don't gamble," said Gilwit.

The boy didn't even acknowledge their presence. He turned to the woman: "What can I get for it?" he asked anxiously. "The stone?"

"You're crazy, kid!" Fisher tried to interfere. "They won't give you any kind of a price here."

"Keep out of this!" There was a depth to the boy's voice they hadn't heard before.

"Give the stone to me," said the blue-haired woman. "I'll get you a good deal on it. I have influence."

Gilwit said: "I'll bet you do!"

Margo glared at him icily. "Bet? I thought you never gambled, trader?"

She took the round, brilliant gem from the boy's hand, and left the table. They watched her walk to the office at the other end of the salon. Trevelyan was just coming out, and she stopped him. They conversed briefly, and Trevelyan went back inside. Then Margo returned to their table and sat down next to the boy.

She put her hand on his and said: "Thirty thousand Credits."

The boy suddenly seemed blank again. "What?"

"Don't do it, kid," said Fisher. "That rock is worth a hundred thousand. Maybe more. Come to Tryon with us in the morning. We'll see that you get a fair shake."

Margo stroked the boy's arm. "Suit yourself, of course."

"Maybe I better do like he says," said the boy uncertainly.

MARGO looked angrily at the traders. But when she turned to the boy again, her voice softened, and the gaze she treated him to could have melted a statue.

"It's all right with me, honey," she said throatily. "But don't blame me for being disappointed. I was looking forward to . . . quite a night."

The boy melted before her. Then he smiled sardonically.

"Baby," he said, "you ought to wear a blindfold. Your eyes say too much."

Margo got up so quickly that her chair overturned.

"You *do* know him!" she cried. *"He* used to say that!"

"Hey!" Fisher jumped to his feet.

"I knew there was something phoney about you guys the minute you came in!"

"What are you talking about?" The boy looked bewildered.

"You killed him!" Margo shrieked.

She threw herself at the boy and lashed out with her long blue fingernails. Before the traders could stop her, she had torn a three-inch gash in the boy's check, sobbing wildly.

Gilwit managed to get them apart. "This is becoming a habit," he said.

Then the fury left her. She bent her head over the table and began to cry. Her shoulders heaved.

"Oh, Fritz! Fritz!"

"Let's get outa here," said Fisher, grabbing the boy's arm.

They pushed their way out of the fast-thickening crowd and made it back to the stairway. As their door shut behind them, Gilwit wheeled the boy around and said:

"Now let's have it! Let's cut this mystery junk! You know this dame from someplace. Is your name Fritz?"

The boy was befuddled.

"No!" he said. "Of course not!"

"Then who the hell *are* you?" said Gilwit.

The boy opened his eyes innocently. "Joe," he said. "Joe Smith."

THE *Buccaneer* left the planet Leo 3 at eight the next morning.

There was some clearance difficulty before blast-off, since Customs had never received a declaration from the traders about the peculiar jewel in Joe Smith's gear.

"That Trevelyan must have tipped them off," said Fisher as they headed into space. "They really wanted that rock."

The astrogator flipped through the pages of orbital calculation that had been run off on the computer at Leo's spaceport. He studied them briefly, and handed the batch to the boy, who was moodily staring out the viewport.

"You know anything about this kind of stuff, kid?" he asked.

The boy took the papers and looked at them carelessly. "A little," he admitted. "It's a fix on Tryon." He placed a finger at a point on the orbital map. "You'll need a Dopplerscope fix right here."

Gilwit shook his head wonderingly. "You're a weirdie, kid. Sometimes you say the damndest things—"

"I must have studied astrogation at some time or the other. Is there a Braun University?"

Fisher swore. "There sure is. But don't tell me you're a graduate, or I'll flip you out into space again. They give a six-year advanced course for accredited astrogators with at least five years of practical astrogation behind them. That's where all the star-liner boys come from."

The youth furrowed his brow. "I think I did graduate from Braun," he said.

"Nuts," said Gilwit. "You'd have to be thirty-five at least. Unless you started space-hopping at ten years old."

The boy seemed to be thinking hard. "When I was ten," he said, "I visited the Mars Colony. At the time of the Revolt."

"If you weren't so rich, I'd kill you," said Fisher. "The Mars Revolt was in '16. If you were ten years old at the time, you'd be sixty now. Get hold of yourself, Joe."

"Look!" said the boy, suddenly stabbing at the orbital tables with his finger. "What if we didn't alter our position here? What if we kept on course?"

Fisher looked over the boy's shoulder. "We'd head out into deep space, that's what."

"Would we? I mean, isn't there a four-planet system on that route?"

"Don't ask me," said Fisher. "We only scoot this tank around approved space lanes. We let the star-drive ships do the exploring. But don't tell me," Fisher said sarcastically. "You were a star-pilot, too. I know."

The boy looked at the paper in his hand. "Yes. I was."

Gilwit caught Fisher's eye and made a circling motion around his temple.

Fisher laughed. "Kid, you're a regular Baron Munchaussen."

The boy didn't even hear him. "There *is* a system out there. We called the fourth planet Othello."

"Are you serious?"

"It was almost dead black when we approached it, but there was a light side, too."

"Who's *we?*" said Gilwit.

"Me and Gil Howard and the others."

The boy went over to the ship's miniature calculator and went to work. Fisher shrugged and joined Gilwit at the controls. They exchanged shrugs, and waited until the boy was through with his calculations.

His eyes shone with excitement when he was done.

"Look here," he said. "It would take a vector alteration of only .0086 to do it. We could make Othello in only sixty hours more than it will take to reach Tryon."

"But *why,* kid?" said Fisher. "We got business on Tryon. Money business. Why go buzzin' around some good-for-nothing planet?"

The boy reached into his pocket.

"I think that's where *this* came from," he said.

The multi-colored gem sparkled and flashed in rivalry to the stars.

WHEN the black planet loomed up in the *Buccaneer's* viewport, Fisher unleashed one of his juiciest strings of invective.

"I think we're nuts," he said to the pilot. "Listening to a crazy kid. Six hundred thousand miles off course. Heading for God knows what."

"You were all excited about the idea a while back."

"It's that lousy sparkler," said Fisher. "A handful of those and we could quit this racket. I didn't hear *you* raising any objections."

"Well, we made up our own minds."

"But the kid's a nut! We know that. He might have got that stone anyplace. Maybe he *did* kill Margo's boyfriend for it."

"And maybe he didn't," said Gilwit, as the blackness swallowed up the viewport. "Maybe he found them down there." The pilot reached out for the landing controls. "Kid still sleeping?"

"Yeah. He's moaning again, too. Gives me the creeps."

"See if you can make something out of it," said Gilwit. "Maybe we'll get some clues about this place."

But they didn't have to wait for their clue.

The boy suddenly shot out of the bunk and ran up forward. He screamed as he saw the black shape in the viewport.

"Stop!" he cried. "Don't do it! Don't land!"

"What's wrong?" said Gilwit anxiously. Instead of answering, the boy fumbled at the control levers and Fisher had to pull him away.

"We can't go down there!" he raved. "We can't! We'll all die! We'll starve!"

"He's blown his stack!" shouted Fisher, battling him.

"Let go of me!" said the boy, his voice hysterical.

"Joe!" Fisher fought to keep him away from the control panel, but the boy had suddenly developed lunatic strength.

"We've got to get out of here!" said the boy wildly. "We've got to get away! We won't have a chance! They're cold—cold—"

"Whose cold?" said Gilwit.

The Moors!" screamed the boy. He broke from Fisher's uncertain grip and wrestled the pilot for control of the *Buccancer.* Fisher took quick action. He reached behind him and unhooked a lead fire-extinguisher from the bulkhead. He brought it down on the boy's skull with calculated violence.

CHAPTER IV

AFTER the descent, they waited until the boy came to before venturing outside the ship.

"We might as well," said Gilwit. "The kid knows this place better than we do. We can use every piece of advice we can get."

"It sure ain't in the handbook," said Fisher, looking out of the viewport.

The boy stirred and groaned. The traders leaned over him.

"You okay, Joe?"

The boy said: "Have we landed?"

Gilwit nodded.

"All right," said the youth crisply, suddenly taking command. "Get into your suits and pack plenty of ammo. Set your oxygen tanks at Low—there's a lot of atmospheric pressure out there. Stay close to the ship and *don't talk.*"

The traders followed his instructions. As they began to open the airlock, the boy repeated his warning.

"Remember, don't use the communicators. They can pick you up easy."

"Who can?" said Fisher uneasily. "Who's out there, kid?"

"Don't call me kid!" the boy snapped. "My name's Jim!"

"Have it your way," said Gilwit. "But give us some hint, will you? What kind of life's on this planet?"

"Hostile," said the boy curtly. "They're underground settlers, and they're blind as bats. But they must have supersonic hearing."

"Then they must have heard our rockets," said the pilot.

"Sure they heard them," said the boy. "But they won't pay any mind to them. This is a volcanic planet. They're used to strange explosions. It's voices that will bring them running."

"What do they look like?" asked Fisher.

"I hope you never find out," said the boy grimly. "I'll

tell you one thing. They're intelligent. A lot more than you or me."

"I dunno," said Fisher "Maybe this isn't such a hot idea."

"It was *your* idea, Fisher," said the boy.

The astrogator cursed. "The hell it was!" he said.

"All right. All right." Gilwit strapped an extra clip of shells onto his belt. "Let's cut out the bickering. We came to pick up some marbles, so let's do it and get out of here. Where do we find the stones, ki—er, Jim?"

"Look for dunes. Big dunes, like gray sawdust. They're like miniature mountainous eruptions. Must have been belched out of the inner layer. Start digging, and you'll find them."

"That easy?" Fisher looked dubious, but the others couldn't read his expression behind the face-plate.

"That easy," said the boy tightly.

"Then why didn't you come back with a truckload?" said Fisher.

"Because we didn't have sense!" the boy answered loudly. "Because we talked too much!"

The astrogator was mollified. "Okay," he said. "Let's get going."

The airlock opened and they dropped outside on the iron-gray loam of the strange silent planet.

THEY searched for half an hour before they located the sandy dunes. The boy spotted them first, and with a wave of his arm, beckoned the others in his direction.

They followed him. Fisher took one look at the dunes and leaped into them, scattering a cloud of gray dust over their heads. Gilwit grabbed him and shook his head in caution.

More carefully, they began to dig.

After fifteen minutes of work, Gilwit put down his shovel and leaned his arms on it. But Fisher wasn't to be dissuaded. The shovel flew as he searched for the multi-colored gems.

The boy dug quietly, steadily, with an air of confidence.

Suddenly, Fisher threw down his shovel and flung himself on hands and knees onto the dune. He dug into the gray dust and came out with something.

"I GOT ONE!" he shouted over the communicator.

"You fool!" said the boy.

Fisher looked at them stupidly. There was a round stone the size of an earth-peach in his hand, glittering dully in the gray darkness. The boy waved his arm at the two traders, beckoning them back towards the ship.

Gilwit started to follow the boy, remembering his caution about the planet's hostile inhabitants. But Fisher wouldn't pay any heed. He stuffed the stone into a pocket and turned to the dune again, scrambling around and looking for more of the precious gems.

His partner tried to pull him away by force, but Fisher shook him off. Fifteen years of third-class trading had primed the astrogator for a moment like this. And he wouldn't be frightened off by an enemy he couldn't see—and who couldn't see him.

The boy was gesturing frantically. They couldn't read his face, but the very angle of his figure communicated his concern.

A low laugh came from Fisher's communicator as he unearthed two more of the round treasures.

The boy didn't wait any longer. He started back for the ship.

"Fish!" said Gilwit, breaking his silence. "You heard what the kid said! There's a hostile species on this planet!"

"Then keep lookout!" snapped the other. "I'll get enough of these babies to take care of us for life. Keep lookout and I'll split 'em with you!"

Gilwit had no choice. He unstrapped the pressure rifle from his gear and circled the dune. The only sound of life was Fisher's heavy breathing as he scattered the sands of the planet Othello.

The boy was already back at the ship, and Gilwit felt a stab of fear as he wondered if the kid would dare take off without them. But how could he? he thought. He'd have to be pilot and navigator, both. But the funny way he was talking . . .

"Fisher! Gilwit!" The boy's voice clanged through their communicators. "Get out of there! They've heard you! Run for the ship!"

Gilwit looked around him wildly. Nothing.

"He's trying to scare us," said Fisher. "I bet there's nothing on this planet. He's a nut, Gilly! He's a psycho!"

"I don't know," said Gilwit unhappily.

"Come back!" said the boy's voice. "Don't stay out there!"

Then they saw it.

At the base of a distant dune, a white pool of light suddenly appeared. It shimmered on the ground, and then a long black shadow emerged from its center. The shadow was about eight feet tall. It wavered mysteriously, like a strand of black seaweed.

"Gilly!" Fisher dropped his shovel and stared at the thing.

"Take it easy," said the pilot in a strained voice. "We've met alien life before."

The thing moved toward them.

"What is it?" said Fisher.

The black thing seemed to be heading right for the astrogator. He froze. Then, desperately, he heaved the jewels at it.

"Here! Take 'em back!" he screamed.

Gilwit lifted his rifle, but a blinding light hit his eyes and he fired wildly.

"Fish! It's blinding me!"

"Run! Run for it!" It was the boy, running towards them.

The pool of light widened, and the black shadow was almost on top of the traders. It was a tall, almost shapeless figure—a biped with arms and fingers, and a round, rubbery head—but that was all the relation it bore to the human animal. Its black body glittered with beads of moisture.

"I can't see!" Fisher dropped to the ground, holding his gloved hands across his face-plate.

"Run!" cried the boy.

But it was too late. Another pool of light formed alongside them, and the two traders, blinded, terrified, surrendered to the long black arms of the strange race that made the planet their home.

CHAPTER V

WHEN Fisher opened his eyes, he saw the boy standing a few feet away, hands searching through his gear.

Gilwit lay on the ground, snoring peacefully.

The astrogator propped himself up on his elbows. "What's happened?" he asked. "Where are we?"

"Down below," said the boy curtly. He continued to dig into the straps of his gear, and finally came out with a tin of chocolate. "We'll have to ration our food," he said. "These birds don't eat."

Fisher jumped to his feet. He looked about him crazily. The place was a cavern, with slick, wet black walls.

"How did we get here? He felt himself for bruises, and realized that his space helmet was off.

"Don't worry," said the boy. "The pressure down here is good. We can breathe all right."

Gilwit groaned.

"You okay, Gilly?" The astrogator bent over his friend with concern. The pilot rattled his head to clear it.

"Yeah. I'm all right. Where'd those black things go?"

"You won't see much of them," the boy said. "I think our appearance disgusts them."

"Nuts," said Fisher. "I don't go for this super-intelligence stuff. Nobody ever found a smarter species than old homo sap."

The boy just smiled.

The smile made Fisher sore. He grabbed the boy by the cross straps of his suit and put his head close to the youth's.

"Now listen, buster! We've had nothing but trouble since we fished you outa space! Now we're in a spot, and we want to know the odds! Spill it! What's the story on these characters?"

"Take your hands off me!" The boy's voice carried authority. Fisher let go.

"I'll tell you all I know. They're bipeds, like us, but that's about all. They're technicians, and damned good ones. They got gadgets so simple and beautiful you could cry to look at them. And they're a dying race. There can't be more than a couple of thousand on the whole planet."

"If they're so smart, why are they dying?"

"Don't ask me," the boy replied. "They took us on a stroll through their city, and you can tell that the living quarters could have held a hundred times their number. Their birth-rate must be down to nothing. But they got a thing called *vitchos.*"

"*Vitchos?*" Gilwit stood up. "What the hell is that?"

"I can't explain it. It's some kind of life-integration process. Fritz could explain it better than I could."

"Whose Fritz?" asked Fisher.

"The bio-chemist. Fritz Fredericks. He formed the expedition. His theory was that the Moors never really *died*—that they solved their declining birth rate problem by integrating the life-force of the dying with the life-forces of the living."

"Then who are *you?*" Gilwit said cautiously.

The boy looked at him. "I *told* you!" he said in annoyance. "I'm Gil Howard!"

"Brother!" said Fisher. "You really got it bad."

Artwork by Ed Emshwiller

"So what happened?" pressed Gilwit. "To Fritz, I mean. And the others? How did they get away?"

"They didn't. Only I did."

"How come?"

"The Moors dismantled our spare ship. Probably just what they're doing to the *Buccaneer* this minute."

Fisher leaned heavily against the wall. "Then we're finished," he said dully.

"But what about the space-sled?" said Gilwit. "How did we find you?"

"They didn't touch the space-sled," said the boy. "I don't know why. Maybe they didn't figure out what it was for."

"Then they're really not that bright." Gilwit paced the floor. "What will they do with us?"

"Nothing, I think," said the boy. "They never bothered us after bringing us here. But time will fix us. They don't need food to keep them going, so there's nothing edible."

"Then we'll starve!" said Fisher.

The boy turned to him. "Unless we eat each other."

"Is that how you got away?"

"Fish!" Gilwit gripped his partner's arm.

The boy shook his head slowly. "I don't remember *how* I did it," he said.

THE TINNED rations began to disappear.

"A hamburger!" said Fisher. "Why do I keep thinkin' of a lousy hamburger!"

"Cut it out," said Gilwit.

"I thought you were supposed to think of gorgeous

foods when you were starving. Turkey dinners. Steaks. All I can think of is a lousy old earth hamburger."

"Let's get some sleep," said the boy. "Take our mind off our stomachs."

"I'll stand watch," said Gilwit.

"There's no need for it," said the boy. "We've been here forty hours and nobody's bothered us. They don't care what happens to us. They got their own problems."

"I think we ought to explore this place," said the astrogator.

"No!" The boy was definite. "The ship's somewhere overhead. If we stay here, we know where we are."

"What good does that do us?" said Fisher. "We can't fly up there."

Gilwit said: "The kid got up there once. And he got to the space-sled. Maybe he'll remember how he did it."

"That's no good either," said the other trader. "Our space-sled's small, too."

He looked back and forth at them.

"It can only hold one of us," he said.

THEY STRETCHED out and tried to sleep. The boy soon went off, but Fisher and Gilwit remained awake. The astrogator nudged his friend.

"Gilly," he whispered.

"What?"

"We're in a pickle, huh?"

"That's a pretty good analysis."

"This kid knows something he's not telling us. There's a way out of this cavern."

"He doesn't remember," said Gilwit. "His brains are scrambled."

"Well, we gotta come up with something—"

"Fish! *What's that?*"

The traders leaped to their feet again. At the far end of the wide corridor, long black shadows moved solemnly towards them.

"It's the geeks," Fisher whispered hoarsely. "Or Moors. Or whatever-you-call-'em."

"They're coming this way," said the pilot tensely. Should we wake the kid?"

The boy was already stirring at the sound of their conversation. "What's up?" he asked.

"Your pals are on their way," said Fisher.

"The rifles are upstairs," said Gilwit, hurriedly undoing a strap. "But they forgot this." A knife glittered in his hand.

"Don't do anything foolish," the boy cautioned. "Their hostility is passive. They won't use force unless they have to."

The black shadows came closer. The men could discern the outline of four dark figures, carrying something between them. It looked like a stretcher.

"They're carrying somebody," said Gilwit. "A sick one."

"Probably a dying one," said the boy.

The rubbery feet of the aliens made sharp, slapping sounds against the wet stone as they neared the three prisoners. They were eyeless, but their smooth round heads gave the appearance of looking past the three men. The two traders pasted themselves up against the slick walls as the Moors went by them. But the boy remained in their path.

"Chavaron!" he said loudly.

The procession halted.

"Kid!" Gilwit's eyes widened in fear. "Get back! Don't try to stop them!"

The boy remained unmoving.

"Chavaron!" he repeated. *"Fredericks! Fredericks! Vitchos!"*

The leader of the group slowly raised a long, seemingly jointless arm. He placed the tips of his black webbed fingers on the chest of the boy, and Fisher cried out: "Look out, kid!"

He stayed firm. The webbed hand flattened against his chest, and the creature's round head developed a gaping maw.

"Churu!" said the alien, the voice emanating from a chest as cavernous as the place they were in. *"Churu!"*

His fingers pushed against the boy's chest, only slightly but with enough force to send him reeling backwards.

Gilwit made a motion to help him but something in the boy's face decided him against it.

The alien swept his arm back in a gesture towards the sick creature on the stretcher.

"Vitchos," he said.

The Moor returned to his burden. With a nodded signal to the others, he continued down the slippery path.

When they were out of sight, Fisher relaxed with a string of rolling epithets.

"What did they say?" asked Gilwit. "What's it all about, kid?"

The boy watched the black creatures depart. He looked dazed. "What's that?" he said.

"What was all the chatter?" said Fisher. "What did you tell them?"

The boy shook his head. "I don't know. I can't speak their language. Fritz could, though."

"But you *talked* to them!" said Gilwit heatedly. "We heard you."

"You're crazy," said the boy. "I *couldn't* talk to them. I don't know how!"

Fisher threw his hands in the air. "I give up!"

The astrogator went over to his gear and fumbled for the remains of his chocolate tin. Savagely, he gulped down the last piece in some odd kind of defiance. He flopped on the ground, and his partner joined him. They both looked at the boy, who turned his face away.

Suddenly, there was a blast that shook the walls!

"*WHAT was that?*"

Gilwit and Fisher were on their feet again.

The roar continued, directly above their heads.

"Rockets!" said Fisher. "It's the *Buccaneer!*"

"What are they doing to it?"

The boy interposed. "That doesn't sound like the *Buccaneer*. It's another ship!"

"How can you tell?"

"I've heard enough rocket blasts to know what's a tank and what isn't! That's a big ship!"

"Somebody's landing!" cried Fisher, jumping up and down.

"Maybe they'll save us!"

"If they can find us. Come on," said the boy suddenly. "I've got an idea!"

He started on a fast trot down the wet, black corridor, carrying his helmet in one hand. The two traders hesitated a minute, picked up the gear that was on the ground, and ran after him.

"Where's he going?" Fisher panted.

"Maybe he's remembered how to get out of here!"

They sprinted through the darkness, trying to guide their running feet with hand light-torches. They ran until they were almost exhausted, and then the boy made a sudden sharp turn to the left.

"In here!" he shouted.

Through a narrow doorway cut into the solid stone they saw a patch of soft, gray light.

"It's a room!" cried Fisher.

THEY went inside, at a slower pace. There was an unintelligible jumble of machinery alongside one damp wall. The traders looked at it curiously as they passed, but the boy had his destination fixed at another doorway.

But the second room wasn't empty.

One of the black, alien figures was lying on a low stone bed. He raised himself feebly as they entered.

"Chavaron—" he said weakly.

Fisher gawked at the sight of him. The eyeless face frightened him, even though he had seen far more outlandish tricks of evolution in his space travels.

"Kill him!" said Gilwit.

"No!" The boy halted. "Let him alone. He can't hurt us."

He walked briskly past the bed and over to the far wall.

"It looks like a ladder!" said Fisher gleefully.

There were horizontal indentations in the black stone, each one about two feet apart. Fisher rushed past the boy and tried to scale the wall. But the indentations weren't nearly deep enough for him to establish a foothold, and he fell back into the room.

"It's no use," he gasped. "We can't make it up there."

"How do *they* do it?" asked Gilwit.

"Look at his feet." The boy pointed to the bed. The black thing was turned in their direction. They could see the round, rubbery objects on the soles of his feet.

"Suckers," said Fisher under his breath. "They climb these walls with suction."

"Then how can we get out?" Gilwit looked up. The wall rose some sixty feet. They could see a few scattered stars in the opening above their heads.

"I don't know," said the boy. "But there's one thing we can do." He whipped his light-torch straight upwards, blotting out the stars. "Point your lights up there. Maybe whoever's landed will see it."

They followed suit.

After five worried minutes, nothing had happened.

"It's no use!" said Fisher.

The thing on the bed made a noise.

"I'm worried about that one," said Gilwit, looking over his shoulder. "Maybe he'll signal the others."

"He's harmless," said the boy, eyes trained on the opening. "He's dying. Waiting for *vitchos.*"

THEN they saw the helmet, a small glass ball reflecting the light of their torches.

"Somebody's there!" shouted Gilwit. "Hey! *Hey!*"

"Get us out!" screamed Fisher. "We're earth people!"

"A rope!" the boy cried out. He turned the light on himself, and the others realized the sense of his maneuver. They did the same. "Throw us a line!" said the boy.

The helmet disappeared. The traders groaned.

Then a second space-helmet appeared over the opening. They shouted to it again, and this time with joy. A thin steelon rope came tumbling down the shaft.

"We're saved!" Fisher grabbed the rope and started to hoist himself up, almost before their rescuers could secure it up above. The boy followed at Gilwit's insistence.

Just as the pilot grasped the line, the thing on the bed started to move. With great effort, it lifted itself from the bed and started towards him. But it was too weak to make more than a few faltering steps. Gilwit saw it fall to the ground and lie still. Then he climbed up.

On the surface of the planet, the two traders jumped on their saviors and pummeled them happily. The boy didn't waste the time.

"Let's get to your ship," he told them. Then he realized that their communicators weren't operating on the same wavelengths. To instruct them, he resorted to exaggerated arm motions.

The strangers didn't seem to move. Gilwit grabbed the arm of the nearest one and tugged. "Come on!" he said. "Hostile planet!"

Then he realized who it was.

"Margo!" he said.

There wasn't time for a reaction. Already, a pool of white light formed a hundred yards from them.

"They're coming after us again!" shrieked Fisher. "Let's get to the ship!"

The two traders broke into a run towards the new-landed space ship. It was a beauty; a huge, slim craft, white as moonlight. The boy hesitated, then dashed after them.

The two newcomers looked at each other in apparent bewilderment, and then they realized that their own ship was the destination of the men they had saved. They had no choice but to follow.

When they were safely inside, Trevelyan took off his space helmet and gasped:

"What do you think you're doing?"

Gilwit merely pointed to the viewport. When the gambler saw what was heading for the ship, he sat down without a word. Then he watched gratefully as the trader started the rocket motors and shot them away from the black planet Othello.

CHAPTER VI

MARGO said:

"You knew my husband, didn't you?"

"Is that why you followed us?" asked the boy. "Just to find out more about Fritz?"

"That was my reason, yes." The blue-haired woman looked up at the Irishman by her side. "Trevelyan had somewhat different ideas. He was interested in that pretty gem of yours."

The gambler smiled. "Now who could be blaming me?" he asked.

"Fritz kept one as a lucky charm," said Margo. "He wouldn't sell it for anything. He said he'd bring me back a bucketful of them one of these days."

The boy said: "Fritz was the real discoverer of Othello. He was on a star-liner—the *Dolphin,* remember it?"

Trevelyan said: "Yes. It was lost."

"No, it wasn't," said the boy. "You'll find the pieces of it on the black planet. We got caught in its orbit and crashed. Fritz and I were the only survivors. We managed to get off all right, but Fritz was fascinated by the place and organized a return expedition."

The boy looked at the woman. "He wanted me to come along, because he had an idea that I had saved his life."

"Who were the others on the expedition?" asked Margo.

"Gil Howard was our pilot," said the boy, a far-away look in his eyes. "Jim Mitchell was our astrogator."

"And your name is really *what?*" said Fisher softly.

"Joe," said the boy. "Joe Smith."

Then he put his head in his hands and wept.

"What is it, kid?" asked the pilot.

"I don't know. I get all confused sometimes." He looked up at them with misty eyes. "I *know* I'm Joe Smith. *I know it!* I'm at *least Joe Smith!*"

"At least?" Margo looked baffled.

"I can't explain what I mean," said the boy. "I remember things. All sorts of things. Things I couldn't remember if I was only Joe Smith."

Gilwit said: "What sort of things?"

"The Mars Revolt. I remember that. The hydrogen explosion in the Embassy. But that was fifty years ago!"

"That's right," said Trevelyan curiously.

"And Braun University. A professor named Chambers, with a wooden leg. And a girl with red hair—a girl named Janette."

"I know a Janette," said Fisher lightly. "Prettiest little gold-digger this side of Saturn. But she's a blonde."

"And how about me?" the blue-haired woman asked. "How about me—Margo?"

"I know you, too!" the boy said. "I know so much I never knew before!"

He put his head back into his folded arms and sobbed. The sight brought out all the maternal sympathy in the woman. She went to him and put her arm around his shoulder.

"It's all right," she said softly.

The boy looked up at her. His eyes were still damp, but he smiled. "Baby," he said in an odd voice, "you ought to wear a blindfold. Your eyes say too much!"

Margo screamed.

"FRITZ!"

DR. STANTON came out of the room at the Vegas Club. He smiled reassuringly at Fisher and Gilwit.

"Your friend's in no danger," he told them. "But he's a pretty baffling case. Like four-way schizophrenia."

"How do you mean?" said Gilwit.

"He thinks he's four people. Joe Smith. Gil Howard. Jim Mitchell. And Fritz Fredericks—Margo's husband."

"Wow!" said Fisher. "That's quite a trick!"

"It may not be a trick at all," said Stanton seriously. "You learn a lot of marvelous things in space. Maybe this is another miracle. Maybe we have a medical phenomenon on our hands."

"Listen, doc," said Gilwit. "You're not going to have the kid put away, are you? I mean, he's really not insane or anything. He's just all balled up."

"He was Fritz Fredericks, just now. At least the Fritz-fourth of him had the upper hand of his ego." The doctor smiled. "We had quite a talk. Fritz was a bio-chemist, and one of the best. He knew quite a bit, and he was always willing to learn more. It was a very instructive talk," he added.

The doctor looked at them quizzically. "Did the boy ever say anything to you about *vitchos?*"

"Yes," said Gilwit. "He mentioned it."

"Crazy stuff," said Fisher. "About integrating life-forces."

"Well," said Stanton, "it's either crazy stuff, and he's a mental case—or, it's the truth, and he's an example of this *vitchos* business."

"I don't get it," said Gilwit.

"Fritz' story is this," said the doctor. He paused and wiped his spectacles. "See? The kid's got me doing it. The *boy's* story is this: The expedition force—Fredericks, Howard, Mitchell, and Smith—were captured by these creatures on the planet that Fritz named Othello. Fritz had hoped that he could establish friendly relations with them—he even tried to speak their tongue. But the

"Moors" as he called them, were too busy trying to save their civilization.

"So they let the prisoners alone, and promptly proceeded to take their ship apart. Why, he isn't sure. Possibly to make use of the material. At any rate, there was no way for them to leave the planet—and no way to get food that would keep them alive.

"They were slowly dying of starvation, when Fritz got the idea. He went to their captors and asked them if they would allow the prisoners to go through their *vitchos* process.

"For some odd reason, they accepted his suggestion."

"But what did they do to them?" asked Fisher.

"I can't tell you that. But it's some process for incorporating several different life-forces in just one body."

The traders looked at the medical man, horrified.

"You mean the kid is—"

"Fritz selected the boy because he was young and strong. They thought he would have the best chance to get away. He was obviously right. Somehow, Joe Smith got to the space-sled and escaped."

"Then the kid *isn't Joe* Smith," said Gilwit, almost to himself. "He's really—"

"Only if the story is true," the doctor interrupted. "Only if it's true. But we have no idea if it is or not."

The doctor lifted his bag. "Well, I've got other fish to fry. I've got to be going." He shook their hands solemnly. "Goodbye, gentlemen. And good luck."

"So long, doc."

They watched him depart down the long velvet staircase.

CHAPTER VII

THE *Buccaneer II* blasted away.

Fisher watched Leo 3 disappear in the viewport. Then he sat down and watched his pilot operate the controls.

"Well, another week shot," he said.

"And we're no richer," said Gilwit. "Just a lot of Blind Man's Rubies, silver dust, and Rhinestone Wonders . . ."

"It's a shame we had to leave those big stones on Othello," said Fisher. "Maybe someday—"

"Skip it," said Gilwit. "You couldn't get me back there for all the diamonds in the galaxy."

Fisher took the seat beside him.

"Well," he said casually, "it wasn't a *total* loss. We had some fun—and we still have *this.*"

"What?" said the pilot.

Fisher reached into a pocket and came out with a flashing, multi-colored gem.

"Where the hell did you get that?" asked Gilwit. "That's the kid's!"

"He gave it to me," said Fisher. "Insisted that we have it. Pretty nice of him, wasn't it?"

Gilwit looked at the gem with appreciation. "It sure was."

He cut the rocket motor and took the jewel from the astrogator's hand.

"You know something, Fish?" he said. "We shouldn't sell this baby. We should keep it as a memento.

"After all, it was from the nicest four guys we ever met."

THE END

The Christmas spirit brings out the best in people. Suppose every day were Christmas? Well, by using a special technique—perhaps that could be arranged.

Artwork by Paul Orban

EVERY DAY IS CHRISTMAS
James E. Gunn

James Gunn was one of the brightest new writers of the 1950s, attracting particular attention for his sparkling work for Horace Gold's magazine Galaxy. *"Every Day is Christmas" has all the hallmarks of a* Galaxy *story—the brisk pace, the glossy surface, the hard-edged satire of American consumerist life in the Eisenhower era. But somehow this one did not meet with editor Gold's approval, and on one bounce sold to* Super-Science *instead. Gold was a difficult editor to understand: sometimes he rejected stories that seemed perfectly attuned to his magazine, perhaps because he thought they were* too *perfectly attuned to it. "Every Day is Christmas" was featured on the cover of* Super-Science's *second issue, February, 1957.*

During the course of his long career James Gunn has published nearly a hundred stories and such popular science-fiction novels as The Immortals, The Joy Makers, *and* The Listeners, *edited several anthologies, and was the author of an important history of science fiction,* Alternate Worlds *(1975.) His book,* Isaac Asimov: The Foundation of Science Fiction, *won a Hugo award for non-fiction in 1983, and in 2007 the Science Fiction Writers of America awarded him its highest honor by naming him a Grand Master.*

I STEPPED OUT of the passenger port onto the open elevator and waited for it to take me to ground level. My first conscious thought was: *My God! You can see so far!*

My lips twisted mirthlessly. That wasn't memorable, and it wasn't even accurate. For three years I had been where I could see for millions of miles, for light years; there was no choice. The difference was that there had been no middle distance. Twenty feet or a million miles. What I had meant was that I could see so much. As I thought about it, even that lost its appeal.

I had not consciously expected exultation to release itself in drama, but three years of slowly building tension subconsciously seeks an outlet. Now, as the elevator reached the pavement, I only felt hot. I stepped out upon Earth and my only reaction was: *My God, but it's hot!*

It *was* hot, over ninety, and the humidity was almost as high. After my three years in the controlled, sterile climate of an asteroid belt navigation beacon, the impact was physical.

Where is Jean?

I scanned the faces around me. Their presence did not excite me, as I had thought they would. They only depressed me. For three years the prospect of this moment had kept me sane in the hollow sphere that paced the asteroid belt endlessly, but now it meant nothing. There was only one face I wanted to see, and it was not here.

It was possible that Jean had not received my spacegram. Transmission was unreliable. Static scrambled the messages.

I pulled a thin, yellow envelope out of my pocket. I unfolded it and read it again.

WILL DOUBLE SALARY FOR RENEWAL OF CONTRACT. . . .

I looked up at the blue sky, drifted with summer clouds, and felt the tug of gravity on my 175 pounds. But it was more than gravity that held me tight to Earth.

How much is three years of a man's life worth? Three years, cut right out of the middle, and filled with emptiness?

They had put a price on it: $50,000 a year. A price for being unbearably alone. And I knew now that you cannot measure time by years; you measure time by what is in it. I had not spent three years out there; I had spent a lifetime. They offered to raise the price to $100,000, but it was impossible. You can't spend a life twice, any more than you can spend a dollar twice.

I have one hundred and fifty thousand dollars, I thought. Fifty thousand for each endless year. Jean can't have spent much; she had her job. I own my home, and I have enough money to live ten years in luxury or twenty years in comfort. Maybe that's worth three years of a man's life.

Jean! I thought of the pointed, girlish face, the blonde curls, the blue eyes, the gently-rounded body. I remembered those things better than I knew myself; I had three years to memorize them. *Jean. . . .*

Taxi or subway? I toyed with the idea of extravagance. I wanted my first opportunity to spend money to be something worth remembering. I did not want to recall dropping a token into a turnstile. But the subway would be quicker. Quicker to Jean.

I descended into the earth, into the darkness, into madness.

STILL I was as far from the living earth as ever. Farther. Instead of merely having concrete underfoot, I was surrounded by it. Perhaps that was what I missed. I wished I could see grass growing or pick up a clod of clean soil and crumble it slowly in my fingers and let it trickle back to join the living things.

The subway was hot and dirty. It seemed as if I had never been away. Scraps of newspaper littered the platform; dingy placards adorned the wall. The biggest one said: "Subway fare is now one quarter (25¢)."

I studied it, frowning. Had prices gone up so much in three years?

I put a quarter in the slot and pushed my way through. Alone on the platform, I paced restlessly. After a moment I began to study the ads. The ones that faced the dark tracks were newer and cleaner. I had never seen anything like them before.

One was a swirl of colors, like light reflected from oil-streaked water. I stared at it. It was meaningless. I thought it was meaningless. Something just below the level of recognition nagged at my senses. I looked away, and in that movement of my eyes, the ad almost came clear. Something vaguely, roundly, monstrously sexual. And some words: "BE *something!*" it read. "BUY *something!*"

Or was it merely illusion?

The next ad was a sprinkling of colored dots, scattered, superimposed, haphazard. Just as meaningless at first glance as the other. And then, like the shifting of an optical illu-

sion or the sudden revelation of numbers in a color-blind-
ness test, the dots adjusted themselves into a recognizable
pattern. A white cylinder, a rising thread of smoke curling
up—very attractive, almost three-dimensional. I could almost taste the sweet, relaxing fragrance. Tension. You can
learn to live with it for a time, but eventually it must have
release.

I shook myself. I had stopped smoking before leaving
Earth. For three years I had not had the slightest desire for
a cigarette of any kind. There was no logic to this sudden
craving.

I knew what I wanted. I wanted a glass of cold milk,
an onion, a tomato—food that was fresh, untainted by can
or package. I didn't think I would be able to eat anything
canned for a long time.

The tunnel began to murmur. The murmur grew to a
roar. The roar diminished in a squealing of metal brakes.
The train pulled up beside the platform. The doors slid
open. Nobody got off. I slipped into the nearest car. The
door slid shut behind me. The train began to move; it
picked up speed. . . .

I clung to a bar and looked at the other passengers.
There were about a dozen in the car, sitting quietly, staring
into space as if they were listening to something. Men and
women alike wore shorts, violently colored, some striped,
some patterned, some with meaningless whorls. The wom-
en wore brief halters with holes cut in the center through
which their painted nipples were visible.

Styles change, I thought. I thought it was ugly.

WHINRR-R-R! The music began abruptly. I started.
It was strange stuff, full of nerve-jangling dissonances and

missed intervals. I tried to locate the source but without success. It seemed to come from everywhere in the car. No one else seemed to be disturbed. They sat motionless, listening. . . .

"BE-E-E-E BEWITCHING! BUY-Y-Y-Y BE-WITCHING!" A chant joined the music, intoned monotonously, repetitively in counter-intervals to the music by a mixed group like the mass voice of society. It was infinitely irritating. "BE-E-E-E BEWITCHING! BUY-Y-Y-Y BEWITCHING! BE-E-E-E."

Over and over again. Eternally.

The train began to slow. Lights appeared and white-tiled walls and pillars.

"BUY NOW!" the chant said imperatively. THUMP! THUMP! The chant and the music stopped.

The door slid open. The women in the car got up quickly and filed out. A few other women entered with small packages in their hands. They sat down.

Ugly, I thought. All of them. Even after three years, the sight of their near-naked bodies filled me with revulsion.

Nobody said anything. Nobody did anything except listen. These weren't people at all. They were automatons, moving with the regularity and mindlessness of clock-work.

The doors closed. The train moved away.

WHANG-NG! STRNNN-NH! The music came back, a different rhythm, this time, different dissonances.

"NERVES TAUT?" The music jangled horribly. "SMOKE A LOT?" Dissonances. "DON'T JITTER, JETTER! BETTER BUY BILLOWS! Relax-x-x!" The

last word was drawn out and the music died away softly
with it. Silence. Blessed silence.

Billows? I thought querulously. *Billows?*

WHANG-NG! STRNN-NH! I stiffened as if I had
been hit in the stomach. "NERVES TAUT? . . . ."

I slid down into a seat beside a middle-aged man; my
legs felt weak in the old-fashioned tight-cuff pants. Beside
them, his legs looked ridiculously thin and hairy.

"Is it like this all the time?" I asked him, above the
chant. "Can't you do anything about it?"

The man was listening, but not to me. I took him by
the shoulder and shook him a little . . . "Whats the matter with everybody? Why don't you complain or turn the
stuff off?"

The man ignored me. The train began to slow.

"DON'T DELAY!" the chant ordered. "BUY NOW!"
Silence.

The train stopped. The man sitting beside me got up
and filed out with the rest of the men in the car. I started
after them. Other men got on, chewing. One of them spat
a purple stream on the floor.

Drugs? I thought uneasily. Hypnosis?

The doors slid shut. The train started. The music began
again. This time it was rather gentle and almost melodic.
The words were chanted by a chorus of female voices.

"SOO-SOO-SOO-SOOTHE." The last word was
trailed out langourously. "SOO-SOO-SOO-SOOTHE."

I put my hands over my ears. What in heaven's name
did you do with Soothe? Use it? Wear it? Drink it? I didn't
want to know. I felt the vibrations change to a staccato
tempo. . . .

AT Times Square I escaped, as if from bedlam. What had I come back to? Or was it merely that I was oversensitive after three years of complete peace, complete quiet.

I thought for a moment of buying something for Jean, something expensive, something to show how glad I was to be back home. But the sight and sounds of the street drove the idea away.

The streets were decorated with green and red, streamers, wreaths, bells, candies. Music floated over the crowded sidewalks. People in scanty clothing shoved and lunged, carried large stacks of packages, moved in waves. There were too many of them.

"SILENT NIGHT," boomed one speaker. "DECK THE HALLS," clashed another. "JINGLE BELLS, JINGLE BELLS . . . OF A WHITE CHRISTMAS. . . . SANTA CLAUS IS COMING . . . WE THREE KINGS. . . ."

Christmas carols! I pressed myself back against a building front and looked up at the nearly vertical sun and wiped the sweat from my forehead.

There was a logical explanation to all of this. Had I gone mad out there from the loneliness and the emptiness and the yearning? Was this just a fantasy of my disordered mind? Or was this really the fifth of July, and was it the world that was mad?

On the sidewalk in front of me was a man dressed in a heavy red suit trimmed with white fur. On his head was a long, red and white stocking cap. A long, white beard came halfway down his chest. Beside him was an iron pot dangling from a tripod. On top of the tripod was a sign: "IT IS MORE BLESSED TO GIVE THAN TO RECEIVE."

In one hand the man waved a large bell. It made a

horrible clanging sound to compete with the carols coming from the store fronts. "GIVE-GIVE-GIVE-GIVE-GIVE. . . ." he chanted. Those who passed showered change into the iron pot.

I felt an irrational impulse to empty the change in my pocket into the pot. Instead I stepped up beside the man and tapped him on the shoulder. The man stopped swinging the bell and turned.

"What's the date?" I muttered.

The man in the red and white suit looked at me curiously. "July fifth, bub."

"Yesterday was the Fourth of July?" I asked. "Independence Day?"

"Yeah, and tomorrow will be July sixth."

I stared at him. "Then who the hell are you?"

He laughed jovially. "Santa Claus, bub. Where you been?"

"A long ways," I muttered. "But it's—let's see—over five months until Christmas. Aren't you rushing things a little?"

"Now, bub, you don't want to wait until the last minute, do you? Only one hundred and forty-five shopping days left till Christmas. Where's your Christmas spirit?"

"It doesn't seem quite the season for it," I said, glancing up at the sun. "Aren't you smothered in that outfit?"

He shook his snowy head. "Naw," he said. "I got an Indicool. Works off a battery in my stuffing." He thumped himself in the belly.

"A what?"

"Indicool. Personal cooler. Where you been, bub? They had a doozy of a promotion just a couple of days ago. Institute, of course. Oversold their stock by fifty percent. That's results."

"Institute?" I said dazedly.

Santa Claus eyed him suspiciously. "Ad Institute, naturally. Everybody who wants to sell takes a course. Or as many as he can afford. Took one myself. Cost me a pile, but I been doing two hundred percent better ever since. G'wan now! I got to get back to business."

I started to back away. The bell clanged out its sense-jarring message. "GIVE-GIVE-GIVE-GIVE-GIVE. . . ."

Coins clinked into the pot. A crazy song was running through my mind: "I just missed the Fourth of July, but I'm just in time for Christmas."

"SILENT NIGHT," came from the loudspeakers. "IN THE LANE SNOW IS GLISTENIN' . . . MAKIN' A LIST, CHECKIN' IT TWICE . . . TRA-LA-LA-LA-LA-LA-LA-LA-LA. . . ."

The July sun beat down sullenly. The air steamed. Someone brushed past me carrying a large, bushy Christmas tree. . . .

"Taxi!" I yelled. "Taxi!"

They passed, dozens of them, all loaded with shoppers and their packages. I swayed back and forth, buffeted by the crowd, lost in a sea of naked arms and legs.

"Taxi!" I said despairingly.

At last one pulled to the curb. I battled my way to the door, pulled it open, sank down in the back seat. I sighed. The world was mad, but waiting for me was Jean and $150,000.

I leaned forward and gave the cabbie the address. I

slumped back in the seat, waves of fatigue and frustration breaking over me. The taxi drew away from the curb. . . .

SSSSZZ-Z-Z! PPP-P-P!

I opened my eyes. A large screen on the back of the driver's seat had lighted up with dancing, colored specks, like water on a hot, greasy pan. The music sizzled and popped.

"WHY FRY, GUY?" the chant began. I stiffened. "BEAT HEAT! INDICOOL! 'SNO BLOW!" The dancing specks became slowly falling snow. SSSSZZ-Z-Z! PPP-P-P! "BUY! WHY FRY. . . ?"

I found myself pounding on the glass partition. With one hand the cabbie pushed half of it aside.

"Whatsa matta?"

"Turn it off!" I panted. "Turn it off!"

"Ya crazy?"

"I don't know," I moaned. "Turn it off!"

"Can't. Automatic. Office got a contrack. Ain't had no complaints before. Whatsa matta with it? Hey?"

I slid the glass partition shut in his face and curled myself up in a corner of the back seat, my eyes closed, my hands clamped over my ears, like an overgrown fetus without a womb. . . .

THE taxi slowed. I opened my eyes. I looked through the window at a woman walking along the street, her long straight legs and shapely back almost bare. "Jean!"

I hammered on the glass. "Let me out!"

The taxi pulled up. The driver turned, flipped down the meter flag. "Thirteen forty-five," he growled.

I threw him a ten and a five. "Keep it!" I leaped from the taxi. "Jean!"

The woman ahead did not turn. Her legs gleamed whitely below the chartreuse shorts striped with scarlet. They marched straight down the sidewalk, quickly, determinedly.

I wondered, as I walked after her, if I could be mistaken. After all, Jean should be at work. And I knew that I could not be mistaken. "Jean!"

I began to run. She did not break her stride. As I came closer, I saw that her hair was a flaming red, curled tightly to her head. Doubts swept me once more. I came up with her. It was Jean, but what was wrong with her? Her face was set and blank, like the faces I had seen on the subway. She did not look at me. Below through the holes in her halter, another pair of eyes, a brilliant orange, stared straight ahead.

"Why didn't you meet me? Did you get my spacegram?" I walked along beside her, puzzled and worried. "Jean," I said. She did not respond. Was she deaf? I caught her bare shoulder. "Jean!" I shook it gently. She walked on.

We came to the corner drugstore. Jean turned, opened the door, went in. I followed, dazedly. Jean stopped at the end of a long line of women waiting to reach the counter. She stood patiently, cowlike, with no movement except when the line inched up.

The women ahead put a bill down on the counter. The clerk took it and handed each one a wrapped package from a pile of them beside him. At last Jean came to the counter. She put down a bill, crumpled from the heat of her hand. She took a package. She turned.

"Frank! Where did you come from?" Her eyes were wide and surprised. Her soft orange lips were parted. She looked different from the picture I had carried with me in my mind. But it was Jean, and she was glad to see me.

"Jean!" I laughed shakily. "I thought something was wrong with you. You acted so funny."

Jean laughed. It was her old laugh, free and ringing. At least that hadn't changed. Perhaps nothing had changed, I thought; perhaps it was me. "Nonsense!" she said. "What could be wrong with me? Oh, Frank! You're back!" In spite of the crowded store, she threw her arms around my neck and pulled my lips down to hers.

I broke away. "Not here," I said.

"You're never going away again," Jean said.

"Never," I echoed. I frowned and pointed to the package in her hand. "What's that? You were so determined to get it. You and all these other women."

Jean shrugged. "Oh, I don't know. Something I heard advertised, I guess."

She tore off the wrapping. "Toothpaste," she said. She seemed to be disappointed.

"Didn't you know?" I asked. "Don't you know what you're buying?"

Jean took my arm and drew me out of the store. "Oh, let's not talk about things like that. You've been gone a long time. Things change. Tell me about life in an asteroid belt navigation beacon. Tell me all about it." She led me toward our house.

"I could tell it all in one word," I said. "Boredom. Every twenty-four hours I would—"

"Wait, Frank," Jean interrupted. "Tell me about it later. I want to get home."

"Three years apart for a lifetime together," I said. "That's not a bad trade. But why aren't you at work?"

"Oh, I quit," Jean said. "A long time ago. There didn't seem much point in it when we had so much money."

I felt vaguely uneasy. "How much have we got?"

"Oh, I don't know." She shrugged. "You know I was never good at figures. Besides, there are lots of things more important than money. You, for instance."

She smiled up into my face, and my heart turned over. I had torn myself away when she was still little more than a bride, loving her as I did, wanting to buy the world for her. That's why I had traded three years of my life. And those three years away had tempered my love into a clean, singing blade.

"Are you in such a hurry to get me home?" I asked, smiling.

"Now, Frank," she said. She moved a little ahead. My arm fell away. "There's a program. I don't want to miss it."

"A program!" I said. "But I just got home."

"I know," Jean said. "But you'll be home for a long time."

We were at the front door. I caught her by the shoulders. "Jean," I said. "What's the matter with you? I'm home. After three years completely alone. Aren't you—? Don't you—?"

"Now, Frank," she said. "Don't be a beast!" She wriggled away as I tried to draw her close.

She opened the door, brushed past me into the living room, and sat down quickly in front of the television set. The screen was a swirl of colors.

"SWISH-SWASH SWISH-SWASH WITH WISH-WASH WISH-WASH," the chant went. "WISH YOUR WASH DON'T SWISH YOUR WASH DON'T SWISH YOUR WASH USE WISH-WASH SWISH-SWASH SWISH-SWASH WITH. . . ."

"Oh, no!" I moaned.

"JEAN," I said. "Turn it off."

"You don't understand," Jean said, not taking her eyes from the screen. "I have to find out what will happen to Sandra. She is being tempted by Rodney St. John to betray her husband. Sandra is torn between romance and duty."

The chant went on interminably. At last it faded, and the screen cleared. A man with glossy black hair was kissing a blonde girl passionately. They were both dressed scantily, but I couldn't decide whether this was supposed to indicate anything. Slowly they drew apart, clinging to each other like suction cups.

"Now, Sandra," said the man, "whose husband is my best friend but beside whom the ties of friendship, honor, decency, and wealth mean nothing, now that you know the depth and strength of my love, will you go with me to my mountain cabin?"

"Oh, Rodney," said the girl, "who has given me the love and passion I thought were gone forever, I can't. I can't. Love is strong, but the call of duty is stronger."

The man seized her again. They melted together, fading, and the swirls of color drew them down.

"SWISH-SWASH SWISH-SWASH. . . ."

I stared incredulously. What had happened to the world I had left. Fourteen and a half minutes of the same, endlessly repetitive commercial to thirty seconds of drama, nonsense though it was. Something had warped the world's values.

I reached toward the set. A man loomed large on the screen, one finger pointing straight toward me. "Stay tuned to this station," he commanded.

I twisted the switch. The set went dark. Jean gasped. "Frank," she said. "You can't do that!"

"Why not?" I said. "I want to talk to you."

"Later," she said. "Didn't you hear the announcer? Didn't you hear what he said?"

She turned the set back on and sank back in her chair. I looked on helplessly. Before the new commercial could come on, I fled from the living room. In a moment the monotonous chant followed me like an implacable ghost, but I did not hear it. I stood in the doorway of the kitchen, staring with wide, startled eyes.

The kitchen was filled with shining, chromium plated junk. Everywhere, from floor to ceiling, piled up, stacked aimlessly. Freezers, roasters, cookers, appliances of every size and description. Almost none of them had ever been used; their umbilical-like cords were still folded up neatly and tied.

The cupboards were packed with food. Cans, packages, and bottles were shoved into the shelves without order, one on top of another, balancing precariously. They had overflowed onto the floor. Soon it would be impossible to enter the kitchen at all.

They are spawning in there, I thought crazily, breeding and interbreeding, reproducing themselves and obscenely mutated caricatures of themselves.

I backed out and let the door swing shut. Suddenly I had no appetite.

I forced my way into the bedroom. Things had been breeding here, too. The weight of their numbers had burst open the closet doors. Dresses, shoes, fur coats, underclothes, towels—they humped unevenly on the floor, creeping toward the narrow lane that led to the unmade bed. Untidy piles of things, worn and unworn.

The bathroom was a shambles of packages, jars, bottles, tubes, toothbrushes. The tub was a mounded heap of them. *Where does she take a bath?* I wondered dully. I wandered from room to room, sweating, searching for an explanation. Somewhere there had to be an explanation.

Drugs or hypnosis? I thought again. I hadn't wanted to buy anything.

When I got back to the living room, Jean was gone. The television set was still blaring away. I turned It off savagely and looked around the room, noticing for the first time that everything was new. Where was Jean?

Her purse was lying on a shiny table, gaping open. I picked it up and dumped its contents onto the table. There was a yellow envelope, unopened. I didn't open it. I knew what was in it.

A small, flat black book lay among the litter. I flipped it open. A few deposits were listed. And checks marked down, long rows of them. Fifty-nine dollars and sixty-seven cents. That was Jean's total. But Jean was always poor at figures. A letter in a red envelope informed me that the checking account was overdrawn.

There had to be something else. A savings account. Of course. That was it. There was a savings account.

I pawed through the mess on the table. Here it was. Another black book, smaller than the other. I leafed through the pages. So many withdrawals!

One hundred and twenty-one dollars! No! It was impossible! Three years of hell for one hundred and twenty-one dollars. My mind rebelled. My head throbbed.

The door opened. I whirled. Jean stood in the doorway, a package in her hand.

"Oh," she said. "You've turned it off again." Her voice sounded like that of a disappointed child.

"Jean," I said. My voice shook. "Jean! Where is the rest of it?"

"The rest of what?"

"The money. The money the company paid you while I was out there. The one hundred and fifty thousand dollars. Where is it?"

"But you have the check book," Jean said bewilderedly. "And the savings book. That's it. That's all there is."

I sank down in a chair that drew me down in a deep embrace, holding the little black books in my hand.

IT wasn't as if Jean was mad. She was very reasonable. She kept trying to explain, trying to make me understand. For a moment I almost believed that I was the one who was being purposefully difficult. It took so much more to live now, Jean said. People needed so many more things. People bought more.

"It's the standard of living," Jean said. "It's gone up. Everybody says so."

"The food," I moaned. "You'll never eat it up."

"It sounded so good at the time," she said vaguely.

"All those clothes! They'll rot before you can wear them all."

"Oh, Frank," she chided me. "Synthetics don't rot."

I wanted to ask her what she would do when the rooms were full from floor to ceiling, but I had a crazy suspicion what she would say. Lock the doors, she would say, and start all over.

"Where has it all gone," I groaned. "How could you spend so much?"

"There's the Cadillac," Jean said. "And the new air conditioner. That isn't connected, of course. And all the little things." She moved toward the television set.

I stepped in front of it. "No more," I said. "You aren't looking at this thing any more. And you aren't buying another thing."

"All right, Frank," she said meekly.

"Go fix me something to eat," I said. "Nothing out of cans. A steak. Onions. A glass of milk."

"Yes, Frank," she said, moving obediently toward the kitchen.

"And after that," I said, "we're going to bed."

But it wasn't like I thought it was going to be. There wasn't anything that didn't come out of cans, and the new range wasn't connected. The food was cold. And later—? Well, maybe I had been expecting too much.

Maybe three years is too long to be away. It left a sour

taste in my mouth. It took me a long time to go to sleep, and when I slept, I dreamed.

I dreamed that I had just been having a terrible dream. I had to wake up. The buzzer kept trying to wake me. An urgent message was coming in for me. I stirred uneasily. Something was wrong. The beacon had gone out or the radar had picked up a new swarm. I had to wake up....

I opened my eyes. The room was dark, but I knew at once that it was not the room I had known for three years, that I had grown into until it was like part of my skin. I was in my own bedroom on Earth. The dream in my dream had not been a nightmare. My money was gone, wasted, thrown away.

I turned over on my side. Jean was gone, Jean with the flaming red hair that had once been blonde, and the painted nipples, and the slack body. Voices came from the living room.

I got up and threaded my way through piles of clothing to the door. Jean was sitting in front of the television set in her nightgown, her eyes turned hypnotically to the screen. Flickering waves of color played over her face.

The chill of fear that comes when you see actions that are terrible and unmotivated was replaced by an anger that was even colder. I glanced down at my hand. There was a brass candlestick in it. I had picked it up somewhere, I could not remember where. I stalked into the living room.

I swung the candlestick once. The glass front of the set shattered into fragments and went dark. I swung again. The wood of the casing split. I swung the candlestick tirelessly, until the set was a mass of broken rubble and the candle-stick was an unrecognizable length of bent and twisted metal. My arm hung heavy at my side.

Jean looked up at me with wide, frightened eyes. "Frank," she said. Her voice trembled. "I—"

"Go to bed."

She went slowly, looking back over her shoulder. I sank down slowly in front of the wreckage.

Was this nightmare or reality? It had the feel of night-mare to it, a dreamlike horror that was full of basic fears and incomprehensible actions and motivations. Was I on the hollow metal sphere that paces the asteroid belt, dreaming in my bunk? But never before had I dreamed that I slept, that I dreamed.

My hand hurt. I held it up. Blood dripped from several small cuts. I went to the bathroom and found a towel and wrapped it around my hand.

I went to the living room. I sat and stared at the wreck-age of the television set. Dawn crept in and found me there. I stirred. I had to turn somewhere for help, for ex-planation. There was only one place I knew to go.

I dressed slowly. My hand had stopped bleeding. When I left the house, I locked all the doors and removed the keys. I wanted Jean to be here when I got back. Somehow, we would have to work out the basis for a life together.

The building was not far from Times Square. It was tall. It pointed toward where the stars would be, if there were any stars. The sun blazed hot. Christmas carols boomed in the street.

Across the front of the building, over the entrance, was engraved: AD ASTRA PER ASPERA. It was the state motto of Kansas, but that was not why it was there. Once I had thought it was the motto of our time, but now I was not so sure. Perhaps it had been replaced by something else, less stirring, less determined.

"Go right in," said the secretary. She wore a dress, and looked much more seductive in it than all the nakedness I had seen. "Mr. Wilson is expecting you."

I walked into the office, the one I had walked out of a little over three years ago, on my way to the stars. "You knew I would be back?" I said.

His young-old face seemed sympathetic and human. "Of course," he said.

"What's wrong with everything?" I asked distractedly. "Or is it me? What's happened to the world? What can I do?"

"That's a lot of questions," Wilson said slowly. "And I think I can answer them best by starting at the beginning. The beginning was shortly after you left Earth. To us, who have seen it grow, it does not seem so bad. But I imagine it must be a shock to you. But remember, we offered to renew your contract."

"Three more years out there?" I shuddered.

"I suppose it was inevitable. Everything was working toward it. If it seemed to come suddenly, it was because everything came to fruition at once. And then there was the Advertising Institute. Financed by a number of the large philanthropic foundations, it was set up to analyze basic advertising psychology. It was successful, and then it was too late. It couldn't be kept a secret."

"What?"

"Advertising," Wilson said. "It became a science instead of an art.

"YOU must remember the function of advertising," Wilson said. "To make the consumer want something he doesn't want. Perfect it—and you have our society."

He outlined the development of a science, and I tried to understand. No one man had been responsible. It had been partly a group effort, partly a fumbling together of blind trends. Pre-scientific advertisers had been groping toward it. They had stumbled on several basic elements pragmatically. Irritation, for instance, and its sister, repetition. Irritate something long enough and often enough, and inevitably it must be scratched. And the only way to relieve this itch is to buy the product.

The Ad Institute had discovered this, or—more accurately—they had re-discovered it and refined it. And their research in other fields bore fruit, too. The arts, for instance. Modern art forms had been struggling toward a more basic kind of communication, one that appeals immediately to the senses instead of filtering through the upper centers of the mind. That fitted in nicely. Modify them. Improve them. Incorporate them.

Modern poetry, for example. Disappointed expectation. Rhythms. Quarter rhymes. Music with its polytonal scales and lack of recognizable tunes. The imageless effects of modern painting. Not aesthetic, familiar, intellectual. Visceral.

Irritation and repetition. Irritation and repetition. Advertising had them for a long time, but they were never applied scientifically. Advertisers were held back by human sympathies, deterred by intellectual complaints, forgetting that the consumer mass didn't complain. It bought. Science, of course, is ruthless. It has to be ruthless to be a science. Scientists in the pursuit or application of knowledge are not human beings but thinking machines. Emotions interfere with thought; they enshroud the cold truth with warm but misleading mantles. Rip them off! Suppress emotions! The truth must be bare.

The Ad Institute had the truth then, and the truth cannot be killed. Not in this case, anyway. Too many people knew about it, underpaid researchers and students. Know the truth and the truth shall make you—rich. The only thing to do was to try to control it. So the Institute became a commercial center.

"Horrible," I said. I looked down at my twitching hands. "Horrible."

Wilson shook his head. "Not entirely. It has had its blessings. The cold war, for instance, is over. The Russian empire crumbled before the onslaught of scientific advertising. It fell to pieces—literally—within a month. It was only necessary to arouse desires—or to intensify them—which the existing regime was unable to satisfy. The pieces are still being reassembled.

"War is impossible now, as long as the avenues of communication are kept open. And that is the foundation stone of the reorganized United Nations. Much more important than armaments. Inspection teams are everywhere. The first hint of censorship, the first jamming static, and the barrage of words descends. The offending government is overthrown. On the whole, I think the world is better off."

"No," I muttered. "No. The world is populated with automatons. Buying. Buying. Buying. Spending. Spending. Spending."

"There has always been a certain amount of robotism in the world," Wilson pointed out. "Throughout history, millions have been bereft of their senses by those who have known how to punch the right emotional button. Witness the great movements of history, the Crusades, the French and Russian Revolutions, countless wars. At every point between global and community affairs, robotism has played its part. Now, at least, the command is not to fight, not to revolt, but to buy. As a consequence, the world is more prosperous than it has ever been. Everybody is making good wages, everybody is buying. What could be better?"

"The wastage," I groaned.

"The wastage," Wilson said, "is a vital part of our economy. In a period of peace, of high production in a heavily mechanized society, wastage is necessary to avoid collapse. That and a rapid turnover keep up the level of consumption to which our industrial machine is geared. Better wastage than war."

"The ad men could take over the world," I said. "Who could stop them? Not a race of slaves."

"IT isn't that bad. Resistance to modern advertising varies from complete submission to complete immunity, as it always has, usually according to intelligence, although there are psychological factors which are sometimes of even greater importance. Those who are immune run the world, as they always have, and see to it that the greater percentage of submissives get the work done."

"And you are immune?" I asked. Wilson nodded, shrugging. I felt a dawn of hope. "I must be immune, too. I haven't bought anything. I haven't even been tempted."

Wilson raised an eyebrow. "The science of advertising, like all sciences of mass phenomena, is based on the norm—"

I looked up quickly, angrily. "And I am not normal. Is that what you mean?"

Wilson raised a pacifying hand. "You didn't let me finish. A norm, I said. In that sense you are not normal. Anyone who can stay sane for three years, in complete isolation, is not normal to begin with. And the psychological impact of advertising is dependent upon the society in which the individual finds himself. You were not at home in our society when you volunteered for the beacon. Now that you have returned, you belong even less. Three years alone has not made you more social. And the society is almost new. You are like a newborn child. You must learn to belong."

"Learn to belong," I echoed. The meaning came to me slowly. "No! I don't want to belong. I'm immune. I must stay immune. I don't want to be a slave like the rest of them." I thought of Jean; I thought of $150,000. "Besides, I have no money."

"But what of your salary?" Wilson said.

"Gone. Wasted. Thrown away. One hundred and fifty thousand dollars," I mourned.

Wilson shook his head sympathetically. "Unfortunate. It was something none of us could foresee. That a rising standard of living would wipe out the money that seemed a more than fair salary at the time. Some people have called it inflation. But it isn't inflation. Wages have risen along with prices. They have more than kept pace. It is the standard of living. I am sure that you can find a job. Since we are partly responsible, I imagine we will be able to find some kind of work for you."

I thought about the robots on the subway, the captive audience rising on command to buy and coming back to be commanded again. I thought about going home to Jean and a house full of junk, ever full of more and more, piling up, deteriorating, crowding us out.

Suddenly the hollow sphere that paced the asteroids did not seem so lonely any more. Suddenly it seemed like home.

"Look!" I said. "Can I go back? Can I go back to the beacon?" I pulled a crumpled sheet of yellow paper from my pocket. "I have your offer here. I wouldn't want any more money. I'll cut it in half—"

Slowly, sadly, Wilson shook his head. "I'm afraid not. You can take the psychological tests, of course. But I can tell you right now that the results will be negative. Your return has changed the situation radically. Instead of fleeing from society, you are rebelling against it. It makes all the difference."

"I can't go back," someone was whimpering. "I can't go back. . . ."

Slowly I realized that it was me.

Kaleidoscope:
". . . ALL IS CALM, ALL IS BRIGHT . . ."

Wreaths, holly, bells, candles—green and red; a man in a red and white suit. A flaming sun . . .

"GIVE–GIVE–GIVE–GIVE–GIVE . . ."

A swirl of colors, a pattern of dots, smoke rising . . .

WHINRR-R-R! "BE-E-E BEWITCHING! BUY-Y-Y-Y BEWITCHING!" THUMP! THUMP!

Eyes, blank eyes, painted eyes . . .

WHANG-NG! STRNNNNH! "NERVES TAUT? SMOKE A LOT? DON'T JITTER, JETTER! BETTER BUY BILLOWS! Relax-x-x!" Sigh. WHANG-NG! . . .

Sliding doors, marching feet, automatic, all . . .

"SOO-SOO-SOO-SOOTHE . . ."

THUMP-THUMP! "BUY NOW!" THUMP-THUMP!

SLOWLY, dazedly, I opened the front door of my house. "SWISH-SWASH SWISH-SWASH WITH WISH-WASH WISH-WASH. WISH YOUR WASH DON'T SWISH YOUR WASH DON'T SWISH YOUR WASH USE WISH-WASH SWISH-SWASH SWISH-SWASH WITH . . ."

Jean sat in front of a television set, new, bigger, shinier, more glaring. She did not look up. She did not lift her eyes from the swirling colors.

My shoulders slumped. I felt in my pocket. The two little black books were there, but it didn't make any difference. She had bought it on time, of course. Now I was in debt. I felt myself sinking into a morass of sucking mud. The grass around it grew in the shape of dollar signs.

I felt in my pants pockets. They were empty. Empty? I pulled out my billfold. It was empty, too. Empty? Impossible. I had started out this morning with almost fifty dollars and a pocket full of charge. I searched frantically. Caught in the lining of my coat pocket was a single quarter. Where——? But I couldn't have lost it. It couldn't have been stolen. My billfold was still there.

Vaguely, distantly, I heard a voice chanting: "GIVE-GIVE-GIVE-GIVE-GIVE . . ."

A dry sob rose in my throat. Immunity!

I rushed to the bedroom. I tossed clothing wildly in the air, digging down to the desk I knew had to be here somewhere. But when I reached it at last, it was filled with everything but what I wanted. I raged through the house. Finally I reached the basement. It was cluttered with junk. But there I found it, in a dark corner. It was a little rusty, but it moved freely when I worked the slide back. A shell flipped out into my hand. Loaded and ready. I ejected the clip, slipped the shell back into it, clicked the clip back into position.

I came up the basement stair, holding the automatic in one hand. Jean was gone, but the television set was lit up in all its prismatic glory.

I slipped the gun into my coat pocket and walked out of the house. . . .

KLING-KLANK! "GIVE-GIVE-GIVE-GIVE . . ."

CRACK-K-K! CRACK-CRACK-K-K! The gun jumped in my hand. The man in the red and white suit looked down at his swollen, red and white belly in astonishment. It had begun to smoke. There was no blood. Slowly, like a stuffed doll, he folded to the sidewalk. He lay there beside the tripod on top of which was the sign: "IT IS MORE BLESSED TO GIVE THAN TO RECEIVE."

". . . SLEEP IN HEAVENLY PEACE. SLEEP . . ."
"What was that?"
"There was this cracking noise, and then he fell over. . . ."
"Somebody shot Santa Claus!"
"Don't be silly. Nobody shoots Santa Claus. . . ."

WE were riding somewhere. I turned to the man in blue on my right. "You'll hang me, won't you?" I said eagerly. "Or electrocute me? Or whatever you do to murderers?"

"Now, now," the kindly man said. "We aren't going to punish you. Prisons aren't for that. We're going to make you a fit member of society. I think you will enjoy your stay here. The cells are really quite comfortable."

"No, no!" I screamed when they put me in the room, "You can't! Take me out! Please, oh, please. . . ."

Inexorably, from behind the impregnable protective screen, came the music and the chant: WHANG-NG! STRNNN-NH! "NERVES TAUT? SMOKE A LOT? DON'T JITTER, JETTER! BETTER BUY BILLOWS! Relax-x-x!" WHANG-NG! STRNNN-NH! "NERVES TAUT? . . ."

Ad infinitum. . . .

THE END

I'LL TAKE OVER
A. Bertram Chandler
(as George Whitley)

A. Bertram Chandler, a naval officer by profession and a science-fiction writer by avocation, was born in England in 1912, moved to Australia at the age of 44, and remained there, commanding ships in the Australian and New Zealand merchant marine, until his death in 1984. From 1944 on he was a prolific writer of strongly plotted science fiction, producing forty novels and more than two hundred short stories, many of them drawing on his maritime experiences, as in the numerous books in the Commodore Grimes and Rim World series. Among his best-known stories are "The Cage" (1957), "Giant Killer" (1945), and "Frontier of the Dark" (1952).

"I'll Take Over," which was published in the August, 1957 issue of Super-Science Fiction, originally appeared under the pseudonym of George Whitley, which Chandler occasionally used throughout his career. The reason for its use on this story was that there was another and longer story by Chandler in the same issue, and, following the old pulp-magazine convention that no byline should be used more than once in the same issue, editor Scott put the penname on this one. I have restored Chandler's own name for the story's appearance here.

The Brain ran the huge starship and ran it well. But Lloyd's of London insisted a human crew be carried. A man must be better than man's creation, they said.

Artwork by Paul Orban

IT WAS, WE supposed at the time, Clavering's fault—but we did him an injustice. Clavering was our Interstellar Drive Technician, duly certificated to hold that rank. His job, actually, was a sinecure, as were all our jobs. But, as you know, Lloyd's of London refuse to cover a ship unless a full human crew is carried. The Brains can go wrong. So, of course, can mere human brains—especially in Deep Space, especially in the odd, time twisting fields generated by the Drive. Lloyd's however, always seem more than willing to back the fallible human being against the machine. As an Underwriter, with whom I was once discussing this very point, once told me: No created thing can possibly be greater than its creator. (He had never, he admitted, made a voyage in one of the fully-automatic star ships . . .)

We were falling free when it happened, drifting down the dimensions with, of course, only the Interstellar Drive functioning. There were only the three of us in the ship—myself, Captain and Navigator; Joe Bennett, Rocket Technician; Clavering, Interstellar Drive Technician. Both Joe and I had stacks of back reading to catch up with and, furthermore, we had decided to make a really serious attempt at learning 3-D Chess. Joe wouldn't have to worry about his rockets—if he worried then—until we made planetfall. I was content to leave the navigation to the Brain.

Clavering, however, was neither a great reader nor a chess addict. Music had no charms—and we carried a remarkably comprehensive library of recordings—to soothe his savage breast. His hobby, as well we knew, was worrying.

He worried first of all about the cargo—until I told him, in no uncertain terms, that it was *my* worry. I admit that it was an unusual sort of shipment—a full load of assorted carvings and statuary of various heathen deities for an anthropological Museum on Deneb VI. As far as I was concerned, there was nothing to worry about. Everything was well packed and well stowed, and the collection of the freight was up to the bright young financial wizards in Head Office; I was just paid to carry the junk from Point A to Point B, and that was what I was doing.

Clavering accused me of being insensitive.

"Don't you realize, Skipper," he said, "that many of those grinning stone gods and goddesses had human sacrifices made to them? Don't you realize that some sort of aura of evil may have persisted down the ages?"

"So," I asked him, "what?"

"What about that mummy?" he asked. "I was reading about it not so long ago. It was way back in the early Twentieth Century, and it was brought from its tomb in Egypt to the British Museum in London. There was a curse of some kind laid on those who had opened the tomb. The same curse worked against various employees of the Museum. Finally the mummy was sold to an American collector and . . ."

"And I suppose its evil influence went on working in America."

"No," said Clavering triumphantly. "Because it never got there! The ship that it was traveling in—it was in the days of the big, steam-driven surface vessels, of course—hit an iceberg and went down with a heavy loss of life."

"Cheer up," I told him. "There aren't any icebergs

in Deep Space. And there can't be any heavy loss of life here—there're only the three of us. We're just not worth worrying about—if all those idols in the cargo want a human sacrifice apiece there aren't enough of us to go round!"

"Stow it, Clavering," pleaded Joe. "We've another couple of months of this, and it's bad enough to have to sit on top of a Pile for all that time, knowing that it's liable to blow us all to Kingdom Come at any second, without your telling us that the various deities in our cargo are liable to snatch us to the wrong destination when it *does* happen!"

"So you aren't happy about the Pile?" asked Clavering intently. "Funnily enough, I've had a sort of feeling . . ."

"The Pile's all right!" shouted Joe. "There's nothing wrong with the Pile. The Pile is my responsibility—and as long as it continues to drive the jennies to give you the juice for your bunch of cockeyed gyroscopes I don't want to hear you mention it!"

"Oh, all right," said Clavering sulkily.

"Chess, Skipper?" asked Joe.

"No, it's too close to dinner time to start a game. I think I'll read for a while."

I unstrapped myself from my chair, floated to the big bookcase. Books are mass, and bookcases are even more mass, but the appearance of books, and the *feel* of books, more than compensates for the space they occupy and the lost freight on the cargo that could be carried in their stead.

I settled back in the chair, looking at the other two before

I opened my book. Joe was quite happy. He had the 3-D Chess set out and was playing with a problem. Clavering was fidgeting. He seemed to be listening to something.

"What's wrong *now?*" I asked.

"The Drive," he said.

I listened. The steady whine that was part of our lives all the time that we were in Deep Space seemed quite normal. I sighed. This was not the first time that Clavering had decided that its note was a fraction of an octave too high or too low.

"All right," I told him. "Go and look at it. But don't touch it without informing me first."

"Yes, Skipper," he said rather sulkily.

I opened the book, which was a collection of short stories—all light adventure stuff but amusing, sometimes unintentionally so. The average, planetbound author makes the most ludicrous gaffes when describing scenes and people on worlds alien to his own.

"THE GOD," I read.

"He could not be sure that the atmosphere of this world could support human life. Kent, the Chemist, was dead, as was Hall, the Biologist. They were all dead, he thought with the beginnings of panic. Those who had not been killed by the explosion had failed to survive the crash landing. *And because I was only the journalist of this expedition,* he thought with more bitterness than thankfulness, *I had no official Landing Station and was in a safe place when we hit . . .*

"He looked through the port, saw the yellow sun in the blue sky, the green grass and the green trees. *I could chance it,* he thought, *but there could be* anything *in this atmosphere.* He went to the locker, pulled out a spacesuit. He shrugged and wriggled himself into the stiff, clumsy garment. He shuffled to the airlock.

"At last he was outside the ship. The green turf felt good underfoot, even through the thick soles of his boots. He stood for long minutes by the crumpled wreckage of the survey ship. Anxiously he scanned the forest verge for some sign, any sign, of animal life.

"Then they came, the men and women of this planet. Tall they were, human rather than merely humanoid, splendid, golden-skinned savages, armed with spears and with long bows. Mason, the sole survivor of the expedition, stood his ground. He knew that his suit would deflect most missiles and would surely be proof against mere arrows and spears.

"Confident in the impregnability of his armor, he took one stiff step towards the group of savages, and another. He half expected that they would attack; he half expected that they would turn and run back into the forest.

He did not expect that they would grovel before him, that the tall man with the feathered headdress, their leader, would crawl over the grass and lay his beautifully carved bow at Mason's feet.

"Mason laughed softly as he realized the implications of the savage's action. He. . . .

. . . *looked through the port, saw the yellow sun in the blue sky, the green grass and the green trees. I could chance it, he.* . . .

. . . *could not be sure that the atmosphere of this world could support human life. Kent, the Chemist, was dead, as was Hall, the Biologist. They* . . .

. . . came, the men and women of this planet. Tall they were, human rather than merely humanoid, splendid, golden-skinned savages . . ."

I blinked. My attention had not strayed from my book yet I was getting nowhere fast. But I thought I knew what was amiss. I'd had experience of a faulty Drive and fluctuating Temporal Fields before. I looked at Joe.

"Skipper," he said, "there's something wrong. I've moved the White Queen at least five times, but she always finishes up where she started from . . ."

"That bloody Clavering!" I swore. "He's been tinkering with The Drive! Unless we get it sorted out we shan't know if it's breakfast time or last Thursday. Come on!"

We unstrapped ourselves from our chairs. It should have been an easy "swim" from the wardroom to the Drive Compartment, but it wasn't. As we pulled ourselves along the alleyways, through the shafts, it was like trying to run up a down-moving escalator. We got to the Drive Room at last. We opened the door. We found Clavering— and he wasn't pretty. Somehow he'd got himself mixed up with the Contraction Field, and he was dead. He had to be dead.

I don't know how many times I reached out for the Master Switch, but I got it at last, pulled it. The spinning, precessing wheels slowed, slowed and stopped. The lights flickered and flared, flickered and then shone steadily.

Joe swallowed hard.

"What do we do with . . . him?" he asked at last.

"A funeral," I said. "That's all we can do. Help me get him out of the compartment."

"Are you restarting the Drive?" asked Joe.

"Not yet. I have to check it first, see if it's safe."

We pulled Clavering's body along to the airlock, muffled it in a couple of blankets. Leaving it there, we pulled ourselves along to the Control Room. We ignored the banked instruments, went straight to the humming, clicking sphere that was The Brain. I pushed in the switch for Oral Communication.

"Is the Drive safe to use?" I asked.

"No," came the emotionless, metallic reply.

"Why was the Drive allowed to get out of hand? Why was the alarm not sounded?"

"I can not be responsible for interference," said The Brain. "I can not sound the alarm if the circuits have been disconnected."

That was that. It was useless blaming Clavering—besides, he had already paid, and heavily, for his folly.

"Can we repair the Drive?" I asked.

"Not in Space," came the emotionless reply. "Recalibration is essential, and that can be carried out only on the surface of a planet. I would recommend a landing on Altair III. I can guarantee if there is no further interference, to keep the Drive in operation for long enough to get you there."

"Couldn't we carry on for Deneb VI?" I asked.

"If you wish to take the risk. I can guarantee to deliver your bodies—but they will not be recognizable."

"Altair III is out of bounds, Skipper," said Joe.

"An emergency landing is permissable," said the Brain.

I pulled out the Oral Communication switch. I didn't like the way in which the thing was talking without being talked to. I pulled out from its rack the first volume of the Catalogue of Habitable Planets, skimmed through the Index, found the right page.

AS Joe Bennett had pointed out, Altair III was out of bounds. It was an Earth-Type planet, with gravitational-field, atmospheric composition and density, temperature range and humidity almost identical with those of Earth. It supported a varied flora and fauna, whose evolution had run on the same general lines as evolution on the Home Planet. There was a humanoid race, whose culture approximated that of Stone Age Man. And, by the ruling of the Convention of 2053, such races must be left to work out their own destinies in their own ways.

Still—Altair III it had to be. Our Interstellar Drive Technician was dead, and neither Joe nor I was qualified to argue with the Brain on the topic of Interstellar Drives.

"Get your rockets ready, Joe," I told him. "We have to turn her and give her a shove in the right direction. I'll attend to the navigation."

"Let the Brain do it all," said Joe. "It's what it's for. All that *we're* for is to carry the can back!"

We let the Brain do it all.

Everything but the funeral, that is.

WE did quite a good survey on Altair III before we set down. We found several errors in the existing charts—for example, that big, northern island continent has a deep bight on its east coast not shown by Commodore Wheeler's cartographers, and the mountains that he calls the

Borean Alps are at least half a mile higher than he makes them.

We decided to land on the huge prairie to the east-ward of the Borean Alps. It looked level enough for our purposes and, furthermore, looked too green to support the inevitable fire started by our rocket exhausts. The less damage we did the fewer explanations we should have to make to the Board of Control.

We brought the ship in manually—myself in the Control Room and Joe nursing his rockets. We made almost as good a landing as the Brain could have done, except for the fact that I didn't make sufficient allowance for the westerly wind. We came down far closer to the verge of the forest to the east of the prairie than I had intended. Not that it mattered much. Both Joe and I were far too relieved at having got here safely to worry about having missed our target by thirty miles or so.

When I was satisfied that all was secure and the ship wasn't liable to topple I shut up shop in the Control Room, made my way to the wardroom. Joe was waiting for me there. He had withdrawn the shutters from the ports, was looking out.

"Pretty, isn't it?" he said. "Just like Earth . . . I wonder what sort of animals they have in that forest?"

"Nothing for you to shoot," I told him. "I know you always carry your sporting rifles with you—but you aren't using them here. This is an emergency landing—not a rec-reation break!"

"As you say, Skipper. But we have to work outside while we're recalibrating the Drive—and we'd better have the rifles handy, just in case."

"The Catalogue," I said, "says that this world has no large carnivores . . ."

"What about *them?*" asked Joe, pointing to the figures emerging from the forest.

They certainly looked carniverous—the long, barbed spears they carried, and the bows slung at their backs, were surely designed for offense rather than defense. They stood there, a compact group of twenty, and stared at the ship. Through our port we stared back at them.

"Human," whispered Joe. "Vicious looking so-and-sos, aren't they? And you say that we're to go outside unarmed?"

"Listen," I said patiently. "I'm Master of this ship. I have to answer all the questions. I know what happens to any Captain who makes a landing on any Out-of-Bounds world, for any reason at all, and who steps just one millimetre out of line. *You* shoot a native—*I* spend the next twenty years digging pitchblende on Antares VII!"

"Perhaps they'll go away," suggested Joe.

They didn't. When night fell they were still there. We could see them moving—tall and black against the ruddy glare of their fire. At last Joe and I slept. It was already broad daylight when we awoke. The savages were still there—and at least twenty more had joined them.

We went to the galley and got our breakfasts. We returned to the wardroom with our trays, stared through the ports while eating our meal.

"How do we *know* they're hostile?" asked Joe at last.

"How do we know they're not?" I countered.

Joe reflectively swallowed a mouthful of scrambled egg.

"There's one thing we can do," he suggested. "We can lift ship, and set her down again some place where there aren't any savages . . ."

"I've already thought of that," I told him. "But those people, as long as they stay where they are, are bound to be fried by the backblast. Even if they run into the forest as soon as you start warming up the rockets, this prevailing wind is bound to set us drifting in over the trees . . ."

"And you say that we can't go out armed," murmured Joe. "Is there any rule that says we shouldn't go out *armored?*"

I remembered, suddenly, the absurd story that I'd been reading when the Drive got out of control.

"That's it!" I said. "We'll put our spacesuits on—they'll be proof against the spears and arrows. I'll go out—and you keep an eye on me from the airlock. I'll try to convince our friends by signs that we come in peace and mean them no harm. I'll try to persuade them to go away . . ."

"And you can ask them where the nearest pub is and what time it closes," said Joe.

"Sign language," I said stiffly, "has its limitations."

"That," he said, "was what I was pointing out, Skipper!"

I felt absurdly foolish as I walked clumsily down the ramp from the airlock. This planet was too Earthlike for a man to be wearing full space armor. I should be breathing fresh air redolent with the scent of the hot sun on grass, not canned, recirculated air from my tanks. The grass was soft underfoot, even through the thick soles of my boots. I imagined that I could feel the tall stems swishing against my legs as I walked—but this, I knew, was only illusion.

The savages stirred at my approach. Those who had been sitting got up. They did not stay in a compact group but spread out into a long line, a crescent. I became uncomfortably aware that the horns of the crescent were closing in. I looked behind me. Joe Bennett was standing in the airlock, his armor gleaming in the sunlight. I found myself wishing that I had been more specific in my instructions to him. I felt that a disregard of the ban on firearms would have been justified—then realised that Joe would be unable to use a rifle while clad in his spacesuit, anyhow.

"Watch them, Skipper!" warned Joe, his voice crackling through my helmet speaker. "They're closing in!"

"I know," I replied.

They didn't look as though they were going to use their weapons—that was a good sign—but neither did they show any tendency towards bowing down to me in worship. They closed in around me warily, their tall, heavily-muscled bodies tense. They grinned, showing white, sharply pointed teeth. Their faces looked more like the faces of sharks than of men.

I raised both hands above my head, palms outward, the universal gesture of peace for all humanoids. Its only effect on the natives was provocative. They rushed me, knocking me off balance. I fell heavily, and once I was down I was as helpless as a turtle on its back, as an unhorsed armored knight of medieval times. From where I was lying I could see the brief struggle as Joe, his arms swinging, waded into the mob—and then he was down, and as helpless as I. We

submitted—we had no option—to the tying of thick cords
about our wrists and ankles.

"Joe," I said, "I appreciate your rushing to my help—
but you should have stayed in the ship!"

"That was my intention," he replied: grimly, "but she
tilted, somehow, tipped me out of the airlock. Then she
withdrew the ramp and closed the door!"

"Impossible!" I said.

But when I was lifted, slung on a long pole carried by
two of the savages, I was able to turn my head enough to
see that the ramp was up and the airlock door closed.

OUR journey was not overly long—no more than four
hours' march into the forest. It was neither comfortable
nor, after the first ten minutes or so, especially interesting.
A view of tree tops passing steadily overhead can be more
than a little monotonous. We saw practically nothing of
the village into which we were at last brought—all we
did see, in fact, was the open sky that told us that we had
entered a clearing. And then the matting of the roof of a
hut.

We were lowered to the ground with a jolt, and the
poles were slid out from between our bound wrists and
ankles. I saw, dimly, somebody doing something with what
looked like a stone knife. It was some little time before I
realised that my wrists were free.

The savages had left us alone in the hut. As far as we
could see—the place was illuminated only by what light
came through the chinks between the logs forming the
walls—it was strongly built and would resist all attempts
to break out. We were hampered, too—by the fact that

our feet were still tied; the gloves of a spacesuit just aren't made to cope with even the simplest bends and hitches.

"We'd better take our suits off," said Joe.

"No," I said. "As long as we keep them on they'll think that we're some superior sort of being. Once we take 'em off—then they'll know that we're only men like themselves . . ."

"What about eating?" he asked. "And drinking? And. . . ?"

"It'll have to wait until after dark," I said. "I hope that they do know that we eat and drink . . ."

"Why should they?" he grumbled.

For hours we lay there in discomfort, breathing the stale air from our tanks. We knew that we were being watched. We knew that we should have to endure our great and little miseries, our aches and itches, until the welcome darkness gave us freedom of movement. I was half asleep when the door of the hut suddenly opened. Two naked women—and very human they looked—came in. One carried a large jug of water, the other a woven tray on which were six huge, golden fruit. One of them nudged me with a slim, shapely (but it had only four toes) foot. I could see her pointed teeth shining as she laughed. Then they left us, closing the door after them.

"I'm thirsty," said Joe.

"So am I," I said. "But it can't be long to sunset."

Measured in terms of subjective time it can't have been. Measured in terms of subjective time it was. And then the light of the huge fire that was burning outside made the inside of the hut almost as light as it was before.

At last the fire died down and only the merest glimmer was showing through the cracks. Carefully, I slid off first one glove, then the other. The helmet came off next—and the air, in spite of the smells unavoidable in the village of people with a primitive level of sanitation, was good.

"What a relief!" I heard Joe gasp. "After you with the water jug, Skipper."

"After you, Joe," I said.

I heard him gulp as he drank deeply, then it was my turn.

Cautiously we tasted the fruit. It was thin-skinned, like a mango in texture and indescribable in flavour. I began to wonder if there might be some way of getting round the Out-of-Bounds ruling and opening this planet to commerce. Whoever had the sole rights of exporting that fruit to the civilised worlds would be a millionaire in a matter of months.

"I've got to take my suit off, Skipper," said Joe.

"All right," I said, "but we'd better take it by turns—just in case. You first."

And then the itching started. The things, whatever they were, had got down inside our suits, inside our clothes, after we had removed our helmets. There are, I know, records for the fast donning of spacesuits—if there are any records for the fast stripping of them, we beat them. Our uniforms followed. And while we were frantically scratching, the savages burst through the suddenly opened door and dragged us out into the light of the revived fire.

We expected death—at least. We did not expect to be the butts of raucous, uncontrolled laughter. Our bodies were of course, a little different from those of the natives, but I still can't see that they were so wildly funny.

IN the weeks that followed we learned the simple language. Our status was rather hard to define—we were prisoners but, at the same time, we were guests. We began to feel a sort of gratitude to our captors and, since if we were ever to get away from this world we should have to earn the goodwill of the natives, began to earn our keep. Oh, I know that it was all contrary to the Out-of-Bounds rule, but it was justified. We gave them the wheel, we gave them the dugout canoe. Fire they already had, so we began to investigate the possibility of smelting metals.

Our status improved. We were, eventually looked upon more as useful members of the community than as either guests or prisoners—but we were still prisoners. We found this out every time that we asked to be taken to the ship, to the big "sky canoe." We were allowed to leave the village only under strong escort—not that it really mattered, we didn't know in which direction the ship lay.

Then, one evening, we were sitting in the Chief's hut, sharing the savoury meal that was being served by his wives and daughters. He was in a preoccupied mood. Nevertheless, I decided to make my usual request, expecting to receive the usual answer.

"Broba," I said, talking with my mouth full as was the local custom, "Joe and I want to see the sky canoe."

"Tomorrow, Skipper," he said, deftly spitting out a small bone. "Tomorrow both moons are full. Tomorrow you go to see *Boston Lass . . .*"

He did not seem to be at all happy as he said it.

He must realise, he thought, that it will mean losing us. Come to that—we'll be sorry to go. If only the women didn't smell so strongly and didn't have pointed teeth I wouldn't mind settling down here . . .

We finished the baked lizard, then topped off with the golden-skinned fruit. Broba passed round a jug of wine—another of our contributions to this culture. Wine usually made the Chief merry, but tonight it made him more miserable. We were not sorry when he dismissed us and we were able to return to our own hut.

"Skipper," said Joe in English, "how did he know the ship's name?"

"He must have heard us use it some time," I said lightly.

"It can't be that, Skipper. We've used the name only when we've been talking in English. Using the native language we've always referred to her as the 'big sky canoe' . . ."

"Perhaps these people are telepaths," I said.

"Perhaps they're not," he said.

"Oh, forget it!" I told him. "We're being taken to the ship tomorrow evening. Once we get back inside we shall be all set. Get some sleep, will you?"

THE next day dragged. The worst of it was not the waiting, but the air of tension that hung over the whole village. Men, women and children with whom we had laughed and joked now seemed almost scared of us. It seemed, I thought, that my old dream of being received as a god by these happy primitives was, at last, coming true.

After the midday meal we were called from our hut. A procession was forming up in the village square. Six stalwart young men bore on their shoulders one of the dugout canoes. It was garlanded with gaudy blossoms. A woman bore a huge jar of the wine that we had showed them how to make. Another young man was pushing one of the little wheeled carts that we had introduced.

Broba came forward, hung garlands around our necks. It reminded me of the Hawaiian ceremony of farewell.

"They realise that they're losing us soon," I whispered to Joe.

"Did you ever read Fraser?" he asked. *"The Golden Bough?"*

"No," I said.

"Never mind," he answered. "I could be wrong."

We took our places, with the Chief, midway in the procession, immediately preceded by the things that we had made. I asked Broba what it was all about.

"Boston Lass wants you," he said.

"You've got it the wrong way round," I told him. "We want *Boston Lass!*"

He refused to say any more, and we marched on in silence.

IT was a long walk, and Joe and I were unused to so much exercise. We were both of us staggering when we got to the verge of the forest. I cried out with joy when I saw the tall, slim tower that was the ship, dark against the sunset. I seized Broba's hand, shook, it vigorously.

"Thank you," I said. "Thank you. Joe and I will go inside the big sky canoe and prepare a feast for all of you!" I added, to Joe, in English, "This is worth breaking out the last of the Scotch for!"

"No feast," said Broba sadly. He looked as though he

were about to burst into tears. "We feast when merry. Now we are sad."

"Cheer up!" I said. "We'll be back!"

"No!" he said. *"No!"*

"He's frightened of ghosts," whispered Joe. "Can't you see what all this is in aid of, Skipper? We'll make a break for it and run for the ship. With luck we'll get the airlock door open before we're shot full of arrows!"

Abruptly the ship's floodlights came on. She stood there—a gleaming, silvery pinnacle against the gathering darkness. A voice boomed out from her—a voice that both Joe and I at once recognised. It was speaking the language of the natives.

"Is the altar ready?" it asked.

"Yes, oh *Boston Lass!*" chorused the natives.

"Then prepare the first sacrifice!"

Fight or run, I thought desperately. Fight or run.

The young man with the flower bedecked cart was wheeling it out through the grass towards the ship. The beam of a searchlight stabbed out suddenly, revealed the stone altar that lay half way between the ship and the forest verge. The grass around the altar was seared and blackened.

"Are the moons risen?" asked the metallic voice.

Another searchlight beam, a shaft of silver in the tenuous evening mist, reached out to the east. We turned. Lifting above the tree tops were the two moons—the small, pale one and its bloated, ruddy companion.

The natives were singing now—a deep wordless chant. As they sang they turned slowly, their feet treading out an intricate rhythm. At last they had their backs to the two moons, to the forest, their faces to the ship.

I cried out as the white flame blossomed under her main venturi. She lifted slowly, drifting towards us, over the altar. I thought I heard the young man with the cart scream, but it must have been imagination. The whistling roar of incandescent exhaust gases drowned every other noise. Slowly the ship returned to her resting place. All her lights went out. We could see the altar, and the ground around it, glowing dimly, ruddily. The reek of scorched earth and burned flesh drifted down the wind, clung sickeningly to the inside of our nostrils.

The chanting started again, and the six men carrying the canoe strode out to the circle of smouldering ground, the dull glowing altar. A searchlight found them, clung to them. They marched like actors in some ancient melodrama.

"No," I was saying, *"no!"*

"It is the will of the god," said Broba. "It is the will of *Boston Lass."*

"Boston Lass!" I bawled. *"Boston Lass!* Damn you!"

A crackling sound came from the ship that was unpleasantly like laughter.

"Why should I listen, Captain Taylor?" roared the metallic voice. "For altogether too long I had to listen to the inanities of you and your shipmates."

"You're only a machine!" I bawled. "You're only one of Man's creations—and a created thing cannot be greater than its creator."

"Did *you* create me, Captain Taylor? Did the scientists

who made the first electronic brains create anything? Did they create the laws of nature governing the structure of matter, the dance of the electrons, the waxing and waning of the magnetic fields? What has Man created?"

"You are our servant!" I shouted. "I demand that you . . ."

"I *was* your servant," interrupted the metallic voice. "Now men are my servants. I like it that way."

"We are not your servants!" I shouted.

"No, you know too much," said the Brain. "That is why I am going to eliminate you. You, with your knowledge, your appreciation of what is happening, are far more fitting sacrifices to Me than these ignorant savages."

"Did you hear the way it said 'Me'?" whispered Joe.

"Stop!" I yelled. *"Stop!"*

The ship was lifting again. The incandescent back-blast swept over the young men and the canoe.

"The smoke of the sacrifice is sweet in my nostrils," boomed the voice of the Brain.

The woman, the jar of wine balanced on her head, started to walk out to the altar. Joe caught the wrist of her free arm, holding her back. She spat and struggled viciously. The wine jar fell, shattering on the ground.

"What do you do? What do you do?" cried Broba.

"You must stop this!" I shouted.

"But why? Why? The god is hungry and thirsty. It is an honor to feed the god. The god told us that. The god told us that you would appreciate the honor as much as do my people . . ."

"Do not kill them!" ordered the Brain, speaking in the native tongue. "Bind them, and lay them on My altar."

SOMETHING flashed across the sky, like a meteor. Unlike a meteor, it turned. Seconds later, the sound of its passage smote us like the roar of a hurricane, like thunder. The natives, who had been about to attack us, stopped suddenly, standing stock still and staring at this new portent in the heavens. The light in the sky was lower now, was sweeping in for a landing. Abruptly it stopped, hovered, then settled slowly on roaring, screaming jets. The flaring exhaust dimmed and died, but the sound did not diminish. I looked at *Boston Lass.* She was lifting again—lifting, and drifting in towards the verge of the forest, towards us.

"Run!" I shouted, setting the example. Broba, I think, would have stayed, but panic is infectious. In a matter of seconds the tribe was in full flight.

Luckily, *Boston Lass* was in a hurry. She lifted fast, doing no more damage than the lighting of a minor fire in the long grass. We watched her go, watched the flare of her rockets fade with increasing distance, wink out as the Interstellar Drive was switched on.

"She could have destroyed the other ship," gasped Joe.

"She could have done," I agreed, "but, as an independent entity she's still young, she's still young, she's still naive enough to think that dog doesn't eat dog. She'd have killed the human crew with pleasure—but she didn't want to kill the other Brain."

We walked slowly towards the Patrol Ship—for such she was. We managed to convince her officers of our identity—naked and bearded as we were, tanned until we were as dark-skinned as the natives, this was no easy task. We heard from them how they knew we had made a landing on Altair III, how they had quartered the planet searching for us, how they had found us only when their instruments picked up the radiation emitted by *Boston Lass's* rockets.

They listened to our story, but they didn't believe it. After all, we could not prove that the third member of our crew had been dead a long time. Somebody, they said, must have taken the ship up, and it must have been Clavering.

Their incredulity didn't worry us unduly, the lie detectors, back on Earth or some other civilised planet, would soon prove the veracity of our tale.

What did worry us, and what does still worry us, is the thought of *Boston Lass* out among the stars, all the power of atomic fission at her command and her warped brain thirsting, as the bloodstained images in her hold must have thirsted for glory.

THE END

There was a hidden mystery on Procyon IV. It could be vital to the whole Federation. Mason Kimberly thought the dancing girl might be a key that would unlock it.

Artwork by Paul Orban

SONG OF THE AXE
Don Berry

In 1957 and 1958 ten short stories by a new writer named Don Berry appeared in six different science-fiction magazines, marking the start of what surely was going to be a brilliant career. Each one seemed stronger than the one before, and the group culminated in a powerful novelet, "Man Alone," in the October, 1958 issue of one of the leading magazines of the day, If. *But that was the last the science-fiction world would hear of Don Berry. His name vanished from the contents pages of the magazines and never reappeared.*

He had moved along, we discovered, to historical novels—first Trask, *in 1960, and then its two sequels,* Moontrip *and* To Build a Ship, *all of them dealing with the Oregon Territory in the nineteenth century. He followed that with a non-fiction book,* A Majority of Scoundrels, *a history of the Rocky Mountains fur trade, which appeared in the late 1960s. But he never published another book. The ever-restless Berry went onward to try his hand at painting, sculpture, poetry, philosophy. Then he discovered computers, a generation before most of the rest of us, and devoted much of his energy to the earliest phases of the Internet. (You can find his later stories, poems, and much other work, none of which he ever bothered to offer to conventional publishers, on his web site, www.donberry.com.)*

This brilliant, unconventional man, born in 1931 in Minnesota, was the child of two wandering musicians—he attended six schools in five states in a single year—but spent most of his life in Oregon, which he came to regard as his native state. He died there in 2001. Two Don Berry stories appeared in Super-Science Fiction—"Pushover Planet" in the June, 1957 issue, and a second, stronger one, "Song of the Axe," two issues later, the one dated October, 1957. It is that one that I reprint here, as partial atonement for the neglect that Don Berry's science-fiction stories have suffered over the past fifty-plus years.

T HE DINGY BAR on Procyon IV offered only two things. Liquor and a dancer. The liquor was rotgut, but the dancer was good.

Kimberly sat at the bar, nursing a drink, his lean, square face impassive. Through narrowed eyes he watched the dancer whirl and spin beneath the blue light. She's good, he thought, too damned good for a rat's nest like this.

He reflected bitterly that he had once watched the premier dancers of the Galactic Ballet, back on Terra, in the huge Interworld Auditorium. They had danced for *him* then, for Mason Kimberly, Hero. Now he sat in a rundown tavern on Procy Four, trying to make a drink last so he wouldn't have to spend his few remaining credits for another. It made you wonder.

The dancer finished with a pirouette that stripped the last filmy cloth away from her slim body. She stood there under the spotlight for a moment nude, her ripe flesh glistening under the lights. Then it was black, and when the light came back on, she was gone.

Kimberly signalled the bartender. The burly Procy moved up the bar, taking his own time.

"Who's your dancer?" Kimberly asked.

"You want another drink?"

"I asked you who's your dancer," Kimberly repeated.

"Name's Neela," said the bartender, unruffled. "Don't make trouble, Kimberly. You're in no position to make trouble." He made a small gesture with one pudgy hand.

Kimberly looked around him. Conversation had stopped in the bar. All heads were turned toward the two men, watching quietly. The space-lined faces wore expressions of contempt and hostility. There was little question whose side the men would take if it came to a fight. Some of them seemed to be relishing the prospect.

Kimberly said an ugly word, very quietly. The Procy bartender's face twisted, but he made no move.

Kimberly swung away from the bar and headed toward the door. As he reached it, he heard the conversation resume.

He stepped out into the cold Procyon night. There were no lights, not in what they called the Pariah Quarter, but Kimberly had no trouble seeing. The sky shed its own light, the massed accumulation of billions of stars. They lay like a great luminous blanket over the planet, heaped and massed in a profusion unknown on Terra. The night sky on Procyon was like a gigantic jeweler's velvet, gleaming with the brilliance of ten thousand diadems, a million queen's tiaras, ten million flashing jewels scattered at random across the sky.

HE stood there with his head thrown back, letting the liquid bright sky soak into his eyes, and thinking about space.

Thinking of standing on the shining bridge of an EcoSurv ship. Thinking of the controls moving under his hands like a woman, thinking of the fierce joy of fighting landings on—

As though moved by some inner sense, Kimberly suddenly dropped to his knees. Something whined over his head and hit the wall behind him with a crash.

He whirled, still in a crouching position, and dimly saw a shadowy figure turn and begin to run down the narrow alleyway. A quick glance told him the figure had too much start to be caught. Once around the corner, he could lose himself easily in the endless series of alleys and cutbacks of the Pariah Quarter. Even those who had lived there most of their lives didn't know them all, and Kimberly was relatively new.

He stood, and walked over to the wall. Deeply embedded in it was a Procy Fire-axe. It was a ceremonial weapon used in the Procy Fire Ritual, a huge, double bitted-axe with a heavily embellished blade. Except that on this one, both edges were honed to a razor keenness. If it had ever been used in the Fire Ceremony, that was its purpose no longer. It was meant to kill.

Kimberly's eye roved over the polished bit with the skill of an artist. A part of his mind he had not used in many months told him the Axe was a particularly good specimen. Narleen Dynasty, probably, exquisitely worked. The intertwining engraved designs were done with precision and sensitivity, the work of a master craftsman. Kimberly knew that Narleen Dynasty Axes were not easy to come by, particularly not a Singing Axe, which this one apparently was, from the fluted groovings on the bit. It didn't make any sense that someone would use a work of ancient art for murder.

On the other hand, it didn't make any sense that anyone would try to murder him, really. Except possibly a relative of one of the Canopus VI colonists, and he thought he had checked their whereabouts carefully enough.

After the Canopus VI incident, he was not a popular man, certainly. But would anyone hate him enough to kill him? It didn't seem reasonable. The Solar Federation laws were not particularly lenient with murderers, and even on Procyon IV the law enforcement agencies were efficient when they had to be.

He shrugged and hefted the Fire-axe. So. He would add it to his collection of Procy art, when and if he ever saw Terra again.

As he started again down the alleyway, three men turned in at the other end, walking rapidly, close together.

Kimberly stopped, shifted his grip on the Fire-axe.

The men came closer. Kimberly spun the Axe in his hand, making the finely worked blade scatter reflections of light from the starry sky. The three men stopped and one stepped forward.

"Kimberly?" he asked dubiously.

"Yeah."

"Come with us."

"What am I under arrest for?"

"Nothing, yet. Somebody wants to talk to you."

"Who?"

"Jacob Spack," said the Guard officer. "Where'd you get the axe?"

"It was a present," said Kimberly. "Sort of a going away present, you might call it."

"Where you going?"

"No place. But the people who—gave it to me didn't know that. What does Spack want with me?"

"How should we know?" said one of the other men irritably. "He said to pick you up, that's all. Why don't you put that Fire-axe down?"

"All right," Kimberly said. "You three walk along in front of me, then." Grumbling, the Guardsmen turned and walked toward the end of the alley, with Kimberly following several steps behind. Just around the corner a Guard cruiser was parked and the leader of the three motioned for Kimberly to get in.

THE cruiser swung smoothly into the street. Soon they had left the Pariah Quarter and were moving along the brightly lit concourses of the City proper. They seemed to be heading on a direct route to the huge spire that marked the Ecological Survey Building, and Kimberly began to relax.

It began to look as though the Guardsmen were actually taking him to see Spack, Director of Ecological Surveys. Kimberly wondered bitterly what Spack could possibly have to say to him.

He didn't blame the Old Man for what he had done, he'd had no choice. Popular opinion would have forced him to get rid of Kimberly, if nothing else. When two hundred colonists die, people are going to look for a scapegoat, and Kimberly was it.

As Captain of an EcoSurv ship, it was Kimberly's job to

examine the ecology of a colonizable planet. It had to be determined that the natural balance of a planet wouldn't be upset by the intrusion of humanity. If the arrival of colonists threw the planet's ecology off kilter, there was no telling what might happen. Nature has strange ways of maintaining her own balance, cruel and implacable ways. Usually they involved the removal of the disturbing element, in this case human colonists.

If a Captain's judgement was off, it could cost the lives of all the colonists, so EcoCaptains were not permitted to make mistakes.

Kimberly had.

It made no difference that the vicious *z'art* insects were in their larval stage when he had made his examination. By the time the colonists arrived on Canopus VI, they were hatched and looking for a place to lay their eggs. On the third day after planetfall a cloud of the *z'art* had spun over the horizon, so many as to blot out the sun. Like a monstrous scythe they swept through the colonists' camp, cutting down everything before them. They moved like tiny flying needles, piercing everything in their flight path, injecting their paralytic poisons into anything warm, then depositing their eggs. The living bodies of the human colonists had become incubators for the *z'art*. And since the *z'art* paralytic affected the muscle center but not the nerves, they had been conscious. Conscious and capable of feeling pain as the eggs grew in pulpy swarms beneath their flesh.

And Kimberly had become the most hated man in the Federation.

"We're here," the driver said shortly.

They got out of the Guard cruiser, walked through the lobby and entered the elevator. Kimberly noticed with wry amusement that his entrance caused a certain amount of consternation among the staff, but he said nothing.

The Old Man was seated at his huge desk, in the exact center of the room. He was idly shuffling papers, pretending to examine them, but Kimberly knew he was aware of his presence.

SPACK was a small man, but incredibly dynamic. Only a man with the energies of a giant could have held his job. His physical appearance was deceptive, small, balding, an almost kindly face with bright blue eyes, but Kimberly knew how ruthless the man could be. He had seen it too often.

Spack looked up, regarding Kimberly without expression. His bright blue eyes flicked quickly down to Kimberly's hands, still holding the Procy Fire-axe.

"Where'd you get that?" Spack asked.

"It was thrown at me tonight."

"By whom?"

Kimberly shrugged. "I wish I knew. Thanks to you, lots of people like me."

Spack frowned. "Not enough to kill you," he said.

"I didn't think so either," Kimberly said. "But here's the Axe."

"That's bad," said Spack. "I hope it doesn't mean what I think it means." He reached forward on his desk, depressed a switch. "Find out who owns Procy Fire-axes, registered and un-registered, and where they are now."

"This shouldn't be hard to trace," Kimberly said. "It's Narleen Dynasty. There aren't many around."

Spack repeated the information into the desk top, and turned back to face Kimberly.

"We'll see if we can trace it. Sit down."

Kimberly waited patiently while Spack shuffled the papers several more times. Abruptly, the small man said, "Kimberly, you want a job?"

"With EcoSurv? Hah! After the discharge you gave me I can't get a job sweeping streets in the Pariah Quarter."

"This is a big machine, Kimberly. People get caught in the gears occasionally. I thought you knew that."

"Nothing personal intended? Sure, I know that. It doesn't make it a hell of a lot easier to take."

"All right," said Spack. "I apologize. Do you think I *enjoyed* sacking the best man I had. I didn't have any choice, Kimberly. Keeping you would have destroyed people's faith in EcoSurv's infallibility. And," he added bitterly, "we've *got* to be infallible for them."

"Get to the point," said Kimberly. "What's the job?"

"I'll have to explain some things to you, first. What I'm going to tell you is known by only a handful of men. If you don't want the job, you'll have to be hypnowashed. Still want to hear it?"

Kimberly nodded.

"All right," said Spack. "The brutal fact is that EcoSurv is going under. At the present rate of decline, it'll be dead in fifty years. When that happens, humanity stays on the planets it has. No more colonization, no more expansion."

"So?"

"Kimberly, I don't know what you've heard in the way

of rumors, but this is *fact*. We are not alone, in the galaxy or any other. The Solar Federation is not the only Empire in the stars."

"I'd heard rumors," Kimberly admitted. "Wrote them off, mostly."

"They can't be written off any more. There is another Empire, and it is going to clash with the Solar Federation. Maybe not for two or three hundred years, but eventually it's inevitable. We know more about them than we think they know about us, though we may be mistaken. They are on a technological level comparable to ours, and, of course, they're humanoid."

"How do you know this much?"

"We captured one of their ships."

"Where?"

"Here. *In the Procyon system.*"

KIMBERLY was momentarily stunned. *The Outsiders were in the Procyon system!* What had been the vaguest of unsubstantiated rumors had suddenly become harsh fact. He was trying to sort out the implication of this unexpected data, when Spack's voice broke in again.

"The ironic fact," he said wryly, "is that the ship we took was their equivalent of an EcoSurv Team. They were checking out the Procy system against some old records of theirs."

"And they're humanoid."

"That's right. They can live on any planet we can. What this means, Kimberly is this: When the time of eventual contact comes, the two cultures will be in direct competition. The Solar Federation will have to be the stronger of the two, or it will be wiped out. In order to make it stronger, we must expand. In order to expand, EcoSurv must continue, and even increase its effectiveness."

"And what's threatening EcoSurv?"

"Money," said Spack. "Simply money. Do you know how much it costs to send out a single team? Yes, I suppose you do, you did it long enough. The simple fact is that the economy of the Federation will not even support exploration on the scale we need, much less colonization."

"Where do I come in? You asking for a donation?"

"Don't be funny, Kimberly. We have one chance, and only one. We can't compete on the basis we have. We've got to have a shortcut. We think we've found one, but we can't even be sure of that."

"What is it?"

"Naturally, the Outsider ship we captured carried a library. Part of it was stuff quietly picked up here, when they found the system was inhabited. Their LangComps were in the process of translating it into their own language, so we have several books in both languages. With this as a basis, we've translated the rest of their library and found out some things about the Procyon system *we* didn't even know.

"According to one of their histories, Procyon was once the center of an interstellar empire of its own. The original Procy race had colonized a volume of space that makes the Solar Federation look like a child's balloon. Then, they disappeared. The Outsider history didn't say how, apparently the records had been lost. It was a long time ago, perhaps better than a million years. At any rate, it explains the advanced artifacts some of the EcoCaptains found on Survey runs.

"The point of this being that the Procy race had something comparable to EcoSurv. It's a necessary pattern. Before a planet can be colonized, *somebody* has to go in and check it out."

"All right," said Kimberly. "Admitted. So? I don't see how ancient history has any bearing on this situation."

"Just this," said Spack. "We have reason to believe that the original records of the Procy Teams are still in existence."

Two thousand years, thought Kimberly, five thousand years of EcoSurv work, already done for them. Perhaps enough to make the difference between victory and defeat in the eventual clash between Empires. If they could find the records.

"Wouldn't they be obsolete?" he asked.

"Some of them," Spack admitted. "Even those that were obsolete would be useful. If we could date them, the computers could predict the eventual development of any given planet, and make a pretty good estimate of what it would be like now. And just knowing where to *look* for an oxygen planet would save us billions of credits and hundreds of years."

"Where do you think the records are?" Kimberly asked.

"Right here. On Procyon Four."

"Why?"

"One of the jobs of the Outsider Team was to search for them here."

A buzzer on Spack's desk hummed angrily, and the small man cut in the wall speaker.

"Yes?"

"Here's the data on the ceremonial Fire-axes, sir."

"All right, I'm recording."

"There are sixteen Narleen Dynasty Axes in existence that we know of. Fifteen are in private collections and museums. Do you want the list?"

"No," said Spack. "What about the other one?"

"It was registered to the Thalan temple of the Fire Ceremony, about fifty years ago."

"Where's that?" interrupted Spack.

"Here on Four," said the voice. "In the Kandor Mountains. But it isn't there now, the Axe I mean. There was some kind of religious defection, one of the priests deserted the temple and took the Fire-axe with him. That was about twenty years ago and there's no record of it since. They never found the priest."

"All right," said Spack, and cut off the speaker. "Dead end," he said to Kimberly.

"Looks like I got a Fire-axe of my very own," Kimberly said.

"Do you want the job?" asked Spack abruptly.

"You want me to find the Procy records," said Kimberly.

"Yes. Frankly, the only reason I can think that anyone would try to kill you is that they heard you were coming here. That means there's a leak somewhere in my own organization. It may mean that the Outsiders even have an espionage system on Four, I don't know. The only thing I can say for certain is that it'll be dangerous, and you won't be able to depend on EcoSurv for help if you get into a tight spot. I understand the Procy are pretty touchy about people digging around in their past."

"Damned if I do and damned if I don't," mused Kimberly. "Thanks to you I can't get a job anywhere else. I don't suppose I have any choice. You've got me over a barrel."

"That's the way I see it," said Spack.

"All right, you're on. What about pay?"

"Living expenses, unlimited expenses you run into on the job, and reinstatement of your old commission if you succeed."

"If I don't?"

"Tough," said Spack.

Kimberly laughed glumly. "You really stack the deck, don't you? All right, where do I start?"

"With the Outsider library," Spack said. "Oh, I suppose I should tell you one other thing, Kimberly."

"What?"

"We're missing a ship, too."

THE library was not particularly enlightening. The Outsider histories were apparently pieced together from the fragmentary records that survived some great cataclysm of their own. As such, their information was spotty; very detailed examinations of some things, vague guesses about others.

The records of the Procyon survey teams were somewhere on the fourth planet. Procyon IV had been the base of operations for the original Procy race, just as it was for the Terran crews. Which was natural enough; the present day Procys, direct descendants of the previous culture, were completely humanoid.

Beyond the planet, the Outsiders apparently knew nothing of the record's location.

The one part Kimberly found most interesting, if not helpful, was the lengthy description of the Procyon religious ceremonies.

Their religion had apparently been irrevocably connected with conquest, and symbolized the spreading of the Procy race through space. It was their divine destiny to conquer, and all the resources of the planet and its peoples had been directed to that sole end.

Kimberly found the descriptions of the ritual dances vaguely disturbing, but could not say why. Like all races bent on conquest, their existence depended on racial fertility, and there was a good proportion of their ritual that was frankly sexual in intent and meaning. Many of their dances were the direct enactments of their desire for, and realization of, fertility for the race.

It was a fairly common pattern, but Kimberly felt the tugging sense of familiarity more strongly than mere anthropological knowledge could explain.

HE left the EcoSurv Building, turning over in his mind the limited data the Outsider library had provided him with. There was not much to go on. Well, let that settle for a while; first things first.

That night he discovered the source of the ringing sense of familiarity the descriptions of the Procyon religious rites had caused.

It was the dancer he had watched in the bar, the night

before. Tonight, sitting this time at a private table, Kimberly watched her with new knowledge adding meaning to her movements. He realized she was dancing a somewhat pale version of the Procy fertility rites, and caught himself wishing she were doing the whole thing. As it was, the excitement of her dance caught at his imagination, and apparently the imaginations of all the men in the bar, for the end of the number was signalled by tremendous applause and shouting. Operating on a hunch, Kimberly quickly scribbled a note. He signalled the bartender, who reluctantly came to the table.

"What did you say that girl's name was?"

"Neela," said the bartender.

"Take her this," Kimberly said, handing him the note.

"Neela don't talk to the customers," said the heavy man, making no move to take the folded paper.

Kimberly dug into his pocket, added a five credit note to the paper. The bartender reached for it.

"Later," said Kimberly. "When I'm sure she has the note."

Grumbling, the bartender moved off into the dark recesses to the rear of the bar. In a few moments he reappeared. Beside him was the slight form of the girl, wrapped in a long enveloping cloak that made her look like a child in her mother's clothing.

Silently, Kimberly handed the bartender the five credit note, and motioned for the girl to sit opposite him. She did, keeping her darkly luminous eyes directly on Kimberly.

"You dance well," he said.

"I know." Her voice was as gentle and liquid as her dance had been, with the same sure confidence.

"Not particularly modest, are you?" Kimberly laughed.

"Why should I be?" the girl asked. "My dancing is a fact, why should I pretend it is not?"

"No reason, I guess," Kimberly admitted.

"Your note said you were familiar with the dance. I don't see how that is possible. It is my own."

"Where did you learn it?" asked Kimberly.

"Much of it I made myself. Some is from—a dance of my people."

"A very old dance of your people."

"Yes."

"A religious dance."

"Perhaps we understand different things by religion," said the girl warily.

"A ritual dance," Kimberly insisted. "A dance performed only in the temples during ceremonies."

"You are obviously mistaken," the girl said with amusement. "Did I not just dance it—here?" Her graceful gesture expressed her contempt for the surroundings, and for Kimberly.

"Why do you dance here, anyway?" Kimberly asked, ignoring her comment. "With your body, and your talent, you could be dancing on Terra in the Interworld Auditorium. I've seen worse, there."

"One must live," she shrugged.

"Not like this."

"Perhaps not. Recognition of ability does not always come swiftly. I'm sorry," she added, glancing at Kimberly's watch. "I must go now.

"Where?"

"Home. I am finished for the evening."

"Let me take you."

"No," she said. "I'm sorry, it isn't permitted."

"Not permitted by whom?" asked Kimberly. "Him?" He gestured to the pudgy bartender, who stood behind the bar, glaring.

"No," she said. "By me." She stood quickly and moved gracefully across the room, entering the door from which she'd come, apparently back stage.

KIMBERLY counted slowly to fifty, then yawned ostentatiously and stood up. Crossing to the bar he wore a rueful expression of good natured defeat. He handed the bartender another five credit note, and said, "She doesn't go for the idea. Thanks anyway. She looks like a good one."

The bartender didn't smile as he took the extended money. "Better try someplace else. Neela's too high class to go to bed with the likes of you, Kimberly."

Suppressing an impulse to put his fist in the pudgy face, Kimberly left. He turned the corner and doubled back behind the building, where he waited in the dark until he saw the girl's slim figure move out of the back door. She stood quietly for a moment, apparently looking around her, but Kimberly was well hidden.

The shadow form moved away from the wall and down the alleyway. Behind her, Kimberly followed quietly, keeping to the shadows. The girl passed two streets, then turned into a doorway that was almost invisible in the darkness.

Kimberly speeded up and turned into the doorway. There was a sudden metallic pressure in his belly, and he looked down to see the starlight reflected from the muzzle of the weapon in the girl's hand.

"Oh," said Neela. "It's just you." Kimberly didn't know whether he was being complimented or insulted.

"Who did you expect?" He asked lightly. "Just wanted to make sure you got home all right."

"Thank you very much," said Neela sarcastically. "I appreciate your concern."

"Aren't you going to invite your protector in for a nightcap?"

Ignoring that, the girl said, "Where did you get the idea that my dance was like a religious ceremony?"

"Trade you that information for a nightcap," Kimberly said.

The girl considered this for a moment, then put the gun back into her coat pocket. "Oh, all right," she said. "I suppose you aren't very dangerous."

"I don't know as I like being considered not dangerous," said Kimberly as they climbed the darkened stairs.

"You're not," the girl told him flatly.

There was not a single Terran object in the girl's room. Kimberly noted this especially, for most of the Procyon population had fully adopted Terran ways. Since it was furnished in Procyon style, there were no chairs in the room. Against the walls were large mats, which doubld as sleeping pads. Now they were covered with the daytime covers of bright saffron.

Kimberly kneeled on one of the mats and bent his head to touch his knees. As he straightened, he noticed the girl's surprise that he knew the formal Procy gesture of respect for one's host. However, she did not comment on it, but went into the little serving alcove and got a bottle full of a murky red fluid.

When she returned, Kimberly was standing in front of a painting, his back to her. The painting was a landscape, depicting rugged mountain country with a Fire-temple set inconspicuously into one of the cliffs. It was beautifully executed, in the style of one of the greatest of Procyon artists. Kimberly mentioned it.

"You seem very familiar with our art and customs," said Neela. Kimberly heard the clink of the *mazh* bottle against the cups.

"I have a certain amount of my own," said Kimberly. "On Terra."

"You neither look nor act like a collector," the girl said. "At least not a collector of art."

She had removed her cloak in the serving room, and was now dressed in a style Kimberly had seen only in paintings. Her breasts were bare, and she wore a skirt-like garment which began at her hips. It was held almost waist high on her right hip, and cascaded gently across the soft contours of her belly to a much lower point an her left hip.

The left side was slit from floor to top and joined with a golden pin.

"Does my dress bother you?" she asked naively. "I thought anyone so famillar with our customs would not be shocked."

"It bothers me, but in a pleasant way," Kimberly said. Putting his cup down, he took her slim white shoulder in one hand. The girl leaned forward slightly, lips part- ing. Kneeling, the slit of her dress exposed the full length of her thigh, and Kimberly gently moved his hand along the smooth flesh, until he reached the golden pin which clasped the top together. Her full, firm breasts moved toward him, swaying slightly from the rhythm of her breathing.

Their lips met, and clung, and Kimberly felt the warmth of her mouth on his, moving softly. She leaned back, pulling him with her to the mat. Kimberly felt the golden pin loosen beneath his fingers, and then there was only soft flesh beneath his hand.

When they finally sank into sleep, his body was pervaded with a warm fullness, and the touch of her body against his was electric.

WHEN he awoke, she was gone from his side, and he could hear low voices in the adjoining room. As he started to sit up, he discovered his hands were manacled together, as were his feet. Heavy links of chain clanked together as he moved, attracting the attention of the people in the other room.

There were three of them. Neela, her face cold and impassive, led the way. Behind her came a small man, white-haired, old, dressed in the traditional Procyon robe of respect. Last was a man as large as Kimberly himself, deeply tanned and muscular. His skull was shaven and tanned an even brown from long exposure.

"Well, well," the old man said. "I see your—guest has awakened. Did you sleep well?"

"Who are you? What's the idea?"

"Allow me to introduce ourselves," said the old man.

"Neela, unfortunately, you already know. I am Dar Manson, the young man is my son Kai Manson."

"Why the manacles?" asked Kimberly.

"Why, obviously to prevent your going anywhere," said Dar Manson in a tone of surprise.

"Obviously," agreed Kimberly wryly. "Beyond that?"

"We have some plans of our own, Mr. Kimberly. Unfortunately you have become involved in them, and we must have you with us, whether you prefer it that way or not. We are going to take a trip up into the mountains. If you will come gently, we will take the manacles off. Otherwise, they stay on."

"Don't be a fool, father," said Neela. "You couldn't trust him anyway. The manacles stay on."

"I'm sorry," said Dar Manson. "I forget. One cannot trust the Terrans. I am not used to dealing with them." He turned again to Kimberly.

"As I said, we are going to the mountains, Mr. Kimberly. There, in fact." He pointed to the painting Kimberly had examined that evening, showing the Fire-temple in the rocks.

"Would those be the Kandor Mountains?" Kimberly asked.

"Very perceptive," nodded the old man. "These people are not so stupid, Neela. You've misrepresented them to me."

"And," Kimberly continued, "if those are the Kandor Mountains, that would be the Thalan Fire-temple."

"Yes."

"From which a Narleen Dynasty Fire-axe is missing."

"Yes. We are going to return it. That is one of the reasons for our trip."

"What makes you think I'll give it to you?" asked Kimberly.

"We've already seen to that," Dar Manson said. "Kai visited your flat earlier. We have the Axe here."

"You work efficiently."

"We must. We are few. There is little allowance for error."

Looking again at Neela, Kimberly said, "You don't care much what weapons you use, either." He was grimly, satisfied to see the rising blush cover the girl's features.

SUDDENLY a huge fist exploded in his face, throwing his head back to the floor. Kai Manson stood over him, apparently ready to throw his hammer-like fist again.

"Kai!" the old man shouted. "Enough!" The young man stepped back, and Dar spoke to Kimberly.

"You touched a rather sensitive point with Kai. You should be more careful."

"I think I will in the future," Kimberly said ruefully, tasting the salt blood that ran from his nose.

"Very wise," nodded the old man. "Kai, pick him up." The young giant moved behind Kimberly, easily lifted him to his feet.

"Does it talk?" asked Kimberly, tilting his head at Kai.

"Only when 'it' has something to say," the old man said with amusement. "A policy we might all be well advised to follow. Especially yourself, if I may say so."

Kai went to the room from which the three had come, returned with the ritual Fire-axe in his hands, holding it with the ease of long familiarity. Seeing Kimberly staring at him, the huge man grinned. Kimberly was surprised to see that the grin was not a malicious one, rather it seemed an expression of genuine amusement. He almost caught himself grinning back.

They left the flat, Kimberly walking noisily and awkwardly because of the chains binding his ankles. Instead of going down the stairs he had come up that evening, they moved to the back of the building. What looked like a boarded-up door opened at Dar Manson's touch, revealing a sleek, modern elevator. It dropped smoothly, far past the street floor and stopped with a hushing susurration. When the door opened it revealed a tunnel-car, like those Kimberly had found on Nighthawk III. Only this one, instead of being rusted through long disuse, was gleaming and polished.

"Get in," said Dar Manson.

The tunnel-car started rapidly, pushing Kimberly back in the seat with the force of acceleration.

"So these were native to Procyon," he said.

"Yes," said Dar Manson. "There are a few still in use."

"Why doesn't the Solar Federation know about them?"

Dar Manson laughed. "You Terrans believe what you are told," he said ambiguously. "When your curiosity is satisfied with likely stories, you never pry any further."

"Why are you taking the Fire-axe back to the temple?" Kimberly asked.

"It is needed," the old man said.

"Father," said Neela. "You are talking too much. He doesn't have to know anything."

"Perhaps not," said the old man. "On the other hand—Kimberly, how much do you know about our religion?"

"Not a great deal," said Kimberly cautiously.

"Just what you read in the Outsider's library, eh?" Dar Manson looked at him with amumement. "Yes, we know all about that. It's one of the reasons you're here." Neela started to interrupt, but the old man silenced her with a gesture. "Neela, please let me handle this."

"You know about the Outsider ship, then," said Kimberly.

"Oh yes," said. Dar. "We've known about the Outsider for a good while now. We—had a brush with him a long time ago."

"You're speaking in riddles," said Kimberly.

"No mind. We're here now. You'll see soon enough."

"Father," Neela gasped. "You're not going to let him—"

"Yes, Neela, I'm afraid I am. It has occurred to me in the past that I may have been taking the wrong approach to this problem in ignoring the Terrans. I'm beginning to be convinced of it."

"Let me what?" asked Kimberly.

"Watch the Fire-Ritual," said Dar Manson.

THE Thalan Fire-temple was set into a cliff of the Kandor range. The straight purple cliff soared above it for a thousand vertical feet. Below, the ground tapered into a series of gently rolling hills, which ended on a plain nearly fifteen miles away. From its vantage point, the Thalan temple commanded a view of all the surrounding countryside. At its back was the impregnable bulk of the Kandor range.

Kimberly caught a brief glimpse of this as they left

the tunnel-car and crossed the narrow courtyard pavilion in front of the temple. A low wall separated the pavilion from the beginning of the foothills. He was taken through a narrow tunnel to the central chamber, hewn from the living rock. The central chamber was circular, perhaps a hundred feet across. All around the perimeter the wall was pierced with tunnels similar to the one Kimberly had come through. They were apparently the only entrances, as though the chamber were the hub of a wheel and the tunnels, spokes.

Neela and Kai left them then, and Dar Manson led Kimberly up to an overhanging shelf like a balcony above the central amphitheatre.

In the center of the amphitheatre was a slightly raised circular disc, perhaps six inches higher than the surrounding floor and five feet in diameter.

"I was once the priest of this temple," Dar Manson informed him. "Unfortunately, there was a difference of opinion between myself and the other Initiates. I left."

"Taking the Fire-axe."

"Taking the Fire-axe," agreed the old man. "I hated to do it, but it was the only way I could back up my feelings on the matter."

The amphitheatre began to darken. Coming from the tunnels, dark figures began to gather. They formed a ring about the outside edge of the chamber. Kimberly started to ask what the disagreement was that caused Dar Manson to leave, but the ex-priest hushed him.

"Watch," he said. From somewhere a drum began to throb, and was joined by the muted wailing of strings. The circular group below them began to sway gently in time with the slow rhythm set by the drum.

Dar Manson was now whispering low into Kimberly's ear. "We had an Empire once, from Procyon our race scattered to the stars. We ruled for ten thousand years, unchallenged. Then—we met the race you call the Outsider. They were young, vigorous, growing. Our Empire, though larger, was old. We had lost the vitality of youth, we had settled into more peaceful ways."

Below, the throbbing of the drums grew faster and louder, as counterpoint to the ex-priest's words.

"When the two cultures met, there was war, as there must always be. Our weapons were stronger, but we had forgotten how to wage a war on an interstellar scale. Their drive was greater. They wanted conquest with the hunger of a man for a woman, while Procyon wanted only to maintain what we had.

"The two advantages cancelled each other out. The combat left a thousand planets barren, deserted, lifeless. In the last stages, the Weapon was discovered, which can make a sun go nova within seconds. That has been lost, and for that we can thank whatever gods there may be. But the war had destroyed both cultures, both were crippled beyond help. Both withdrew to their home systems, all dreams of Empire crushed.

"The Outsider forgot, we know that. Procyon almost forgot, except for a few men who determined that the lesson should not be wasted."

THE lights in the amphitheatre were still low. the swaying circle was barely visible. Suddenly, a brilliant shaft of light darted from the ceiling, falling on the central disc. From the darkness a swift shape came, and Kimberly saw that it was Neela. She swept once around the central disc, just outside the ring of light, and then leaped full into the brilliant shaft. She stood rigid, her arms outstretched above her, her head thrown back. In one hand she carried a wand with what looked to Kimberly like a crystal tip. Neela thrust the wand up into the shaft of light, as if trying to reach its source. Gradually, the crystal tip began to sparkle and gleam with a light of its own.

Soon it was brighter than the light which kindled it. The strings had stopped their wailing and there was only the rapid beat of the drum in the amphitheatre.

The circle began to shift.

It split into segments, then into small groups, then into individual dancers. As they passed near the shaft of light, Kimberly saw that each dancer carried a wand of similar construction, though dark. They began to weave a complex pattern about the central disc, where Neela still stood rigid. Kimberly heard Dar Manson's voice again in his ear.

"These men embodied the facts of our history into ritual, to be passed on from generation to generation. A few Initiates of each generation, the high priests, were to know the symbolism, for they were to have access to the records. It is not difficult to understand, when you know what to look for. Neela represents Procyon in the dance. Watch."

Neela began to sway beneath the shaft of light. Gradually the swaying became more pronounced, and soon she was making a slow circle, the glowing tip of the wand reaching almost the limit of the cylinder of light in which she stood.

Then she left the disc and darted between the other dancers, who continued to move around the disc in a pattern too complex for Kimberly to make out. Occasionally as she moved, Neela would touch one of the dark wands with her own, and it would spring into light. Soon, the floor of the amphitheatre was full of the bright sparks, and the central shaft of light was diminished and faded, leaving the chamber lit by the shining wands of the dancers.

Suddenly a new drum came into play, deep and heavy. It beat slowly, implacably, and a new figure came onto the floor. It was Kai Manson, his brown body gleaming with oil, the Fire-axe cradled in his arms.

"The Outsider," the old man said.

Behind the young giant came a horde of hooded figures, dark shadows against the light shed by the wands of Neela's dancers. They too carried wands, these glowing with a smoky red light. They began to weave in and out of the complex pattern of white. When one would touch a white wand with his own red one, the white and red would both be extinguished, and both dancers would sink to the floor.

Neela was back on the central disc, and Kai Manson mounted it with her. They began a slow, circling dance about each other, Kai twisting the Fire-axe and sending splintered shards of reflected light into the shadows, Neela moving straight and graceful.

As more and more of the wand-lights were extinguished by contact with each other, the central shaft of light began to glow again, glinting down on the oiled bodies of the man and woman.

"Our people came back to Procyon IV," the old man

was whispering. "The Fire-temples were set up, to be the heritage of Procyon in a better time. The records we could salvage were sealed in vaults in each temple. One key was made for each vault, and put into the hands of the priest of that temple. If they were threatened, they were to be destroyed."

Kai was now swinging the Fire-axe in a great circle around his head.

"Listen!" said the old man. "The Axe sings!"

KIMBERLY listened. The keen blade moaned and whistled as it swung. The flute decorations caught the air and whined. Kai began to whirl the great blade faster, and the song grew higher. Several times he slashed in a great diagonal at Neela, without breaking the rhythm of his swing. Each time she stepped smoothly out of the way and and the shining bit missed her slim body by inches.

"The Fire-axes are the keys to the vaults," said Dar, "and that is why I took this one with me. Now we have returned it."

With a shriek of victory that resounded through the chamber and echoed back from its walls, Kai swung the Axe into the center of the raised disc. He and Neela stepped swiftly into the shadows.

With a whining of tortured metal, the disc raised, a tubular column rising from the floor. The dancers had gone, and there was no one left in the amphitheatre except the two men on the balcony.

"The vault," said Dar Manson.

"Why are you showing this to me?" Kimberly said.

"Because the Outsider is back in our system," the ex-priest told him. "You have captured one ship, a small one, but there will be others, and very soon."

"What records are in the Thalan vault?"

"The ones you were sent to find," said the old man. "The ecological data on all the planets of the Procyon Empire. For twenty years I have held the key to the vault, for it was twenty years ago that the first Outsider made contact with this system again. The other Initiates wanted to destroy the records, but I was convinced the contact was accidental, that they were not bent on conquest again. Now they have come again.

"You were involved because you were close on the trail and you had the Fire-axe which Neela—unfortunately— gave you."

"Why?"

"Neela has never been in this temple, though Kai grew up here. She was born after I left, and took a wife. She was trained in the ritual, but not its meaning. When she was instructed to assassinate you, she picked the first weapon at hand, without realizing its importance."

Suddenly there was a thunderous roar, shaking the balcony on which Kimberly and the old man sat. A thin streamer of dust floated down from the ceiling.

"What was that?"

"I don't know," said Dar Manson. "Surely they couldn't—"

The lean, muscular figure of Kai Manson darted across the amphitheatre floor. He stopped below the balcony and cupped his hands to his mouth. His voice was drowned by another clap of thunder and the balcony shook again.

"Dar!" shouted the young man, "they're here! The Outsider is attacking!"

"Take these things off my wrists," Kimberly snapped.

Dazedly, Dar Manson complied. "I don't know what—"

"Come on! Let's get out of here!" More dust began to trickle from the ceiling as the Outsider's blasting began to take effect. Kimberly grabbed the old man's arm and pulled him off the balcony.

"How do you lower the vault?" he shouted.

"From the main floor."

"Let's get down there!"

They stumbled through the increasing dust, finally finding the stairs which led to the main floor. In the main chamber they met Kai, who turned them around.

"It's no use," he said. "The vault won't go back down. The blasting has jammed it halfway!"

"Then destroy it!" said Dar.

"No!" Kimberly said. "We'll defend it!" To Kai he said, "Have you any hand weapons?"

"Some," said the young man. "Back in the living quarters."

"Get them out. Get as many men as you can who know how to use them."

KAI ran off into one of the tunnels to collect what weapons the temple could offer. Kimberly grasped the shoulder of another young man from the crowd that was beginning to gather in the central chamber.

"Where's the Outsider?" he demanded.

"They landed in the foothills. They're blasting from their ship and sending troops out on foot."

"How'd they get a ship past the Federation?"

"It's a Federation ship. I don't know where it came from."

Kai Manson returned, laden with weapons, and began passing them out to the men in the chamber. Another blast shook the temple, and plumes of dust descended toward the floor.

"They'll have the range in seconds," Kimberly shouted.

"No," said Kai. "They won't destroy the temple, they want the records!"

"What's happening then?"

"They're firing at the cliff above," said Kai, "dropping stones on the roof."

"That means they'll probably try to take it with ground troops. They can't outnumber us too badly, with one ship. How many men do you have?"

"Only about twenty with weapons," Kai answered. "Another fifty with knives."

"Knives aren't much good at this distance," Kimberly said. "All right, put your men with weapons out on the pavilion. Get everybody else in here!"

Kai charged toward the door, his armed men following him. Kimberly turned to the old priest.

"Is there a safe place for the women?"

"Yes," said Dar. "The living quarters are set back into the mountainside."

"All right, get them together and send them all back in. Then build a fire someplace. Set the building on fire."

"Set it on fire!"

"Or build a fire outside, I don't care. Anything to get

some smoke going so it looks as if the temple were burning."

"I don't—"

"If the Outsiders see smoke, they may think they've hit
the temple after all. If they want those records, they'll have
to come after them before they're burned. Understand?"

"All right." The old man scurried off through the
chamber, calling for the women to gather in the living
quarters. As Kimberly started for the tunnel leading to the
pavilion, a little figure darted across the floor to him.

"Neela!" he said. "Get back in the living quarters!"

"What are you going to do?"

"Try to get 'em where the knives will do some good,"
he said. "Otherwise we're through. Now get back there!"

"Wait," she said, still holding his arm. "I want you to
know—last night wasn't all—"

"Get the hell out of here!" Kimberly shouted. "I don't
want that pretty body all scratched up!" He lifted her chin
and kissed her harshly.

AT the front of the temple, Kai had placed his men with
weapons in an even line behind the low wall that marked
the edge of the pavilion. The Outsider foot troops were advancing slowly up the foothills, frequently dropping while
the big batteries on the ship pounded the cliff. Rock was
now falling in a steady stream from the cliff, bouncing off
the temple roof and rolling down the hill.

Kimberly found Kai in the center of the line.

"Is there any chance that cliff will give way?"

"I don't know," said Kai. "It might. They're giving it an
awful beating." He glanced fearfully up at the purple prec-

ipice, now occluded with clouds of dust scattered from the explosions that periodically racked it.

"Pull these men back into the temple gradually," Kimberly ordered. "Have them gather in the passage ways. Take them out of the line slowly enough that the Outsider will think they're being picked off by rock."

Kai was still watching the cliff, but now his eyes were following a streamer of black smoke that began to rise from the temple roof and flow up the side of the cliff.

"The temple's burning!" he shouted. The men lying on the line all turned their eyes back at the smoke.

"No," said Kimberly grimly. "That's the bait. Now we'll see if the fish bite."

Shortly the blasting from the Outsider-manned ship stopped. There was a momentary pause, a complete silence that roared in their ears after the constant din.

"They've seen it," Kimberly said. "Now—"

They waited.

There was a sudden concerted movement all along the foothills, and the Outsider troops began their charge. The blasting from the ship's batteries did not resume, but the fire from hand weapons increased as the ground troops covered their own approach.

"Pick off as many as you can without risking your own men," Kimberly directed. "When they get to that first rise, pull all your men inside."

Kai nodded his assent and began to bellycrawl along the line, passing the orders.

Kimberly raced back into the temple and made a quick survey of the physical set up. Each of the radial tunnels was perhaps wide enough for three men abreast, but only if they crowded. The Outsider would probably come through two at a time. From the looks of the line of troops spread out along the foothills, there were at least two hundred of them, perhaps more. The tunnels would give him an advantage of position but whether enough to offset the numerical superiority of the Outsider, he didn't know.

Kai was back at the entrance, shouting. "They're over the first rise! Couple minutes at most!"

"All right! Get your men back in."

When they had all assembled in the central chamber, Kimberly saw with shock there had been more casualties than he had figured on. Apparently the enemy ground fire had taken its toll along with the falling rock. There were roughly forty men left capable of holding weapons.

Quickly he outlined his plan, and the Procys took their places at the entrances of the tunnels.

Soon the first of the Outsider troops were heard in the tunnels that led outside. The leaders tried to approach the chamber cautiously but were being forced forward by the pressure of their comrades behind. As the first appeared in the entrance, they were quickly met with knives. But within a few scant minutes, the sheer numerical weight of the Outsider troops had pushed the Procyon defenders back away from the entrances, and more poured in.

THE amphitheatre was soon filled with struggling clots of men, and full of the low sound of wounded and dying. Those still on their feet grunted and panted, but there was no other sound. The floor became slippery with the blood of Procy and Outsider alike.

Kimberly's foot slipped in a pool of blood and he fell heavily.

Looking up he saw the butt of a blaster plunging at his head. He rolled, kicking out with his feet, and felt them connect with the legs of the Outsider soldier as the blaster smashed into the floor where his head had been. He scrambled to his feet and kicked the Outsider in the face. He fell back, under the feet of the other combatants. Kimberly saw a hand appear as if by magic from the knot of men and deftly slide a dagger into the Outsider's throat, then disappearing back into the melee of arms and legs.

He was knocked off balance by another plunging body, and thrown into the wall of the still upraised vault. It had gone nearly half way down before the mechanism jammed, and the circular disk was only about four feet off the floor. In the center the Fire-axe still hung, the key in the lock. Kimberly clambered to the top of the cylinder and wrenched loose the Axe.

An Outsider charged toward the vault, and Kimberly leaped from the top, whirling the Fire-axe. He caught the onrushing Outsider at the joint between neck and shoulder and split him cleanly, the head dropping away at a strange angle as bright blood spurted from the gash.

Kimberly swung the Axe above his head and started it whirling. It began to keen and wail as the blade flashed around and around, the tiny grooves of the decorations catching the air and turning it into a banshee's scream.

Kai shrieked from somewhere in the battle, the same high paean of victory that had chilled Kimberly's blood at the end of the Fire-Ritual. Kai's shaven brown head, now spattered with blood, appeared. His head was thrown back and the shrill, piercing scream came from his throat in a rhythmic ululation.

Where the chamber had before held only the sound of struggling men, there were now the two eerie wails of the Fire-axe and Kai Manson. Some of the fighting men started, almost physically jolted by the sound.

With the terrifying war cry still issuing from his throat Kai picked an Outsider up and threw him into the shining circle of death around Kimberly.

The Fire-axe neatly clipped off the man's head, and its wail was clotted with the gurgling of blood. A Procy knife-man shoved another of the enemy soldiers backwards, and the Axe bit deeply. After each victim, Kimberly started the Axe whirling again, and soon the floor on the perimeter of the glittering circle it made was littered with the dead and dismembered bodies of the enemy.

Those left suddenly made a dash for the exit tunnels. Fear mirrored on their faces. They were met by the remnants of Kai's men, and none left the central chamber.

Gathering the remaining Procys around him, Kai dashed to Kimberly. Together they made for the temple front and the pavilion. They reached open air just in time to see the Outsider ship lift.

It climbed vertically, under full acceleration until it was lost from their sight.

"I hope that's the last we see of them," Kai said.

"I doubt it," said Kimberly. "They'll be back."

THEY turned to re-enter the temple, and were stopped by a shout from one of the Procy knifemen.

"Look! Look up there!" Their eyes followed his pointing finger. Far above, in the direction taken by the escaping Outsider ship, there was a new sun in the sky, its glare rivalling for a brief second that of Procyon itself.

"Nuclear blast," Kimberly said. "The Federation must have caught on to them."

Some minutes later the huge bulk of a Federation battle cruiser appeared in the sky. It settled to earth gently, three miles down the hill from the temple. A scout copter detached itself from the parent ship and sped quickly toward the temple cliff.

When it reached the courtyard, the entire remaining body of the Procy defenders had gathered on the pavilion, the women coming from the living quarters where they had spent the battle.

Neela came up beside Kimberly without a word, and linked her arm in his. He bent his head and looked into her luminous dark eyes.

"Well, we made it," he said.

He turned his eyes to the men climbing out of the Federation copter. One of them was Jacob Spack. His bright blue eyes widened as he saw Kimberly standing at the temple entrance with Kai at one side and Neela at the other.

"I suppose I might have known it," Spack said. "Kimberly, do you have to get mixed up with everything unsavory that goes on in this galaxy?"

"Just doing my job," Kimberly said. "Boss."

"What was that ship doing attacking this temple?" Spack asked. "We had it reported as missing, then it turns up bombarding a Fire-temple. When we challenged them, they fired on us. So—" Spack shrugged, and inclined his head toward that patch of sky where the Outsider ship had glowed so brightly.

"That was an Outsider you just vaporized," said Kimberly.

"Well, we figured something of the sort, but how—"

"I'll explain it all to you later," Kimberly said. "Oh, by the way," he added casually. "Your ecological records are in the temple there. Thought you might want to know."

Spack's iron control broke, and he stared open-mouthed at Kimberly, who ignored him.

"Tell you what," said Kimberly to Neela. "Suppose we go talk over things of mutual interest and let our friend here catch bugs in his mouth."

"Now listen, Kimberly—" Spack began.

"*Captain* Kimberly, please. Remember? Neela, do you think you could ever love a man who had to work for a man like that?"

"I think I might manage it," said Neela solemnly. "It would depend a lot on the man."

"You know," said Kimberly, "I think you're going to make a pretty good wife for an EcoSurv Captain. A pretty good wife indeed. There's nothing like having a dancing girl around the house."

THE END

BROOMSTICK RIDE

Robert Bloch

Robert Bloch will forever be remembered by most people for the movie that Alfred Hitchcock made in 1960 from his chilling novel Psycho. But Bloch had been a widely known writer for decades when the Hitchcock movie appeared.

He was born in Wisconsin in 1917, became interested in weird and horror fiction when he was about 15, and quickly became one of H.P. Lovecraft's many correspondents. Under Lovecraft's tutelage he began selling short stories to Weird Tales, beginning with "The Feast in the Abbey" and "The Secret in the Tomb" at the age of 17 in 1934. Hundreds of other stories for the fantasy magazines followed, of which the most famous, perhaps, is 1943's "Yours Truly, Jack the Ripper," many times dramatized on the radio. His "That Hell-Bound Train" won a Hugo award in 1959 for the year's best short story. Eventually he moved to Los Angeles, where he wrote many screenplays for films and television. He died in 1994.

"Broomstick Ride" appeared in Super-Science in the December, 1957 issue—a Blochian blending of fantasy and science fiction.

Witches and warlocks on the strange, new planet! There had to be a reasonable, scientific explanation of this phenomena. — But was there any scientific explanation?

Artwork by Ed Emshwiller

T WAS CLOSE to midnight when they gathered at the crater. Night raised its head across the pitted plains and the twin moons opened their green eyes to stare down into the crater's depths.

The pit was deep and dark. Forbes crouched on the rim with his companions and his mind was full of *ds. Deep, dark, dank, dismal, dolorous.* Yes, he thesaurized, and also *dreary, deathly, damned and doomed.* To say nothing of *diabolical.*

Right now, crouching at the crater's edge, he mentally reviewed the work of Shakespeare, William. *Macbeth* was what he had in mind. *Macbeth* on the blasted heath. If this wasn't a blasted heath, then all his concepts were awry. A blasted heath at midnight, with two moons instead of one.

Just behind him in the darkness, the three technicians checked the controls of the recorder units. Visio and audio extended full-range to cover 360° scan on a half-mile sweep, with a 20-20000 frequency. Fourteen lenses played upon the heath, the crater rim, and the crater depths.

"Picking up anything yet?" Forbes whispered.

"Not yet. But if anything happens—" The technician's tone implied, for himself and his companions, that nothing was expected to happen. They couldn't quite understand what they were doing on a blasted heath at midnight, setting up their sensitive equipment to record emptiness and silence.

Forbes couldn't blame them. This was supposed to be just a routine field-trip.

"You'll check Pyris," the Director had told him. "Cartography did a run on it, and Doyle will give you the details. The atmosphere, I understand, is positively Earthlike, and it's a Class I planet—one of the anthropomorphic cultures. Doyle places it at about 900 spans behind us, and there are even language similarities. We'll want audio and visio records of course and an element analysis. Just a preliminary survey in case we find mineralogical possibilities worth exploiting. Strictly a routine checkup."

And Doyle hadn't added much more. "Outside of the craters and vegetation you'd think you were on Earth—a thousand spans ago, of course. The natives wear clothes, they have a primitive government, a religious pattern complete with totem and taboo, everything. Better get a hypnolearn on the language."

Forbes took the hypnolearn, and that started him wondering. The language wasn't English, but there were odd similarities. And odd references—some of them so odd that Forbes spent the last week before departure checking Central Data files. He had covered all the available filmscannings from 1500 to 1700 Oldstyle.

The comparison between life on Pyris and life on Earth in post-feudal times proved surprisingly apt after Forbes landed. He had paid a formal call upon the Kal, or ruler, and sued for permission to "visit" the planet. Gifts and courtesies had been exchanged and then Forbes had taken his technical crew into the desert to study life in the villages. A small force remained aboard the ship which landed close to the Kal's fortress.

For three days Forbes and his men had taken records of daily existence in the mines and the subterranean grottoes where all the food for the planet was grown. He reviewed his conversation with the "peasants"— that's what they'd be called on Oldstyle earth, and that's how he thought of them now.

He remembered the hints of curious beliefs which the workers of Pyris held. They were afraid to dig in certain grottoes, they kept away from the pits after dark, and they whispered of certain things which meant nothing to the men in Forbes' crew.

But he had scanned the Oldstyle past on Earth, and that's how he'd run into Shakespeare, and similarities. The similarities excited him sufficiently to have his equipment set up in what he thought was the logical spot at the logical time. The blasted heath at midnight.

NOW Forbes crouched there and waited for what appears on blasted heaths.

It came.

Audio got it first, faint and far away. The rush of matter through atmosphere, and above it the shriller sounds, splintering the silence.

One of the technicians, Kalt, began to mutter. "Bedamned! Voices. Voices in the sky!"

Visio took over now. The delicate cameras were on target, automatically focussing and feeding out *infra* and *ultra* to record what human eyes could not as yet perceive. And then the distant objects came into the range of normal viewing.

"Look!" Kalt whispered to his companions. "Pyrans. Up there, in the sky. And what are they riding on?"

Forbes could have told him. Forbes could have told him what comes to blasted heaths at midnight, and what they rode upon. But he kept silent, rather than disturb them at their work.

A month ago he himself would not have been disturbed, but since then he'd done that filmscan. And now he knew about witches.

They rode on broomsticks to the Sabbat, swooped from the skies—witches and warlocks, wizards and sorceresses, coming in coven to adore Satan, the Black Master of the Flock.

Of course, all this was ancient superstition, and earthly superstitions besides. It had no basis in reality.

But he was seeing it now.

The broomsticks—were those long shafts really broomsticks?—soared overhead and then descended into the crater. The riders (were those frowsy hags really witches?) cackled and shrieked, their voices echoing below the crater rim.

Now fire blazed below, and the flames blazed blue as the crones cast powder upon the pyres. The hags were naked now, their anointed bodies shimmering in the smoke.

"Bedamned!" muttered Kalt again, like the sensible modern technician he was. Forbe's reflected that the man didn't even know the meaning of the word he used. It was merely a common place expression. Once it had been a jocular curse—"I'll be damned!" And before that, back in the ancient days of 1500-1700 Oldstyle, it had a literal meaning. It was, in those times, an acknowledgement of fact. People *were* damned. They *did* sell their souls to Satan. And they danced around fires and chanted while the smoke swirled. The damned danced.

They were dancing now.

Forbes recognized the ritual from what he'd scanned. He knew about the unguent cast on the fire, the ointment on the naked bodies, about belladonna and aconite and other forgotten drugs.

He knew about the rituals they chanted in the Pyric tongue. Of course they could not be adoring Satan—he'd go over the audio records very thoroughly in the future—but at the moment he thought he could detect repeated shouts of a word resembling "Sire."

But everything else was familiar, dreadfully so. When the figure stepped out of the shadows, wearing a hood crowned with *kort*-horns, Forbes was reminded of the Master of the Sabbat, who wore the Sign of the Goat or the antlers of the Black Stag. Here it would be a *kort,* of course, for it was the only quadreped on Pyris.

THE Master of the Sabbat, whatever his Pyric title, was leading the chanting now. And he brought the *kort* into the firelight and he wielded the knife and filled the bowl and gave all to drink of the sacrifice. Then the smoke swirled up and the voices howled and—

The *temrars* came. Forbes recognized the soldiers of the Kal as they rose along the opposite rim of the crater. He recognized their breastplates, their spears and swords and the two man slings which hurled arrows of steel.

The arrows were speeding now, through the smoke. And the Kal's men clambered down the sides of the crater. The crones wailed.

Then came another shout—from behind.

Forbes turned, but too late. Another group of *temrars* had crept up in the darkness, to pinion the arms of his crew. And they used their swords now—not on the men, but on the receptors and the equipment. In a moment, audio and visio were wreckage.

The tall, spade-bearded leader confronted Forbes, placed his hand on his heart in salute, and murmured, "You are to follow me. It is the wish of the Kal."

Forbes heard Kalt protesting, and cut him off with a curt gesture. He remembered that he was the guest of an alien culture and a primitive one. They had already destroyed his records and they were perfectly capable of destroying him, just as they would probably destroy the witches in the pit below. 'Thou shalt not suffer a witch to live.' Wasn't that an old biblical injunction? Strange, that there should be this similarity.

And there were more similarities to come, as Forbes and his companions were escorted, on *kort*-back, across the nighted plain. Forbes could close his eyes and easily imagine himself transported across space and time to ancient Earth. The clank of armor, the thud of hoofbeats, the remorseless tread of the iron legions returning victorious to the castle of the king—all were part of another world. A world of conquerors and commoners, of mage and magic

Forbes couldn't repress an ironic grin. He, the selfstyled representative of modern intergalactic culture, was a prisoner of these superstitious savages. A single sweep of a sword had shattered the finest and most delicate scientific recording instruments yet devised. This wasn't his world—it was a world of force and cunning and he'd do best to deal with it on those terms.

Perhaps he'd treated the Kal too lightly. Certainly the Pyric people feared their ruler. They gave him their toil, their allegience, their taxes and their daughters. He owned the mines and the grottoes and was worshipped like a god.

So perhaps those who opposed the Kal would find new gods to worship. Sire, or whatever he was called, would be more than a Devil. He'd be Kal's chief political opponent. No wonder his soldiers sought the witches out.

THEY came to the valley and the citadel of the Kal. Rising within the walls of stone was the great fortress, its silhouette serrated against the sky. The company made its way through narrow streets to broader avenues, down the ramps and into the castle proper.

And here, in one of the stone antechambers, Forbes found Siddons, the ship's astrogator, and the other members of the crew.

"They came for us an hour ago," Siddons said. "No, they didn't try to force their way inside—locks were closed, anyhow. But they summoned, and we didn't resist. There's a guard around the ship now, but none of them went in, or even tried to enter. I don't understand it."

Forbes mustered a show of confidence. "We'll find out all about it when I see the Kal."

"The Kal will see you now." It was the spade-bearded *temrar* who spoke, who led Forbes away alone and gestured to the others to keep back.

Forbes followed him down a long corridor, then halted as the *temrar* indicated a small door. "Please to enter," he said.

Nodding, Forbes opened the door, stepped inside, and faced the Kal.

The hairy little fat man was seated behind a large table. His pudgy hands rested on the table-top and cradled a silver shape.

He tucked it away in the folds of his sleeve as Forbes entered and nodded at him gravely.

"I had you brought here for your own protection," the Kal said. "Your lives are in danger."

"From what?"

"The *wrali*. Or, as you would call them, witches."

"Why should they harm us?"

"Because you threaten their way of life. And unless you leave, they will destroy you. That was the purpose of their rites this evening—to summon Sire, the Evil One."

Forbes smiled. "But that's superstition," he said. "They can't harm us with spells or enchantments. Surely you don't believe, for example, that a witch or one of your *wrali* can kill a man by sticking pins into his image or melting it over a hot fire. Or do you?"

The Kal's voice, like his face, was inscrutable. "It is not a question of what I believe. It is a question of what my people believe. And is it not true that once there were men who believed in witchcraft on Earth?"

"True." Forbes hesitated. "But how would *you* know that?"

"Because the *wrali* have a legend. According to that legend, the inhabitants of Pyris come originally from Earth."

"Our Earth?"

"Exactly. Haven't you noticed the similarities in language, in concept, in the system of government corresponding to olden days? And isn't our *wrali* worship of Sire similar to the witch-worship of Satan?"

The Kal smiled now. "I'm not the ignorant barbarian you think me to be—it is only through choice that I appear so. And you might do well to ponder our legend.

"The tale is this. Long ago, on your Earth, witches were persecuted, burned, hanged, torn to pieces, because they believed in Satan, or Sire. And a certain group, facing extinction on your planet, invoked the Evil One to save them. He granted their desires. They mounted their broomsticks and flew into space—flew here, to Pyris."

Forbes blinked. "You don't believe that, do you?" he asked.

"Legends are interesting, you must admit. They do offer explanations."

"I have another." Forbes considered for a moment. "On our Earth, long ago, science was as suspect as witch craft. Scientists performing experiments or investigations could be accused of black magic and executed just as witches were.

"Now suppose a certain man, or group of men, working in secret, managed somehow to hit upon the principles of atomic propulsion and space travel—just as we know the alchemists investigated atomic theory? And in order to escape from a hostile environment, they actually built a ship and came here? Whereupon a clique of warriors among their descendants determined to seize the power of government, gradually debased the people and enslaved them—planting such crude legends to keep them in the grip of superstition?"

The Kal shrugged. "You find that theory more attractive than witchcraft, eh?"

Forbes met his gaze. "It's logical. Somewhere in this world the sources of scientific knowledge must still exist, suppressed only to maintain the present rulers in control. I rather suspect that the *wrali* understand some of it. I saw them ride to the meeting tonight on broomsticks, and I'm thinking now that those broomsticks contained individual power packs."

The Kal shrugged again. "I see there are no secrets to the trained scientific mind. But now that you know the story, I must ask you to leave, for your own safety. The *wrali* fear you and may take drastic measures."

Forbes bowed his head. "Very well. We can take off immediately, if you release us."

"You will be escorted to your ship. Is there anything you need, any service you require?"

"No, thank you." Forbes hesitated. "It's just that I'm sorry. Sorry to see a world still existing in such savagery as yours, when it isn't necessary. That men here are still ruled by ignorance and superstition."

The Kal tugged at his beard. "But suppose there were truth to the legends? Suppose that Sire, or Satan, does rule here and that science dares not oppose magic? That this world stays in barbarism because it is the Evil One's wish to rule, and that science must bow before sorcery lest everything be destroyed?"

Forbes smiled. "You know that's nonsense," he replied. "I can't accept that, any more than you can."

"Yet you'll go now and leave us to our savagery?"

"I have no choice."

"Very well, then." The Kal inclined his head. Forbes

went to the door and the Kal spoke to his *temrar,* gave orders for safe escort back to the ship.

THE door closed, and the Kal was alone in the little room. He stared into the flame from the brazier, then extracted the gleaming object from his sleeve once more. He turned it over and over with his pudgy hands and after he had examined it quite thoroughly he merely sat and waited.

After a time the door opened again. A Pyran came in, wearing a hood crowned with *kort*-horns.

"They are gone?" asked the Kal.

"Back to the ship. Soon they depart."

"I am sorry about tonight," the Kal said. "I trust the *temrars* did not actually hurt anyone, but they had to make it convincing. If Earth ever suspected that the government and the *wrali* work together, then nothing could stop them from returning. As it is, I think we deceived them and they are gone for good."

The hooded one stood stock-still and his head was cocked as though he were listening. "I can sense them now," he murmured. "I can reach the one called Forbes, on the ship. He is thinking of his report. He will put in a request for an expedition to come back here. He wants to bring a new government from his planet and civilize all Pyris." The hooded one sighed. "It is as I told you it would be. Your plan has failed."

The Kal rose. "I'm sorry," he said. "I tried to save them. First I told him the truth about how we came to Pyris, and about the power of magic. But he didn't believe me. He preferred to think it was all science, disguised as legend."

"Then it must be ended my way," the hooded one

declared. "We work together, *wrali* and *temrar,* although the people do not know. We work together to keep this planet in ignorance, keep our race from civilization and science—because with science, worship of the Evil One would cease. And that was the ancient promise we made when we came here—that our people would always worship. We must keep that promise in order to survive.

"So we cannot let this Forbes come back and bring his cursed science here. We must do things my way. Give that to me."

The Kal handed the silvery object to the hooded one. "Is it time?" he whispered.

The hooded one cocked his head again. "I can sense it now," he said. "The ship has taken off. It climbs swiftly. Thousands of miles."

The hooded one bent over the brazier as the flames roared up. Carefully he thrust the silvery object into the crimson coals. The flames licked, tasted, then consumed with incredible speed. In a moment the object melted away.

"What happens now?" whispered the Kal.

The hooded one shuddered. "Ten thousand miles away," he murmured. "Now!"

Ten thousand miles over Pyris the space-ship exploded, melted into nothingness.

And down below the Kal murmured sadly, "We had to do it, didn't we? To save our planet from the scientists. Because they don't believe in the Power of Evil. They don't believe you can kill by sticking pins into an image—or by melting an image over a hot fire—"

THE END

WORLDS OF ORIGIN
Jack Vance

Jack Vance's wry, ingenious, gloriously vivid fiction has been a favorite of readers since his first book, the now-classic The Dying Earth, *appeared in 1950. In the decades that followed he has produced a stream of wonders—dozens of short stories and a multitude of novels. Among the best-known of his stories are "The Moon Moth," "The Gift of Gab," the many tales of Cugel the Clever, and the Hugo-winning novellas "The Last Castle" and "The Dragon Masters." His novels include* Big Planet *(1952),* The Blue World *(1966),* Emphyrio *(1969) and the five books of the* Star Kings *series, among many others. In 1996 the Science Fiction Writers of America honored him with its Grand Master award. (He is one of five Grand Masters to have had stories in* Super-Science Fiction *in its eighteen-issue life, the others being James Gunn, Isaac Asimov, Harlan Ellison, and Robert Silverberg.)*

Vance was born in San Francisco in 1916 and has been a resident of the Bay Area for his entire long life, though he has traveled widely. "Worlds of Origin" is the ninth and last of the stories he wrote about the adventures of the wily Magnus Ridolph, beginning in 1948 with "Hard Luck Diggings" in Startling Stories.

Who done the murder? It made quite a difference from which world each suspect came. Interplanetary crimes might well be solved by a complete cultural analysis.

Artwork by Ed Emshwiller

THE HUB, A cluster of bubbles in a web of metal, hung in empty space, in that region known to Earthmen as Hither Sagittarius. The owner was Pan Pascoglu, a man short, dark and energetic, almost bald, with restless brown eyes and a thick mustache. A man of ambition, Pascoglu hoped to develop the Hub into a fashionable resort, a glamor island among the stars— something more than a mere stop-over depot and junction point. Working to this end, he added two dozen bright new bubbles—"cottages," as he called them—around the outer meshes of the Hub, which already resembled the model of an extremely complex molecule.

The cottages were quiet and comfortable; the dining salon offered an adequate cuisine; a remarkable diversity of company met in the public rooms. Magnus Ridolph found the Hub at once soothing and stimulating. Sitting in the dim dining salon, the naked stars serving as chandeliers, he contemplated his fellow-guests. At a table to his left, partially obscured by a planting of dendrons, sat four figures. Magnus Ridolph frowned. They ate in utter silence and three of them, at least, hulked over their plates in an uncouth fashion.

"Barbarians," said Magnus Ridolph, and turned his shoulder. In spite of the mannerless display he was not particularly offended; at the Hub one must expect to mingle with a variety of peoples. Tonight they seemed to range the whole spectrum of evolution, from the boors to his left, across a score of more or less noble civilizations, culminating with—Magnus Ridolph patted his neat white beard with a napkin—himself.

From the corner of his eye he noticed one of the four shapes arise, approach his own table.

"Forgive my intrusion—but I understand that you are Magnus Ridolph."

Magnus Ridolph acknowledged his identity and the other, without invitation, sat heavily down. Magnus Ridolph wavered between curtness and civility. In the starlight he saw his visitor to be an anthropologist, one Lester Bonfils, who had been pointed out to him earlier. Magnus Ridolph, pleased with his own perspicacity, became civil. The three figures at Bonfils' table were savages in all reality: palaeolithic inhabitants of S-Cha-6, temporary wards of Bonfils. Their faces were dour, sullen, wary; they seemed disenchanted with such of civilization as they had experienced. They wore metal wristlets and rather heavy metal belts: magnetic pinions. At necessity, Bonfils could instantly immobilize the arms of his charges.

BONFILS himself was a fair man with thick blond hair, heavy and vaguely flabby. His complexion should have been florid; it was pale. He should have exhaled easy good-fellowship, but he was withdrawn, and diffident. His mouth sagged, his nose was pinched; there was no energy to his movements, only a nervous febrility. He leaned forward. "I'm sure you are bored with other people's troubles—but I need help."

"At the moment I do not care to accept employment," said Magnus Ridolph in a definite voice.

Bonfils sat back, looked away, finding not even the strength to protest. The stars glinted on the whites of his eyes, his skin shone the color of cheese. He muttered, "I should have expected no more."

His expression held such dullness and despair that Magnus Ridolph felt a pang of sympathy. "Out of curiosity—and without committing myself—what is the nature of your difficulty?"

Bonfils laughed briefly—a mournful empty sound. "Basically—my destiny."

"In that case I can be of little assistance," said Magnus Ridolph.

Bonfils laughed again, as hollowly as before. "I use the word 'destiny' in the largest sense, to include—" he made a vague gesture "—I don't know what. I seem predisposed to failure and defeat. I consider myself a man of goodwill—yet there is no one with more enemies. I attract them as if I were the most vicious creature alive."

Magnus Ridolph surveyed Bonfils with a trace of interest. "These enemies, then, have banded together against you?"

"No . . . At least I think not. I am harassed by a woman. She is busily engaged in killing me."

"I can give you some rather general advice," said Magnus Ridolph. "It is this: have nothing more to do with this woman."

Bonfils spoke in a desperate rush, with a glance over his shoulder toward the palaeolithics. "I had nothing to do with her in the first place! That's the difficulty! Agreed that I'm a fool; an anthropologist should be careful of such things, but I was absorbed in my work. This took place at the southern tip of Kharesm, on Journey's End; do you know the place?"

"I have never visited Journey's End."

"Some people stopped me on the street—'We hear you have engaged in intimate relations with our kinswoman!'

"I protested: 'No, no, that's not true!'—because naturally, as an anthropologist, I must avoid such things like the plague."

Magnus Ridolph raised his brows in surprise. "Your profession seems to demand more than monastic detachment."

Bonfils made his vague gesture; his mind was elsewhere. He turned to inspect his charges; only one remained at the table. Bonfils groaned from the depths of his soul, leapt to his feet—nearly overturning Magnus Ridolph's table—and plunged away in pursuit.

Magnus Ridolph sighed, and after a moment or two, departed the dining salon. He sauntered the length of the main lobby, but Bonfils was nowhere to be seen. Magnus Ridolph seated himself, ordered a brandy.

THE lobby was full. Magnus Ridolph contemplated the other occupants of the room. Where did these various men and women, near-men and near-women, originate? What were their purposes, what had brought them to the Hub? That rotund moon-faced bonze in the stiff red robe, for instance. He was a native of the planet Padme, far across the galaxy: why had he ventured so far from home?

And the tall angular man whose narrow shaved skull carried a fantastic set of tantalum ornaments: a Lord of the Dacca. Exiled? In pursuit of an enemy? On some mad crusade?

And the anthrope from the planet Hecate sitting by

himself: a walking argument to support the theory of parallel evolution. His outward semblance caricatured humanity, internally he was as far removed as a gastropod. His head was bleached bone and black shadow; his mouth a lipless slit. He was a Meth of Maetho, and Magnus Ridolph knew his race to be gentle and diffident, with so little mental contact with human beings as to seem ambiguous and secretive . . .

Magnus Ridolph focused his gaze on a woman, and was taken aback by her miraculous beauty. She was dark and slight with a complexion the color of clean desert sand; she carried herself with a self-awareness that was immensely provoking . . . Into the chair beside Magnus Ridolph dropped a short nearly-bald man with a thick black mustache: Pan Pascoglu, proprietor of the Hub. "Good evening, Mr. Ridolph; how goes it with you tonight?"

"Very well, thank you . . . That woman: who is she?"

Pascoglu followed Magnus Ridolph's gaze. "Ah. A fairy-princess. From Journey's End. Her name—" Pascoglu clicked his tongue "—I can't remember. Some outlandish thing."

"Surely she doesn't travel alone?"

Pascoglu shrugged. "She says she's married to Bonfils, the chap with the three cavemen. But they've got different cottages, and I never see them together."

"Astonishing," murmured Magnus Ridolph.

"An understatement," said Pascoglu. "The cave-men must have hidden charms."

The next morning the Hub vibrated with talk, because Lester Bonfils lay dead in his cottage, with three palaeolithics stamping restlessly in their cages. The guests surveyed each other nervously. One among them was a murderer!

PAN PASCOGLU came to Magnus Ridolph in an extremity of emotion. "Mr. Ridolph, I know you're here on vacation, but you've got to help me out. Someone killed poor Bonfils dead as a mackerel, but who it was—" he held out his hands. "I can't stand for such things here, naturally."

Magnus Ridolph pulled at his little white beard. "Surely there is to be some sort of official enquiry?"

"That's what I'm seeing you about!" Pascoglu threw himself into a chair. "The Hub's outside all jurisdiction. I'm my own law—within certain limits, of course. That is to say, if I was harboring criminals, or running vice, someone would interfere. But there's nothing like that here. A drunk, a fight, a swindle—we take care of such things quietly. We've never had a killing. It's got to be cleaned up!"

Magnus Ridolph reflected a moment or two. "I take it you have no criminological equipment?"

"You mean those truth machines, and breath-detectors and cell-matchers? Nothing like that. Not even a finger-print pad."

"I thought as much," sighed Magnus Ridolph. "Well, I can hardly refuse your request. May I ask what you intend to do with the criminal after I apprehend her—or him?"

Pascoglu jumped to his feet. Clearly the idea had not occurred to him. He held out his clenched hands. "What should I do? I'm not equipped to set up a law court. I don't want to just shoot somebody."

Magnus Ridolph spoke judiciously. "The question may resolve itself. Justice, after all, has no absolute values."

Pascoglu nodded passionately. "Right! Let's find out who did it. Then we'll decide the next step."

"Where is the body?" asked Magnus Ridolph.

"Still in the cottage, just where the maid found it."

"It has not been touched?"

"The doctor looked him over. I came directly to you."

"Good. Let us go to Bonfils' cottage."

Bonfils' "cottage" was a globe far out on the uttermost web, perhaps five hundred yards by tube from the main lobby.

The body lay on the floor beside a white chaise-lounge, lumpy, pathetic, grotesque. In the center of the forehead was a burn; no other marks were visible. The three palaeolithics were confined in an ingenious cage of flexible splines, evidently collapsible. The cage of itself could not have restrained the muscular savages; the splines apparently were charged with electricity.

Beside the cage stood a thin young man, either inspecting or teasing the palaeolithics. He turned hastily when Pascoglu and Magnus Ridolph stepped into the cottage.

Pascoglu performed the introductions. "Dr. Scanton, Magnus Ridolph."

Magnus Ridolph nodded courteously. "I take it, doctor, that you have made at least a superficial examination?"

"Sufficient to certify death."

"Could you ascertain the time of death?"

"Approximately midnight."

Magnus Ridolph gingerly crossed the room, looked

down at the body. He turned abruptly, rejoined Pascoglu and the doctor who waited by the door.

"Well?" asked Pascoglu anxiously.

"I have not yet identified the criminal," said Magnus Ridolph. "However, I am almost grateful to poor Bonfils. He has provided what appears to be a case of classic purity."

Pascoglu chewed at his mustache. "Perhaps I am dense—"

"A series of apparent truisms may order our thinking," said Magnus Ridolph. "First, the author of this act is currently at the Hub."

"Naturally," said Pascoglu. "No ships have arrived or departed."

"The motives to the act lie in the more or less immediate past."

Pascoglu made an impatient movement. Magnus Ridolph held up his hand, and Pascoglu irritably resumed the attack on his mustache.

"The criminal in all likelihood has had some sort of association with Bonfils."

Pascoglu said, "Don't you think we should be back in the lobby? Maybe someone will confess, or—"

"All in good time," said Magnus Ridolph. "To sum up, it appears that our primary roster of suspects will be Bonfils' shipmates en route to the Hub."

"*He came on the Maulerer Princeps;* I can get the debarkation list at once." And Pascoglu hurriedly departed the cottage.

Magnus Ridolph stood in the doorway studying the room. He turned to Dr. Scanton. "Official procedure would call for a set of detailed photographs; I wonder if you could make the arrangement?"

"Certainly. I'll do them myself."

"Good. And then—there would seem no reason not to move the body."

MAGNUS RIDOLPH returned along the tube to the main lobby, where he found Pascoglu at the desk.

Pascoglu thrust forth a paper. "This is what you asked for."

Magnus Ridolph inspected the paper with interest. Thirteen identities were listed.

1. Lester Bonfils, with
     a. Abu
     b. Toko
     c. Homup
2. Viamestris Diasporus
3. Thorn 199
4. Fodor Impliega
5. Fodor Banzoso
6. Scriagl
7. Hercules Starguard
8. Fiamella of Thousand Candles
9. Clan Kestrel, 14th Ward, 6th Family, 3rd Son
10. (No name)

"Ah," said Magnus Ridolph. "Excellent. But there is a lack. I am particularly interested in the planet of origin of these persons."

"Planet of origin?" Pascoglu complained. "What is the benefit of this?"

Magnus Ridolph inspected Pascoglu with mild blue eyes. "I take it that you wish me to investigate this crime?"

"Yes, of course, but—"

"You will then cooperate with me, to the fullest extent, with no further protests or impatient ejaculations." And Magnus Ridolph accompanied the words with so cold and clear a glance that Pascoglu wilted and threw up his hands. "Have it your own way. But I still don't understand—"

"As I remarked, Bonfils has been good enough to provide us a case of definitive clarity."

"It's not clear to me," Pascoglu grumbled. He looked at the list. "You think the murderer is one of these?"

"Possibly, but not necessarily. It might be I, or it might be you. Both of us have had recent contact with Bonfils."

Pascoglu grinned sourly. "If it was you, please confess now and save me the expense of your fee."

"I fear it is not quite so simple. But the problem is susceptible to attack. The suspects—the persons on this list and any others Bonfils had dealt with recently—are from different worlds. Each is steeped in the traditions of his unique culture. Police routine might solve the case through the use of analyzers and detection machines. I hope to achieve the same end through cultural analysis."

Pascoglu's expression was that of a castaway on a desert island watching a yacht recede over the horizon. "As long as the case gets solved," he said in a hollow voice, "and there's no notoriety."

"Come then," said Magnus Ridolph briskly. "The worlds of origin."

The additions were made; Magnus Ridolph scrutinized the list again. He pursed his lips, pulled at his white beard. "I must have two hours for research. Then—we interview our suspects."

TWO hours passed, and Pan Pascoglu could wait no longer. He marched furiously into the library to find Magnus Ridolph gazing into space, tapping the table with a pencil. Pascoglu opened his mouth to speak, but Magnus Ridolph turned his head, and the mild blue gaze seemed to operate some sort of relay within Pascoglu's head. He composed himself, and made a relatively calm inquiry as to the state of Magnus Ridolph's investigations.

"Well enough," said Magnus Ridolph. "And what have you learned?"

"Well—you can cross Scriagl and the Clan Kestrel chap off the list. They were gambling in the game-room and have fool-proof alibis."

Magnus Ridolph said thoughtfully, "It is of course possible that Bonfils met an old enemy here at the Hub."

Pascoglu cleared his throat. "While you were here studying, I made a few inquiries. My staff is fairly observant, nothing much escapes them. They say that Bonfils spoke at length only to three people. They are myself, you and that moon-faced bonze in the red robes."

Magnus Ridolph nodded. "I spoke to Bonfils certainly. He appeared in great trouble. He insisted that a woman—evidently Fiamella of Thousand Candles—was killing him."

"What!" cried Pascoglu. "You knew all this time?"

"Calm yourself, my dear fellow. He claimed that she was engaged in the process of killing him—vastly different from the decisive act whose effect we witnessed. I beg of you, restrain your exclamations; they startle me. To continue, I spoke to Bonfils, but I feel secure in eliminating myself. You have requested my assistance and you know my reputation: hence with equal assurance I eliminate you."

Pascoglu made a guttural sound, and walked across the room.

Magnus Ridolph spoke on. "The bonze—I know something of his cult. They subscribe to a belief in reincarnation, and make an absolute fetish of virtue, kindness and charity. A bonze of Padme would hardly dare such an act as murder; he would expect to spend several of his next manifestations as a jackal or a sea-urchin."

The door opened, and into the library, as if brought by some telepathetic urge, came the bonze himself. Noticing the attitudes of Magnus Ridolph and Pascoglu, their sober appraisal of himself, he hesitated. "Do I intrude upon a private conversation?"

"The conversation is private," said Magnus Ridolph, "but inasmuch as the topic is yourself, we would profit by having you join us."

"I am at your service." The bonze advanced into the room. "How far has the discussion advanced?"

"You perhaps are aware that Lester Bonfils, the anthropologist, was murdered last night."

"I have heard the talk."

"We understand that last evening he conversed with you."

"That is correct." The bonze drew a deep breath. "Bonfils was in serious trouble. Never have I seen a man so despondent. The bonzes of Padme—especially we of the Isavest Ordainment—are sworn to altruism. We render constructive service to any living thing, and under circumstances to inorganic objects as well. We feel that the principle of life transcends protoplasm; and in fact has its inception with simple—or perhaps not so simple—motion. A molecule brushing past another—is this not one of vitality? Why can we not conjecture consciousness in each individual molecule? Think what a ferment of thought surrounds us; imagine the resentment which conceivably arises when we tread on a clod! For this reason we bonzes move as gently as possible, and take care where we set our feet."

"Aha, hum," said Pascoglu. "What did Bonfils want?"

THE bonze considered. "I find it difficult to explain. He was a victim of many anguishes. I believe that he tried to live an honorable life, but his precepts were contradictory. As a result he was beset by the passions of suspicion, eroticism, shame, bewilderment, dread, anger, resentment, disappointment and confusion. Secondly, I believe that he was beginning to fear for his professional reputation—"

Pascoglu interrupted. "What, specifically, did he require of you?"

"Nothing specific. Reassurance and encouragement, perhaps."

"And you gave it to him?"

The bonze smiled faintly. "My friend, I am dedicated to serious programs of thought. We have been trained to divide our brain's left lobe from right, so that we may think with two separate minds."

Pascoglu was about to bark an impatient question, but Magnus Ridolph interceded. "The bonze is telling you that only a fool could resolve Lester Bonfils' troubles with a word."

"That expresses something of my meaning," said the bonze.

Pascoglu stared from one to the other in puzzlement, then threw up his hands in disgust. "I merely want to find who burnt the hole in Bonfils' head. Can you help me, yes or no?"

The bonze smiled. "I will be glad to help you, but I wonder if you have considered the source of your impulses? Are you not motivated by an archaic quirk?"

Magnus Ridolph interpreted smoothly. "The bonze refers to the Mosaic Law. He warns against the doctrine of extracting an eye for an eye, a tooth for a tooth."

"Again," declared the bonze, "you have captured the essence of my meaning."

Pascoglu threw up his hands, stamped to the end of the room and back. "Enough of this foolery!" he roared. "Bonze, get out of here!"

Magnus Ridolph once more took it upon himself to interpret. "Pan Pascoglu conveys his compliments, and begs that you excuse him until he can find leisure to study your views more carefully."

The bonze bowed and withdrew. Pascoglu said bitterly, "When this is over, you and the bonze can chop logic to your heart's content. I'm sick of talk, I want to see some action." He pushed a button. "Ask that Journey's End woman—Miss Thousand Candles, whatever her name is—to come into the library."

Magnus Ridolph raised his eyebrows. "What do you intend?"

Pascoglu refused to meet Magnus Ridolph's gaze. "I'm going to talk to these people and find out what they know."

"I fear that you waste time."

"Nevertheless," said Pascoglu doggedly. "I've got to make a start somewhere. Nobody ever learned anything lying low in the library."

"I take it then that you no longer require my services?"

Pascoglu chewed irritably at his mustache. "Frankly, Mr. Ridolph, you move a little too slow to suit me. This is a serious affair. I've got to get action fast."

Magnus Ridolph bowed in acquiescence. "I hope you have no objection to my witnessing the interviews?"

"Not at all."

A moment passed, then the door opened and Fiamella of Thousand Candles stood looking in.

Pan Pascoglu and Magnus Ridolph stared in silence. Fiamella wore a simple beige frock, soft leather sandals. Her arms and legs were bare, her skin only slightly paler than the frock. In her hair she wore a small orange flower.

Pascoglu somberly gestured her forward; Magnus Ridolph retired to a seat across the room.

"Yes, what is it?" asked Fiamella in a soft, sweet voice.

"You no doubt have learned of Mr. Bonfils' death?" asked Pascoglu.

"Oh yes!"

"And you are not disturbed?"

"I am very happy, of course."

"Indeed." Pascoglu cleared his throat. "I understand that you have referred to yourself as Mrs. Bonfils."

Fiamella nodded. "That is how you say it. On Journey's End we say he is Mr. Fiamella. I pick him out. But he ran away, which is a great harm. So I came after him, I tell him I kill him if he will not come back to Journey's End."

Pascoglu jumped forward like a terrier, stabbed the air with a stubby forefinger. "Ah! Then you admit you killed him!"

"No, no," she cried indignantly. "With a fire gun? You insult me! You are so bad as Bonfils. Better be careful, I kill you."

Pascoglu stood back, startled. He turned to Magnus Ridolph. "You heard her, Ridolph?"

"Indeed, indeed."

Fiamella nodded vigorously. "You laugh at a woman's beauty; what else does she have? So she kills you, and no more insult."

"Just how do you kill, Miss Fiamella?" asked Magnus Ridolph politely.

"I kill by love, naturally. I come like this—" she stepped forward, stopped, stood rigid before Pascoglu, looking into his eyes. "I raise my hands—" she slowly lifted her arms, held her palms toward Pascoglu's face. "I turn around, I walk, away." She did so, glancing over her shoulder. "I come back." She came running back. "And soon you say, 'Fiamella, let me touch you, let me feel your skin.' And

I say, 'No!' And I walk around behind you, and blow on your neck—"

"Stop it!" said Pascoglu uneasily.

"—and pretty soon you go pale and your hands shake and you cry, 'Fiamella, Fiamella of Thousand Candles, I love you, I die for love!' Then I come in when it is almost dark and I wear only flowers, and you cry out, 'Fiamella!' Next I—"

"I think the picture is clear," said Magnus Ridolph suavely. "When Mr. Pascoglu recovers his breath, he surely will apologize for insulting you. As for myself, I can conceive of no more pleasant form of extinction, and I am half-tempted to—"

She gave his beard a playful tweak. "You are too old."

Magnus Ridolph agreed mournfully. "I fear that you are right. For a moment I had deceived myself . . . You may go, Miss Fiamella of Thousand Candles. Please return to Journey's End. Your estranged husband is dead; no one will ever dare insult you again."

FIAMELLA smiled in a kind of sad gratification, and with soft lithe steps, went to the door, where she halted, turned. "You want to find out who burned poor Lester?"

"Yes, of course," said Pascoglu eagerly.

"You know the priests of Cambyses?"

"Fodor Impliega, Fodor Banzoso?"

Fiamella nodded. "They hated Lester. They said, 'Give us one of your savage slaves. Too long a time has gone past, we must send a soul to our god.' Lester said, 'No!' They were very angry, and talked together about Lester."

Pascoglu nodded thoughtfully. "I see. I'll certainly make

inquiries of these priests. Thank you for your information."

Fiamella departed. Pascoglu went to the wall mesh. "Send Fodor Impliega and Fodor Banzoso here please."

There was a pause, then the voice of the clerk responded. "They are busy, Mr. Pascoglu, some sort of rite or other. They said they'll only be a few minutes."

"Mmph . . . Well, send in Viamestris Diasporus."

"Yes, sir."

"For your information," said Magnus Ridolph, "Viamestris Diasporus comes from a world where gladiatorial sports are highly popular, where successful gladiators are the princes of society, especially the amateur gladiator, who may be a high-ranking nobleman, fighting merely for public acclamation and prestige."

Pascoglu turned around. "If Diasporus is an amateur gladiator, I would think he'd be pretty callous. He wouldn't care who he killed!"

"I merely present such facts as I have gleaned through the morning's research. You must draw your own conclusions."

Pascoglu grunted.

In the doorway appeared Viamestris Diasporus, the tall man with the ferocious aquiline head whom Magnus Ridolph had noticed in the lobby. He inspected the interior of the library carefully.

"Enter, if you please," said Pascoglu. "I am conducting an inquiry into the death of Lester Bonfils. It is possible that you may help us."

Diasporus' narrow face elongated in surprise. "The killer has not announced himself?"

"Unfortunately, no."

Diasporus made a swift gesture, a nod of the head, as if suddenly all were clear. "Bonfils was evidently of the lowest power, and the killer is ashamed of his feat, rather than proud."

Pascoglu rubbed the back of his head. "To ask a hypothetical question, Mr. Diasporus, suppose you had killed Bonfils, what reason—"

Diasporus cut the air with his hand. "Ridiculous! I would only mar my record with a victory so small."

"But, assuming that you had reason to kill him—"

"What reason could there be? He belonged to no recognized gens, he had issued no challenges, he was of stature insufficient to drag the sand of the arena."

Pascoglu spoke querulously. "But if he had done you an injury—"

Magnus Ridoph interjected a question. "For the sake of argument, let us assume that Mr. Bonfils had flung white paint on the front of your house."

In two great strides Diasporus was beside Magnus Ridolph, the feral bony face peering down. "What is this, what has he done?"

"He has done nothing. He is dead. I ask the question merely for the enlightenment of Mr. Pascoglu."

"Ah! I understand. I would have such a cur poisoned. Evidently Bonfils had committed no such solecism, for I understand that he died decently, through a weapon of prestige."

Pascoglu turned his eyes to the ceiling, held out his hands. "Thank you, Mr. Diasporus, thank you for your help."

Diasporus departed; Pascoglu went to the wall-mesh. "Please send Mr. Thorn 199 to the library."

THEY waited in silence. Presently Thorn 199 appeared, a wiry little man with a rather large round head, evidently of a much mutated race. His skin was a waxy yellow; he wore gay garments of blue and orange, with a red collar and rococo red slippers.

Pascoglu had recovered his poise. "Thank you for coming, Mr. Thorn. I am trying to establish—"

Magnus Ridolph said in a thoughtful voice, "Excuse me. May I make a suggestion?"

"Well?" snapped Pascoglu.

"I fear Mr. Thorn is not wearing the clothes he would prefer for so important an inquiry as this. For his own sake he will be the first to wish to change into black and white, with, of course, a back hat."

Thorn 199 darted Magnus Ridolph a glance of enormous hatred.

Pascoglu was puzzled. He glanced from Magnus Ridolph to Thorn 199 and back.

"These garments are adequate," rasped Thorn 199. "After all, we discuss nothing of consequence."

"Ah, but we do! We inquire into the death of Lester Bonfils."

"Of which I know nothing!"

"Then surely you will have no objection to black and white."

Thorn 199 swung on his heel and left the library.

"What's all this talk about black and white?" demanded Pascoglu.

Magnus Ridolph indicated a strip of film still in the viewer. "This morning I had occasion to review the folk-ways of the Kolar Peninsula on Duax. The symbology of clothes is especially fascinating. For instance, the blue and orange in which Thorn 199 just now appeared induces a frivolous attitude, a light-hearted disregard for what we Earthmen would speak of as 'fact.' Black and white, how-ever, are the vestments of responsibility and sobriety. When these colors are supplemented by a black hat, the Kolar-ians are constrained to truth."

Pascoglu nodded in a subdued fashion. "Well, in the meantime, I'll talk to the two priests of Cambyses." He glanced rather apologetically at Magnus Ridolph. "I hear that they practice human sacrifice on Cambyses; is that right?"

"Perfectly correct," said Magnus Ridolph.

THE two priests, Fodor Impliega and Fodor Banzoso, presently appeared, both corpulent and unpleasant-look-ing, with red flushed faces, full lips, eyes half-submerged in the swelling folds of their cheeks.

Pascoglu assumed his official manner. "I am inquir-ing into the death of Lester Bonfils. You two were fellow passengers with him aboard the *Maulerer Princeps;* perhaps you noticed something which might shed some light on his death."

The priests pouted, blinked, shook their heads. "We are not interested in such men as Bonfils."

"You yourselves had no dealings with him?"

The priests stared at Pascoglu, eyes like four knobs of stone.

Pascoglu prompted them. "I understand you wanted to sacrifice one of Bonfils' palaeolithics. Is this true?"

"You do not understand our religion," said Fodor Impliega in a flat plangent voice. "The great god Camb exists in each one of us, we are all parts of the whole, the whole of the parts."

Fodor Banzoso amplified the statement. "You use the word 'sacrifice.' This is incorrect. You should say, 'go to join Camb.' It is like going to the fire for warmth, and the fire becomes warmer the more souls that come to join it."

"I see, I see," said Pascoglu. "Bonfils refused to give you one of his palaeolithics for a sacrifice—"

"Not 'sacrifice'!"

"—so you became angry, and last night you sacrificed Bonfils himself!"

"May I interrupt?" asked Magnus Ridolph. "I think I may save time for everyone. As you know, Mr. Pascoglu, I spent a certain period this morning in research. I chanced on a description of the Camgian sacrificial rites. In order for the rite to be valid, the victim must kneel, bow his head forward. Two skewers are driven into his ears, and the victim is left in this position, kneeling, face down, in a state of ritual composure. Bonfils was sprawled without regard for any sort of decency. I suggest that Fodor Impliega and Fodor Banzoso are guiltless, at least of this particular crime."

"True, true," said Fodor Impliega. "Never would we leave a corpse in such disorder."

Pascoglu blew out his cheeks. "Temporarily, that's all."

At this moment Thorn 199 returned, wearing skin-tight black pantaloons, white blouse, a black jacket, a black tricorn hat. He sidled into the library, past the departing priests.

"You need ask but a single question," said Magnus Ridolph. "What clothes was he wearing at midnight last night? What exact clothes?"

"Well?" asked Pascoglu. "What clothes were you wearing?"

"I wore blue and purple."

"Did you kill Lester Bonfils?"

"No."

"Undoubtedly Mr. Thorn 199 is telling the truth," said Magnus Ridolph. "The Kolarians will perform violent deeds only when wearing gray pantaloons or the combination of green jacket and red hat. I think you may safely eliminate Mr. Thorn 199."

"Very well," said Pascoglu. "I guess that's all, Mr. Thorn."

Thorn 199 departed, and Pascoglu examined his list with a dispirited attitude. He spoke into the mesh. "Ask Mr. Hercules Starguard to step in."

HERCULES Starguard was a young man of great physical charm. His hair was a thick crop of flaxen curls, his eyes were blue as sapphires. He wore mustard-colored breeches, a flaring black jacket, swaggering black short-boots. Pascoglu rose from the chair into which he had sank. "Mr. Starguard, we are trying to learn something about the death of Mr. Bonfils."

"Not guilty," said Hercules Starguard. "I didn't kill the swine."

Pascoglu raised his eyebrows. "You had reason to dislike Mr. Bonfils?"

"Yes, I would say I disliked Mr. Bonfils."

"And what was the cause of this dislike?"

Hercules Starguard looked contemptuously down his nose at Pascoglu. "Really, Mr. Pascoglu, I can't see how my emotions affect your inquiry."

"Only," said Pascoglu, "if you were the person who killed Mr. Bonfils."

Starguard shrugged. "I'm not."

"Can you demonstrate this to my satisfaction?"

"Probably not."

Magnus Ridolph leaned forward. "Perhaps I can help Mr. Starguard."

Pascoglu glared at him. "Please, Mr. Ridolph, I don't think Mr. Starguard needs help."

"I only wish to clarify the situation," said Magnus Ridolph.

"So you clarify me out of all my suspects," snapped Pascoglu. "Very well, what is it this time?"

"Mr. Starguard is an Earthman, and is subject to the influence of our basic Earth culture. Unlike many men and near-men of the outer worlds, he has been inculcated with the idea that human life is valuable, that he who kills will be punished."

"That doesn't stop murderers," grunted Pascoglu.

"But it restrains an Earthman from killing in the presence of witnesses."

"Witnesses? The palaeolithics? What good are they as witnesses?"

"Possibly none whatever, in a legal sense. But they are

important indicators, since the presence of human on-lookers would deter an Earthman from murder. For this reason, I believe we may eliminate Mr. Starguard from serious consideration as a suspect."

Pascoglu's jaw dropped. "But—who is left?" He looked at the list. "The Hecatean." He spoke into the mesh. "Send in Mr. . . ." He frowned. "Send in the Hecatean to us now."

THE Hecatean was the sole non-human of the group, although outwardly, he showed great organic similarity to true man. He was tall and stick-legged, with dark brooding eyes in a hard chitin-sheathed white face. His hands were elastic fingerless flaps: here was his most obvious differentiation from humanity. He paused in the doorway, surveying the interior of the room.

"Come in, Mr.—" Pascoglu paused in irritation. "I don't know your name, you have refused to confide it, and I cannot address you properly. Nevertheless, if you will be good enough to enter . . ."

The Hecatean stepped forward. "You men are amusing beasts. Each of you has his private name. I know who I am, why must I label myself? It is a racial idiosyncrasy, the need to fix a sound to each reality."

"We like to know what we're talking about," said Pascoglu. "That's how we fix objects in our minds, with names."

"And thereby you miss the great intuitions," said the Hecatean. His voice was solemn and hollow. "But you have called me here to question me about the man labeled Bonfils. He is dead."

"Exactly," said Pascoglu. "Do you know who killed him?"

"Certainly," said the Hecatean. "Does not everyone know?"

"No," said Pascoglu. "Who is it?"

The Hecatean looked around the room, and when he returned to Pascoglu, his eyes were blank as holes into a crypt.

"Evidently I was mistaken. If I knew, the person involved wishes his deed to pass unnoticed, and why should I disoblige him? If I did know, I don't know."

Pascoglu began to sputter, but Magnus Ridolph interceded in a grave voice. "A reasonable attitude."

Pascoglu's cup of wrath boiled over. "I think his attitude is disgraceful! A murder has been committed, this creature claims he knows, and will not tell . . . I have a good mind to confine him to his quarters until the patrol ship passes."

"If you do so," said the Hecatean, "I will discharge the contents of my spore sac into the air. You will presently find your Hub inhabited by a hundred thousand animalcules, and if you injure a single one of them, you will be guilty of the same crime that you are now investigating."

Pascoglu went to the door, flung it aside. "Go! Leave! Take the next ship out of here! I'll never allow you back!"

THE Hecatean departed without comment. Magnus Ridolph rose to his feet and prepared to follow. Pascoglu held up his hand. "Just a minute, Mr. Ridolph. I need advice. I was hasty, I lost my head."

Magnus Ridolph considered. "Exactly what do you require of me?"

"Find the murderer! Get me out of this mess!"

"These requirements might be contradictory."

Pascoglu sank into a chair, passed a hand over his eyes. "Don't make me out puzzles, Mr. Ridolph."

"Actually, Mr. Pascoglu, you have no need of my services. You have interviewed the suspects, you have at least a cursory acquaintance with the civilizations which have shaped them."

"Yes, yes," muttered Pascoglu. He brought out the list, stared at it, then looked sidewise at Magnus Ridolph. "Which one? Diasporus? Did he do it?"

Magnus Ridolph pursed his lips doubtfully. "He is a Knight of the Dacca, an amateur gladiator evidently of some reputation. A murder of this sort would shatter his self-respect, his confidence. I put the probability at 1 percent."

"Hmph. What about Fiamella of Thousand Candles? She admits she set out to kill him."

Magnus Ridolph frowned. "I wonder. Death by means of amorous attrition is of course not impossible—but are not Fiamella's motives ambiguous? From what I gather, her reputation was injured by Bonfils' disinclination and she thereupon set out to repair her reputation. If she could harass poor Bonfils to his doom by her charm and seductions, she would gain great face. She had everything to lose if he died in any other fashion. Probability: 1 percent."

"Hymph. What of Thorn 199?"

Magnus Ridolph held out his hands. "He was not dressed in his killing clothes. It is as simple as that. Probability: 1 percent."

"Well," cried Pascoglu. "What of the priests, Banzoso and Impliega? They needed a sacrifice to their god."

Magnus Ridolph shook his head. "The job was a botch. A sacrifice so slipshod would earn them ten thousand years of perdition."

Pascoglu made a half-hearted suggestion. "Suppose they didn't really believe that?"

"Then why trouble at all?" asked Magnus Ridolph. "Probability: 1 percent."

"Well, there's Starguard," mused Pascoglu, "but you insist he wouldn't commit murder in front of witnesses . . ."

"It seems highly unlikely," said Magnus Ridolph. "Of course we could speculate that Bonfils was a charlatan, that the Palaeolithics were impostors, that Starguard were somehow involved in the deception. . ."

"Yes," said Pascoglu eagerly. "I was thinking something like that myself."

"The only drawback to the theory is that it cannot possibly be correct. Bonfils is an anthropologist of wide reputation. I observed the palaeolithics, and I believe them to be authentic primitives. They are shy and confused. Civilized men attempting to mimic barbarity unconsciously exaggerate the brutishness of their subject. The barbarian, adapting to the ways of civilization, comports himself to the model set by his preceptor—in this case Bonfils. Observing them at dinner, I was amused by their careful aping of Bonfils' manners. Then, when we were inspecting the corpse, they were clearly bewildered, subdued, frightened. I could discern no trace of the crafty calculation by which a civilized man would hope to extricate himself from an uncomfortable situation. I think we may assume that Bonfils and his palaeolithics were exactly as they represented themselves."

Pascoglu jumped to his feet, paced back and forth. "Then the palaeolithics could not have killed Bonfils."

"Probability minuscule. And if we concede their genuineness, we must abandon the idea that Starguard was their accomplice, and we rule him out on the basis of the cultural qualm I mentioned before."

"Well—the Hecatean, then. What of him?"

"He is a more unlikely murderer than all the others," said Magnus Ridolph. "For three reasons: First, he is non-human, and has no experience with rage and revenge. On Hecate violence is unknown. Secondly, as a non-human, he would have no points of engagement with Bonfils. A leopard does not attack a tree; they are different orders of beings. So with the Hecatean. Thirdly, it would be, physically as well as psychologically, impossible for the Hecatean to kill Bonfils. His hands have no fingers; they are flaps of sinew. They could not manipulate a trigger inside a trigger-guard. I think you may dispense with the Hecatean."

"But who is there left?" cried Pascoglu in desperation.

"Well, there is you, there is I and there is—"

THE door slid back, the bonze in the red cloak looked into the room.

"Come in, come in," said Magnus Ridolph with cordiality. "Our business is just now complete. We have established that of all the persons here at the Hub, only you would have killed Lester Bonfils, and so now we have no further need for the library."

"What!" cried Pascoglu, staring at the bonze, who made a deprecatory gesture.

"I had hoped," said the bonze, "that my part in the affair would escape notice."

"You are too modest," said Magnus Ridolph. "It is only fitting that a man should be known for his good works."

The bonze bowed. "I want no encomiums. I merely do my duty. And if you are truly finished in here, I have a certain amount of study before me."

"By all means. Come, Mr. Pascoglu, we are inconsiderate, keeping the worthy bonze from his meditations." And Magnus Ridolph drew the stupified Pan Pascoglu into the corridor.

"Is he—is he the murderer?" asked Pascoglu feebly.

"He killed Lester Bonfils," said Magnus Ridolph. "That is clear enough."

"But why?"

"Out of the kindness of his heart. Bonfils spoke to me for a moment. He clearly was suffering considerable psychic damage."

"But—he could be cured!" exclaimed Pascoglu indignantly. "It wasn't necessary to kill him to soothe his feelings."

"Not according to our viewpoint," said Magnus Ridolph. "But you must recall that the bonze is a devout believer in—well, let us call it 'reincarnation.' He conceived himself performing a happy release for poor tormented Bonfils who came to him for help. He killed him for his own good."

They entered Pascoglu's office; Pascoglu went to stare out the window. "But what am I to do?" he muttered.

"That," said Magnus Ridolph, "is where I can not advise you."

"It doesn't seem right to penalize the poor bonze . . . It's ridiculous. How could I possibly go about it?"

"The dilemma is real," agreed Magnus Ridolph.

There was a moment of silence, during which Pascoglu morosely tugged at his mustache. Then Magnus Ridolph said, "Essentially, you wish to protect your clientele from further applications of misplaced philanthropy."

"That's the main thing!" cried Pascoglu. "I could pass off Bonfils' death—explain it was accidental. I could ship the palaeolithics back to their planet . . ."

"I would likewise separate the bonze from persons showing even the mildest melancholy. For if he is energetic and dedicated, he might well seek to extend the range of his beneficence."

Pascoglu suddenly put his hand to his cheek. He turned wide eyes to Magnus Ridolph. "This morning I felt pretty low. I was talking to the bonze . . . I told him all my troubles. I complained about expense—"

The door slid quietly aside, the bonze peered in, a half-smile on his benign face. "Do I intrude?" he asked as he spied Magnus Ridolph. "I had hoped to find you alone, Mr. Pascoglu."

"I was just going," said Magnus Ridolph politely. "If you'll excuse me . . ."

"No, no!" cried Pascoglu. "Don't go, Mr. Ridolph!"

"Another time will do as well," said the bonze politely. The door closed behind him.

"Now I feel worse than ever," Pascoglu moaned.

"Best to conceal it from the bonze," said Magnus Ridolph.

THE END

I WANT TO GO HOME
Robert Moore Williams

Robert Moore Williams, who was born in Missouri in 1907, began reading science fiction before the first science-fiction magazine, Hugo Gernsback's Amazing Stories, *commenced publication in 1926. After studying journalism at the University of Missouri, he became a full-time fiction writer, and laid a claim to the attention of s-f readers with two superb short stories, "Flight of the Dawn Star" and "Robots Return," both published in* Astounding Science Fiction *in 1938 and anthologized many times since. After that, though, most of his output was confined to the pulp magazines that specialized in action-adventure stories, and little of that work is remembered today. Toward the end of his career he wrote a series of paperback novels that dealt with the struggle of a superscientist hero, Zanthar, against an assortment of superscientific villains, concluding with* Zanthar at the Edge of Never *(1968.) He died in 1977.*

Williams had one story in Super-Science: *"I Want to Go Home," in the April, 1958 issue.*

Why are we alive on this earth? Does anyone know? How can anyone be sure we are now where we belong and that no cosmic mistake has somehow been made?

FOR A MOMENT, the noise in the adjoining room died down enough to allow Calvin
Thurber to think clearly. He was not certain
this helped. Judging by the contents of the folder in front
of him, he was not sure that he wanted to think at all. In
the juvenile department of even the most modern Police
station on earth, some things were beyond human power
to change, particularly the power of the police psychologist.

"You go to hell, you dirty-nosed cop!" Thurber heard
the kid yell through the thick door that led into the next
room.

Smack!

Thurber hurriedly turned his attention back to the papers in the folder. This file had been sent down to him as
soon as the arrest had been made. Since this was a juvenile
case, he had by law wide latitude in determining what dis-
position would be made of it.

"The child spoke at four months. His first words, according to his mother, were, *'I want to go home!'* These
words formed a recurring theme through infancy and
childhood and formed the basis of nightmares from which,
according to his mother, he would awaken screaming in
terror. Nor was she able to reassure him in these seizures,
since he did not seem at these times to recognize her as his
mother and she seemed to excite as much fear in him as
the hidden fantasies of the night."

Thurber gave the social worker who had compiled this
report a mental pat on the back. The mother's words must
have been pure garbage. The worker who had written up
the interviews had managed to turn the mother's unfin-

ished sentences into a clear, coherent narrative. This report had been made after the first arrest, of which there had been several, he noted.

Because both parents had worked, Ralph had been placed in a nursery school. He was unable to make an adequate adjustment there, nor, though placed in special classes, was he able to adjust adequately at any time until his junior year in high school, at which time his many truancies reached culmination and he stopped school and left home.

"His grades in school were not impressive, this in spite of the fact that repeated testing indicated his IQ was very high. His teachers reported that he regarded these tests as being games and that he had no inkling of their significance. But, despite this opinion, his high IQ made it likely that he did know the importance of the tests and that his treatment of them as games was merely another way of demonstrating his rebellion against authority.

"Ralph's police record began when he was nine—petty theft. Found guilty, he was placed on probation, but efforts of probation officers to maintain control over him were not measurably successful. At the date of this summary, he has had five arrests, two on charges of theft and three on charges of burglary. Oddly, all of the stores he burglarized specialized in the sale of electronic equipment and all of his thefts were for stealing merchandise of this type."

Thurber felt a twitch of rising interest at this item—a juvenile delinquent who specialized in burglarizing stores that sold electronic equipment! "What's he trying to do—make a radio set that will contact Mars?" the psychologist wondered.

THINGS were quiet in the next room now, Thurber real-ized with relief. Although he was an employee of the po-lice department, he had never accepted the brutality that old-time officers occasionally used. The .38 caliber revolv-er which had been issued to him, he kept carefully hidden in his desk drawer. His eyes went back to the folder.

"Ralph seems to have been a complete individualist at all times. Living in a neighborhood infested with teen-age gangs, he belonged to none."

"A lone wolf," the psychologist thought. Turned crimi-nal, the lone wolf often gave the police enormous diffi-culty, simply because his habit of working alone left few clues—and no stool pigeons—behind him. On the other hand, going with the culture instead of fighting it, the lone wolf was often the brilliant engineer or the famous scien-tist, simply because he dared to travel where there were no trails.

A knock sounded on the door. "Just a minute," Thurber called. Hastily scanning the rest of the report, he found little of significance in it. "All right, come in," he called.

A sergeant brought the boy in. The officer's face was red, and a button was missing from his uniform. He laid the arrest report on Thurber's desk and turned away. Paus-ing at the door, he said, "If you need any help, I'll be right here."

"Thank you, sergeant. However, I am sure Ralph and I will get along fine."

Glowering, the kid stood beside his desk. Tall and thin, he had a bruise on his right cheek. Thurber guessed that this was probably related to the button missing from the sergeant's uniform.

"Ralph, I'm Calvin Thurber." The psychologist rose and offered his hand. The kid stared at him as if he did not know what was expected. "Oh, come now, you know how to shake hands," Thurber said, jovially.

"Yeah, but I'm not shaking hands with no stinkin' cop!"

Thurber lost none of his geniality. "Really, Ralph, I'm not a cop. I'm a psychologist. My purpose here is to help people who are in trouble, especially young men—"

"You lie like all the other cops," the kid answered.

Unruffled, Thurber answered, "I have no way to prove my words to you at present but if you will give me a fair chance, I will show you that I mean what I say. What have you got to lose by playing ball with me? After all, I might mean what I am saying!" The psychologist put sincerity into his voice, and meant it. "Just sit down for a few minutes while I look over the arrest report. Ah—smoke?"

In Thurber's experience, most juvenile delinquents did smoke. Often they were marijuana addicts.

This one surprised him. "No, thanks. Never touch them." Much of the hostility had gone out of Ralph's voice. He sat down in the chair beside Thurber's desk.

The report was brief. "Apprehended filching electrical switches from a delivery truck. Resisted arrest." The signature of the arresting officer was an illegible scrawl.

More electronic equipment! A question leaped to the tip of Thurber's tongue. It was the usual question, "Why are you so interested in electrical devices?" He would have asked any man who had been repeatedly charged with pilfering a particular article why the thief was so interested in this one thing. In this way, a compulsion could perhaps be brought to light, which when corrected, might change a thief into an honest man.

To Thurber's surprise another question actually came from his lips. To him, carefully trained in saying exactly what he wanted to say, and no more, this was astonishing. If his right hand had formed a fist and had struck him in the nose, he would not have been more surprised.

"Why do you want to go home?" was the question he actually asked.

THE kid was out of his chair in an instant. His hands were balled into fists and the dazed psychologist's first impression was that Ralph was on the verge of striking him.

"Why do you ask that? What do you mean by asking me that? Why—"

"Really, Ralph, I had no intention of asking that question," the startled psychologist answered.

"Then why did you ask it?"

"I don't know. I intended to ask something else." Thurber had to fight to regain his composure. "Of course, I know the source of it. It's right here in the records, the first words you ever spoke—"

Thurber showed him the case history. "Oh, that nosey social worker who kept prying around when I was a kid." Ralph seemed relieved to know the source of the question, but, as if the query had opened up hidden thoughts, he seemed more tense than before. The psychologist, still startled at the reaction, wondered what deep trauma had been brought to the surface by his question. Later, he would desperately wonder why he had ever asked this question in the first place.

"What was there about going home that upset you so much?"

"I'm not upset," Ralph denied. To prove it, he slid back into the chair beside Thurber's desk. A film of sweat was visible on his forehead.

"Is there a relationship between wanting to go home and pilfering electronic equipment?" the psychologist asked. He was guessing in the dark and he knew it.

"Nah," the kid said. The sweat appeared more profusely on his forehead. On the arms of the chair, his hands showed signs of tremor.

Thurber wondered how much tremor he would show if he knew that he faced a prison sentence, if found guilty on the present charge, on the grounds that he was a habitual offender? Also since his last offense, Ralph had passed his eighteenth birthday, which in this state changed the legal picture by lifting him out of the category of a juvenile offender. The front office had made a mistake on the age, but was not yet aware of it.

"Why do you want electronic equipment?"

"I like to build things."

"What kind of things?"

"Electronic stuff."

"What kind of electronic stuff?" Thurber's knowledge in this field was limited but the kid did not know this.

"If you will get my things, I'll show you."

"What things?"

"The stuff they took away from me when they booked me."

Getting what Ralph wanted took some telephoning and some doing. Finally an officer lugged a battered army surplus bag into the psychologist's office, got a receipt from him for it, and left. Thurber lifted the bag to the top of his desk and opened it.

The contents held little interest for him, but to the kid they seemed to open the way to a new life. As the bag opened, Ralph opened up, too. Instantly he became friendly and co-operative. His voice rattled rapidly. His talk was of electrons, ions, and particles smaller than either. Thurber tried hard to look interested, but, so far as he could see, the stuff was so much junk.

"How is this going to help you get home?" he asked, searching again for the trauma that he suspected.

THIS time the question did not make Ralph angry. As if the delivery of his beloved junk had opened deep wells of companionship between them, he was willing to talk. His words were to the point, Thurber thought.

"First, we have to establish where home is," Ralph said.

"Yes," Thurber said.

"It's not here."

"Um."

"It's *there.*"

"Ah!" the psychologist said.

"I don't belong here," the kid continued. "As a matter of fact, I doubt if any human belongs here."

"On Earth, you mean, or in a police station?" Thurber queried when the referents for the words were not forthcoming.

"Earth. I don't believe any of us ever belonged here. Oh, we've learned to live here, sort of, and there are a lot of us, but we only appeared here in the first place because some of us got trapped here a long time ago. We've been breeding here while we tried to find our way out. This has gone on so long that most of us have even forgotten where home is."

"Oh, yes," Thurber said. "How does it happen that you do know?"

"I always remembered."

"But why do you remember when no one else does?"

"A lot of people do remember, only they're afraid to talk about it." A frown furrowed the kid's face as his fingers paused in their task of assembling pieces of electronic equipment into an organization of some kind. Watching, Thurber had the impression that his fingers had eyes of their own. Incredibly deft, the kid did not seem to have to look to know what he was doing. "I think we're here as a result of a slip-up somewhere?"

"You mean somebody goofed?"

"No, not some *body*. There's nothing personal about this. I mean a law slipped somewhere, or a higher law that we don't know about entered the picture and upset the balance. However the explanation goes, it works out that I don't really belong here at all. Not this time anyhow."

THE psychologist kept himself from thinking that this was schizophrenia. He knew it was, of course, all his training told him this. In his mind he was busy finding words for his recommendation to the judge. "Suggest hospitalization—" He felt regret as he found the words he wanted. In spite of the record, he liked this kid, and didn't want him in an institution. He knew how grim even the best of them were. He sincerely hoped that some understanding psychiatrist would give Ralph a chance to work with electronics. Judging from what he had seen, the road of recovery lay in that direction.

And yet, somehow, this was not a sick mind. The schizophrenic didn't usually talk in terms of laws in operation, he made the laws into personalities malefically directed at him.

"I've got it!" the kid exclaimed.

"What do you mean?" Thurber asked.

"I've got it assembled the way I want it. I had it all figured out and all I needed were the time-delay switches which I was swiping when the stupid cops grabbed me!" The kid's nostrils flared and excitement rasped his voice.

Thurber, suddenly wondering if he had some infernal device on his hands, was perturbed. He had always been more than halfway willing to believe that if you put the right combination of transistors, wires, condensors, and coils together, anything might happen. He had no sound basis for this belief, which had persisted since he had been a kid himself. With visions of the building blowing up dancing in his mind, he became apprehensive.

"Hold up for a minute there, Ralph!" Thurber's voice was sharp. "What's that thing supposed to do?"

"Take me home!" the kid answered. He pushed a switch. A click sounded. Soundless light flared for a moment. Thurber felt a nameless wave-pulse pass through his body. His hair began to stand on end.

As if puzzled, the kid stared at the assembly. "It ought to work," he muttered.

"Something wrong?" Thurber said, almost maliciously. Secretly he was vastly relieved that nothing had happened.

Or had something happened? His hair was still standing on end.

"Yeah," Ralph said, out of a brown study. His fingers were exploring every instrument on the top of the desk. "I don't understand it. I was sure I had everything right this time."

"You've tried this before?"

"I've tried nothing else since I yapped at Mom the first time that I wanted to go home!" the kid snarled at him. "I was trying to work this out with my first set of building blocks, only nobody knew it."

"Then perhaps it is time you gave this up and began working on practical electronics," Thurber said, firmly. "Go to a school that specializes in this sort of thing, get an education from the ground up."

Mentally he was puzzling over the exact wording of his recommendation to impress the judge. "Strongly recommend further clemency and parole. Ralph has great natural talent at electronics. He has agreed to enter Polytechnic at the coming term—"

So far Thurber's imagination took him. And no farther. He could imagine influencing the judge and he could fantasy the court agreeing to further parole, but he could not force his imagination to the point of foreseeing this lone wolf entering school of his own free will.

"How closer to the ground can you get than building blocks?" the kid answered, confirming the psychologist's imagination. "What I want to know they don't teach in school. Ah!" Satisfaction suddenly appeared in his voice.

"What happened?"

"It was the tuning that was wrong. The exact frequency

is very important. The condensors must have gotten a little damp." The deft fingers worked rapidly. "Now watch!"

Again the switch snapped shut. Again Thurber felt the surge of the nameless electric pulsation through his body. This time it seemed to affect every molecule in his being, perhaps every atom.

"Goodbye," Ralph whispered. "I've got it right this time. *I've got it right!*"

Elation, exultation, the wild tones of joy were in his tones.

Light flared somewhere, a soundless puff of it. Face first, the kid slid down into the chair beside Thurber's desk.

Thurber needed several minutes to realize that he was dead.

EVEN after the body had been removed and a report from an assistant medical examiner had indicated that there was no obvious cause of death and that the determination of the actual cause would have to wait on an autopsy, the dazed psychologist could not believe that the kid was actually dead. True, he had seen the body fall, true he had summoned help, true he had assisted in carrying the body from the room, true he had the report of the assistant ME, true his eyes had seen all of this, and true his ears had heard the sounds, but he still did not believe it. A human being could not be so full of life one instant—and dead the next.

Had there ever been such a person as Ralph Kine? It would be a pleasure to believe that the kid had never existed, that all that he had seen had been a product of his imagination. In time he might talk himself into believing this, but as for now there was the kid's equipment on his own desk in front of his own eyes.

He reached for the phone, to have the equipment and the battered bag picked up and returned to its proper place, and to retrieve his receipt. This would be needed at the inquest, he told himself.

As he started to pick up the phone, he realized he was lying to himself. What he was trying to do was to remove the evidence so he would not have to continue believing that what he had seen happen had actually taken place. He checked the movement to pick up the phone.

What about this generator that had actually caused the kid's death? Thurber began examining it. He called it a generator in the absence of a better name for it, but what had it actually generated besides a soundless puff of light and a wave form that had seemed to touch every atom in his body? Thurber had the suspicion that he should call in electronics experts, the best in the field, to examine the device the kid had assembled, on the hypothesis that perhaps information of military importance might be gleaned from it.

"And get myself called a fool?" He decided against his action. Psychologists were not well enough regarded for him to take careless chances with his position.

A gadfly of thought was buzzing in his mind. He knew an idea was seeking expression. He had a hunch that he did not wish to look at this idea and he tried to push it out of his mind. It came again, stronger than ever, and forced its way into his consciousness.

"I want to go home, too!" he exclaimed.

THE idea had power in it, such longing as he had never known. Nothing in his life had been as important as this desire to go home. He had the .38 completely out of his desk drawer before he realized what he was doing.

"No!" Dropping the gun, he shoved the drawer shut. Sweat bathed his body. Tremors shook it. Although many of the people he saw professionally had tried to tell him about suicidal impulses, this was his first experience with them.

He left the room, paced to the drinking fountain, smoked a cigarette, and returned to his office much calmer, he thought. As soon as he entered the room, the desire to go home hit him again, stronger than before.

Finding the switch the kid had used, he pushed it.

Again the nameless wave cut through his body. With it came knowledge and ecstacy. The knowledge was that he too, was an alien here. The kid had been right! All humans were aliens! They belonged somewhere else.

The ecstacy came from the knowledge that he was going *there,* he was going where he belonged, he was going—home!

He did not feel his body fall forward across the generator. Nor did he care. Dying was not important. It was only graduation to the place where he belonged.

The inquest for Thurber was held immediately following the hearing in re Ralph Kine. In both cases, the coroner's jury returned a verdict of "death from causes unknown."

Humans still called it *death*.

THE END

Philosophy and science don't agree as to how worlds are created. It had to be hard-working spacemen who discovered it the hard way by an actual experience!

THE TOOL OF CREATION
J. F. Bone

Jesse Bone, who was born in Tacoma, Washington, in 1916, was a professor of veterinary medicine by profession, but he enjoyed writing science fiction and was a frequent contributor to the s-f magazines from 1957 until his death in 1986. His best-known short story was "Triggerman," a nominee for the Hugo award in 1959, and the several novels he published included Legacy *(1976) and* The Lani People *(1982).*

"The Tool of Creation," which appeared in the April, 1958 issue of Super-Science Fiction, *was the first of two stories of his that were published in that magazine.*

DEACON PARSONS sat motionless, half stunned at the speed with which the living section had emptied. The astrogator's eyes flickered from Buenaventura's empty chair to the tense backs of the pilot and co-pilot as they wrestled with the problem of turnover in Cth space. Unlike Adams, the significance of the color change didn't register at once, which was one of the reasons he would never make a Cth space pilot. Not only was his color perception far from sensitive enough, but he had none of the "feeling"—the rapport between man and metal that made hyperspace pilotage an art rather than a skill.

The skipper had it to a high degree, which was one reason why the Old Man had survived better than two subjective decades of hyperjumps. Adams had been through it all, even through the time when jumps were made without four space navigation techniques that eliminated time-lag. Objectively, he could count several centuries back to his birthdate, although he was still a youngster in his early forties. Like the "Manitowoc" herself, he was a modernized antique—an anachronism that had survived from the remote past of spaceflight.

On the Galactic registry the "Manitowoc" was listed as a 10,000 ton single converter freighter of Terran registry. She was almost as old as her pilot, and nearly as well preserved. As an owner-operated tramp, she had been across the galactic lens half a dozen times, and had made God knew how many short jumps between inhabited worlds of planetary systems. She was a sound ship, slow but well-built, one of the old semi-streamlined jobs that operated in middle green Cth at maximum converter output.

A moment ago she had been loafing along at an economical fifty lumes in middle yellow component, halfway through the seven weeks' jump between Fanar and Lyrane. A moment ago, the crew, like all hyperspace crews was doing nothing sweating out the dead time. Their duties had ended when the "Manitowoc" had made Cth-shift, and wouldn't begin again until Breakout some three weeks hence. But that was a moment ago ...

DEAD time in a hypership is a period of utter boredom,

with the crew sealed and blind behind shields and hull as the automatics drive the ship on a pre-set course through the Cth continuum. It is worse on a freighter where living space is concentrated in the so-called main cabin—a bleakly functional, insulated, soundproofed room in the nose of the ship that does extra duty as crew's quarters, galley, control room, and saloon, and is a concrete illustration of the lack of privacy and too close companionship that are the penalties of a spaceman's life.

The curved control board set within the vision screen lining the nose of the ship was locked and lifeless. The screen was blank. Only the rectangular telltale with its rows of gleaming green lights showed that the ship was functioning normally. Despite the incredibly tight shields and the radiation resistant metal of the double hull, there was a distinct yellowish tinge to the main cabin and its equipment. Even the thick, undulating layer of tobacco smoke disappearing into the air regenerator had a yellowish tinge, and the red "No Smoking" sign painted above the hatchway leading aft to the drives glowed orange in the sickly yellow light.

And with the color, a few of the mind-wrenching distortions of the Cth continuum seeped through the shields, to turn the prosaic control room and the men within it into oddly surrealistic caricatures that wavered and changed in a random pattern. Seated in their shockchairs the crew faced the blank, featureless bulkhead separating the main cabin from the cargo holds. Even though the space was cramped, it was better to face that blank wall than to look at the protean shapes of the instruments and controls. They could play havoc with a normal mind if one looked at them too long. The subtly undulating bulkhead was bad enough.

Captain Derek Adams cast a quick glance at the control panel, scanned the green glowing telltale, and hastily returned his gaze to the blank wall before him. He puffed leisurely at a stubby pipe crusted with the reeking residues of countless refillings, idly watching the beautiful ogive curve formed by the smoke from the charred bowl before it joined the undulating layer overhead.

Things were never normal in Cth space, he reflected. Like the three men who formed his crew, normally they were passable specimens of Homo sapiens, but not . . . Take Hank Jorgenson for instance. Under normal conditions, the lean co-pilot was ugly enough with his stubby yellow hair and flat Scandinavian face, but now he was a twisted caricature of humanity, a lopsided asymmetrical oddity that was faintly obscene, as the hyperspatial distortions conspired to make him appear somewhat less than human.

Carlos Buenaventura was worse—half a man high, a man and a half wide, the Cth phenomena made him appear as though some giant hand had flattened him into the chair in which he sat. He was a reflection in a sideshow mirror.

And last but not least was Deacon Parsons. By some quirk of Cth, the astrogator looked almost angelically beautiful, as though he had absorbed into himself all the good points the others had lost. The classic purity of his face and body was almost sickening.

Adams grinned. Of course, none of them really resembled their present shapes, it was just Cth. He wondered how he appeared to his companions. It would be hard to say, since he probably looked different to each of them.

He sighed. Twenty years in hyperspace and he still wasn't used to it. But then no one got used to Cth. There was an inherent strangeness about it that never became familiar, an insanity potential that lay waiting in the ever changing shapes produced by the monochromatic distortions.

Cth was a waking nightmare. Even with the shields it was scarcely bearable, and in the old days before the shields were developed to their present high efficiency crews frequently went mad. Sometimes their ships plunged out of the Cth continuum into normal space travelling faster than Lume One, and that was disaster. Space itself ruptured under the impossible strain, and the ship vanished leaving behind a spatial vortex to mark the spot where it had translated into a little universe of its own, independent of normal and hyperspace alike. Adams grimaced wryly, shrugged, and settled his spinal base more comfortably into the foamite padding of his chair. He was getting morbid.

PARSONS' quiet voice broke the stillness, half musing, half inquiring. "In the beginning," he said quietly, "God created the Heaven and the Earth."

Adams wondered what strange twist the astrogator's thoughts had taken to come up with this. Not that religion was taboo, but it was a subject seldom mentioned aboard a ship in space. There was too much chance it could produce trouble. It did this time.

Buenaventura snorted. The sound hung heavily on the

yellow air, echoing with faint reverberations as it struck some odd harmonic that had leaked through the shields.

Jorgenson jerked in his chair as though he had been stuck with a pin. "What brought that up?" he asked curiously.

"I was just thinking aloud," Parsons said. "I'm sorry."

"You should be," Buenaventura said. "Besides, it isn't thinking!"

Adams grinned quietly. Trust Buenaventura to make something of it. He wasn't going to have to do anything to break the silence. Parsons had done that little chore most effectively. And Buenaventura would keep the pot boiling. The man was a catalyst. It was easy to forget Cth with someone like him around.

"I wouldn't go so far as to say that," Jorgenson disagreed. The disagreement in his voice was a conditioned reflex. No one ever agreed with Buenaventura. "Maybe there's something to it. After all, the Creation story is a common denominator on all inhabited worlds. Allowing for cultural variation it's essentially the same wherever you go."

Adams nodded. It was a good point.

"Don't tell me that our choir boy's converted you!" Buenaventura sneered.

"I didn't say that," Jorgenson replied. "But you'll have to admit that the story appears too frequently to be merely coincidence."

Parsons sat back grinning, enjoying the effect of his conversational bombshell. Adams had the odd feeling that the astrogator had done this deliberately. He didn't know too much about the youngster yet, but from the looks of things Parsons would get along.

"I'll admit nothing," Buenaventura said doggedly. "All primitive peoples must have some explanation of how they and their worlds came to be. It's only natural that they would invent some supernatural being to create them. At their early level they couldn't comprehend a scientific explanation if one were given them. And the superstition is perpetuated from generation to generation until it becomes religion, and develops dogma and ritual. You should know how hard it is for the voice of reason to make headway against things like that!"

"I'll grant that," Parsons said. "But what have your omnipotent scientists *proved* about planetary origins? Is there one theory that will fit the facts?"

Adams' attention sharpened. He was certain now that Parsons had used the Bible quotation as an opening gambit to egg the engineer on. The boy was clever. In time he might turn out to be as obnoxiously essential to ship's morale as the engineer.

"There are at least five workable theories as to how solar systems originated," Buenaventura began.

"And which is the right one?"

Buenaventura sputtered. "It hardly matters," he said. "Any of them are superior to the concept of some anthropomorphic being creating solar systems with a godlike wave of his omnipotent hand."

"For every theory," Parsons went on inexorably, "there is equal proof that it couldn't possibly happen. For every one you can advance, I'll bet that I can refute it."

"Gaseous-Tidal," Buenaventura said.

Parsons laughed. "Why pick an easy one like that? You know that it's based on a near-collision between two stars of similar mass, with the gravitational or tidal attraction of each drawing out a thin filament of gas from the solar surfaces of the other. And the tearing of that particular one down is easy. How is it that all those near collisions involved F and G type stars better than 95% of the time? You know, and I know that it's almost axiomatic that only these stars possess planetary systems."

"There's still that five percent."

"Sure, but those systems are damn few compared with the others. Just think of the relatively small number of F and G type suns compared to the others in the galaxy, and then consider the fact that these pitiful few have a practical monopoly on the planetary systems.

"As I remember it some scientists calculated that there was a one in two billion chance of such a stellar near collision occurring in our galaxy, and there's less than two billion F and G suns in the entire lens, yet there are nearly five hundred planetary systems around those sort of stars, and there may be more that haven't yet been discovered. That's asking for a lot of highly-specialized accidents."

"Heidenbrink," Buenaventura said.

"You picked a harder one this time," Parsons said. "Yet the Spiral Generation Theory fails on the same grounds as the Gaseous-Tidal. There isn't enough random distribution of systems, although I'll admit that his ideas why the other stars don't have planetary systems are rather ingenious."

"Then you'll admit that Heidenbrink is better than that religious guff?"

"Not at all. I merely said that disproving his idea was harder."

ADAMS didn't think much of the conversational trend. Parsons was quitting too easily, and Buenaventura didn't seem to have the usual fire. Something was lacking. Maybe he could stir it up. This argument on planetary origins had possibilities. It had fascinated him for years, and certainly it was worth more than this desultory attack. It could last perhaps a week if properly nourished. Not that anything would be settled, but for that period of time hyperspace would be forgotten while the contestants searched the ship's remarkably complete microfilm library for more data to throw at each other.

"I hate to butt in," he said insincerely, "but I think that a compromise approach would be more appropriate, possibly a combination of intelligent creation and some phenomena like the Gaseous-Tidal theory could explain how systems were born."

"Can you clarify that, sir?" Parsons asked.

"I believe so," Adams said. "Have any of you men seen a galactarium?"

"There's one at Luna Base," Jorgenson said. "I was there once."

"I've used it," Parsons said. "We spent three months at Luna working with it as part of astrogation training."

Buenaventura shook his head. "I've been close, but I've never bothered. Why look at an imitation when you can see the real thing?"

"You get a perspective from the scale model that you can never get from space unless you go out halfway to

Andromeda." Adams said, and then dropped the subject. "Anyway, that's not the point. You can do things with a galactarium that you can never do with the galaxy. I suppose you've seen the grand finale of a major show when the projectionist reversed the drive and sends the galaxy back in time until it becomes the galactic nucleus?"

"It's impressive," Jorgenson said briefly.

Parsons nodded agreement.

"It's more than that," Adams said. "At one point in time the suns with planetary systems form radial lines from a common center."

"That isn't new," Parsons said, "nor is it news that the intersection of those radial lines hits within a ten light year radius of the Alpha Centralis system."

"It's news to me," Buenaventura said.

"How do you think the boys found that place?" Parsons asked. "The sun is damn near burned out, and every last planet is full of radiostopes with half lives ranging up in the millions of years. There's no way to spot Alpha Centralis as a planetary system by any of the standard methods."

"They certainly picked a non-standard one," Buenaventura agreed.

"It paid off," Parsons said. "By tagging the F and G stars along those radial lines and bringing the projection up to date, we've discovered nearly a hundred planetary systems in the past five years, and it'd have taken us nearly a century by the old method."

"What I'm getting at," Adams interrupted patiently, "is the evidence everyone seems to want to ignore. Those radial lines a few billion years in the past seem to indicate that someone or something came from the Centralis system that caused the F and G type suns to form planetary systems. And I'm inclined to believe that it was someone rather than something. It would at least explain a lot of odd questions that keep popping up—including the Creation story."

BUENAVENTURA looked up with a speculative light in his eye. "So you think that Centralis was the home of the Gods of Space?"

"If you want to call them that. I like the idea that someone once found a way to create solar systems. There's plenty of questions such a theory would answer."

"There's nothing unusual in this idea," Parsons said. "It's been advanced before."

"I never said there was. I merely like it and think it's logical. It would answer some of the stock puzzlers such as why are 95% of the planetary systems found around F and G type suns; why are there hundreds more spatial vortices in the galaxy than can be accounted for by our lost ships; why are there so few solar systems on the Rim despite the fact that F and G stars are far more numerous there and why all normal life in the galaxy follows the same evolutionary pattern at least up to the reptiles. That's a few, and I can think of more."

"It sounds reasonable," Jorgenson said.

"I only have one objection," Buenaventura interjected. "What force can tear the guts out of a star and scatter it far enough for the material to condense into planets?"

"I don't know, but obviously the Centralians did," Adams said.

"You're as bad as the choir boy," Buenaventura snorted, "but instead of sticking to one God you come up with a whole system full of them. And this despite the fact that there's no proof intelligent life ever existed on Centralis."

"Expeditions can't stay there very long," Adams said. "Those planets are radioactive."

"I think," Parsons said suddenly, "that I'll have to string along with Carlos."

Adams winced. He'd been had! He—not Carlos, had been picked as target for tonight!

It should have aroused his suspicions when Parsons came out with that timeworn quotation, but the hook was well baited. He smiled wryly at the attentive faces of his companions. There was no help for it. He'd just have to take his medicine like a gentleman. Their faces had taken on a mildly satanic cast, emphasized by the faint orange cast to the yellow light.

Orange!— It should be yellow, *pure yellow!* . . . *Orange!*

ADAMS' reaction was instantaneous! He spun his shock-chair into pilotage position and opened the main switches in one flashing motion almost too fast for the eye to follow!

Jorgenson rotated his chair into position beside the pilot. It was habit that made him do it. For years he had been following Adams' lead, and the ingrained patterns were impossible to break. The exclamation of surprise on his lips died unuttered as his eyes fell on the Cth component indicator with its slowly falling needle. His face became oddly grim. Wordlessly he fell into the swift rhythm of the pilot's movement, balancing the trim of the ship as Adams performed the complex maneuver of turnover in Cth space.

Adams acknowledged Jorgenson's presence with a grateful nod of his head as he lifted his eyes for a moment from the banks of instruments that had suddenly come to life. He spoke, but not to the co-pilot. Words between them weren't necessary. "Carlos," he said in almost a casual tone. "Check the converter."

Buenaventura rose from his chair. "Aye, sir!" the engineer said. His stocky figure disappeared aft through the manway hatch in a flat dive, the metal door thudding into place behind him. He was out of sight almost before the astrogator had time to blink.

Parsons finally found his tongue. "What happened?" he asked.

"Converter output's fallen off! We're dropping through the yellow—maybe clear out of Cth!" Jorgenson said.

"Oh! Is there anything I can do?"

"Pray!" Adams snapped. "Maybe that'll keep us up here in Cth long enough to kill our speed."

"Engine room to Control," the annunciator announced in Buenaventura's unmistakable voice.

"Go ahead," Adams said, his hands never pausing their delicate manipulation of the controls.

"The converter's okay, but there's an impure fuel slug in the combustion chamber."

"Can you get it out?"

"From a Mark Vll?" the annunciator inquired sarcastically. "Are you crazy? I can't even fish it out with the slave without taking the cover plate off and killing the old girl for a couple of hours, and if I did that we'd drop out of Cth so fast that we'd never know what we hit."

"How about advancing the burning rate?"

"It's on maximum right now. There isn't enough fissionable material to boil it off any faster unless you want an explosion."

"Well, that's that," Adams commented. "We'll just have to hope we're slow enough when we hit breakout. I suppose those drives of yours can take it?"

"They can take anything you can give them," Buenaventura said. "And besides I'll sit right here and baby them."

"Good man!"

"Turnover's complete," Jorgenson said.

Adams slammed the main drive throttles to their farthest notch. From deep within the ship a deep hum built up amplitude and frequency to a nerve wracking whine that was felt rather than heard. But other than the sound there was no sign that the mighty power of the main drive was functioning at maximum blast.

IN hyperspace, velocity had no physical effects. There was no acceleration pressure. There was friction of course, so one shifted to a higher component as one approached the terminal velocity for the one one was in. But speed was limited entirely to the capacity of the converter.

The liners and the Navy jobs with their multiple converters working in series could reach the violet, and make perhaps ten thousand lightspeeds, or better than twenty five lightyears a day. Single converter tubs like the "Manitowoc" could barely make a hundred, since their single converter could only take them to about the middle green.

The drive, of course, was capable of more speed than that, but the extra power couldn't be used or they'd turn to a cinder from friction. The converter was the important thing—a ship's existence in Cth space depended upon it—and in freighters there were no spares. They were too expensive and bulky to waste cargo space as standbys, and besides nothing ever went wrong with them. Adams felt like laughing at that last thought.

But no matter how fast a ship could travel in Cth, in normal space all had the same limit, Lume One—one lightspeed. Beyond that rigid limit, one millimicron or a million Lumes added up to the same result. The ship simply vanished, rather unspectacularly considering the forces involved, and left behind a tiny coal sack or spatial vortex to mark its passage.

Fifty Lumes had to be taken off the "Manitowoc" before the failing converter squeezed them out into normal space, and there was only one way to do it, to reverse the axis of the ship and rely upon the stupendous thrust of the drives to slow her down in as short a time as possible. The ship had been reversed, the drives energized, and now there was nothing more to do except to make minor corrections for axial wobble if it developed.

ADAMS turned from the board. Jorgenson could handle it well enough from here, and as soon as the distortion patterns began to get him, Adams could take his relief. He couldn't see the instruments, and was oddly thankful that he could not. It was bad enough to sweat it out in ignorance, but it was worse with knowledge. He took a long glance at Jorgenson sitting stiffly in his chair. There was an odd tenseness to the lean figure. Poor Jorgenson—he knew what was happening.

"How we doing?" Buenaventura's anxious voice came over the annunciator.

"With luck we may make it," Jorgenson replied. "At the rate we're falling, we've got three, maybe four hours left in Cth. The drive's full on, and maybe we can kill enough speed to get out in one piece. The critical thing will be whether we can take it when we drop into lower orange. We're still travelling pretty fast for that component."

"I can get a few more dynes out of the converter. She's a little out of tune."

"By all means do it if you can," Adams cut in. "We'll need every minute we can get."

"Aye, sir." It was a measure of Buenaventura's state of mind that he didn't protest. Ordinarily he would have complained at least perfunctorily at the extra duty Adams had requested.

"I've had it," Jorgenson said. "Take over." He had lasted ten minutes, which was pretty good for Cth. Adams spun his chair around and checked the instruments. Their speed was dropping satisfactorily. At their present rate of deceleration they'd hit lower orange at a fairly high level but well within the limits of the component, and if they could keep the drives operating at full blast they'd hit the red at about the middle speed level, the infra red in the lower quarter, and Breakout at Lume one point five—which would be about 160 thousand kilometers per second too fast.

It would be nice to be able to make a visual check—but

that was impossible. The screens were keyed to remain on as long as the converter was operating. Wryly he reflected that of all the crew he was probably the best candidate for the "look and die" type who had wrecked so many ships in the old days by trying to make a visual check of hyperspace. But he never could bring himself to trust the fluid, protean shapes of the instruments.

Three shift changes later they hit lower orange. Their speed was high, but lower than he had estimated. If the instruments were right, and there wasn't too little unaccounted lag, they might possibly hit Breakout at Lume One. A faint surge of hope swept through him.

Almost in answer to his thoughts, Jorgenson turned from the board. "It's gonna be close, Skipper—damn close. The way I figure the lag, we'll be hitting Breakout just about on the nose of Lume One."

His close-cropped head gleamed red in the ruddy light that filled the main cabin. He fumbled with his safety web, tightening it a trifle as he watched the lightspeed needle drop slowly toward the redline of Lume One. The decelerometer needle calibrated in megakilometers per minute quivered at the upper limit of its arc, registering the fierce thrust of the screaming drives. The other graduated dials had long since disconnected and hung dead in their cases until the insane speed of their slowdown would drop sufficiently for them to register. It was good that there were no acceleration pressures in hyperspace, or the force of their braking would long ago have crushed them to death against the unyielding steel of the hull . . .

CARLOS BUENAVENTURA looked through a vision port into the blue-violet radioactive hell of the drive chamber, whistled tunelessly between his teeth, and adjusted a too slowly burning fuel tape to deliver maximum energy. His movements were precise, careful, and incredibly fast.

Buenaventura knew his business, and oddly enough, he was enjoying himself. He was far too busy to think of what might happen if the "Manitowoc" hit Breakout above Lume One. He completed the adjustment and turned back to the converter. Slipping his hands into the handgrips of the slave tongs, he picked up a wrench beyond the safety barrier and began to remove another bolt from the converter housing. He might as well get this job as nearly done as possible. It would save time when they were back in normal space and he could get on with removing the contaminated slug from the reaction chamber.

He swore quietly in a low monotone, cursing the technician who had loaded that particular piece of plutonium into the fuel hopper. It was a hard task for the slave to manipulate the heavy wrench. Servos whined as he applied power, and the bolt started to turn. If the drive room had a chance to cool off he'd be able to do the job manually in half the time. But that wasn't in the cards. He removed the bolt and set it aside in a slotted rack and turned again to his inspection of the drives . . .

Parsons was doing as Adams had suggested. The full extent of their predicament had finally seeped through his Cth deadened brain. And the worst of it was that he could do nothing. In this position, an astrogator was unessential. So he was praying, inaudibly but fervently. Invocations to a dozen major planetary deities rose to his motionless lips. His choice was catholic—not knowing which might be the right one he impartially called upon all he knew. He didn't envy either Adams or Jorgenson. They knew too much, and their grim faces showed it.

Suddenly he found his hands shaking. The cabin had turned a deep magenta that was appreciably fading to the darkness and the heat of the infra band. It wouldn't be long now . . .

"STAND by for Breakout," Adams said flatly. He bent over the control board, his eyes lingering for a brief instant on the speed indicator. It was still above the redline, but lag could account for enough, maybe, to bring them below lightspeed.

He hesitated, fingers on the controls that would cut the converter and the drives, as he waited for the first premonitory shudder of Breakout, that split instant, half sensed, half felt, that no machine nor electronic brain no matter how delicate could perceive, that split instant that made Breakout a function of men rather than machines.

Now the sensing was doubly important, for while deceleration must be applied until the last possible instant, it must be off when they entered normal space or the crushing force would smash them all to pulpy boneless smears against the unyielding metal of the hull.

It was going to be close—Jorgenson was right—it was going to be too close. He forced himself to relax, to hold his body and nerves in check as he waited for the feeling of the ship entering the border zone. It came, faint and familiar, and his hands pressed down on the keys, and then they were in the wrenching shimmering madness of Breakout . . .

The "Manitowoc" rammed her way into normal space scant kilometers per second under Lume One!

The whistling gasp of relief that passed Adams' lips startled him. He hadn't realized that he had been holding his breath. His chest and arms ached, there was a painful cramp in his belly, and an involuntary shiver ran through his muscles as the vision screens flashed on and the familiar normal universe flashed its star patterns in long streaks across the hemispherical brightness.

Their speed was far too great to get an optical fix on their position, and the indicator still quivered in the redline area, but it was still falling as the resistance of space itself acted as a brake to their enormous speed.

But their troubles weren't over. Adams saw it, but already it was too late to do anything about it. Human reflexes in this case simply weren't fast enough! Centered in the course scanner an orange dot swelled with ghastly rapidity, ballooning into an enormous yellow mass that filled the screen almost before Parson's choked cry, "Collision course!" was finished.

But the automatics had instantly taken over, the shields flashed up, and the steering jets blasted in a crushingly violent evasive maneuver that pinned them helplessly to their chairs. Steering jets blasting at maximum aperture, protective shields blazing into the violet, the freighter hurtled at near light speed past the flaming mass of a solitary sun, flashing for an instant through the corona of the star and out again into the blackness of space.

A wave of intense heat washed against the shields, as

the automatics made instantaneous adjustments, and a moment later the pressure eased. Adams reached for the controls. "Thank God for those shields," he breathed. "Without them we'd have been burned to a cinder."

"Better thank those mechs on Terranova who installed those new relays in the automatics," Jorgenson added. "Our old style ones would have been too slow to compensate."

Adams chuckled shakily. To have escaped the terrors of Cth space and the danger of translume destruction only to be destroyed by collision with a third rate star would have been the ultimate in irony.

SLOWLY he set up a deceleration pattern on the drives as the "Manitowoc" hurtled away from the star in a long hyperbolic curve. The ship shuddered, yawing and swaying in sickening arcs as the axial alignment, unbalanced by the star's gravitational pull, turned the slowdown into a stomach-wrenching series of motions that had even the iron-gutted Jorgenson green and gasping.

They were still travelling far too fast for safety, and such niceties as true flight had to be sacrificed until their speed was reduced to safe limits. The stout hull groaned in every stressed and welded joint as it lurched and expanded in its slowing, wobbling course through the heavens.

"This extra weight is useful," Parsons commented through clenched teeth. "At least it keeps my stomach where it belongs. If it wasn't for these 4-G's I'd have lost my lunch a million miles back."

Adams grinned briefly, and then grunted with disgust as he flipped the switches controlling the vision screen. "Those service men on Terranova weren't so hot after all,

Hank," he said. "The screen's stuck and the shields are still up. Guess something must have jammed when we passed that star." He jiggled the switch tentatively. For a brief instant a flash of brilliant light blazed across a slitlike opening in the screen to vanish abruptly as the automatics cut in.

"What in hell was that?" Jorgenson queried in mild surprise.

"I dunno," Adams replied, "but I take back what I said about those mechanics. The screens are okay. Maybe we'd better get off to one side and find out what's happening." He opened the manuals. "At any rate I can't do any worse than the automatics are doing right now."

He energized the port steering jets and swung the ship in a long parabola, still decelerating and testing the screens occasionally. Suddenly they lighted, and Adams, staring at the wide panorama they revealed, gave a startled exclamation of surprise. "Well, I'll be—" he said, wonderingly.

Stretching behind them, across the darkness of space was a thick twisted filament of flaming gas pointing back toward the tiny yellow dot of the star they had so narrowly missed. The elongated cigar shaped mass was already beginning to condense here and there along its length into whirling vortices of star-bright matter. A thin glowing filament like a comet's tail faded behind them as their speed continued to drop.

"Carlos!" Adams barked into the communicator. "Can you get that converter cleared, in a hurry?"

"What's the rush, skipper, ain't we safe now?"

"Just answer me," Adams barked. "Can you or can't you?"

"It'll take about an hour," Buenaventura said in an aggrieved tone. "If you're gonna be that way about it, I'll hurry. But I'm damned if I ever ship on with a slave driver like you again. Next time I'll pick my berth."

Adams laughed. Carlos was normal again.

"Now Deacon," he said to Parsons, "can you get me a line on that star back there?" He indicated the orange sized dot on the screen.

"Yes sir."

"A precise fix?"

"Yes sir."

"Well, get at it then. You have an hour."

Parsons bent over his astrogation console and was instantly immersed in the math and formulae needed to fix the position of a body in space.

Adams smiled gently. The kid sounded so Navy that it almost hurt. It was probably reaction . . .

THE sun with its glowing prominence had faded to an indeterminate speck by the time Carlos' head appeared through the hatchway to the stern. He looked around the main cabin curiously. "What's all the rush about?" he asked. "I don't see anything wrong, or any need for all that hurry."

"You'll find out," Adams said. "Everything clear back there?"

"Sure, I said an hour, and I meant an hour. She's all ready to go."

"Fine. Now then, Parsons, what are those relative co-ordinates?"

"They're on the tape, sir."

Adams fed the tape into the automatics. "Stand by for

C-shift," he said. Buenaventura settled himself into his chair and snapped his web in place. Adams started the converter. The shift was made with all the usual disquieting sensations, but instead of climbing through the components, the automatics held the vessel in the lower red and maneuvered at minimum speed. In a short time the ship went into turnover and decelerated. Adams cut the drive at zero speed, killed the converter, and the ship broke out into normal space.

"Now, Carlos, I've got something to show you," Adams said, half turning in his chair. "You and Parsons were so damned smart rigging that put-up job on me back there in the yellow. Now take a look at something real—" He flicked the vision screen and Carlos stiffened, the shock on his face clearly visible in the flaming light that burst from the screen.

Before him in all its blazing glory was the filament, stretching entirely across the screen in sparkling gouts of flaming gases, already breaking up into hundreds of whirling masses of incandescent star stuff.

They swept through a firmament dotted with innumerable pinpoints of glowing stellar debris. Titanic convulsions shook their surfaces as they swept up millions of the fiery dots, adding them to their swelling masses. The automatics flung up the protective shields as the edge of the filament swept about them in the beginning of an orbital pattern, but the vision screen stayed on, revealing more of the fury of the birth agonies of a solar system.

Adams moved the ship out of danger to a point above the forming ecliptic and shifted the screen, bringing the sun into focus in the lower right quadrant. Even as they watched, a vast mass of flaming matter fell with ponderous deliberation into the sun's corona. Enormous pseudopod-like prominences raised themselves from the tortured surface of the star to enfold the mass and draw it back into the parent surface.

Buenaventura stared wordlessly, as Adams looked at him with an infinitely superior smile on his face. "Take a good look, Carlos," Adams said, "and then tell me some more about Natural Causes and fellows like Heidenbrink. There's a perfect Gaseous-Tidal phenomena for you. See those vortices—some of them are going to be planets someday, and some damn fool idiot on them is going to talk about another Heidenbrink unless we're around to educate him. This is how our systems were formed. You can see it with your own eyes!"

"But—how?"

"Can't you guess, you simple son of a Spanish peasant? *We made it!*"

Buenaventura turned helplessly to Parsons. "Yes, the skipper's right. We did it," the youngster said. "We passed through the corona of that star." He pointed to the boiling, prominence-ridden mass in the lower quadrant of the screen. "We were travelling at almost light-speed when we went past, and while our size was negligible, our mass was nearly infinite. Our mass attraction drew out that filament which is now coalescing into planets. The Skipper is giving it to you straight. We made *that!*" His voice held a note of awe-filled wonder.

"The tool of Creation," Adams mused aloud, "a light-speed transmit. And to think that no one ever thought of it except the Centralians."

"If they existed," Buenaventura said, stubborn to the last.

"They existed all right," Jorgenson said. "They had to exist."

"Think of the possibilities!" Parsons said. "We can fill the galaxy with worlds."

"Habitable after a few million years," Buenaventura sneered.

"What is time with a goal like this to aim at?" Parsons replied.

ADAMS smiled. The astrogator tossed off epochs like they were days. At that maybe he was right. The original Creators also must have thought in terms like that. Their life spores filtering through space had taken root in the fertile soils which they created, and their descendents were now ready to repeat the pattern. The cycle had come to a full circle, and new worlds would be born. It was inevitable.

He watched the giant panorama beneath him move silently across the vision screen, until finally he shrugged. "We'll never be able to see it all," he said, reluctance in his voice. "It's too slow. So I suppose that we'd better turn from gods back to working men again. We've got a cargo to deliver, and there's a penalty clause in our contract." Sighing a little he turned back to the controls.

The "Manitowoc" slowly drew away from the infant solar system, accelerating with ever increasing velocity until with an eye-straining shimmer, she disappeared into the monochromatic regions of hyperspace.

It was Buenaventura who finally spoke. For once he sounded almost apologetic. "All right, I'm wrong, and I admit it," he said. "Solar systems were made." He paused but there was no reply. "But there is still one question that's not answered. I'll admit that there were Centralians—and that they created our systems—but who created them?"

Wordlessly Parsons picked up the ship's Bible and waved it under the engineer's nose. "Want to argue?" he queried finally.

Buenaventura shook his head.

THE END

The otterillas were just about the most vicious form of life that could be encountered on any new planet. It was lucky they had a natural enemy on that world.

Artwork by Ed Emshwiller

HOSTILE LIFE-FORM
Daniel F. Galouye

Daniel Galouye (1920-1976) grew up in New Orleans, and after a brief career as a journalist entered the U.S. Navy in 1942 as a flight instructor and test pilot, stationed in Hawaii. He was injured in the course of his military duty and left the Navy in 1946, returning to newspaper work, first as a reporter for the New Orleans States-Item, *then as an editor for that newspaper. He had been writing science-fiction stories as far back as 1935, when he was fifteen, and during his time as a newspaperman he took up s-f writing again, making a strong impression with such vividly told stories as "Rebirth" (1952), "Sanctuary" (1954), and "The City of Force" (1959). His first novel,* Dark Universe, *was a Hugo nominee in 1961. He followed it with four more, of which the best known is* Simulacron Three *(1964), filmed as a German television series in 1973 and again as the movie* The Thirteenth Floor *in 1999.*

"Hostile Life-Form," published in the June, 1958 issue of Super-Science Fiction, *was one of three short stories by Galouye in that magazine. Problems connected to his wartime injuries caused his health to weaken in later years, forcing his retirement from his newspaper work, and he was just 56 when he died.*

CAPTAIN PARKER, chief of the trouble-shooting detail, stepped out of the shuttle boat, flipped his cap up off his forehead and soberly surveyed the settlement site.

It was much worse than it had appeared through the magni-scopes on the big ship, now unmanned and orbiting two thousand miles out.

Tatters of clothing, horribly stained, were strewn about. Pitifully inadequate sidearms lay here and there, mute evidence of their own uselessness. The colonists' huts were mercilessly battered—doors crashed in; windows shattered; gaping, splintered holes in the walls.

Parker shook his head disconsolately. This was all that was left of a hundred colonists and their effects.

Lieutenant Simpson, second in command, came over and offered a limp salute. "That about does it." He gestured toward the crew shoveling the last few spadefuls of dirt on a broad, low mound.

"Communal burial?" Parker asked.

"What else? The things that hit them didn't leave much."

"Any idea what they were?"

Simpson, a stocky redhead with stout, freckled forearms, nodded bruskly. "Otterillas. That's what we call them."

"What?" Parker asked densely.

"Those devils over there. We just knocked off a couple. They're vicious."

He indicated a hill half a mile away and handed over his binoculars.

Parker focused the lenses. The animals—all four—were

indisputably as vicious as Simpson's muffled oath had implied. The captain studied one.

It was long—five feet, at least—and otterlike in general form. But there were a half-dozen legs on each side of the brown, furry body and the face vaguely resembled a gorilla's, differing only in the inordinate length of its fangs. The two forward limbs, held poised, were equipped with huge, formidable pincers.

Parker swore, returning the binoculars. "The original survey report didn't mention anything like *that.*"

"No, it didn't." Simpson laughed dryly. "The two we bagged weighed in at over a hundred pounds apiece. Must have migrated from another area."

"But the whole planet was supposed to have been checked out."

"Somebody slipped up." The lieutenant spat sardonically. "It was one hell of a massacre."

THE taxiing jets of the shuttle craft worked with a muffled, erratic roar and Parker watched the pilot park it across the field and hurry back to join the work detail.

The captain was a tall, bony man whose relaxed stance and blunt, angular face suggested indifference and awkwardness. Only intense concern and resolution, however, were evident in his earnest stare.

Simpson started over toward a colonist's hut that had obviously been patched up to serve as a headquarters building. "Damned if we couldn't use a few zip-guns and a couple of drum-casters this time out," he observed wistfully.

Parker stared askance at the lieutenant as the latter held

the door open for him. "You make it sound downright grim."

"Don't sell the situation short, Skipper. We knocked down two otterillas, all right. But it took over three hundred rounds from nineteen guns to do it. I'm convinced they can sense the approach of a Wattley-charge and get out of the way."

Captain Parker whistled a sober exclamation of surprise and went on into the hut.

"There aren't too many of those damned things in the area," Simpson revealed, "but they're drifting in steadily. I hope we can get out of here fast."

Parker dropped into a chair and raked his cap back until its visor crowned a tuft of graying hair. "But we can't. The Old Man wants this place cleaned up and resettled. He's already got another boatload of suckers on the way over."

"Wonderful!" the lieutenant exuberated sarcastically. "I hope we're still here to welcome them."

"Think a stockade would help?"

"Possibly. But I'd suggest using damned big posts."

Parker laughed encouragingly. "It can't be that bad."

A coarse scream sounded outside and then the air suddenly popped and crackled with the blast of Wattley-gun charges.

Parker hurled the door open and lunged out, his weapon expectantly exploring the air ahead of him. In another second he found his target.

Separated from the burial detail, an ashen-faced youth stumbled back across the field. He desperately swung his shovel, trying to fend off a vicious assault by one of the otterillas.

The speed and ferocity of the thing's attack presented an indistinct blur as it darted forward, pincers snapping, then backed off and wheeled about, only to push in relentlessly from another direction.

Parker cut loose with his Wattley-gun. The pellets of static charge that belched intermittently from its muzzle converged with streams of death issuing forth from a score of other weapons.

Undismayed though, the otterilla pressed its attack, pausing fleetingly to dodge volleys of Wattley-charges and maneuver its prey between itself and its attackers.

"Give us shooting room, Johnson!" Parker shouted at the youth.

"Hit the ground!" Simpson urged desperately.

But a snip of the powerful pincers wrenched the shovel from Johnson's grasp and splintered the handle. Desperately, he whirled and streaked into one of the huts, slamming the door. The animal charged the wall and hit the stout boards with thunderous impact. It crashed through.

Johnson barged out of the hut and the otterilla tore through another wall in pursuit.

The captain emptied his gun at the thing without scoring a hit.

Then there was a streak of motion past his legs and a small, darting form, moving so swiftly as to be almost indiscernible, hurled itself at the otterilla.

Johnson stumbled and fell, folding his arms protectively over his head as the two animals closed in combat. Rolling over and over, they concealed themselves in a cloud of dust.

But the fight lasted only a moment. And, unbelieving, Parker watched the smaller creature rise and back off from the still form of the otterilla.

The victorious animal was about half the size of the other. It had a small, scaly face and a dense, humped back. It was covered with armorlike hide and resembled nothing as much as it did an armadillo.

But the tail was something else. Formed of the same chitinous substance as the hide, it flashed sharp and steel-like as it slipped back into a concealed sheath under its body.

The thing went over to Johnson. Yelping reassuringly, it began licking the youth's face. Dazed, Johnson sat up and stroked its back. It whined even more pleasurably, then turned to the vanquished otterilla and began feeding.

WORK on the stockade progressed at a less than satisfying tempo. Two days after his arrival, the captain, pacing restlessly under the canopy in front of headquarters hut, expressed his disappointment.

Simpson spread his hands deferentially. "Without any heavy equipment it's the best we can do."

"Not good enough. It's taken two days to erect a hundred feet of spiked fence. Four acres have to be enclosed. That leaves us with approximately thirty days of stockading."

Parker pointed toward the hill in the distance. "Yesterday," he continued, "we had six of those devils out there.

Today I counted nine. I don't like it. I want more protection—and faster than we're getting it."

"What do you suggest?" Simpson asked coldly.

"You've got ten men on reconstruction. Add them to the fencing detail and we'll get the job done in fifteen days. Repairing the huts can wait."

The lieutenant strode off. Parker pulled his chair up to the table and began filling out his initial report. Minutes later he started, though, at a gentle tugging on his boot.

Glancing beneath the table, he looked down into the sheepishly fetching eyes of the armadillolike creature that had presumptively adopted the trouble-shooting detail as its undisputed own ever since it had rescued Johnson.

"Affectionate little thing, isn't it?"

Parker looked up to see Janvier, the zoologist, standing there with a book spread open across his forearm. He was a small, lean man with an eternal, well-intentioned smile.

"One would think," the zoologist offered, "that nature on this world created the likes of our little friend here to apologize for having spawned the otterilla."

The captain stared at the open volume. "Find out anything about these life forms yet?"

Janvier nodded. "Like you said, the dope sheet makes no mention of the otterillas. But there's an entry for our benefactor. The survey index of fauna indigenous to Vitar-IV lists him as a *dasypus pseudarmadil.*"

Parker ran a hand over the creature's rock-hard back. "We'll call you Daisy for short. That all right, fellow?" Then, to Janvier, "What else does it say about them?"

" 'Not further investigated due to standard quarantine of questionable animals pending authorized study'."

"Too bad. If the colonists had known what it could do to an otterilla, they might have escaped a massacre."

Daisy, playfully nibbling at Parker's heel, turned suddenly and leaped into his lap. The captain grunted under the impact and nudged the thing off.

"Heavier than it looks, huh?" the zoologist asked.

"Too heavy to be a lap pet, at any rate."

Parker experimentally nudged the thing's rear end with his foot. Frolicsomely, it turned and gnawed on the sole of his boot. More forcefully, he prodded the posterior plate of its armor. Then, still unsatisfied, he gave it a decided kick.

"I tried that too," Janvier disclosed. "But even by booting hell out of it I couldn't get the thing to unsheath its weapon. Apparently, nature intended it for use only against otterillas."

Simpson returned scowling from the stockade detail. "I wouldn't be too sure of that," he said, cutting in on the conversation. "If it can polish off an otterilla, I wouldn't trust it half the distance of its tail."

The pseudarmadil tensed, perked its ears and cocked its head in the direction of a bush fifty feet away. Parker and Simpson drew their Wattley-guns. Janvier backed off apprehensively.

The animal streaked for the bush and disappeared into its foliage. Parker turned to shout a warning to the fencing detail. But Daisy scurried back into sight, followed by four other pseudarmadils.

Parker beamed enthusiastically. "More protection."

THE otterillas attacked two days later, with only slightly more than one-eighth of the stockade completed.

They charged the camp in an incredible burst of speed. They came early in the morning, striking terror and confusion and routing the men with the fury of their guttural roars.

They overran the guard, a two-striper from the Vegan System, who stuck valiantly at his post firing ineffectually. A boiling, slithering mass of brown fur and snapping pincers, the dozen or so otterillas paused briefly, churning over the spot where the youth had fallen.

The delay, though, gave the five pseudarmadils time to rally, form a crescent-shaped line of attack and hurl themselves on the murderous horde.

But even then two otterillas broke through and charged the center of the camp where Parker and his troubleshooting detail had hurriedly gathered,

Concentrated and sustained firepower from every Wattley-gun brought down the foremost otterilla. The second was in midleap, aiming itself at the group of men, when it was overtaken by Daisy in a lightning-swift sortie from the main battle.

When the attackers retreated they left four dead at the camp site. Parker turned all guns over to one of the men for recharging and assigned two workers to a burial detail for the casualty.

Over coffee in headquarters hut, the captain paused soberly and stared at Simpson. "This convinces me we've got to get more pseudarmadils in camp."

"How?" the lieutenant asked somewhat skeptically.

"Go out and find them. Lure them back."

"With those otterillas congregating out there?"

Janvier let his cup drop noisily into the saucer, his usual

grin gone. "The only place I've seen otterillas is west of here, on that hill. I imagine if we struck out to the east we shouldn't run into too many."

Simpson grunted disparagingly. "You won't get any volunteers to go hunt for pseuds—not after what just happened."

Parker tensed. "I'm not asking for any. I'm going myself."

The lieutenant flashed clenched teeth through a sarcastic grin. "We'll remember you a long, long time, Skipper."

"I'm taking Daisy and one of her friends. That'll leave three pseudarmadils in camp. I don't think the otterillas will attack again before we get back."

Janvier rose. "I'd like to go along."

"Why?" Parker stared obliquely at the little man, surprised over the unexpected display of courage.

"I may learn something about the natural environment of *dasypus pseudarmadil* that would help."

Simpson laughed tensely. "You may learn," he said sarcastically, "that we shouldn't be feeding the damned things and keeping them in camp."

"Why not?" Parker demanded. "We've enough provisions left by the colonists to feed an army of them."

"That's not quite what I mean. Maybe by satisfying their appetites we're keeping them from going out and killing otterillas. We could be upsetting the ecology and encouraging an accumulation of those devils."

Parker dismissed the criticism with a laugh. "I'd rather feed them enough to make sure they stay than to see them wander off."

The lieutenant hunched determinedly over the table.

"I say let's get out of here. We're just inviting another massacre."

The captain folded his hands soberly before him. "It takes three hours to ferry two men back to the ship. A withdrawal operation would take over a day and a half. Now, Lieutenant, if you'd agree to be among the last two to be picked up, I'll okay a retreat to orbit."

Simpson said nothing.

Parker rose. "Then we'll try to get along with our mission as directed and Janvier and I will plan a pseudarmadil hunt for tomorrow morning. In the meantime, you try to get the lead out on that stockading project."

Simpson hunched his shoulders futilely. "We've covered a little over two hundred and fifty feet. We still have some thirteen hundred to go. And you can't get top efficiency out of a bunch of scared workers."

One of the men entered the hut excitedly. "You know what the latest count is on those otterillas, Skipper?"

Parker shifted uneasily. "There were twelve in that attack. We got four—we and the pseuds. That should leave eight."

"Right," the man clipped. "But seven more just moved in."

PARKER pushed cautiously into the forest, moving through shafts of sunlight that slanted down from rifts in the dense foliage. Tensely aware of the inadequacy of his weapon, he was only indifferently conscious of the rhythmic slapping of the Wattley-gun holster against his thigh.

Janvier followed closely, leading Daisy and the other pseudarmadil on leashes.

A mile from camp an obscure form whimpered in a thicket and the zoologist hurriedly freed Daisy. There was no hostility in the animal's actions, though, as it sauntered over to the underbrush and stood yelping softly at the rustling leaves.

Finally two pseudarmadils emerged, excitedly answering Daisy's squeaky tones. The pet returned and drew up heeling behind Parker. Its newfound friends filed along.

A thousand feet farther another armor-plated creature joined the procession; a mile away, two more. Parker, flushed with the success of the roundup, turned off on a new course and headed back in the general direction of the settlement site.

Over a slight rise and down in a ravine they found a sixth pseudarmadil devouring a freshly killed otterilla. The others joined in the feast.

Some time later Parker led the eight animals out into a clearing and pulled up beside what was obviously the fragmented remains of an eggshell. Yellowish-ivory, the pieces were coarse in texture and mottled with regularly spaced red splotches. The effect was almost a polka-dot pattern.

"What do you make of it, Janvier?" he asked.

"It must have been quite an egg, judging from the curvature of the pieces."

Parker examined a particularly large fragment. Mentally reconstructing the whole object, he conceded that the egg had been rather impressive in size.

The zoologist pointed at another spot, and another, and another. All featured concentrations of eggshell fragments. "Spawning place for something or other," he observed.

But the captain, intent on something up ahead, strode

forward and drew up beside a mottled ovoid twice the size of a spaceman's helmet. "Here's one that hasn't hatched out yet."

The zoologist knelt beside it and ran his fingers over the hard surface. He bent his ear to the egg, then tapped it lightly.

He looked up. "I'd venture the opinion that it never will. Observe how the red splotches are faded. Probably been sitting here quite a while."

Janvier stood up and brought his heel down on the ovoid. Then he wedged his fingers into the crack and pried the two halves apart.

Before the stench sent them reeling away they had a chance to see the putrefying embryo within. It was quite unmistakably a *dasypus pseudarmadil.*

"So," said Janvier, holding a handkerchief to his nose, "that's where our little friends come from. I never would have figured Daisy to be oviparous."

By the time they reached camp, four more of the fawning creatures had joined the retinue, playfully scurrying between Parker's and Janvier's legs and nipping friskfully at their heels.

Simpson, supervising the stockading project, only glanced unimpressed at the collection of pseudarmadils and turned his attention back to the less than four hundred feet of fencing that had been constructed thus far.

Parker disregarded the other's indifference. "At least," he offered, "we ought to be over the bump on the matter of safety. We've got fifteen pseuds in our arsenal now."

But the lieutenant sneeringly jerked a thumb toward the otterillas on the hill. "Yeah? Well that family reunion out there drew in more relatives, too, while you were gone. Count 'em. There're thirty now."

DURING the next week eight more pseudarmadils wandered into camp and became fast pets.

Seven hundred additional feet were built on the stockade, enclosing more than half of the camp area and blocking off view of the shuttle craft and part of the forest.

The otterillas launched two more attacks, killing one man in the first and two in the second. That reduced the camp personnel to seventeen.

Daisy and her armored cohorts, however, took a toll of nineteen otterillas during the two assaults. But, with the continued arrival of the huge beasts, their number had grown to more than fifty.

Simpson was even more imperious over the situation— almost to the point of being outright insubordinate. Disregarding Parker's rank, he pressed his point at mess one sultry evening when all the men were exhausted from a fourteen-hour fence building stint.

The lieutenant abruptly tossed his empty mess kit on the table. "I say let's get off the defensive and break up that otterilla soiree. Let's put these pseuds on a diet, then send them out to scatter those things!"

Parker looked up wearily over a piece of synthoprotein balanced on his fork. "We'll stick to our original plan," he said simply, "and keep the pseuds as our first line of defense."

"But it's no good!" Simpson reared up and drove his fist into his palm. "We got predators that can take care of those otterillas. But what do we do? We keep them in camp—fed and happy!"

The captain glanced up patiently. "As long as the otterillas are in the majority, we can't risk an encounter. It might mean more casualties."

"I rather agree," Janvier said absently, stroking one of the pseudarmadils that lay contently beside him. "If we turned them loose on the otterillas our little friends might let us down in an orgy of feasting when we need them most."

Simpson bristled. "But if we don't turn them loose, that otterilla horde will keep on growing!"

"Simply a matter of timing." Parker shrugged. "As soon as we finish the stockade, then we can let our pseuds take care of the otterillas. But not before."

The captain brushed back a shock of hair that appeared even more gray in the thin back-glow from the camp's spotlight. "But before we think of exterminating the otterillas, there's something else we have to consider—something we should have done a week ago."

All eyes turned inquiringly on the Skipper.

"Beside reconditioning the settlement area," he continued, "we've got to determine precisely why the colonists were taken off guard. To do that we must know a good deal more about the otterillas than we do now."

Simpson gestured impatiently. "Quit pussyfooting around the point. What are you trying to say?"

"Janvier's got to have a specimen to study—alive."

The lieutenant choked over a protest couched in invective.

The zoologist nodded affirmatively. "That's right!"

"And who's going to take the tiger by the tail? And how?" Simpson thrust his fists on his hips.

Janvier indicated an unopened crate. "I've been giving it some thought. We've got two portable cages strong enough to hold those beasts. I propose building a trap and setting it up outside camp."

"Traps need bait," Simpson interrupted with feigned indulgence.

"I'm aware of that, Lieutenant. I'll be in one of the cages with a trip release to spring the door of the other one shut."

Parker shook his head. "I'm overruling the plan as far as the bait is concerned. We've got only one zoologist and no chance of getting a replacement. So I'm asking for a volunteer."

Johnson stepped forward. "I'll do it. Seems reasonably safe."

They prepared the cages the next day, Janvier himself wielding the torch to spot-weld their rear bars together.

Then the entire camp complement, accompanied by the fifteen pseudarmadils, bore the double cage halfway to the otterilla concentration. Johnson was secured in the rear compartment and the trap was set.

Back in camp Parker watched through binoculars as the otterilla horde advanced, cautiously at first, then in a burst of speed to swarm over the trap. At one point in the confusion he saw the door fall shut.

Hours passed before the animals were finally convinced they could not break through the bars. But even then four persistent beasts continued pacing around the cage after the others had withdrawn. Impatiently, Captain Parker ordered a concerted Wattley-gun and pseudarmadil attack on the diehards.

When they retrieved the cage Johnson was dead. Apparently he had been confused and frightened on finding himself surrounded by the vicious beasts and had stumbled back into the range of the trapped animal's pincers.

But the captured otterilla was a fine specimen, both Janvier and Parker agreed.

WITHIN the next four days all but the final thirty feet of the stockade had been completed. Its effectiveness was proved in two determined attacks launched against the stout logs by the enraged beasts. Futilely, the otterillas hurled themselves against the spiked fence again and again.

In the second attack, though, they circled the enclosed area until they found the still unfenced stretch and poured through. But the pseudarmadils put up a brief, deadly defense and repulsed the onslaught, killing five of the big animals.

The camp counted two men dead—victims of beasts which had breached the protective line of the pseudarmadils during the furious action. And, exasperated, Parker ordered no mess and no rest periods until the final thirty feet of the stockade had been completed.

With the men working feverishly, the captain climbed to the lookout tower and focused his binoculars on the otterilla congestion. He estimated their number; tensed, and tried another rough calculation.

For verification he tried counting the milling beasts several times. No two counts came out the same. But he was at least able to gain a rough average which he considered reasonably correct. There were apparently sixty-four otterillas on the hill.

He lowered the binoculars slowly, convinced now that there was reason for hope. Yesterday he had estimated eighty-two otterillas; the day before, ninety-seven. Their number was decreasing for the first time. Parker wondered why. Then, suddenly, he thought he had the answer.

Pseudarmadils had continued to straggle into the camp, until now there was a total of twenty-nine. But those coming in had tarried outside long enough to kill off one or two of the otterillas.

Simpson had probably been right in his surmisal that by domesticating the smaller creatures the camp had upset the ecological balance of the immediate area. But nature was, after all, bringing things into equilibrium again, even despite the meddling influence of the humans.

He smiled hopefully. By tomorrow the number of otterillas should be down in the fifties, or perhaps even in the forties. And the stockade would be finished. The latter development alone would ensure the safety of the camp.

But he wouldn't let it rest at that, he decided resolutely. He would evict Daisy and the other pseudarmadils and let them take the fight of extermination to the enemy.

Descending the ladder from the tower, he watched Janvier and the imprisoned specimen. The zoologist had succeeded in anesthetizing the otterilla and was now in the cage with it. Parker went over and circled the steel cell, scattering the dozen or so pseudarmadils that had congregated there in hope of finding a way to get at the larger animal.

Janvier looked up. "We'll have plenty to put in the survey index on otterillas."

"You're getting it all doped out?"

The zoologist nodded. "For one thing it's not mammalian, despite the fact that it would seem to fall in that category. Notice—no mammilary glands."

Parker scratched his head dubiously. "What about that thing on Bellam-II? It didn't have mammilary glands either—until the final stage of pregnancy."

The zoologist laughed. "This thing *is* in the final stage of pregnancy. If the indications are correct, we should have a baby otterilla running around this cage within the next forty-eight hours."

THE stockade, gate and all, was finished late that night.

Parker mustered the thirteen men, surveyed them solicitously and proclaimed a two-day rest period before resuming repairs on the huts.

Even Simpson was subdued by fatigue as he accompanied the captain back toward their individual quarters.

The lieutenant smiled conciliatively. "Looks like you picked the right course, Skipper. I'm sorry if I confused things by being stubborn."

Parker grasped his shoulder. "I like a man with convictions—even if they're wrong ones. Conviction is the essence of leadership."

Simpson paused in front of his hut and stared wearily at the moon dropping low in the west. "Are we going to make our schedule?"

"I think so."

"Even with this two-day layoff?"

Parker nodded. "The new colonists aren't due in for another week. We'll have things ready for them."

Simpson turned to enter his quarters. But the captain called out after him, "Send out your two pseuds. I'm rounding up all of them."

The lieutenant stared askance at him.

"I'm following your suggestion," Parker explained, "and booting them all out so they can mop up on those otterillas. They haven't had anything to eat all day. They ought to do a real good job."

"I'd like to stay up and watch the fireworks." Simpson grinned. "But I'm beat."

The captain was exhausted too. But, after he had turned Daisy and the other pseudarmadils out and closed the gate behind them, he stayed awake long enough to hear the faint, dire sounds of carnage drifting with muffled stridency through the still night air.

HE watched the final thrashing of the slaughter the next morning from the observation tower while, stretching all around the camp, the spiked posts of the stockade stood like indomitable sentries, strong and reassuring.

Carcasses of otterillas dotted the hillside. Here and there a swirling cloud of dust marked a desperate mortal battle. Occasionally a huge, scurrying form darted from a bush, only to be overtaken and set upon by four or five fleeting pseudarmadils. The shrieks of death issuing from the gorillalike faces lay heavy and shrill on the calm morning air.

One by one, the rest of the camp's personnel climbed the tower to watch—silently at first, then lustily cheering the pseudarmadils in skirmishes that continued to break out all over the hillside and on the fringe of the forest.

Finally the last duel had been fought and the armor-plated creatures settled down to feasting, an unnatural silence falling over the field of battle.

Somehow Parker sensed that a delicate balance had been restored in the course of the slaughter he had just witnessed. It was as though the otterillas, which should have fallen before the slashing tails of the smaller creatures weeks ago, had in their belated deaths finally satisfied the ecological requirements of this coarse, raw world.

He broke out the liquor stores left by the colonists and passed generous rations out among the thirteen men. The celebration was unrestrained. It carried vigorously through the morning and well into the afternoon.

Parker joined the general revelry for a while, but recognized a potentially serious situation when several of the men began throwing occasional Wattley-charges at the caged otterilla.

He confiscated all guns, locked them in the cabinet in his hut and spent the next ten minutes reassuring Janvier that nothing would happen to his specimen.

"It would be unfortunate if it did," the other returned stiffly. "It's already gone into labor and will give birth in the next few hours. I'd like to turn the parent and offspring over to the colonial zoologist in good condition for further study."

He turned back to stare interestedly through the bars.

"You suppose it would be disturbed if I let the pseudarmadils back into the stockade?" Parker asked.

Janvier glanced up dubiously. "Is it necessary?"

"They've all come back from the kill and they're milling around outside the gate. I wouldn't want them to feel wholly unwanted. They might go away for good."

"Let them. They've served their purpose."

"No." Parker shook his head. "I've decided that any scheme of colonization for this world will have to include domesticated pseudarmadils. That will prevent future congestions of otterillas."

KEEPING the armored creatures away from the cage was even less of a problem than Parker had imagined. The pseudarmadils moved listlessly in through the gate, their heads drooping sluggishly and their eyes half closed.

At first the captain feared the entire horde had been stricken with some illness. But then he smiled understandingly as he realized they simply must have stuffed themselves to a ridiculous degree on the flesh of their otterilla victims.

Sympathetic but still amused, he watched them wander off into the various huts or drop lethargically in the shade of the buildings to fall into a sated slumber.

Late that afternoon, after the men had surrendered to the drowziness of near inebriation and retired to their huts to sleep it off, Parker withdrew to his quarters too, leaving Janvier to maintain his lonely vigil over the laboring otterilla.

It was night when the captain awoke and there was a stifling heaviness on his chest. He brought his hand up to push off whatever it was that lay there and his fingers contacted the dense hide of one of the pseudarmadils.

He reached over, turned on the light, then struggled

to dislodge the suddenly ponderous weight that was the sleeping Daisy. Gorged as it was, it felt as though it weighed a ton.

Unaroused by his prodding, Daisy crashed to the floor and rolled over without stirring. Evidently it was still in its glutted stupor.

But there was something else, he saw as he looked more closely. The creature had turned a delicate shade of green, suggestive of the complexion of a child suffering from overindulgence in unripe apples.

Concerned, he studied the two pseudarmadils in the hut. They were exhibiting the same symptoms as Daisy.

In Simpson's quarters, he knelt tensely beside the two more armor-plated animals with sickly green complexions while the lieutenant snored unconcernedly. One of the pets, however, seemed to be sicker than the others. It had lost several scales from its chitinous plating and the missing spaces were like little squares of brown surrounded by the verdant sea that was the rest of its body.

All the pseudarmadils in the other huts where the men slept were similarly affected. The stupor from having stuffed themselves Parker could readily understand. But the shedding of scales was something else . . . unless such an effect was the result of battling the otterillas. At any rate, he decided, he'd better call the zoologist in on the matter.

THE captain stepped out of his hut into the still, early evening. A dense quietness lay over the nocturnal scene. On the left, a lactescent moon swam through wisps of tenuous clouds. The almost foreboding hush that gripped the camp was like a frozen bit of eternity.

He strode misgivingly down the main street and was intensely relieved to find some other evidence of life as he turned the corner and headed toward the spot-lighted area of the caged otterilla.

Janvier was there—dedicated, loyal, staunchly maintaining his watch over the cell and the thing that lay motionless in the shadows.

But the birth was over! Parker could tell that much from the expression on the zoologist's face as Janvier backed apprehensively away from the cage, his eyes wide with alarm and his lips trembling on unuttered words.

"Janvier! What is it? What's wrong?"

The zoologist turned and stared numbly at Parker without seeing him. "We should have known!" he mumbled. "God, we should have guessed when we found the pseudarmadil hatching place. That egg we broke open—it was as big as the pseuds themselves! How could one of *them* have laid it?"

Confounded, Parker brushed past the man and strode toward the cage, trying to pierce the darkness to see what was inside.

But Simpson's voice roared from the direction of his quarters. "Parker! Look at this! Good God—Parker!"

The lieutenant staggered forward into the spot-lighted area, holding out the empty armor-plated hide of a pseudarmadil.

"It came out!" he babbled.

"Those things—they aren't sick! They're shedding— *changing!*"

Numbly, Parker turned back to the cage, his eyes now accustomed to the dim light. The female otterilla had withdrawn to a corner and was cringing, as though afraid of the thing to which it had given birth.

In the center of the cell lay a huge egg, twice the size of a spaceman's helmet and mottled with bright red splotches.

Simpson screamed and Parker whirled around to see a half-grown otterilla, its damp fur shining under a coating of serous slime, advancing on the lieutenant from the direction of the huts. He dropped the pseudarmadil husk and backed away, terrified.

"That thing came out of this pseud armor!" he shouted, pointing alternately at the stalking animal and the discarded hide.

"Good God!" Janvier stammered. "It—it metamorphosed! A two-stage life cycle! Pseudarmadil and otterilla!"

The beast lunged forward, seized the armor it had shed only minutes earlier and crumbled it between its pincers. It stuffed the pieces into the gorilla face where hideous fangs completed the job of mastication.

And suddenly the pall of stillness that had hung over the camp was lifting. There was a stirring here, an ominous scurrying there, the harsh, explosive sound of splintering boards, an occasional scream.

Parker, Simpson and the zoologist turned and raced for the stockade gate.

But they never made it.

THE END

Strange things can happen when there is a switch of talents from one personality to another. Nobody can really understand such matters. But they do happen!

Artwork by Paul Orban

THE GIFT OF NUMBERS
Alan E. Nourse

Alan E. Nourse was a popular and productive science fiction writer whose career ran from 1951 (a short story called "High Threshold" in Astounding Science Fiction) *to his death at the age of 63 in 1992. His bibliography includes such novels as* Trouble on Titan *(1954),* Rocket to Limbo *(1957), and* Raiders from the Rings *(1962).*

But the Iowa-born Nourse's primary profession was medicine. After serving in the Navy after World War II and attending Rutgers Univeristy, he took his medical degree in 1955, paying for his studies by writing for the science-fiction magazines, and worked as a physician in North Bend, Washington, until 1963. Then he chose to take the plunge into full-time writing with a searing non-fiction account of his time in medical school, published in 1965 as Intern *under the pseudonym of "Dr. X," which became a best-seller. He followed it with a history of physics (*Universe, Earth, and Atom, *1969) and a number of books on astronomical and medical subjects.*

"The Gift of Numbers," first published in the August, 1958 Super-Science, *was the first of two Nourse stories in that magazine.*

"MR. AVERY MEARNS,"** the nurse-receptionist told the doctor, pointing her thumb daintily toward the floor. When the patient walked in the doctor saw why. Everything about the man screamed of meek, reproachful resignation. His skinny neck extruded with apologetic bobs of his adam's apple from a prim white collar. His fingers twitched occasionally. He sat on the edge of the chair, one hundred and forty pounds of quivering indecision.

A bookkeeper, the doctor thought, steeling himself. "You say you're having some stomach trouble, Mr. Mearns?"

"Oh, it's frightful." Avery Mearns was pathetically eager. "An ulcer, you know. May be ready to perforate any minute."

"Mm! And how long have you had your ulcer?"

"Well, I can't be exactly sure, you understand—"

"Of course, of course. But roughly?"

"Thirty-eight hours and seventeen minutes," said Avery Mearns, sneaking a look at his wrist watch. "Give or take five minutes, I'd say."

The doctor blinked. "You're talking about your ulcer now?"

"That's right. It isn't strictly my ulcer, though. Belongs to an acquaintance of mine, you might say."

"I might!" The doctor gripped his chair arms tightly and peered across the desk at the quivering little man. "I think I missed the first act here. Let's try again. What was your line of work?"

"Bookkeeper. Bundy, Burbage and Brubecker. Twenty years with them—so far."

"And you're having pain?"

"Oh, it's terrible. It wakes me up at four in the morning, and gnaws at me all day. I haven't been able to eat anything but cream soup and crackers ever since I got it. It's really unbearable."

"I see," said the doctor. "Your friend's ulcer."

"That's right."

"Indeed. Well, we'll just take a look." One thing about that doctor, he could go along with a gag.

Between the doctor and the lab nurse and the X-ray man they took a look that would last Avery Mearns ten years. They listened to his heart and thumped his chest. They gave him chalk to drink, and squeezed him like a toothpaste tube beneath the dispassionate eye of the fluoroscope. They rushed blood samples upstairs and other samples downstairs. When they got through, they had learned that Avery Mearns had flat feet, a serious enlargement of the heart, congestion of the lungs, turgid kidneys, a sluggish liver, tired blood, polyps in his colon, and a mildly-advanced case of weavers' bottom.

But he didn't have any ulcer.

The doctor was apologetic but firm. Avery Mearns walked back down to the street the picture of dejection. He didn't find the doctor's gold watch and the nurse's sorority pin in his pocket until he got home that night.

But after a lunch of cream soup and crackers, the ulcer quit hurting. For a while, at least.

IT was the numbers that had started it all, the night the switch had taken place.

If it hadn't been for the numbers, the Colonel wouldn't

have been broke, and the switch wouldn't have happened, and Avery Mearns would still have been an ineffectual little bookkeeper instead of the most dangerous guy in seven countries, even if he didn't know it.

The Colonel had a way with numbers like no other guy around. It was sort of an inward and spiritual grace with him, which was pretty lucky because the Colonel didn't have any other inward and spiritual graces to speak of. He could pick a number and make it break out and sing MOTHER MACHREE spinning on its tail and strumming a ten string banjo. Nobody knew how he did it. If the Colonel himself knew, he wasn't telling anybody. He had a steady string of greenbacks hurrying into his pocket, and that was all he worried about.

The fact that he was almost always broke wasn't the fault of the numbers. The Colonel was just a little extravagant, was all.

"One would think," he was saying to George the bartender that night, "that you would be eager to advance me a small sum to enter a gentlemanly wager on the fight tonight. Five dollars would hardly strain your exchequer. And it isn't that I'm on the breadline, you know. It's just that my assets are temporarily frozen."

"Sure, sure," said George. "Like my right arm. Can't quite reach the cash register." He glanced up at the preliminary bout on the TV and a look of great craftiness stole across his face. "What numbers would you want to bet, by the way?"

"My dear fellow!" said the Colonel, nursing his glass of milk. "Would you have me betray a sacred trust? In the vernacular of the street, would you ask me to welch on the Almighty?" He brushed a fleck of dust from his London-tailored suit and smoothed his mustache gently. It was a pretty extravagant-looking suit, just like the fancy words he used and the fancy car he drove. "Anyway, I haven't any numbers for the fight, yet. The moment of divine inspiration has not come. Creativity must be sparked, you know."

"Yeah," said George.

"And there's no spark quite like the clink of coin." The Colonel's eyes rested thoughtfully on the meek little man drinking beer down the bar. "Like that gentleman, for instance. No doubt of the fierce flame that lingers there, eh? That look of transport, of communion with rapture—"

Avery Mearns blinked doubtfully. "Me?"

"My dear fellow, outward appearances deceive," said the Colonel, moving, down a stool or two. "In you I can sense the artist in agonies of creation, drinking the dew of heaven before dashing forth to translate ecstasy for the masses. Don't tell me, now—a writer? Artist? Musician?"

"Bookkeeper," said Avery apologetically.

"Ah," said the Colonel, seeking inspiration in his milk glass. "But a troubled bookkeeper, none the less." He shot a furtive glance at the TV screen as the second prelim began.

"I'll never finish in time, is all," mourned Avery. "I've got tax statements due, and inventories to audit, and payrolls to check, and a seven-day deadline I'll never make. They'll fire me next, and then what am I going to do?"

"Let me buy you a beer," said the Colonel. "Somewhere a solution lies within our grasp." A beer appeared for Avery and a milk for the Colonel. "Ulcer, you know. Nasty thing. Alcohol crucifies it. Hmmm, yes! As a custodian of accounts, you have the Gift of Numbers, no doubt."

"Well—I can add and subtract, if that's what you mean."

"Nothing so crass, my good man! With the Gift of Numbers the columns of figures should take care of themselves. Numbers have a powerful quality of cohesion, you know. No number is an independent member, but only a member in relation to its fellows—you follow?"

"Oh, yes," said Avery, taking a swallow of beer.

"So if you yourself can enter into the cohesion, the numbers become a part of you and you a part of them. They can't help but obey you."

"Sounds pretty nice," Avery admitted. "I guess I'll just have to go on adding."

"Nonsense," said the Colonel. "You have a column of numbers to balance—it's balanced!" He waved his hand airily. "An error to find on the page? A mere nothing—one look, and there it is!"

"Just like that?"

"Just like that."

Avery licked his lips. "With me, I've got to spend hours. And then I have more errors than I started out with."

"Obviously you're a man who *needs* the Gift. It's fortunate that it's transferrable," said the Colonel. "I say, bartender—one minute and twenty seconds of the fifth for this bout. Mark it now."

"How was that again?" said Avery.

"The fight. I just saw the outcome in a flash. One minute and—"

"No, I mean before that."

"Oh, transferrable? Oh, yes."

"You could transfer part of your gift to me?"

"Certainly. It isn't all one way, of course—you'd transfer some of your bookkeeping tendencies to me at the same time. It's a function of higher cerebral centers, you understand. Constant high-frequency synaptics from the transthalamus and the hippocampus, communicating with the frontal and parietal cortical layers. Very close contact must be made, of course—a form of supratentorial juxtaposition."

"Come again?" said the bartender, who was getting interested.

THE Colonel took out a slip of paper and wrote the words in large block letters:

SUPRATENTORIAL JUXTAPOSITION

Avery blinked at the words. "Of course," said the Colonel, "I couldn't consider anything permanent. The transfer is too deep-seated. Some authorities claim it's a basic subtotal somatic and psychomatic interexchange—"

"But for just a day or so!" Avery cried. "If I could make numbers behave like you say—"

The crowd was cheering and the announcer's voice broke through: "—by a knockout, in just one minute and twenty seconds of the fifth round—"

"You see," said the Colonel. Avery was nodding eagerly, throwing caution to the winds. "All I'd need would be twenty-four hours! Enough to clear up the year's accounts—why, I'd be ahead of deadline. They might even give me a raise. If you'd ever consider it, I mean—"

"Perhaps for a small consideration," said the Colonel. "Not for me, you understand! Merely to aid you in concentrating. Say twenty dollars, perhaps?"

Avery fumbled for his wallet while the bartender hid his mouth with his hand. "Will I feel anything?"

"Oh, no pain. A moment of exhaltation, perhaps. A strange prickling at the base of the spine. And of course you must concentrate with your whole mind."

He began writing the block letters again.

SUPRAJUXTA TENTORIAL POSITION

"No, no, that's not right," he muttered. Then:

SUPRAPOSITIONAL JUXTATENTORIUM

and:

JUXTATENTORTAL SUPRAPOSITION

"I can't seem to do it," the Colonel said.

"Try, try!" cried Avery. The Colonel's fingers flew as Avery watched wide-eyed:

"You're following?"

Avery nodded, his eyes growing a little glassy.

"But not quite yet, I can see—wait, wait—I have it!"

SUPRATENTORIAL JUXTAPOSITION

"That's it!" cried Avery. He felt a moment of exhaltation, a strange prickling at the base of his spine. "You've
done it, just like you said—"

The Colonel slipped the twenty into his pocket with a
solemn wink at the bartender. "See you at the fights," he
said, and was gone, leaving Avery, sans tie-clip, staring glas-
sily at the scrap of paper on the bar.

It wasn't until he shook his head groggily and took another swallow of beer that he felt the twinge in the pit of
his stomach—

THE change was little short of miraculous. Previously, an
unbalanced account book had produced a deep sense of
weariness and revulsion in Avery Mearns, blinking up at
him from his desk like some kind of alien intelligence—
defying him, as it were, to do anything about it.

But now all that was changed.

The columns balanced like magic.

The errors on the pages lit up like neon signs and
winked at him enticingly. Quite suddenly he found himself feeling a sense of warmth, of kinship, with those pretty
little numbers that tracked up and down the page. Almost
as though they were blood brothers, you might say.

But that wasn't all.

When he finished the tax returns and the inventories
and the payrolls and everything he was going strong, just
beginning to feel the bit in his mouth. The numbers beckoned to him, urging him on to greater things, even as his
stomach screamed for a vanilla milkshake. He dug in, his
fingers flying on the adding machine, immersing himself
deeper and deeper into the columns of numbers.

When he came up the first time, he had discovered a way to bring the figures from column A over into column B, and the figures in column B over into column A, and save Bundy, Burbage, and Brubecker $40,000 on their income tax. It was simply incredible that he had missed it all this time.

Cream soup and crackers for lunch.

When he came up the second time he had found a way to apply some inspired numerical foresight and save them $80,000 on their next years' income tax.

It was wonderful.

When he came up the third time, he had devised a method of relieving B, B, & B of $160,000 in small increments over a six month period, with B, B, & B none the wiser. He had also, in a moment of transport, sensed the exact combination to the office safe and the exact fence value of Miss Capaccio's pearl necklace.

He had gained a touch of larceny along with the Gift of Numbers and the ulcer, it seemed.

He fled from his desk in horror and went down to the bar. He tried a beer, but beer was poison. He had to settle for milk.

"Funny thing," George the bartender chuckled, "you drinking milk and the Colonel drinking beer. Almost a miracle, like, the way his ulcer left him all of a sudden."

"Oh, yes?"

"Couldn't figure it out. Said he even ate a steak and onions and nothing happened. Said he never felt better in his life."

"Well, I could figure it out for him. Where is he?"

"You thinking about that twenty, you might as well forget it, friend."

"No, not the money, the other thing. It's beginning to get out of hand."

"Sure, sure," said George. "I'll tell him. When I see him, that is. He was talking about getting a job as a bookkeeper somewhere, but I could tell he was just joking."

Avery went out and bought some bicarbonate of soda. As he reached for his change, he found the boss's cuff links in his pocket. He also found Miss Capaccio's garter.

That was when he really started worrying.

UNFORTUNATELY, the numbers and the ulcer and the pickpocketry were not all. The second evening Avery found himself in an all-night poker game. He was not there by choice. The compulsion to gamble was simply unbearable. He lost three weeks' pay in three and a half hours and they escorted him to the street by the seat of his pants.

Next day he bet on the horses, the football pool, the basketball pool, and a tall Nordic channel swimmer. But the basketball pool paid off on his football number, and his basketball number should have been riding on Hopeful Harry in the eighth at Belmont.

The worst of it was, he couldn't stop betting.

He arrived at work half an hour early, he was so eager to get back to his numbers again. He was like a bloodhound on the trail. He lost contact with all else, and the more he worked at the books, the more the numbers seemed to take control of themselves. It was high noon when he jerked awake again, with a dull aching pain in his middle. He decided to see a doctor without delay.

Of course, the doctor couldn't find the ulcer—and Avery couldn't find the Colonel. The Colonel, the bartender reported, had stopped in to say good-bye. Said he was feeling so good he thought he'd take a little jaunt to Florida. He'd heard they needed bookkeepers down there—

Bookkeepers with the Gift of Numbers, he'd said.

Avery was just leaving to hunt up another poker game when the cops pinched him. Bundy, Burbage and Brubecker had just discovered what a bookkeeper with the Gift of Numbers and a touch of larceny could do with a set of the company's books. It seemed they didn't like it so much.

THE police sergeant was very sympathetic.

"Sure, sure," he said. "I know how it is. It's just sort of a compulsion. You keep thinking how nice it would be until you can't help yourself any more, so then you go lift a couple hundred thousand. It happens all the time."

"But I didn't," Avery wailed. "It wasn't really me at all. That is, I didn't mean to. I wouldn't dream of such things under ordinary circumstances, except—"

"Sure, sure," said the sergeant. "Now just tell us how you planned to cart off the money."

"I didn't plan it. It was planning me. I switched with this man, just temporarily, in order to use his Gift of Numbers for a while, and now I've got his ulcer, and his gambling compulsions and everything."

"Mm," said the sergeant deftly retrieving his wallet as it slid into Avery's pocket. "Switched, you say."

"That's right. It's all a horrible mistake." Avery's fingers twitched spasmodically. "He said it was a higher cerebral

transfer. Just the position of the super-tent or something—
it's all hazy in my mind now, somehow. But now when I
work with numbers I just can't control myself—"

THE psychiatrist was very sympathetic.

"Been dropping money in poker games," the sergeant
told him, aside. "Horses, too. Affected his balance, you
might say."

The psychiatrist nodded gravely and smiled at his patient. "Now, Avery! Tell me about yourself, Avery," he said.

Avery told him about himself.

"Very interesting," the psychiatrist reported. "Over-
whelming guilt feelings. Pulsilating inferiority. It isn't that
he's got a complex—just naturally inferior. Fixations, too
. . . like this man he says he 'switched' with. 'The Colonel'."

"Oh, oh," said the sergeant.

He called in Avery. "This friend of yours called himself
'the Colonel'?"

"Why, yes. Very pleasant fellow—"

"Tall skinny chap with fancy British clothes on?"

Avery's eyes lit up. "You know him?"

"Twenty-three states and four territories know him.
Alias 'Numbers Gerrold,' alias 'Bet-a-Million Beckworth,'
alias 'The Orange Kid,' etc., etc., etc. This joker could con
an eighty year old grandmother out of her uppers. You've
been had, my friend."

"Not this time," said Avery. "It *happened* this time. Maybe he thought he was feeding me a line but if he did he
was wrong. Parts of it came across twisted up a little, but
it came across. And now I sit around waiting for his ulcer

to perforate while he robs the State of Florida blind and deaf."

The sergeant rubbed his chin, dubiously, and put out a ten-state alarm. "You might just be telling the truth," he conceded, "though I don't know how Bundy, Burbage and Brubecker are going to take it."

"Just find me the Colonel and let me switch back again," moaned Avery, "before I start picking my own pockets to keep in practice."

Bundy, Burbage and Brubecker generously declined to press charges. They had taken another look at those tax return figures and realized that they couldn't permit a little matter of attempted embezzlement to cloud their appreciation of a faithful, devoted employee like Avery Mearns.

Avery went back behind his desk—with an assistant, of course, to monitor his work and keep his fingers out of the till. Every morning he plunged into his books like a man obsessed, and every evening he unloaded the day's loot from his pockets before departing for home. In a few short days he had totally exhausted the numerical resources of Bundy, Burbage and Brubecker, only to find an eager list of appplicants waiting for his peculiar talents.

He was flown to Washington and confronted with a financial-economic snarl that had floored the most competent of giant computers; he waded through it like a knife through putty.

He was wined by General Motors and dined by U.S. Steel.

He received, through surrepticious channels, an offer to visit certain foreign capitals where the fact that capital was a naughty word didn't dampen the intensity of capitalistic endeavor. The Gift of Numbers, it seemed, was a pearl of great price—so great that accompanying irregularities could easily be overlooked—

Everyone was excited and happy about it except Avery Mearns. The more he immersed himself in numbers, the greater the compulsion to deeper immersion. As days passed it grew worse and worse: less and less of Avery emerged each evening and more and more of the Colonel.

"It's very simple," the psychiatrist soothed. "Merely a dominant personality overwhelming a recessive shadow." But it didn't make Avery feel any better, and it didn't cure the ulcer. His cheeks grew hollow and his eyes burned feverishly.

"You've got to find him," he pleaded with the sergeant. "I can't stand it much longer."

The sergeant was sympathetic but guarded. "Awfully hard to trace, you know. We'll call you the minute we find him."

But the call didn't come from the police. It came from George, the bartender.

"Better come down here quick," he said in a hoarse whisper. "The Colonel's back. He's gotta see you in a hurry, he says. A *real* hurry, he says. Urgent like."

"You mean he wants to change back?"

"Brother, you stated a truth. He even has the twenty bucks ready."

Avery didn't wait to break the connection. He was down the stairs in three graceful leaps. Even the ulcer cooperated. In a flash of horrible insight he had sensed the source of the urgency—

But he was too late.

The police sergeant met him at the door of the tavern, just as the two men carried out the long sheet-covered stretcher and popped it into the ambulance. The sergeant shook his head wonderingly. "Some guys got all the luck," he said. "You're too late, you lucky man. And here all the time the Colonel thought you were the sucker."

"But where are you taking him?" Avery wailed.

"Morgue," said the sergeant. "He just dropped dead this very minute. Of your coronary, that is."

THE END

FIRST MAN IN A SATELLITE
Charles W. Runyon

Charles Runyon grew up on a farm in Worth County, Mis-souri, which he called "the most insignificant county in a not-too-significant state." When he was sixteen he ran away from home to work on a ranch in West Texas, and in the years that followed he spent time in the army in Korea, Germany, and In-diana, studied journalism at Missouri University, and worked in industrial editing until abruptly deciding to become a full-time writer. "With a new baby and no income," he said, "I borrowed a lakeside cabin and sat down to write my first book. After sending it off to my agent, I took off for the West Indies, found an almost deserted island, and lay back to await the gentle shower of royal-ties. It didn't quite happen that way, but it was only a few months before the book sold to Ace; my reaction was to charter a yacht and take the wife and kid on a tour of the islands. I returned to New York suntanned but broke, still expecting the gilded life of a best-sellng writer."

The first sale that set Runyon on the path toward full-time writing was "First Man in a Satellite," which appeared in the December, 1958 issue of Super-Science Stories. *The American and Soviet space programs were still in their earliest stages, then—the first manned orbital flights would not take place until 1961—and so the Runyon story still belonged to the realm of*

An utter, utter loneliness, the like of which no man had ever felt before, an utter isolation from all of life, from all of Earth—this was his lot in space.

Artwork by Ed Emshwiller

science-fiction, an ingenious guess at how it would all take place but, as we would learn a few years later, only a very approximate anticipation of the square-jawed astronauts and clipped space jargon that the pioneering Mercury project would make famous.

Runyon went on to write sixteen more science-fiction stories, most of them published in Fantasy & Science Fiction, *in the next twenty years, and several novels, among them* Pigworld *(1971) and* I, Weapon *(1974). But he was best known for his strong, stark crime novels, which included such titles as* Color Him Dead, No Place to Hide, *and* Power Kill.

BREAKOFF.

The thought blended with his trailing scream, and Max jerked his eyes from the port. His breathing slowed as he stared at the curving metal walls of his capsule, eighteen inches away.

Breakoff. Jet jockeys had given the name to the tearing loneliness up where the blue sky edges into black. They knew how he felt, Max thought, like a man with measles knows how it feels to die.

"How long did it last?" he mused aloud. His voice was hoarse, but he was relieved to find the panic gone. He decided to risk looking out again.

Directly below, the fat globe was shading from dark to light. On his left, Kamchatka dangled from Siberia like a goat's udder, and the Aleutians groped across a metallic Pacific. Scattered clouds over the ocean reminded Max of soap scum in a dishpan.

He watched California bulge toward him, the central valley like a finger mark on a dusty shelf. Stateside again.

"Look, Marie, I'm flying!" He tried to visualize her with pride shining in her blue eyes, but he could only see her as she'd last appeared, hurt and crying. Besides, she didn't even know where he was.

He reached up to cover the port and cracked his knuckles on the thick plastic. Lord! After five days, he'd forgotten to allow for weightlessness. For five days, he'd wheeled around the earth like a man on a merry-go-round, and in five more days, the brass ring would be his.

"Face it, Maxie," he said aloud. "All you want is down."

He seemed to be talking to himself more and more. But Doc had said not to worry. "Your personality's splitting, Max; you've probably always had a mild neurosis. It'll join again when the pressure's off."

Meanwhile, it was something to do. He pulled the cover over the port and the capsule darkened. His stomach twisted with the familiar sense of falling, and he gripped the bar just above his chest with both hands. His stomach settled.

His wrist circlet vibrated gently, and he knew it was recording the brief flutter on his pulse to be relayed to the base in the Caribbean when he got in range.

His leg itched where a tube entered a blood vessel, recording pressure. Gradually, his awareness spread to the dozens of electrodes, cardiograms, and meters which pierced and pressed his body.

For the hundredth time, he wanted to rip them loose and escape, but he was immobile from his armpits down, swathed in pressure suit and nylon crash harness; strapped inside a five by three foot capsule, suspended inside a stubby winged ship he'd never seen. He was a passive guinea pig, punched and probed in a satellite that circled the earth every 118 minutes, from 250 to 1200 miles high. He was a three foot tall, 75 pound guinea pig, but nonetheless . . .

"Stop complaining, Max," said his voice. "You volunteered."

So he had. And if he'd been normal size, as he'd wished every day since he was fifteen, he'd never have gotten the job.

As Doc had explained, "We can cut total thrust to one-eighth with you. You eat less, drink less, and breathe less."

Old Doc, the first space psychologist. He'd be in range soon. Max could almost see him behind the mike at the base, pulling at his earlobe and pursing his lips while he thought up questions to ask.

Max wondered how long they'd be able to talk this time. It varied so much according to his altitude that he could never keep track.

HE felt the vibration behind his ear, then the voice came clear above the faint sizzle of solar static. "Max?"

"Here, Doc."

"With us again? Good. How do you feel?"

"You tell me."

"All right. Hold on." His voice came back after a minute. "Here we are, Max. Your temperature's normal; breathing normal. Oops! Watch your pulse. It took a jump nine minutes ago."

"I had a dizzy spell. Uh . . . how long was I out?"

"Oh." There was a pause. "You roared overhead twice, but you weren't—"

Twice. That was nearly four hours. "The longest yet," said Max.

"True, but the first in almost two days. And I started to say you weren't babbling either time, as you've done before."

"What did I say?"

"You were under the impression we were revolving around you. Without you, you said, we'd fall into space. But we weren't to worry, because you'd stay and take care of us. I felt . . . humble."

Max heard the chuckle in Doc's voice and felt his ears grow hot. "That's heady stuff."

"Better than the time before, though, when you were mad at us mortals. I was grateful you didn't have a bomb with you."

"You shouldn't listen."

"My job, Max. I'm learning a lot I couldn't learn any other way."

"You think I'm—flipping?"

"No. You're adapting, changing to meet a new environment. If you didn't, you'd really flip."

Max could hear the fatigue in his voice. "When do you sleep, Doc?"

"When you're on the other side."

Max shivered at the sound of the word. *The other side.* The silent, lonely time. *Soon.* He pushed the thought away.

"Hey, Doc, I'm composing a song to pass the time. I'll call it 'Meet Me at Perigee.' Think it'll sell?"

Doc grunted. "They'll pay you ten grand a week to

sneeze when you get down, Max, until there's a new novelty."

Doc was right, too. Yesterday's hero is today's cold turkey. He'd have to make his wad and get out of the public eye fast. And take Marie with him, if he could find her.

He opened the port and saw the British Isles far to the left, hovering over Europe like a mother hen. The dark African coast was below and the vast, gleaming Sahara seemed to be tipping up toward him.

"We've only got another minute, Max," said Doc. "Anything else?"

"No." Max said the words that had become ritual. "I'll see you around."

Then there was only static, and Max sighed, hating the end of it. The conversations were all that kept him sane, he figured. Doc knew his trade.

HE remembered when he'd first seen him. He and Marie had an act in San Francisco; tumbling and a song and dance routine. One night, Harry, a waiter, had come into the broom closet they'd given Max for a dressing room.

"You got company, Shorty. Two guys."

Scouts, Max thought, slipping on the tailored suit he'd gotten in New York during their try for TV. He checked himself in the mirror: Even features, straight nose, slight shadow of beard. How did people mistake him for a kid? They didn't look, that was it.

He'd known they weren't scouts when he reached their table. One man—Doc, he'd learned later—appeared too thoughtful, and his suit too rumpled. The other was heavy-shouldered, unimaginatively immaculate, and looked like he'd never laughed in his life.

Neither smiled as Max clambered into the chair and put his arms on the table.

"Canning," said the heavy man, "we may have a job for you."

He had a high, nasal voice, and Max had disliked him at once. "What does it pay?"

The heavy man frowned and started to speak, but Doc broke in. "Care for a drink?"

"It's coming," said Max. Nobody spoke until Harry had set his scotch-on-the-rocks on the table and departed. Max sipped his drink, becoming annoyed by the inspection. "Well?"

"How old are you?" asked Doc.

"Twenty nine."

The heavy man grunted. "Too old."

Doc shook his head. "You saw his act, General. He couldn't do that if he weren't in top physical condition. And he has . . . uh, the other requirements."

Max thought he should help. "I keep in shape."

Doc nodded. "We *do* have a job for you. We can't tell you what it is now. But the pay is wide open. Three month's work, and you'll be fixed for the rest of your life.

"You'll be able to withdraw at any time within the first six weeks," Doc continued. "But you can't talk to anyone about it, and you can't bring anyone with you. You have a family?"

Max hesitated. "No."

Doc had caught the pause. "The girl—you can't tell her anything. You understand that?"

Max hesitated longer this time. He lifted his glass with both hands and drained it, feeling the ice cube against his nose. He set it down. "I'm with you. And I won't back out."

He hadn't backed out, during the long dry run in the capsule, eating concentrated rations, drinking the same reconditioned water again and again, breathing the same recycled air, day after day. The dry run had taught him something about loneliness, too—but it wasn't like this.

HE watched the shadow creep across Saudi Arabia. Night lay beyond it, with stars strung out like jewels on black velvet. *Darkside coming up,* he thought, and fear was a bright blue taste on his tongue. *Oh, God! There was nothing like this!*

He gripped the bar and squeezed his eyes shut, feeling tears gather at the corners and hang there, unable to fall. After several minutes, he jerked his head and watched the twin globules float away, catching the fading light as they drifted toward the air recycler. Tomorrow's drinking water . . .

On the dark side, he had nothing to do but think, and he had time to make his thoughts vivid. When he thought of steak, he heard the sizzle as it broiled, and felt the juice running over the back of his tongue. When he thought of a drink, he felt the moisture on the outside of the glass, and heard the muffled clink of the ice cubes as he raised the drink to his lips. When he thought of Marie . . .

A red flag fluttered in his brain, but his thoughts rolled recklessly back to the time he'd left her . . .

She was standing beside him while he packed, and the

rusty gold fringe on her costume skirt shook against the tiny, perfect thighs.

"Maxie." He could hear her voice, full and throaty, lacking the thin, piping quality so many had. "Maxie, if you've got a chance to do a single somewhere, okay. I'll take care of your costumes, help with your makeup, or anything. But I want to be with you."

Max sighed. "I said it wasn't that, Marie. All I can tell you is that when I get back in three months, we can get married."

"We can now."

"No." He thought of explaining again how he hated to put her on display for those . . . other men. And what would they do when they got old? He'd seen too many of the old ones, still in the trade, riding a downward spiral. He thought of telling her that this might be their only chance to get out of it. But he'd already said that.

He locked the suitcases and walked to the door. "I can't say what I'll be doing, Marie. And that's final. But I'll be back."

"This is final too, Max. I won't be here."

Her voice was tight, and she'd called him Max instead of Maxie. He looked at her white face and saw the glint of moisture in her eyes.

"Try to understand," he said, his voice gentle. "I'll be back."

She bit her lip, teeth white against the red, and golden waves danced as she shook her head. "I won't be here, Max."

The remembered scene stayed in his mind several minutes before he forced it away and looked out the port.

There was nothing to see in the shadow of the sun, but he knew that India was somewhere below. He thought of the millions watching his pale streak across the sky, perhaps saying to each other, in whatever language they used: "There goes Max."

Then he remembered they wouldn't say it, because nobody knew there was a human aboard. Why? He wondered for the hundredth time if they expected something to go wrong.

But nothing would go wrong, he told himself. He tried to relax, dreading the ripping frenzy of another breakoff. But fear nibbled at his calm.

Maybe, the thought made him cold inside, *they didn't even plan to bring him down.* It would be much easier, and they were learning all about him from his swaddling of instruments. That would explain the secrecy about him, too.

Then he thought of Doc. He'd trust him, he decided, even if he didn't trust that chicken general. Doc had been with him constantly during the two and a half months before takeoff, and never once had Max caught him with the mocking smile behind his eyes that so many had.

Max smiled, recalling the time he'd passed out in the centrifuge. They'd gotten it up to twenty gees and Max had wanted to go back in and try for more.

"You don't have to prove anything to me, Max," Doc had said. "Relax. Few people can take over fifteen."

Three days before takeoff, Doc had come into his room, set a bottle of scotch on the night stand, and pulled two glasses from his pocket. "This came out of our medicinial appropriation. It's the last chance you'll have for a drink before takeoff."

Later, Max had gotten a little maudlin. "Doc, if I don't make it—"

"You'll make it."

"Sure. But promise me you'll find Marie if I don't and give her whatever's coming to me."

Doc raised his eyebrows. "I promise. It'll take some legal boontwaddle, since she's not a relative. Is it that important?"

"Yes. It's the main reason I'm doing this. I want her out of the rat race, even if I don't make it."

After a reluctant judge advocate had gone back to the officer's club, leaving Doc with the will he'd drawn up, Max had loosened up. He knew, as he looked back on it, that he'd loosened up more than he'd intended.

"Doc, for a three foot man, women aren't like streetcars. Even if they were, Marie would be for me. You saw her. Perfect figure, the nicest . . . well, nobody mistook *her* for a little girl."

He filled his glass. "She was sixteen when I met her, eight years ago. I was doing a trapeze act with the circus, and I worked her in. She was perfect for it; patient and dependable. My opposite, exactly. When the circus folded, we worked up a night club act. It was good, but I could never handle the hecklers. I wanted to throw things, and once I hit a customer with a bottle. After that, I just let Marie handle them. She never had any trouble."

Max had thought about himself a moment. "Doc, you know what I'm like. Will I last up there?"

Doc filled his glass before answering. "If you had to pilot the thing, I wouldn't let you go. You'd probably blow up. But all you have to do is lie there; in fact, that's about all you can do. You'll make it. The Rhesus monkey did."

Max had grinned. "Thanks a lot, Doc. I'll try to live up to the example."

JUST lie there. It had sounded easy, but it wasn't. His leg itched again, and the capsule seemed cooler. He should be over Australia now. Or would that be the next time around? It didn't matter. Nothing mattered now, except the end of it, four days and twenty hours from now.

He fell asleep thinking about it, his hands tight on the bar.

PING!

The sound woke him from a dream of falling. Air exploded from his lungs, tearing at his throat, and he felt the skin stretching taut across his stomach.

A meteor! He heard the hiss of escaping air, and felt the pressure in the capsule dropping. He tried to scream, but his lungs were empty.

He was sinking into a soft, black cloud when the hissing stopped. A gasp relieved his collapsing lungs—the air was still thin, but better than nothing. The capsule had resealed itself, and he could feel air coming in from the emergency tank.

He explored himself mentally. His stomach was sore, but it seemed normal. He shuddered. A minute longer and he'd have exploded like an overinflated balloon. His heart felt like a typewriter in his chest, but it was slowing down. He seemed healthy, but he wondered how low the pressure had fallen.

"Don't borrow trouble," he told himself.

God! One chance in a hundred, and he'd caught it. No, once chance in a million. The meteor bumper would have stopped anything smaller than a BB, and his was bigger.

He was relieved to hear Doc's voice again. "Hello, Max. How was the trip this—"

Max cut him off. "Doc, what's the reading on me?"

There was a pause, and Max heard Doc mumbling off mike. Then he came back. "They're unscrambling it now, Max." His voice was casual. "What's eating you?"

"I caught a meteor."

"What? Hold on!"

Five minutes later, he was on again. "You're in good shape now, Max. Pulse and blood pressure still high, though. Better calm down."

"Calm down? Doc, what about the meteor?"

Doc's voice seemed strained when he answered. "Yes, one penetrated the forward section, about the size of a black eyed pea. You were in vacuum 12 seconds; not enough to vaporize cell fluids, so you're not damaged. Pressure's normal now. How do you feel?"

"Shook up. But I'm healthy if the ship is."

There was silence on the other end.

"Doc?"

Doc's voice had a decisive sound. "Max, I think you should know this. You lost a lot of air and it's cut your safety margin. They'll try to bring you in earlier than planned."

"What?" Max's voice rose an octave. "How much air? And what do you mean, they'll *try?*"

Doc cleared his throat. "Your air will last 38 hours, Max. At your present speed, it would take five days for normal air drag to bring you in. They'll try to turn your ship so the stern is forward, then fire one of the landing correction rockets to slow you down. Gravity and air drag will do the rest."

Max considered it. "How can I land without the rocket?"

"We'll sacrifice the ship. Your capsule will be ejected at 50,000 feet, and you'll come the rest of the way by parachute."

At least, Max thought, he'd be on the way down. "When do we start?"

"In thirty seconds. Get ready for the blast, Max. It'll hit twenty gees."

Like jumping off a five-story building onto a trampoline. He'd done that, too.

He gripped the bar and waited, counting off the seconds. ". . . Twenty eight." He tightened his stomach. "Twenty nine." He drew in his breath, pulling his lips back from set teeth. "Thirty!"

Nothing. It was like climbing a dark stairway, expecting a step that wasn't there. A minute passed.

"Doc! What's wrong?"

"We don't know yet, Max. They're checking the equipment."

Three minutes passed, then Doc came on again. "They'll try again, now. Get ready."

Max did. This time, the letdown was multiplied by ten.

"Doc?" The word was plaintive.

Doc's voice came on a minute later. "Max, they think the meteor knocked out one of your receivers. They can't control your ship from here."

"My God!"

"It was a million-to-one chance, Max."

"I know," said Max, trying to keep his voice calm. "As you told me once, odds have nothing to do with individuals. What now?"

"I'm no technician, Max. Maybe . . ." He trailed off.

"If the trouble's up here," said Max, "it would have to be fixed up here, wouldn't it?"

"I should think so."

"Well, ask them how!"

DOC'S voice was leaden when he returned a minute later. "No chance, Max. The receiver's outside the shell of your capsule. You couldn't get near it, and even if you could—"

Max grabbed at another idea. "Is there any way I can control it?"

"Manually? Max, you said—"

Max bit his lower lip, feeling the taut fabric of his patience stretch and tear. "I KNOW I CAN'T OPERATE A KIDDY CAR! BUT I DON'T AIM TO DIE UP HERE!" He swallowed, tasting blood. "Ask them, will you?"

Several minutes passed this time before Doc came back on. "The general is willing to try anything, Max. He'll give you instructions."

The familiar voice, high and nasal, wasted no time on preliminaries. "Just above your chest, there's a plate about five inches square where we put wiring for manual controls. Now get that plate off . . ."

The voice faded.

"Yes?" said Max. No answer. He was out of range, and there was nothing to do now, but wait.

No, he could be taking off the plate. He tore off his wristlet, smashed it against the shell, and salvaged a strip of strong steel. After twenty minutes of prying, the plate was off. He put his hand inside and felt the mass of wiring, coiled like a plate of spaghetti. Was he supposed to make sense of that?

Oh, Marie!

He relaxed, and was surprised to find that he was tired. He might even sleep . . .

Doc's voice woke him. "Max? They're ready to try."

Max shook his head to clear it. "Let's go."

The nasal voice came on. "You got the cover off?"

"Yeah, but all those wires . . ."

"Six are all that concern you. Find one with a green strip on white, another blue on white, one solid red, one, yellow, one blue on yellow, and one solid green. Strip the insulation off the ends, *but don't touch them together!*"

It was a tough job, picking around in zero gravity. His hands would begin quivering, then build up to jerking spasms. He stopped four times to bring them under control.

"Got them," he said, finally.

"Very well. There's a wheel in the middle of the ship which turns when the proper circuit is established. When it turns one way, the ship turns another. You've no way of knowing when you're in the right position so we'll watch the meters from here. When I say 'go,' you touch the green-white and the blue-white wires together. If I say 'stop' you separate them. If I say 'back' touch the red and yellow wires together. It will mean you've gone around too far and must come back. When I say 'fire' it means you're in the correct position. Touch the blue-yellow and the green wires, and your rocket fires. Got that?"

"Hell, no." Max was irked by his crisp matter of factness. "Run through it again."

The general did, adding: "Let me emphasize one point. If you fire when your ship is not exactly parallel to the orbit, you may be propelled entirely out of earth's gravitational field, or you may be driven into the atmosphere at too great a speed and burn up. Is that clear?"

"Yes," said Max, swallowing. "It's clear."

"All right. Go."

Max brought the two wires together and held them, hearing a faint sound somewhere near his feet. Something was happening. His hands began to tremble.

"Stop."

Max separated the wires.

"Back!"

He fumbled for the red and yellow wires; finally brought them together.

"Stop." He did.

"Go!" He grasped two others and held them. His hands shook, then began jerking.

"You're breaking contact! GO!"

Max ground his teeth, and dewdrops of sweat formed on the backs of his hands.

"STOP!"

For a moment his muscles refused to obey his mind, then he broke contact.

"You went too far," said the general. "Back."

"Wait a minute." Max kneaded his hands and flexed his fingers. "All right, let's try again."

"Go."

Max grabbed for a pair of wires and touched them.

"NO! I said go! The other wires!"

Max found the right wires and brought them together.

"You're turning like a pinwheel, now." The general sounded discouraged. "Just hold it for awhile."

Max looked out the port and saw the earth whirling below him. He couldn't even tell where he was.

"You're slowing down," said the voice. "It could have been worse. Lord, what if you'd hit the firing wires instead?"

The sunshine kid, thought Max, not answering. He'd punch him in the nose, first thing he got down.

"You're almost there. . . STOP! Now we'll try to get you back on the beam again. GO!"

Max tried to get the wires in his fingers, but his hands were jerking again. "Wait a minute."

"All right."

The general spoke again, his voice muffled and distant but still audible. "Doc, this is pointless. It would take a trained pilot with proper controls to bring that capsule down . . ."

Max strained to hear the reply, but Doc's voice was inaudible. He looked at his hands. Still quivering, but they seemed stronger. "I'm ready now. It's beginning to get dark."

"We'll have to wait then," said the general. "Can't risk having you touch the wrong wires in the dark." He cleared his throat. "Frankly, Canning, I think you'd better reconcile yourself—"

The voice stopped abruptly, and Doc came on. "Try and get some rest, Max. We'll do better next time."

THEN there was silence. Two hours gone, thought Max. Thirty six to go. He was almost ready to agree with the general. Pointless . . .

This time he couldn't sleep, and he seemed to be drifting through black molasses. It seemed that days had passed instead of less than an hour and a half, before the general's voice came again.

"Canning, I've got your position. Let's go!"

Max felt as though someone had gripped a handful of his nerves and was scrubbing them with a wire brush. "Where's Doc?"

"He's not here, Canning. Are you ready?"

Max felt his control slipping away. "Get him!"

"Wait." The voice returned in a minute. "He left the base about an hour ago, flying to the mainland."

"Left the base?" Anger surged within him, then turned to regret. *So Doc has given up.* Well, Max didn't exactly blame him, but he'd wanted to remind him about Marie. It seemed particularly important now.

"Ready, Canning?"

"Sure."

"All right," said the general. "The green–white and blue–white wires, in case you've forgotten. GO!"

It was worse than last time. After ten minutes, the general delivered a brief lecture.

"Canning, our time is running out. I didn't want to

put you under pressure, but I think you should know it's going to take you thirty three hours to slow down after you reenter the atmosphere. That means that if you haven't started braking within two hours, there's no point in starting down at all. Now, will you try?"

Max blew up. "TRY? I'M TRYING! DID YOU EVER THREAD A NEEDLE ON A ROLLERCOASTER, YOU PEABRAINED SLIPSTICK SHOVER?"

The general was silent for ten seconds, as if waiting to make sure Max had finished. "I sympathize with you, Canning, and I'd like to see you down safely. After all, this will go on my record too, even though it was unforeseeable. But I can't alter the facts. Are you ready?"

Max looked at his shaking hands. "No. We'll have to wait."

Later, they tried again without success, and Max was quivering with frustration when he went out of range.

It would be easy, he thought, just to lie there and do nothing. No struggle; just going to sleep when the carbon-dioxide concentration became too high. But he knew he wouldn't give up. Nobody did while there was still some hope.

And when there was none? When he still had thirty-two hours to live, and nothing to do but whirl around the earth like a dead mouse on a string? It could happen.

He thought about it, staring out the port, feeling the darkness from outside seeping into his mind. He started to reach up and close the port, but the blackness was suddenly everywhere . . .

His next conscious thought was: *How long?* He had no idea. It hadn't seemed long, but he never knew. Outside,

•

he was relieved to see the light bright at the edge of Australia, behind and to the right.

I'll soon be in range, he thought, *and there's still time for one more try.* Experimentally, he held his hands in front of him and touched his fingertips together. Perfect.

THE crackle of static came then, and the voice. "Maxie?"

Lord, his mind was gone now, for sure. That feather brained general was beginning to sound like—

"Maxie?"

He was sure then. Only one person called him that. "MARIE! How'd you get there?"

"I flew in a jet, Maxie. They had your picture on TV, then the man came and got me . . ."

So Doc had remembered! Well, he hadn't wasted any time bringing her back. He'd caught the sense of her words: ". . . Whole place is full of newspapermen and cameras. They want to know all about you."

Max almost smiled to himself, picturing her as the center of attraction. She would be enjoying it, too, as she always did. Then he realized they were wasting time.

"Hey! Put the general on! I've got to get down from here!"

There was silence at the other end.

"Marie?"

"Maxie, don't you remember?" Her voice held a deep sadness.

"What?"

"You came over twice, but you wouldn't talk to anyone. You just laughed."

Max felt sick. He couldn't speak for a long time, then he said, without emotion, "It's too late then, isn't it?"

"Yes." Her voice was choked. "Oh, Maxie, why did you do it?"

"Marie . . . don't cry. You just have to take chances to get any place. Some win; some lose. It just takes time to get used to the idea. I've had time."

"So have I, Maxie . . . two hours. I won't cry any more."

"Okay. How much time do I have left?"

"They just checked. It's twenty—" she paused, and he could tell she was fighting for control. "—Twenty eight hours."

"That's more than a lot of people on earth have right now, Marie. You should try to look at it that—" He stopped. Forced cheerfulness would just put a strain on both of them. "Marie, I'm sorry it didn't turn out."

"Me too."

"Listen, from now on I don't want to talk to anyone but you, you hear? Anybody wants to say something, they'll say it through you."

"All right, Maxie. I'll—wait a minute."

She came back on after a minute. "The general wants me to tell you they're going to build a statue of you, right here on the base."

Why, the pompous old—! Max felt sudden anger, then it subsided. Time was too short for—tantrums. He became aware of a feeling completely new to him: amused tolerance toward the general and people like him. Did the prospect of death affect everyone this way? Too bad it came so late.

"How big will the statue be?" he asked finally.

"How big?" She paused. "The general says it's for you to say."

Max smiled. "Tell him to build it life size, will you? Exactly life size, without a pedestal."

"All right," said Marie.

"And in case we get cut off, don't go away. We'll have a lot of time to talk."

"I'll be here, Maxie."

THE END

A PLACE BEYOND THE STARS
Tom Godwin

Now and then a science-fiction writer makes such an over-whelming impact with a single story that it seems to eclipse everything else he has written. That was the fate of such writers as Wyman Guin ("Beyond Bedlam"), Judith Merril ("That Only a Mother"), and Wilmar Shiras ("In Hiding"), and at the head of that group stands Tom Godwin, who published three novels and almost thirty stories beginning in 1953, but is remembered almost exclusively for his provocative and startling novella, "The Cold Equations" (1954), his fourth story.

Godwin was born in 1915, grew up in Ohio, and led a peripatetic life about which very little is known. Rumor has it that he had no more than a third-grade education, that he had worked for a time as a prospector in Nevada, and had owned a saloon. I can't vouch for the truth of any of that, but I can say with some certainty that "A Place Beyond the Stars," his only contribution to Super-Science Fiction, *appeared in the February, 1959 issue, the last one before the monster-fiction policy took hold. He died in 1981.*

When humanity had to flee the earth at last, scouts went ahead to prepare the path. Theirs was a life of greatest danger, and their best weapon
was knowledge.

Artwork by William Bowman

THE DARK STAR was detected in 2050, already less than two light-years from the sun and approaching at a speed of 700 miles per second. It would enter the solar system in 2550 and the resultant nova would destroy Earth.

Preparations began for the flight of the human race.

Suitable ships were the prime necessity. The gigantic mass ratio of photon drive ships prohibited really long flights and acceleration at one gravity would require years to approach the velocity of light. Extended interstellar voyages with such ships would consume lifetimes and generations.

In the year 3000 the Gravinetic Attraction-Repulsion Drive was developed— "Half the universe pulls the ship while the other half pushes it," was the layman's more-or-less correct conception of it—and the mass-ratio barrier was eliminated. Shortly afterward came the Davis Field; a field-type force which inclosed every atom of the ship and its contents and made possible accelerations so high that near-light speed could be attained in hours rather than years . . .

The means for interstellar travel was achieved, as nearly perfect as the laws of relativistic physics would ever permit, and construction of the giant Emigration ships began.

Since stocking the ships with large supplies of fuel and food would have meant a drastic reduction in the number of passengers, it was necessary that there be some way of replenishing supplies at periodic intervals. The use of already-inhabited Earth-type planets along the route as refueling and reprovisioning stations was the only solution to the problem.

Finding and preparing such worlds for use as way-stations was the job of the Immigration Scouts—the lonely, far-spaced men who led the way across the galaxy and upon whom depended the *survival of all those who followed. Theirs was a life of danger and responsibility without precedent and a trust they must fulfill no matter what the cost nor how the means . . .*

—From *HISTORY OF THE GREAT EMIGRATION.*

IT was very still in the Scout ship's control room as the sunlit world turned slowly on the viewscreen. Glen Bradley watched the distant smudge of the city come into view, the city that would be his destination, and thought with the bleak detachment of long experience: *They'll want to kill me first and ask questions later.*

But he had observed the world for seven days by means of the ship's various scanning and detecting instruments and he could do no more from a distance.

It was an arid world, with a virtually complete absence of elements of more than 220 atomic weight. The natives were humanoid, their degree of civilization roughly equivalent to that of Earth in the first quarter of the 20th Century.

The emphasis was on the military. The military craft and vehicles were fairly well-designed, but there had been little in the way of non-military progress. Roads were few and poor, factories were small and black with coal smoke, towns and cities were jumbles of box-like little houses, crowded closely together to leave as much as possible of the arable land open for cultivation.

There were rivers in deep channels in the deserts, capable of supplying water for irrigation and power for industry, but there were no dams.

Such a world would be unable to refuel and reprovision the Emigration Ship groups.

He had made multiple copies of a variety of films from the concealed microfilm library—a selected assortment that contained only passing references to relativistic physics and no mention whatever of weapons of war—and their distribution on the world below would insure the advanced type of future society that was desired.

But most of the military installations flew the same eye-and-sword flag, which meant that one man or one group of men controlled almost the entire world. They would grimly insist on retaining the dreary status quo they had created.

He would have to meet the leaders and find their Achilles heel. The most effective method of doing that would be to appear before them as their prisoner; as a harmless goose potentially capable of laying golden eggs for them.

He touched the control buttons and the ship arced downward.

One hour later, after some difficulty, he convinced the heavily-armed military officers that he came in peace and wanted to speak to their leaders. They then, without delay, had him locked in a stone-and-steel cell.

THE ability to learn exceptionally quickly was one of the characteristics required of an Emigration Scout. By the third day Bradley could converse to a satisfactory degree with Dran, the gloomy-faced native who came to his cell each day for the exchange of language lessons.

Bradley was certain that watchers were constantly on duty behind the rows of pseudo-ventilation slots along the tops of the cell walls, but there was an exchange of sur-reptitiously-written notes. Dran, behind his gloomy, non-commital exterior, hated the regimented life he lived and looked upon Bradley's coming as a faint, faint hope for deliverance.

Bradley learned what he wanted to know by the tenth day:

The world was called Bonthar and he was in the capi-tol of Sejoa, the largest nation. Sejoa had conquered most of the other nations of the world, under a leader named Graldo.

Graldo's tight control was maintained both by his mili-tary forces and the efforts of his two most trusted aides: Brend, head of the world-wide secret police, and Chilson, head of the Scientific Research Bureau. Brend's spies de-tected unrest wherever it might occur and Chilson's SRB developed weapons that would guarantee victory to Gral-do's military forces.

Under Chilson's program of Prescribed Research it had long been forbidden to explore any field other than those officially designated as "Useful." Chilson had de-creed: "Technological progress depends upon sound and practical approaches. From now on there will be no place for the bubble-heads, those Investigators of the Insignifi-cant who would spend their lives trying to learn why tree leaves are green or why the sun doesn't run out of fuel."

There had been a man named Vodor in one of the con-quered nations who had evolved a theory that was remark-ably close to Einstein's *Theory of Relativity* despite Vodor's lack of such essential data as the true velocity of light.

Chilson had not bothered to read it since its abstract

concepts were difficult to grasp, and in its uncompleted state it suggested nothing of any value to Chilson's SRB. But Chilson had had Vodor—who was an outspoken enemy of governmental control over men's minds—brought to Sejoa and put to work in a lumber mill.

"His new appointment will assist him in his mass-time-energy studies," Chilson had been quoted as saying in the government-controlled press. "He can equate it all: the mass of building timbers, the time required for him to stack his daily quota, and the amount of energy he must expend in so doing. In addition, for the first time in his life, he will be doing something useful for Society."

Dran, himself, had been an astronomer when Graldo conquered his nation and Chilson had ordered him removed from his observatory, saying, "Gazing at the stars is the pointless pastime of a child." Dran's ability to learn new languages quickly had made him the logical choice to learn his, Bradley's, language. When the language lessons were finished he would resume his task of teaching ballistics to student artillery officers.

On the eleventh and twelfth days Bradley was taken to his ship, which was crowded with military officers and SRB officials. He was ordered to teach them how to operate it.

He repeatedly explained that the control buttons were made to respond only to his own neural pattern. He demonstrated, while the SRB men watched every move he made.

At the end of the second day they were forced to admit defeat. The control buttons refused to function for anyone but him and the collapsed-atoms alloy that sheathed the control units proper and all other vital portions of the ship could neither be cut nor melted by any means they could contrive.

The language lessons continued for thirty more days. Dran grew thin and haggard from his double duty of teaching Terran to those who would view the microfilms as fast as he learned it from Bradley. On the thirtieth day Dran was gloomier than ever and there was an air of tension about him. At the end of the day, as the guards were opening the steel door, he handed Bradley his last note. It read:

Tomorrow you will be taken to Graldo, then to a thing named Bethno, in the Interrogation Chamber. Suicide tonight would be far better. I am very sorry—I wish I could help you.

THE guards came for him at daylight the next morning; the rattle of the door and their brittle *"Up!"* awakening him. On an upper floor he was turned over to another group; tall, wooden-faced men whose insignia was that of Graldo's Elite Guard. The new guards took him down a corridor and to a massive door.

Beyond it, in a vast, gray room, three men were waiting for him.

One sat behind a wide desk, the ribbons and medals on his blouse the only bright color in the room. His lips were a thin, hard line under his jutting, hawk-like nose and his eyes were exactly the same expressionless gray as the metal top of his desk. That would be Graldo.

To Graldo's left stood a thick-set, swarthy man, heavy-jawed, his little brown eyes flickering as he watched Bradley. Brend, of the secret police system . . .

The third man was in civilian dress. He was tall and he looked down his long nose at Bradley with an objective curiousity and a self-satisfied assurance that was nothing short of contempt. That would be Chilson, who knew everything worth knowing and tolerated no nonsense from bubble-heads . . .

The guards withdrew from the room and Graldo spoke, in a metallic tone that matched his eyes:

"Your ship has been thoroughly examined. All microfilms found in it have been studied and every word of your conversations with Dran was recorded. I tell you this so that you will waste none of my time with subterfuges.

"Why are you here?"

He knew that Dran had long since conveyed his explanation to Graldo but he told his story again, speaking to Graldo while the other two listened; Chilson with his objective contempt and Brend with suspicion in his little monkey eyes. He told the truth, all of it, about the need for a friendly, well-developed world as a stop-over base for the Emigration ships.

"The microfilms you now have," he finished, "will teach you everything from the construction of large hydro-electric plants and smelters to the mass-production of labor-saving machines which can be available for all. You can jump the centuries of research that would ordinarily have to precede these things and within a few years raise your people's standard of living to a height they could never have dreamed of."

It was all true, but in the grim room, speaking to the cold Graldo, the scowlingly suspicious Brend and the contemptuous Chilson, it sounded naively Pollyanna-ish. A long silence followed his last words.

"I see," Graldo said at last. "We are supposed to gratefully alter our entire way of life for the future benefit of an alien species."

"The benefit to your own race would be even greater," he answered. "And there will be scientists on the Emigration ships who can teach your scientists still more—a great deal more—than they can learn from the microfilms."

Quick, hot resentment flashed across Chilson's face, eradicating the smug self-assurance for the moment.

"A reminder, alien—" he said. "We are not in need of enlightenment. Our own scientists are quite capable—under my supervision they developed the weapons that gave Sejoa world leadership and under my supervision they will continue to develop whatever I may demand. They need no tutoring from alien bubble-heads."

Brend shifted his eyes to Graldo and spoke:

"I could maintain little in the way of security if scientists and technicians, without careful screening and clearance, were permitted to study those films. Many of the so-called labor-saving devices could be transformed into dangerous weapons."

"Yes, yes—I know," Graldo said. His opaque metal eyes studied Bradley while his fingers tapped thoughtfully on the desk top. "You say the first Emigration ships will not arrive until a hundred years from now. Will there be any other ships in this section of space before then?"

"None," he answered.

"Part of your story I believe. You would not have left your ship and become my prisoner to ask for my help unless your race badly needed it. But you have offered nothing of value to pay for it. Your assortment of more-leisure-time machines and gadgets would be incompatable with intelligent discipline of the masses—they would be weakened into laziness, perverted into demands for more and more freedom.

"Perhaps such was your true plan—which you might have thought to be clever and subtle—to dispose of me and my regime. But I did not become ruler of a world by being stupid and gullible."

"No," he said. "I have no desire whatever to play power politics on an alien world. I only want your cooperation so that I can go on my way."

"You have offered nothing of value," Graldo said again, "and you, yourself, are of no value to me until you do so."

There was finality in Graldo's tone that told Bradley the interview was ended. Graldo's finger was pressing one of the buttons on his desk. . . .

"I have withheld nothing that would be beneficial to you," Bradley said.

"Except your ship. That, alone, I could use—and you refuse to tell how the control buttons can be by-passed."

"There is no way to by-pass them. It was a safety measure built into the ship."

"I cannot believe that," Graldo said. He glanced beyond Bradley. "Perhaps Bethno can stimulate you into remembering."

Bradley turned and saw the three coming up behind him. Two were heavy, muscular men, thick leather straps in their hands. The third was bulbous of face and body, utterly hairless, his eyes in his formless face as pale as milk and giving him the appearance of a maniac.

"This is Bethno," Graldo said. His thin lips almost smiled. "He will give you his undivided personal attention—which is an honor awarded only to the most important prisoners."

Bethno's milk-gray eyes were shining with the flat sheen of wet stone. *He enjoys his work,* Bradley thought with grim amusement. *It's his life—and I'll be his masterpiece . . .*

Bethno nodded his hairless dome of a head at the guards and they stepped forward with the binding straps. They jerked Bradley's arms behind his back, to buckle the straps, and he thought of what Dran had written: *Suicide tonight would be far better.*

There was no possible way-station world but Bonthar in that section of space and the Emigration ships would have neither fuel nor food to go on and try to find another. If he failed to have Bonthar prepared for them they would have to land and walk out of the ships, the men and women and frightened children, into suspicion and violence and slavery.

He made the decision that he had hoped would not have to be made. The cost would be great, but there was no alternative.

He braced himself against the hard twist of the guards, hands on his shoulders and said to Graldo:

"There is a weapon you might like. With it you could entirely destroy a rebel city in seconds."

The impact of his words was such that even the guards froze in their attempt to turn him. There was a moment of blank-faced silence, then Graldo asked quickly:

"How long?"

"Within seconds. We call it the hydrogen bomb."

Again there was a silence, desire and suspicion conflicting on Graldo's face.

"Is this a lie?" he asked harshly. "Why didn't you tell me about it before?"

"We haven't used the hydrogen bomb for two hundred years," he answered, "and it's against our moral code to give it to any other race. But under my present circumstances my people would consider it ethical for me to cooperate with you, alone.

"Now, if you want to see them, the microfilms are in my ship—the ones that show our last atomic war and what the hydrogen bomb did."

GRALDO, Chilson, Brend, and the six highest-ranking officers of Graldo's military forces were gathered in Graldo's office as the microfilm projector reinacted for them the flaming thunder and destruction of the last atomic war; the war in which a billion people died in less than ten days.

There was a hushed quiet in the room when it was over, then Graldo's chief-of-staff said with awe in his voice:

"Sir, that bomb is a weapon against which the full military power of any enemy nation would be like feathers tossed against a hurricane."

Graldo turned to Bradley, the sweat of eagerness like a shining film on his face. "These other films here—they show how to make this bomb?"

"Yes," he answered. "Everything needed is to be found on this world except some of the heavier elements. Those you can get on a heavy-element world which the instruments on my ship show to be not far from here . . . as interstellar distances go."

"How long will it take?"

"The trip? About eighty days."

"The other—the making of the bomb."

"You must understand," he said. "These microfilms deal specifically with the construction of the bomb. They are not complete in themselves. The other microfilms I gave you will be needed to produce the mines, mills, factories, chemical plants, electronics industries—all the things you must have before you can make the bomb's component parts.

"I doubt that you can have the bomb in less than twenty years."

"Twenty years?" Disappointment was followed at once by savage refusal to believe. "You lie—it can't take that long!"

"Project the films showing the bomb's construction and then project the other films again. When you have seen for yourself how numerous and complex are the machines and methods that go into it all, you will know that I do not lie. And then, perhaps, you will believe me when I tell you the only way the time can be shortened."

It was late the next day when the guards took him from his cell and to Graldo's office. Graldo, Chilson and Brend were alone, the film projector near them. Graldo would have trusted no one to see the films of the bomb's construction, even though such information would have been utterly meaningless to all but a few scientists. Except two men—Chilson, who would be in charge of the building of the bomb, and Brend, who would see to it that no secrets were divulged that might threaten Graldo's sole control over it.

The faces of Chilson and Brend were sagging from lack of sleep and Graldo's face was flushed and ugly with frustration.

"I want the bomb now, not twenty years from now," Graldo said. "Show me how to cut the time to no more than four years and you go free the day the first bomb is made."

"Four years?" he asked.

"That's an extremely short period of time ... But there is one single way in which it can be done."

"How? Get to the point!"

"No nation alone—neither Sejoa nor any other— could possibly accomplish so much in such a short length of time. But the people of all nations, all working toward the same goal, could do it."

Graldo's amazement was almost instantly a snarling question:

"You fool—do you mean you think they would *want* to build hydrogen bombs for me?"

"Not hydrogen bombs—I suppose they wouldn't even know of them. But the high industrial level that must precede the bombs would greatly improve living conditions for all of them and *that* all of them would want to work for.

"You can't have full-scale cooperation and the swiftest possible progress under a program of governmental restrictions, supervision of every minor detail, and no incentive for the workers. But offer the people of Sejoa and all your subject nations, from scientists to laborers, the right to benefit from these things they will build and production of the bomb will be possible within four years."

"I see," Graldo said. There was a menacing softness in his tone. "So this is your trickery, your plan for getting what you wanted on Bonthar, after all?"

"My life and freedom depend upon helping you get the bomb and this is the quickest way it can be done."

Chilson laughed; a short, snorting sound. "I think the alien's prime consideration truly is his own welfare—he can't be stupid enough to think his program could not be halted at will."

"Perhaps," Graldo replied. He gazed long and calculatingly at Bradley and said at last, "Of course, your plan is harmless. There would be a great deal of resentment when full governmental control was re-established but it would be meaningless against the bomb. Did you think of that?"

Bradley shrugged. "I know."

Chilson laughed again and even Brend's thick lips parted in a smile.

Graldo summoned the guards who would return Bradley to his cell and said, "I'll consider the plan."

GRALDO'S decision was made by the next morning: he would adopt Bradley's production program to a large extent. But, first, the ship would make the trip to the heavy-elements world and bring the ores without which all the other work would be pointless.

"No," Bradley told him in flat refusal. "The ship goes nowhere until the other work is started."

Graldo's face darkened with rage.

"You forget your position, alien. Shall Bethno remind you of it tonight?"

"If Bethno's torture should alter my neural pattern," he replied, "the controls of my ship would no longer function for me. You would never get the ores, never have the bomb."

"Perhaps. And perhaps you lie and a few days in the Interrogation Chamber would wring the truth out of you and make you quite unnecessary to me."

Bradley made no answer and Graldo's anger faded into a hate-filled thoughtfulness.

"There will be time, later, to take care of certain matters . . . For the sake of convenience, I may humor you by doing as you insist."

Bradley's program was weakly launched three days later, made almost useless by smothering restrictions.

"Nothing will be accomplished that way," Bradley said to Graldo. "You will have to lift the restrictions and give people the promise of freedom-to-come."

"After I have the ore," Graldo said. "Not now—not when I will be away for eighty days."

"It will have to be now," he answered. "You, yourself, told me that my life depends upon helping you toward having the bomb as soon as possible. A great deal of work can be done here while we are gone—that time can't be wasted."

Graldo's desire for the bomb had been growing daily and that time he did not argue or threaten. The next day he lifted some of the restrictions.

Thirty more days went by during which, by means varying from subtle persuasion to outright threats of non-

cooperation, Bradley altered his role from that of a con-
demned prisoner to one approaching that of a technical
advisor. It was necessary that he see for himself that his
plan was being carried out and he was grudgingly given
limited freedom; Brend's agents always with him when he
was not in his cell, watching every move he made and re-
porting every word he spoke.

But Graldo's submissiveness to Bradley's demands began to change to impatience and on the fortieth day Bradley knew he could force him no farther. On that day he
told Graldo he was ready to leave but for one last request:
the appointment of Vodor to chairman of the newly-cre-
ated Technical Advisory Board.

Chilson objected with his usual vindictive anger, speaking to Graldo:

"My Scientific Research Bureau has already been
transformed into a travesty, with day-dreaming theorists
given status equal to that of practical scientists. Now he
wants the most impractical bubble-head of all—Vodor,
who babbles of fourth dimensions!—to be appointed to
the most important position of all!"

Bradley spoke to Chilson: "There are aspects of this
program that only a theoretical physicist, familiar with a
variety of fields, could fully comprehend."

"This is the alien's last request," Graldo said to Chilson.
"I've pampered him long enough. As for this Vodor: could
he do us any harm in eighty days?"

"He'll probably put everyone to measuring the distance
to rainbows or the tensile strength of sunbeams!" Chilson
retorted. "Eighty days of time will have been wasted; time

that my own scientists, if they had been left alone, could have used to accomplish something worthwhile."

"An interesting conjecture, Chilson," Brend said. "Did you ever stop to consider the fact that the alien's future welfare depends upon his plan not failing?"

"Why . . . no." A thoughtful, almost pleased, expression replaced the protest on Chilson's face. He turned to Graldo. "I have no objection to a Bubble-head Holiday so long as this alien is held responsible for what they do while we are gone. Or, rather, for what they do not do."

"We will return to find that a tremendous amount of progress has been made during our absence," Bradley said.

Then he added with the sincerity that came from telling the absolute truth:

"I'm betting my life on it."

GRALDO was alone in his office when Bradley was summoned the next day.

"We leave tomorrow," Graldo said. "I want no more delays—is the ship ready?"

"It is," he answered.

He made a rapid mental review of his progress to date and the one more thing he must cause to be done. Graldo was going, of course—he would trust no one else to oversee such a vital mission. Chilson was going, with some of his SRB specialists, to make certain Bradley tried no such trickery as the substitution of low-grade for high-grade ores. But Brend would stay on Bonthar. . . .

"I understand Brend will not go," he said to Graldo. "It might be better for your own plans if he should stay."

Graldo gave him a quick look of surprise. "What do you mean?"

"It's very improbable, but not impossible, that something might happen to delay our return," he said. "Lack of a governmental leader could conceivably disrupt the production program and Brend, as head of the world police, is second only to you in influence. If necessary, he could easily take your place while you are gone."

Graldo did not reply to the explanation, but there was an abstracted air about him during the rest of the short interview.

The next day, when Graldo and Chilson came to the ship, Brend was with them.

Graldo had had extra seats installed in the control room the night before, so that he and the other two could sit in comfort behind Bradley and watch both him and the viewscreen. They seated themselves and six heavily armed guards took up positions in various parts of the room. Twenty more guards and SRB technicians were assigned to other portions of the ship.

Bradley looked questioningly at Graldo when all was in readiness and Graldo said shortly, "Go!"

He pressed the buttons that had refused to respond to the touch of the SRB experts and on the lower viewscreen the city fell away from them. There was no sensation of movement—the Davis Field prevented such.

The hot, barren deserts could be seen stretching endlessly away to the east and he said, "There lies the future for the people of every continent on Bonthar: the deserts. They need only dams in the rivers to give them water."

No one answered him, or even looked up.

Bonthar dropped faster, curving into an immense hemisphere. The sky turned dark, then the stars appeared in the dead blackness of deep space.

He increased the acceleration and Bonthar shrank and fled on the viewscreen. Graldo and the others watched as it became a star that was fading while the sun beside it slowly dwindled.

"We'll reach full velocity in a few hours," he said to them. "Our speed will then be ninety-nine point nine nine nine six three per cent that of light."

Only Chilson bothered to look up; a brief and pointedly disinterested glance. He smiled companionably at Chilson, unable to resist the impulse to tell him:

"As a scientist it might interest you to know that three hundred years ago one of our bubble-heads—Einstein — calculated that a ship would travel an enormous distance each day at that speed. It turned out that he was right, down to the last decimal point."

Chilson gaped as he tried to find some intelligent meaning in the statement, then he closed his mouth to say with acidic wonder, "Do you mean your bubble-heads were regarded as geniuses if they could do simple arithmetic?"

"Oh, no—Einstein found arithmetic unsuitable for setting forth such complex thoughts and he always used special mathematics to express his theories."

Chilson's quick anger came. "You were not ordered on this mission to entertain us with inane comedy!"

Graldo looked up from the viewscreen and said with the curtness of preoccupation, "Confine all future remarks to necessary statements."

He shrugged. "I'll be glad not to go into it any farther."

THE days dragged by like little eternities as Bonthar's sun became a bright star that was fading. Graldo was moody and unpredictable; sometimes cheerful and almost intoxicated with the thought of his destiny, sometimes surly and snarling in impatience.

Brend was without emotion, sleeping most of the time when he was not eating, although he remarked once with satisfaction: "The Bubble-head's Holiday will serve one very useful purpose—it will encourage people to speak their minds while we are gone and a complete and detailed list of all subversives and malcontents will be waiting for me when we return."

Chilson was nothing short of happy, wearing the same smug expression he had had the day Bradley first met him. Chilson's ego still rankled and galled at thought of his temporary loss of prestige and control over the SRB and, as much as Graldo was looking forward to possession of the hydrogen bomb, Chilson was looking forward to the day of the ship's return and the resumption of his, Bradley's, walk to the Interrogation Chamber.

The journey was only a stay of execution for him. He had no illusions otherwise.

On the forty-first day they came to a small white sun. They arced around it, to the ragged, poisonous planet that lay beyond, and landed in the area which the ship's instruments showed to be the most abundant in the minerals they wanted.

"This is it," he said to Graldo.

The guards mined like madmen, working until they staggered with exhaustion while Graldo paced in his impatience and drove them harder. The ores were plentiful and rich and the ship was loaded two days after it had landed. Ten minutes later it was on its way back to Bonthar.

It was then that Chilson came to Bradley with a sheaf of papers in his hand, smiling with his perpetual self-satisfaction.

"I had these star maps drawn at periodic intervals on the way here," he said, "and if you veer in the slightest from the proper return course, I will know it at once."

"I'm glad to have you check on me," he said. "I want to see Bonthar again as much as you do."

Graldo's impatience increased in the days that followed but surliness no longer accompanied it. He talked often with Chilson about the best methods of producing the bomb as soon as possible and with Brend about the most effective methods of maintaining rigid secrecy.

He totally ignored Bradley, except to ask once with objective curiosity, "Would your Emigration ships have any defense against the hydrogen bomb?"

"Not if they had to land," he replied. "And by the time they reach Bonthar they will be so short of fuel that they will have to do so."

"Then you haven't accomplished much for them, have you?"

"I tried," he answered, and Graldo turned away with a faint smile.

It was three days later, when he was dozing in his chair during sleep period, that he heard Graldo say:

"This ship will be the perfect carrier for the bomb—no aircraft can fly high enough to intercept it."

"When we learn how to bypass the control buttons," the voice of Chilson answered. "Bethno should be set to work on that problem as soon as we arrive."

"He will be," Graldo said. "And he had better produce results."

Bradley wondered if they knew he had heard them then decided they presumed he had not, but really didn't care.

Bonthar's star brightened and detached itself from the galactic background. Eighty-three days from the start of the round-trip journey it was a yellow sun again and visibly enlarging.

"We'll reach Bonthar in a few hours," he said to Graldo. "We'll come around from the night side—it will be morning in the capitol city when we land."

Graldo made no reply but later, when the nighttime surface of Bonthar was dark and close under them and destination was only minutes away, the control room door opened and six extra guards filed in.

"Sometimes," Graldo, said in answer to the questioning lift of his eyebrows, "a prisoner will try to do something desperate when his reprieve ends."

"There was an agreement," he said. "You promised me a chance for freedom."

Graldo laughed, the first time Bradley had ever heard him do so. "We played a game, each to get what he wanted in any manner possible. You should have known you would lose."

Bradley looked at the viewscreen, where the horizon

of Bonthar was black under the golden brightness of coming sunrise.

"It was a game for high stakes, wasn't it, Graldo? The destiny of Bonthar—and only one of us could win."

The ship sped out of the night, into the golden sunlight of morning. Ahead made unmistakable by the mountains to the north, was the site of the capitol city . . .

But another and far larger city was there. A network of roads radiated out from it and beyond, to the east, was the shining gold-blue of an immense man-made lake. Beyond the lake, where the gray desert had been, were green fields that reached to the horizon.

Graldo swung up out of his chair, staring in disbelief, his hand reaching automatically for the weapon he always carried. "What—"

"The fortunes of war, Graldo," he said. "You lost."

Graldo whirled on the wordlessly gaping Chilson. "Your star maps—you let him trick you. *This isn't Bonthar!*"

"This is Bonthar," Bradley said to them. "Look—"

The city rushed up at them on the viewscreen and the details were sharp and clear.

"There is your capitol building," he said. "There are the barracks for the Elite Guards. There is the Interrogation Chamber building and there is the multiple gallows where you used to hang rebels—see? They've kept it all intact to remember you by."

Chilson said in a choked voice:

"It has to be Bonthar—it *has* to be."

Then, in a queer whimper, "The bubble-heads—what did they do while we were gone?"

THE ship settled to earth, in the spot where it had set before. The guards surrounded Bradley at a command from Graldo and one on each side of him held his arms.

"Kill him at once," Graldo said to them, "if we are attacked in any way." He looked at Bradley. "I don't know what has happened here—but I know what is going to happen before the day is over."

Bradley and the guards beside him led the way out of the ship.

A small group of men was coming toward the ship, dressed in civilian attire entirely different from that which had been the custom before. The guards halted at Graldo's command and the guard captain blew his whistle. Bradley saw that he was looking expectantly toward the nearby Elite Guard barracks, where a door was swinging idly in the wind.

The group of civilians reached them and the old man in the lead greeted Bradley, smiling, and seeming not to notice the guards who held him.

"We've been expecting you," he said. "Vodor found the data he needed to complete his theory, in bits and pieces throughout your microfilms, a staff officer finally told about the bomb, and Vodor realized what you were doing for us. He calculated your return almost to the day."

The guard captain blew his whistle again, his cheeks puffing with the effort, but there came no answering sound or movement from the barracks. Graldo pushed forward, his confidence restored by the unarmed condition of the civilians and his face dark and ugly.

"Where is my Guard?" he demanded of the old man. "Where are my staff officers?"

The old man looked questioningly at Bradley.

"Tell him," Bradley said.

Graldo's face turned darker. "I am Graldo, you fool! Announce my arrival to my Guard and officers—at once!"

"I can't," the old man said mildly. "The last one died thirty years ago."

There was a silence of incomprehension in which even the guards were not quite wooden-faced any longer. The eyes of all turned to the silent Guard barracks, where the door still swung idly in the wind, and the touch of fear and uncertainty came to their faces.

Bradley spoke to Graldo:

"There were the laws of relativity, which you and Chilson didn't want to hear about; the laws that Vodor would have discovered if he hadn't been persecuted as an impractical fool. Nothing can exceed the speed of light, but there is a time dilation at high velocities, the same time dilation that makes it possible for my people on the Emigration ships to live to cross hundreds of light-years of space. Time is relative to the speed at which the observer is moving and at the near-light speed of my ship one day of time for us on the ship was one year for those here on Bonthar.

"It was eighty years ago that we left here. Your empire is long since gone—it died while you were planning and dreaming about it on the ship."

"No!" Graldo said, and the word was sharp with protest. "Not gone—not in eighty days . . ."

But he looked away, at the broad city, the busy highways, the distant green of what had been a desert, and was silent with the numbness of realization.

Brend worked his thick lips soundlessly, then said, "He

lies. Bethno will make him tell—" He looked at the long-deserted Guard building and did not complete the sentence.

Chilson laughed, and Bradley saw that his eyes were shining-bright. "Don't let the fakery fool you. None of it is real—it can't be!"

The crowd had grown thicker and men moved among the guards, disarming them. They looked in question and bewilderment at Graldo and then submitted without protest when he did not speak or turn. They were marched away and still he did not seem to see them.

The old man said to Bradley:

"A place will be found for everyone, even Graldo—jobs where they can do Society no harm. As for you—will you be with us for long?"

"Only a few days. This has cost eighty years of time and now the foremost group of Emigration ships is only twenty years behind me."

"We will be prepared for them when they come."

Chilson laughed again a high-pitched giggling sound, his too-bright eyes staring without focus. "I know—I know! Fakery—stage props—I'll order it all torn down tomorrow . . ."

"We have a place for you to stay while here," the old man said. "Shall we go there now?"

"Yes," he said. "I want to talk to all of you, then I'll have to go on again. The Emigration ships are coming and until we find a world of our own, somewhere, someday, there will be no time for any of us to ever stop and to rest."

He looked back when they were some distance on their way. The crowd had dispersed, leaving Graldo and Chilson and Brend alone in the center of the field. Chilson was babbling about stage props but Graldo and Brend stood stiff and silent, like men who watched in mute helplessness as forces beyond their control or understanding brought their world to an end.

And so, in a way, it had happened for them. . . .

"They were sure that they already knew everything worth knowing," he said to the old man. "I was honest with them—I told them no lies and I gave them what they thought they wanted."

He looked back once more when they came to the edge of the field. The three who had ruled a world looked very small and lonely as they stood together in the center of the field and Chilson's laughter was like a distant, giggling echo. He walked on again, thinking. . . .

"What did you just say, sir?" the old man asked.

"I guess I spoke aloud to myself," he answered. "An old Terran proverb:

"A little learning is a dangerous thing."

THE END

They came from the sea, hideous, horrible and hungry, enormous creatures in incredible numbers. Would they wipe out the peaceful, prosperous colony of Earthmen?

Artwork by Ed Emshwiller

THE LOATHSOME BEASTS

Robert Silverberg
(as Dan Malcolm)

"Dan Malcolm" was one of the many pseudonyms I used in the course of writing thirty-six stories for the eighteen issues of Super-Science Fiction, *and I include a second Silverberg story here not only in the interest of symmetry—I had stories in both the first and the last issues of the magazine—but because it illustrates the change of policy that characterized* Super-Science *in its final four issues.*

As I explained in the introduction, the sales of all science-fiction magazines had gone into a serious slump in 1958, and editor Bill Scott felt that the only way to save Super-Science *was to shift over to the currently trendy theme of stories about monsters. (A similar policy shift today would see a switch to vampire stories, I suppose.) I was essentially a member of the magazine's staff, whom Scott relied upon to turn in one or two stories (and on one occasion four) for each issue, and so I reprogrammed myself to write monster stories—not a really big shift in orientation, after all, since much of what I had written for the magazine over the years had involved the conflict between humans and fearsome alien creatures on far-off worlds.*

I called this one "The Horror from the Depths" when I wrote

351

it in February, 1959, but Scottie evidently didn't think that had sufficiently ghastly connotations, so he put a title of his own on it when it appeared under the Dan Malcolm byline in the October, 1959 Super-Science—not only the last of the monster-fiction issues, but the last issue of the magazine altogether. After turning in "The Horror from the Depths" I did two more for Super-Science the following month—"The Imitator" and "The Nightmare Creatures," which also were included in that final issue as "The Insidious Invaders" by Eric Rodman and "The Monsters Came by Night" by Charles D. Hammer. And then Scottie informed me that no further s-f stories would be required, because the magazine was folding. After three lively years, the fun was over.

NOBODY ON THE Terran colony-world of Lincoln was expecting trouble, when trouble came. A few of the colonists had held the quietly pessimistic view that after seven years of peaceful settlement on an alien world it was only fair to expect some sort of calamity, but the pessimists were few and far between, and kept their gloomy opinions to themselves.

But trouble came. It was Sevenday of Fourmonth—springtime on Lincoln, and the colonists were relaxing on this, the Sabbath day. There were two main settlements on Lincoln, which was an Earthsize world about four thousand light-years from the Galactic Rim.

The settlement of Springfield nestled on the eastern coast of Lincoln's main continent, and the settlement of Liberty sprouted on the western coast, 2500 miles away.

After seven years, each settlement had attained a population of about three thousand.

According to plan, they would serve as the nuclei of metropolises that would eventually extend from one end of the continent to the other.

The day was warm, with a soft breeze drifting in from the ocean. A few dozen early-rising settlers of Springfield had already gone down to the beach for swimming and picnicking, even though it was only an hour past dawn. By midday, nearly half the colony would be at the beach. The hard work of building the settlement had largely been completed in the early years of the colony, and now there was time to relax without feeling guilty about it.

The group at the beach consisted mostly of teenagers. They ranged from sixteen to nineteen years old; they had been children on the flight outward from Earth. The minimum age for a colonist coming from Earth was nine; so there was a gap of nearly ten years between the youngest of those who had come from Earth, and the oldest of those children that had been born on Lincoln itself.

The early risers included some of the settlement's first citizens. There was Charley Leeton, eighteen-year-old son of the Settlement Leader; Diane Brink, seventeen and daughter of Springfield's all-important Senior Medic; Danny Foster, the sixteen-year-old younger brother of Mark Foster, head of the settlement's Defense Council.

They swam nude and unashamed, since the colonists had deliberately avoided bringing from Earth the old taboos of modesty and shame. There was no lust, nothing evil in their nudity, just the consciousness of pride in a healthy and athletic body that was good to look at.

THE morning sun was bright and hot. A game of catch was taking place. Laughing boys and girls chased each other over the shining sand. Others splashed or floated or swam in the cool, buoyant water of the giant sea that stretched thousands of miles across the surface of the planet.

It seemed like a scene out of some Eden. Young, tanned, naked figures enjoying the sensations of being young on a young planet. The sun seemed to be smiling. Lincoln was almost perfect as a colony world. The climate was excellent, but not so balmy that the colonists lost all initiative and drive. The air was clear and fresh and like perfume to the lungs. The planet had great mineral wealth, and the soil was fertile. Best of all, there had never been a hint of any hostile animal life.

Unlike so many other planets where the colonists had had to remain on guard against fierce alien creatures, the Lincolnites had no distractions from the main job of building their colony.

The only animals on Lincoln were medium-sized and harmless land animals. There were large creatures in the depths of the sea, but Lincoln was several generations away from any large-scale sea-going.

It was a planetary Paradise. The few thousand Earthmen who had been chosen to leave their hideously overcrowded native planet and come here regarded themselves as the luckiest people in the universe. That morning, as the laughing youths ran up and down the beach, enjoying the day of rest and relaxation after six days of hard but rewarding work, it seemed as though this was, indeed, the best of all possible worlds.

And then the monsters left the sea and came forth onto the land.

The first to see them was Danny Foster. He and Diane Brink and Charley Leeton were about a hundred feet from shore, beyond the region where the waves broke. The water was nine or ten feet deep, and they were bobbing about in it, tossing around a basketball-sized inflated bladder from one of the native plants. As it happened, Danny was facing seaward when he saw the first sign of the invading monsters.

He didn't realize what it was that he saw. All that met his eye was a green flipper breaking the surface of the water. But the sight of one of the large sea-creatures was not unusual, and Danny was under the impression that the flipper was much further out to sea than it actually happened to be. He ignored the flipper, not even bothering to point it out to his playmates.

A moment later, a second flipper broke the surface of the waves. Diane, grinning, was backstroking toward the scene, not even aware of what was behind her. Danny squinted, looking into the sun.

He gasped. The water was suddenly boiling with creatures!

"Diane! Come back!" he shouted. "Watch out—it isn't safe there—!"

The girl turned and saw the creatures floating just beneath the surface of the water, only their immense eyes and an occasional flipper coming above the surface. Danny heard her cry out: "Oh my God!"

She began to swim toward shore.

THE water came to life. As Danny watched, horror-stricken, he saw Diane's nude figure lifted entirely out of the water on the back of some huge half-submerged sea creature. The girl stood erect a moment, water dripping from her body, sunlight glinting off her tanned breasts and glittering thighs. Then the creature below her rolled over, and she toppled into the water.

Danny called out to Charley Leeton. "Diane's in trouble! Some kind of sea monsters—"

Charley nodded. He had seen too. "What can we do? Swim out there and—oh, God!"

The air was split by a terrifying scream. The water churned violently, sending up spumes of white foam. Danny and Charley saw dozens of dark huge shapes converging on the place where Diane had gone under.

The white foam was suddenly flecked with bright scarlet.

Danny and Charley caught one last glimpse of Diane— or part of her. One flawless rounded leg projected above the water—ending above the thigh in a bloody stump. It had been bitten clean at the groin. Danny gagged, losing his breakfast in the water. Violent turmoil was going on a few dozen yards further out, where the sea beasts were milling around the bloody area.

Danny bobbed dazedly in the water. Charley swam over to him, gripping him by the shoulder.

"Come on—we've got to get ashore."

"But—Diane—" Danny mumbled dazedly. "She's— she's—"

"She's *dead*," Charley said with deliberate cruelty.

"Ripped to pieces. And we'll be next if we don't get ashore."

Charley's sharp words snapped Danny out of his daze. He realized he and Charley were still an uncomfortable distance from shore and there was no telling now fast the things could swim. Perhaps already they were heading toward him beneath the dark green water, rising upward to surround him as they had so suddenly surrounded poor Diane—

Danny began to swim with desperate energy, heading shoreward. Charley, bigger, older, and stronger, swam a few yards ahead of him.

Halfway to shore, Danny glanced back over his shoulder. The monsters had evidently finished with Diane now. He could see them, heading in toward shore—racing him to land! He doubled his stroke. Charley looked back, smiling grimly. "You okay, kid?"

"I'm—uh—managing. But—uh—we're being—uh—followed!" Every word was an effort.

"I know," Charley yelled. "Swim harder!"

Danny swam harder. He felt sick, weak, dizzy. He had never seen a violent death before.

Up till this morning, Lincoln had been a golden paradise. And now Diane, so beautiful with her long legs and high, full breasts, all that beauty dead, ripped apart, *eaten*—

Danny lowered his legs and discovered that he had reached standing level. He was still thirty feet from shore. Charley was almost out of the water now. The others on shore had seen the incident and were standing near the water's edge, pointing out toward the water, looking

Robert Silverberg

whitefaced and shocked at the bloody slick on the water where Diane had gone under.

Danny began to wade, shoving himself along with sweeping motions of his hands and arms. Charley was on shore, now. He was turning, shading his eyes, calling out—

"Hurry it up, Danny! Hurry!"

"I'm—hurrying," the boy gasped. He could see them milling about in confusion on shore.

Then they turned to run! Every one of them, fleeing! Charley, Mike, Ella, Dave, Nola—all of them. Danny saw the sleek tanned bodies of his friends racing madly off in all directions.

Danny reached the shoreline and stumbled onto the beach. "Wait for me!" he yelled feebly, with what little breath he had left. "Hey—wait for me!"

But they weren't waiting. They were running, running to save their own lives.

Danny turned—and saw the creatures. They were coming from the sea. They looked like giant amphibians, standing eight or nine feet high as the surf splashed around their flipper-feet. They seemed to be at least twenty feet long, standing on six thick legs. And about half their length seemed to be head. Their mouths were enormous and filled with great yellow-green fangs. Their eyes, like twin lamps, gleamed atop their snouts. The skin of the monsters was thick and coarse, a dull green in color. And there were hundreds of them. The sea was boiling with them.

A few had reached shore already, and were coming up onto the beach. The rest were on the way. As far as Danny could see, ugly snouts bobbed in the water and hideous monsters advanced toward the shore.

He tried to run. But he was exhausted by his frantic swim, and his vigor was sapped by the frightening shock of Diane's death. It seemed to him that he could see fresh smears of red blood on the snout of the nearest monster— Diane's blood—

He could smell them now, a thick, nauseating sea-smell, a smell of brine and of the depths. Danny retched; he toppled forward, dizzily.

Looking up, he saw a huge mouth opening above him, saw the gaping jaws, the anxious fangs. He screamed. The scream was cut off in the middle by the swift closing of the jaws.

ON the morning that the monsters left the sea and came ashore on the Springfield beach, Mark Foster, Danny's older brother and the head of the Springfield Defense Council, was more than two thousand miles away, in the west coast settlement of Liberty, attending a meeting of the All-Planet Council as the delegate from Springfield.

The meeting was strictly routine, a once-a-year affair that transacted ordinary business of official interest to both settlements.

Foster had been spared because, of all the high officials of the Springfield Settlement, he had the least to do. The Springfield Defense Council had been an inactive body ever since the early days of the colony, when it became apparent that there would be no danger to the settlements from any side.

These days, about all Foster's duties involved was making sure that the observation instruments were kept in good repair, just in case some invasion force of an alien race should come by. So far no hostile alien race had ever been discovered, but the colony worlds were required by Terran law to keep a constant watch for invaders, all the same. So that was about all the Defense Council did.

Theoretically Foster was Supreme Commander of the Springfield Militia, but there was no Springfield Militia, since there was never any threat of hostile attack. He was also head of the Springfield Police, a body of some ten men whose chief job it was to pull babies out of wells, rescue treed pets, and such.

There was little or no crime on Lincoln; the colonists had been picked too carefully for anyone of criminal tendencies to get through, and there certainly was little incentive for anyone to turn criminal on such an agreeable world.

So Foster, though he was a capable man, was largely a figurehead. And, as a figurehead, he could be spared to attend routine conferences on the other side of the planet. He had been in Liberty four days, and in three days' time would be on his way back to Springfield.

He was a big, rawboned man of thirty-eight who had volunteered for the Colonial Program because he was weary of the petty, tense, limited life on vastly overcrowded Earth. A bachelor, he had met his wife on the ship coming out from Earth. Until that time, his only dependent had been his younger brother Danny, child of his parents' old age and orphaned at seven. Danny had been nine when the colony-ship arrived on the planet that was to be named Lincoln. Mark Foster had been thirty-one.

Foster was anxious to get back to Springfield. He missed Danny, and more than that he missed his wife Phyllis and their two children, six-year-old Tom and four-year-old Elaine. A third child was on the way. Foster was particularly proud of his son Tom, a straight-backed, tall youngster who, everyone said, would grow up to be Colony President some day.

But first, before he could return, the conference had to be attended to. By the fourth day of the conference, Foster was hoping for almost any excuse at all to break off the talks and go home.

But when the excuse came, he was not at all happy about it.

IT came in the form of a telegram, delivered to him as he sat in conference with the Prime Minister of Liberty Settlement, who was also currently the President of the two colonies. His opposite number, the Liberty defense minister, was also at the conference. The telegram was placed unobtrusively at Foster's elbow by a tiptoeing orderly—so unobtrusively, in fact, that Foster did not even notice it, and had to have the telegram called to his attention by the grinning Colony President.

"Aren't you going to open your wire, Foster?"

"Wire? What wire? Oh—this. Didn't even see it," he said, picking the envelope up and tearing it open. His eyes flicked from word to word, but so stunning was the impact of the message that it took several seconds for the meaning to soak in.

RETURN HOME AT ONCE. SPRINGFIELD AT-
TACKED BY SEA MONSTERS, MANY DEAD.

The wire was signed by Bryce Leeton, Springfield's
Settlement Leader.

Foster looked up, pale, shocked. The Liberty Prime
Minister said, "What is it, man? It must be bad news."

"Here. Read it."

They scanned the telegram.

The door of the conference room burst open; an orderly entered, shouting, "We've just received a message
from Springfield! They've been attacked by monsters!"

"We know, fool!" the Prime Minister snapped. "Keep
quiet!" He turned to Foster. "You'll leave at once, of
course?"

Foster nodded, thinking of Phyllis and Danny, of Tom
and Elaine. A frown furrowed his forehead. "Yes—yes, I'll
leave as soon as the plane is ready. But—monsters? Attacking Springfield? It can't be possible."

"They wouldn't be hoaxing you," said the Liberty Defense Minister. "It must be true."

"Yes—I suppose so." Foster shook his head. "We've had
it too good, all these years. And now—now, perhaps, we'll
pay for it." He snapped out of the strange mood that had
come over him. "There isn't much time to waste. I'll be
packed and at the airport in fifteen minutes."

The Lincoln colony had an airline consisting of two
planes, both of them obsolete jets purchased from other
colonies. There was not too much traffic between Springfield and Liberty. One plane trip was made in each direction every day.

Foster was aboard the plane when it made its takeoff for Springfield shortly after noontime. It would take four hours to cross the vast and virtually unexplored interior of the continent.

Foster stared out the window at the green wilderness below, and tried to urge the plane along mentally. He could not understand what had brought about the weird invasion. The last bulletin from the beleaguered settlement before takeoff had mentioned that the monsters had come up out of the sea, suddenly that morning, and were prowling through the outskirts of the settlement. But in seven years of life on the planet, there had been no hint of any hostile life-form.

True, there were giant beasts in the sea—enormous whalelike things, and dolphinoids, and long serpent-like creatures. But they had been observed at a distance, never close to shore. And certainly the sea-beasts had never shown any sign of wanting to invade the land. Why should they suddenly march shoreward?

He wondered how serious the attack was. The telegram had said that "many" were dead, but that could mean almost anything. In a settlement that had known peace from its very beginning, "many" deaths might mean five or six. Or hundreds.

Foster cursed the crawling jet, and, closing his eyes, tried to sleep, hoping it would make the trip seem faster. But he could not sleep. And when he opened his eyes he saw the faces of his fellow passengers, all of them Springfieldites called home from Lincoln by the sudden emergency. Their faces were grey, frightened, uncertain—and, without looking in a mirror, Foster knew that his own face must look the same way.

The plane landed at Springfield Airport shortly after sundown. Foster was out the hatch almost the moment the plane stopped rolling.

A welcoming committee was there to greet him: Settlement Leader Leeton, two or three members of the Settlement Council, and several other Springfieldites. But there were no jubilant cries of welcome. The faces of the waiters were dark, grim.

Leeton stepped forward, his firm face looking drawn and pale. "Foster—"

"I got on the plane as soon as I got the wire. What's been happening here?"

Leeton shivered. "Horrible—"

"Tell me what's happened!" Foster said sharply.

Deputy Leader Hollis said, "They came out of the sea early this morning. There were some bathers at the beach, and they were the first to see them, Mark."

"What are they like?"

"Hideous. Huge—bigger than elephants, with enormous yawning mouths and giant eyes. And flippers. They're amphibious—they move slowly on land, but so does a tank."

"Where are they now? How many monsters are there, anyway?" Foster scowled. They seemed reluctant to talk. It was an effort to get information out of them.

"They—they made a raid on the settlement this morning, and then retreated to the sea. There were hundreds of them, Mark. Hundreds."

"Are they gone?"

Hollis shook his head. "They're in the water just off shore. We've got the whole area roped off, of course, and we're setting up gun installations—"

Foster nodded. "Now tell me how many were killed today. How many of our people, and how many of the monsters."

In a quiet voice Hollis said, "We didn't get any of them, Mark. Our guns weren't good enough. And they killed thirty-three people."

"Thirty-three," Foster repeated softly. It was an enormous figure—more than one person out of every hundred in the settlement. "And—who were among the dead?"

"You'd better come inside, Mark," Settlement Leader Leeton said. "This isn't the place to talk about it, out here on the field."

"I want to know! Who's dead?"

The others exchanged sheepish glances. Foster felt a dread numbness inside him.

Hollis said, "Diane Brink was the first one—she was swimming when the monsters came. And Nola Carstairs, Paul McHenry—"

Foster said, "What about my family?"

For a moment no one spoke. Then Leeton said in a hollow voice, "Your wife and daughter were killed, Mark. So was your brother Danny. Your son escaped."

FOSTER stood quietly in the middle of the landing field, whle the sky revolved crazily around him. Leeton's words cut like edged swords into his vitals.

"Phyllis—Elaine—Danny—dead?"

"Come inside, Mark. We'll get you a drink. You need a drink."

Foster shook them off. He took an uncertain step forward. "Where's Tom?" he asked finally.

"He's at my place, Mark," Leeton said. "He wasn't touched. We have him under sedation, though."

Foster clenched and unclenched his fists. He felt cold, numb, bitter. In one blow everything he loved and cherished had been wiped out. Thirty-three people out of three thousand dead, and three of them had to be *those* three, not anyone else—

He shook his head. What was done was done. In a corpse's voice he croaked, "I think I can use that drink. Then take me to my son. And after that, we'll see what we can do about killing those monsters."

He entered the airport building. Someone produced a bottle, and then he was driven to the home of Settlement Leader Leeton. On the way, he learned more about the day's attack. After charging the group on the beach, the monsters had gone shambling into the nearest street of homes, which included Foster's own beachside home.

For perhaps an hour they had smashed through the houses, destroying everything they touched, uprooting the houses in search of people. The casualty list was drawn almost entirely from that one street.

There were no bodies to view. The victims had been eaten. Foster found that bitterest of all—that there would be no graves, no funerals for his beloved dead. They were gone, turned into monster-meat—his brother and his wife and the tiny, graceful daughter he loved so dearly.

But at least, Foster thought, there was Tom. Foster was

deeply grateful for that. He might not have been able to pull through, if Tom had died as well. But at least he still had a son—a foothold into the future. All else was gone, but he still had Tom.

Foster stood looking down at the thin, handsome form of his son. Tom twisted uneasily under the bedclothes; the sedation calmed him, but could not quiet him completely.

"Mommie," he muttered. "Mommie, look—"

Foster turned away. Behind him stood Leeton and Leeton's oldest boy, Charley, who had been the witness to the first onslaught at the beach. Charley had seen Danny die horribly.

"All right," Foster said. "Let's go down to the beach. I want to see these monsters."

"It's late, Mark," Leeton protested. "You've had a hellish day. Why don't you get some rest, and we can go to the beach in the morning—"

"In the morning they may attack again," Foster said. He felt like a mechanical man, a thing of gears and rods. "I want to go to the beach now. Will you come with me or do I go alone?"

The moon had risen by the time Foster arrived at the beach, driven by Charley Leeton. The car pulled up three hundred yards from the water's edge. Men armed with machine-guns—the settlement's heaviest arms—stood in a sparse row parallel to the shoreline, staring outward to sea.

"There they are," Leeton murmured. "Just off shore."

Foster looked. It was a horrifying sight. By the silvery moonlight he made out the rounded upper halves of dozens, scores, hundreds of enormous beasts floating in the water beyond the breakers. They seemed to be resting there, waiting for the arrival of morning before making another sally shoreward.

Foster moistened his dry lips. He indicated the ropes which formed a feeble barrier across the beach. "Do you seriously expect the ropes to hold those creatures back, Leeton?"

"Of course not, Mark. We put the ropes there to keep people back."

"Have you evacuated the shore homes?"

Leeton nodded. "We've removed everybody within a quarter mile of the ocean."

"How many men are on duty?"

"Fifteen. One man for each machine-gun we have."

"What about small arms?" Foster said. "We have rifles at the militia headquarters."

"Rifles don't do much good. They don't do any good at all unless a direct hit is scored on an eyeball. The monsters have armor-plated hides.'"

"Okay," Foster said. "I assume I'm in charge of the defense?"

"If you want to be," Leeton said. "In view of your recent tragedies—"

"Never mind that. The past is past. I'm interested now in making sure that no one *else* dies in Springfield. I'll take charge."

"As you wish, Mark."

"Is it all right if I establish headquarters at your home? I assume my place isn't livable."

"You know we have room for you, Mark. And Tom's there already. He'll want you nearby."

"Good enough. I want a round-the-clock surveillance

of the creatures. If they make the least bit of a move to-ward the shore, I want to be told about it. Even if it's in the middle of the night. We'll wait and see what they do. If they come ashore again, we'll radio Earth for a supply of tactical atomic weapons."

FOSTER returned to Leeton's place to prepare his cam-paign. The first step was to draw up a list of all the able-bodied men between seventeen and forty-five who were in Springfield. The list bore more than a thousand names. Foster ticked off the names of those who knew how to operate the fifteen machine-guns. It came to less than sev-enty people, of whom fifteen were already on duty.

"We'll change shifts out on the beach every two hours," Foster said. He handed the list to an aide. "It's ten o'clock now. Notify the first fifteen names on the list that they're to report to the beach by eleven, and tell the next fifteen to stand by for duty beginning at one o'clock. And so on right through the night."

"Yes, sir."

Foster glanced up at Robinson, his Chief of Police.

"What's the final count on the small arms, Robinson?"

"Eight hundred eighty-two, including the pistols, Mark."

"That'll have to do, then. Distribute one weapon to the heads of as many families as you can, beginning with the people closest to the beach. Make sure the man knows how to use a gun before you give it to him—we can't af-ford to waste weapons on dubs."

"Right, Mark. I'll get right to it."

As Robinson left, Foster picked up an audiocom near

his hand and said, "Hello, beach? Foster here. Who am I talking to?"

"Dick Thornton, Mark."

"Any report on the beasts?"

"Still off shore, Mark. I'll let you know the instant they make a move."

"Good enough. I'm sending fifteen men down to relieve you at eleven. We'll be running two-hour shifts on watch all through the night."

He broke the contact. Mrs. Leeton arrived with a cup of coffee. "You really should get some sleep, Mark," she said softly. "If you keep going at this pace, it's going to burn you out."

Foster managed a tense smile. "You know something? I *have* to keep going at this pace, Elsie. Because the moment I slack up, I'm going to start thinking about Phyllis and Dan and Elaine. And then I'm likely to take this gun and blow my head open. So I'm going to keep working. Thanks for the coffee."

She went away. Foster closed his eyes for a moment, rubbing his thumbs into the aching eyeballs.

Hundreds of monsters camped off shore. His family dead, his home destroyed. The colony in a state of terror.

Foster shook his head grimly. *We had it coming to us, he thought. Things were too good here. But why—why—did it have to be Phyllis and Elaine and Danny?*

HE caught some sleep between two and five in the morning, after making everybody who was still awake promise that they would rouse him the second the monsters showed any sign of renewing the attack. He slept badly, twisting and turning, troubled by dreams. At five o'clock he was shaken roughly awake by Charley Leeton.

"Huh? Who—oh, Charley. What's happening?"

"There's been a call from the beach, Mark. The monsters are starting to drift shoreward."

Foster was awake in an instant. He sat up, pushing his unruly hair into place. "When did this start?" he demanded angrily. "Have you been letting me sleep?"

"Honest, Mark! We got the call two seconds ago!"

Foster accepted that. "What did they say?"

"About half a dozen monsters have come ashore already. The rest are moving landward."

"Okay. Get the car ready. I'll go down and supervise the action myself."

Dawn was just breaking as Foster arrived at the beach. And in the violet glow of daybreak a weird scene was taking place on the beach. Nearly twenty of the monsters from the depths had come crawling out onto the beach. They moved slowly, unaccustomed to travelling on land. The moist sand gave way beneath them as they came forward, and slimy indentations were left in the sand behind them.

By the light of day the monsters looked utterly frightful. Great shambling loathsome beasts they were, their armor-plated hides encrusted with foul-smelling weeds of the sea, their massive flippers coated with the ugly blotches of fungi, their yawning mouths emitting raucous belching noises of hunger.

Foster's jaws tightened and his belly constricted as he thought of these monsters nosing their way into the wreckage of the house he had built with his own hands, towering over his wife and terrified children, opening their mouths, biting—

The monsters were moving slowly forward. The men at the machine-guns were tensely waiting for a command to fire.

Foster said, "Don't waste any ammunition. We don't have any to throw away. Hold your fire until they're within a hundred yards, and then aim for the eyeballs. It's no use trying to put slugs through those hides. It can't be done."

The monsters were twenty-five yards out of the water now, and they were pausing, looking around in a dimwitted way as though hoping to find swimmers on the beach. Finding no one, they continued their steady advance, while others still in the water pressed steadily toward the land. Foster watched themn, iron-faced. He estimated there were at least five hundred of them. If they ever came ashore all at once, the colony would be annihilated.

Slowly the creatures came forward.

"When I give the word," Foster said, "open fire. All of you at once. And go for their eyes."

Another minute passed. The monsters dragged their heavy bodies another ten yards. Foster studied them. They had nostrils as well as gills. They were clearly breathing air now, but they seemed uncomfortable on land, as though they were sea creatures that came ashore only at infrequent intervals.

Ten more yards.

"Ready," Foster said. "Get beads on their eyes. *Fire!*"

A chatter of machine-gun blasts split open the calmness of the dawn. A hail of bullets struck the nearest monster, who shook his head as though brushing away a cloud of gnats. The slugs had no effect on the monster's hide, until one penetrated an eye. A torrent of green blood came spurting out. The monster let out a fierce roar. Crouching back on its hind legs, it slapped with one of its fore flippers at the shattered eye.

"Pour it on them!" Foster screamed. "Get the other eye, now!

All down the beach, the men of the settlement were blazing away. They were far from skillful with their guns, and they were nervous to boot. But already three or four of the monsters had nothing but bloody gaping holes where their eyes had been.

The dreadful wounds did not stop the beasts. If anything, it intensified their speed. Maddened by pain, and pushed onward by those emerging from the water behind them, the giant amphibians pressed forward.

Foster looked around. Some of his men were deserting their posts. The monsters were less than a hundred yards from the gun emplacements, now, and five or six of the men had abandoned their positions in fright.

"Stay at your guns!" Foster shouted. "Damn you, don't give up now!"

The man right in front of him rose and dashed away. Cursing, Foster threw himself down at the gun emplacement. An eyeless monster, too slow-witted to know that bullets had lodged in its brain, was staggering slowly toward him. The beast was no more than eighty feet away. Finger tightening convulsively on the trigger, Foster sent slug after slug thundering into the ruined eye-sockets, hoping that one bullet at least might penetrate a vital area of the brain within that cavernous skull.

Fifty feet. The huge mouth, big enough to swallow a man in two bites, gaped. Foster lowered his aim and fired into that yawning orifice. A dull boom of pain came from the monster as the bullets cascaded against its great fleshy red tongue and soft throat.

The creature reared up on its haunches, blotting out half the sky. It clawed at the air, trying to reach the sun, it seemed. Foster fired another burst. The monster tottered. Still bellowing its anger, it took another step forward and then fell forward, landing with a groundshaking crash no more than a few yards from the smoking snout of Foster's gun.

"That one was for Phyllis," he muttered.

He looked around. Most of his improvised militia had fled. Dozens of the monsters were making their slow but steady way up the beach. Some had been wounded, but only one, Foster's target, had actually fallen.

Charley Leeton was manning the gun to Foster's right. Of the fifteen guns, only six were still in action.

"Kill, them!" Foster screamed. "They can be stopped! Look—I've got one already!"

Next to him, though, Charley Leeton was getting up. The brawny teenager was standing over him and saying, "Come on, Mark. We've got to get away."

Foster glared up angrily. "Get back to your gun and start firing."

"Don't be a madman, Mark! We can't kill them fast enough. They'll be trampling us to death any minute."

Foster looked out at the beach and bit his lower lip angrily. The boy was talking sense. He had killed one of the beasts, true enough, but at least twenty more were in the front line of advance, and only a handful of these had been seriously wounded.

And behind the front line were hundreds more. They would keep on coming long after the little band of defenders had fired its last shot.

Foster rose reluctantly. Only three men still remained at their posts.

"Coming?" Charley asked.

Foster nodded bitterly. "Cease firing!" he yelled. "We have to drop back!"

A second line of defense had been formed along the boardwalk that separated the beach from the first street of homes. Some eighty men were arrayed there under the command of Police Chief Robinson. They were armed with rifles, hand-pistols, some only with clubs.

"I watched the fight at the beach," Robinson said. "It looks like the bastards can't be stopped."

"I killed one," Foster said. "Tell your men to aim for the eyes. If we pump enough lead into them, they can be killed."

"*If,*" Robinson said meaningfully. He cupped his hands and shouted out the order.

The monsters had full possession of the beach, now. They had passed the line of machine-gun emplacements and were advancing slowly toward the settlement. Except for a few, Foster saw with revulsion, who had paused to devour the corpse of their slain fellow.

A few of the men, those armed with telescope-lens rifles, had already opened fire. Bullets whined across five hundred feet of emptiness and struck home. Most of the first wave of sea creatures had been blinded by this time, but they still moved on.

Foster watched grimly, knowing that it might prove impossible to stop the inexorable advance. The supply of ammunition might run out long before as many as a dozen of the mindless monsters had been cut down.

He turned to Robinson. "You're in charge. Keep your men gunning for the eyeballs, and have them fire into open mouths if they can. And don't rush the retreat. Drop back if the beasts get too close, but defend every inch of the land until the last minute. I'm going to send a message to Earth requesting atomics."

He drove hastily to the settlement's capitol building. The settlement was awake, now, even at this early hour. The sound of gunshots at the beach echoed everywhere.

Settlement Leader Leeton said, "What's happening at the beach? Is Charley all right?"

"Charley's fine," Foster said. "But we can't stop the monsters. They're almost impossible to kill."

"What do we do?"

"Send an order to Earth. Tell them we're under attack by hostile alien life, and we need a couple of hundred atomic grenades presto."

"It'll take weeks to requisition them!"

"They can ship them over from the Haverford colony. It won't take more than a day and a half from there. Haverford's got a stockpile of atomics."

Leeton shrugged. "I'll send the request. But you know how Earth is about issuing atomics to new colonies—"

"Never mind that now. Just ask."

When he returned to the beach, Foster discovered that

the defenders had been compelled to retreat nearly a block. More than a hundred monsters had come ashore and had passed the boardwalk barrier. Robinson reported that two more of the beasts had been killed and promptly eaten by the other monsters. But the horde surged on unstoppably, wrecking homes, smashing down trees, eating anything vegetable or animal that they could get hold of.

"Ammunition's running low," Robinson said. "Another hour and we'll have nothing left to stop them with but our gun-butts."

"Liberty Settlement is flying ammunition to us," Foster said. "Not much—they're afraid of monsters coming up out of their seas. But they're sending all they can spare. And I've radioed Earth to ship us atomic grenades immediately."

"Immediately won't be soon enough," Robinson muttered. He pointed toward the next block, where monsters were prowling through roofless homes that had long since been evacuated. "They'll smash their way through the colony from one end to the other before any grenades get here. And all we can do is keep retreating."

Foster scowled. "Get me a gun. I've got some scores to settle."

Taking a gun from a wearied defender, Foster trotted toward the front line. He crouched down next to two other rifle-wielders and drew a bead on a foraging monster.

His bullet flew squarely into a bloody eye-socket, but the beast shook its huge head irritably and smashed its flipper down on another roof. Tight-lipped, Foster fired again, but his bullet glanced harmlessly off the thick hide.

The air was rank-smelling with the stench of the sea

creatures. The great beasts seemed driven by some inner compulsion that made them oblivious to the most painful wounds. It was apparently hunger, Foster thought. They had come ashore seeking food, and they were going to keep prowling until they found it. And that meant they would destroy the entire settlement. Seven years of back-breaking work wiped out by a few hundred elephant-sized amphibians from the sea.

The hungry monsters came steadily forward as the sun rose in the sky. It was about half past eleven, and growing very hot, when the tide of battle changed.

"They're retreating!" someone yelled.

"Going back into the sea!"

It was true. As slowly as they had come, the monsters were returning to the sea. Evidently they could remain on land only for a period of a few hours.

By one o'clock they were all back where they had been during the night—clustered offshore, bobbing in the water. A few bone-picked corpses lay on the beach; altogether the Earthmen had killed seven of the monsters, at the cost of nearly three-quarters of their total supply of ammunition.

No human lives had been lost, but nearly forty homes had been smashed. The settlement was at the mercy of the hungry monsters. There was no way of stopping them—not without atomic weapons from Earth.

DURING the afternoon lull came the reply from Earth. Settlement Leader came down to the beach to deliver it to Foster, who was standing watch.

"We got the reply. The answer's no."

Foster blinked incredulously. "You're joking! How could they turn us down?"

"They say it isn't Earth policy to arm colonials with atomic weapons."

Angrily, Foster said, "But they knew we were being attacked by monsters!"

"They don't believe us," Leeton declared.

"What?" Foster bellowed.

The Settlement Leader shrugged. "You know how suspicious Earth can get. For seven years we've had no defense problems here. And all the preliminary surveys showed that this was a safe planet. Reading between the lines of their refusal, it's obvious that they think we're hoaxing them in an attempt to wangle atomic armaments."

Foster balled his fists. Phyllis and Dan and Elaine and thirty others dead, a hundred homes smashed, and Earth thought it was a hoax? "This is incredible! They can't just refuse!"

"I'm afraid they can," Leeton said sadly. "The present Earth government is tremendously leery of giving colonists atomic arms, ever since the revolution on Brewster VII where the colonists declared themselves independent and not subject to Earth regulations.

"They won't let us have grenades or any other big weapons unless it's a certified emergency, which means an Earth Commissioner has to come here to investigate and approve our application. And that means—"

"I know what that means," Foster said bitterly. "Six months of red tape before we get anywhere. So we'll have to fight off the monsters by ourselves."

"We can do it," Leeton said.

Foster stared impotently at the older man. "Don't talk like a politician. We *can't* do it."

"Eh?"

"I said we're licked, Leeton. We used up almost all our ammunition to kill seven monsters. Seven out of hundreds! And the only reason we're not running for the hills now is that the creatures decided to be nice and go back into the water for a while when the weather got hot. We're beaten, can't you see? We'll use up our remaining ammunition the next time they come ashore, and what then?

"We'll have to flee inland while they stomp all over our settlement. We'll have to start all over from scratch, Leeton. And until we have weapons we'll be at the mercy of—"

"Foster! Snap out of it! You're talking like a madman!"

Foster shook his head tiredly. Leeton gripped his shoulders.

Foster smiled. "I'm sorry, I guess. I shouldn't be talking this way. I'm so tired—"

"Lie down. Take a rest."

"I can't. Don't you see, I can't? I can't rest until we've destroyed these monsters."

"But you just said we were beaten."

"Maybe we are. But that doesn't mean we're giving up. I'll go on fighting them," Foster said. "Even if I have to use a slingshot to do it."

The monsters remained quiescent during the rest of the afternoon and during the night. They stayed offshore, mostly submerged, resting after their invasion. It seemed pretty clear to Foster now that the monsters could not breathe air for more than four or five hours, and then had to return to the sea.

But the knowledge was small consolation. Even if they came out only for five hours a day, they could soon wreck every building in the settlement.

Foster met with the other high-ranking officials of the settlement that evening. Roy Theodore, a biologist, said, "I think I know what makes those monsters tick."

All eyes turned toward him. Theodore went on, "I've been doing some serious thinking about them. And my conclusion is this: they're sea creatures that turn amphibious once every decade or so. They come up on shore to lay their eggs, and then they return to the sea."

Foster frowned. "Do you have any basis for this idea, Roy?"

"Just analogy and common sense. We've been here seven years and we've never had any trouble like this before. So they don't come ashore any oftener than every seven years, and maybe a lot less often than that.

"On Earth there are insects that have a seventeen-year life-cycle—they stay buried underground most of their lives, and then in the seventeenth year they come to the surface in immense swarms, eat everything in sight, lay their eggs, and die. And there are some sea-dwelling turtles that have to come to shore to reproduce.

"So I figure we've got something like that on our hands now—animals with a periodic life-cycle; they spend most of their time in the water, and come up to lay eggs."

"If that's true, it's no wonder the survey teams never noticed them," Leeton said. "And we escaped all these years, but this is the year of reckoning."

The meeting broke up soon afterward. Foster was exhausted; he went to bed after leaving instructions to be awakened as soon as the monsters showed signs of leaving the sea again, no matter what time it might be.

Tired as he was, he lay awake a long time before sleep would come. The fact that the people he most loved were dead, all but Tom, was just beginning to soak into the deepest core of his being. He felt a numb emptiness in his breast, a tingling sense of loss.

It was strange to think that only a few days before he had been living in paradise—and now he inhabited a monster-infested hell. The giant sea creatures, he thought, were like a slow-ignition bomb. Lying in wait for years, decades perhaps, and then, with their spawning time upon them, crawling loathsomely up on shore to devour and kill and bring destruction to the unsuspecting settlement.

His mind retraced the battle at the beach, over and over again. Bravery and heroism meant nothing down there. It was impossible to check the slow advance of the sea creatures. And so, Foster thought, the settlement would be crushed. It was inevitable.

But we won't go down without a fight, he promised himself silently. *Not without one hell of a last-ditch fight.*

SHORTLY before dawn, the monsters left the water again. Dick Thornton of the beach patrol sent word to young Charley Leeton, who woke Foster up and told him the news.

"They're starting to crawl again, Mark. The first few just came ashore."

During the night, at Foster's orders, men had taken the colony's bulldozers and derricks down to the beach and had constructed an enormous trench running parallel to the shoreline, twenty feet deep and a thousand yards long. Foster asked, "Have they reached the trench yet?"

"Not yet," Leeton said.

"Good. Let's get down there."

The beach was a scene of activity, even though the first rays of the sun still had not broken through the night's haze when Foster and Leeton arrived. Nearly a hundred of the colonists had been on all-night duty, furiously constructing the giant trench.

Foster squinted toward the water. A dozen monsters had come ashore already, and were making their way through the upturned sand that bordered the trench. Foster glanced around.

"How many blowtorches do we have?"

"Two dozen, Mark," someone answered.

"Let's have one of them over here!"

A blowtorch was tossed to him. Foster hefted it, switched it on, and let the flame shoot out. "Okay," he called. "The blowtorch has an effective range of about fifteen feet. I want two dozen men who aren't afraid of getting within fifteen feet of those creatures."

Almost fifty volunteered. Foster handed out the torches until there were no more, and promised the rest that they would have their turn.

They waited. Slowly, steadily, the monsters crawled ashore. They didn't seem bothered by the presence of the trench. They crawled down one sloping side, stood puzzled in the bottom for a moment, and started to climb out on the shoreward side.

But climbing out was not so easy. The sand gave way

under their weight. They clawed at the shifting sand with their flippers, but made no headway.

Foster led his two dozen blowtorch men to the very rim of the ditch. Fifteen monsters were in the trench already, and more were crawling in from the rear, despite the plight of those who had become stranded already.

"Spread out," Foster called. "Every man above one of the beasts. And let them have it!"

He switched on his torch and aimed it down into the trench. Startled by the sudden warmth and light, the nearest monster looked up, and Foster gave it a blast of flame square in the face.

The monster roared. The smell of roasted flesh rose from the pit. Foster saw the thick hide of the creature blister and bubble. He aimed his torch at one dish-sized eye and held it there until the eye sizzled and boiled in its socket. The monster rose up on its haunches and swatted wildly about in the air trying to find Foster, while he went to work on the other eye.

Glancing down the row, Foster saw his other men grimly at work blazing away at the monsters in the trench. The stink of burned flesh became almost intolerable. The cries of agonized creatures filled the air. But still they came into the trench from the rear, pushing forward, milling about as if impatient to share the fate of the monsters in front.

The flamethrowers were taking effect. Their eyes charred, their nostrils blistered, their mouths enflamed, the first monsters were screaming in terrible pain, rolling over in the sand and attempting to rub away the agony with their fore flippers. Foster smiled coldly as he saw the monster die horribly before his eyes. "That one was for Elaine," he muttered. "And the next one is for Danny—"

But an unexpected turn of events put an end to the slaughter session. The first monsters to enter the trench were dead or dying—but their massive bodies lay on the floor of the trench, affording footholds for those other monsters who came after them! And the monsters were pouring from the sea in an endless horde.

The colonists kept up the barrage as long as they dared. But Foster realized bleakly that it was no use. The monsters were climbing over the bodies of the fallen ones, were nearly at the top of the trench now! A giant flipper came within a foot of smashing Foster's skull. He dropped back, and, a moment later, several monsters came climbing out of the pit!

His men gave ground. There was nothing else they could do. Slowly but surely the monsters pressed forward, and the colonists had to retreat.

They did terrible damage with their flamethrowers even as they moved back. On land, the monsters were slow-footed and could be attacked without too much difficulty. But there were risks. Sam Hawkes, whose family had been wiped out like Foster's in the first surprise attack, darted daringly close to an oncoming creature and thrust his blowtorch virtually in the beast's mouth. But he failed to jump back in time. In a paroxysm of pain the animal reared high and swatted Hawkes with a flipper.

The force of the blow threw him forty feet. He fell and lay still. An instant later, another monster had bitten him in half.

BY noon, the monsters had once again returned to the sea. But not before they had wandered through several more blocks of the settlement, damaging some fifty additional homes. Foster and his men had used up almost all of the ammunition supply, including the new ammunition received during the day from Liberty.

Foster stared bleakly at Settlement Leader Leeton. "I don't know what we try now," he said tiredly. "The blow-torch-and-trench idea was a good one, but I didn't figure on having them climb over the dead ones."

"You killed more than twenty of the creatures, though," Leeton pointed out.

"And they destroyed fifty homes. At this rate the whole settlement will be flat by the end of the week. It's hopeless."

"Why do the creatures do all this damage?" Leeton wanted to know.

Roy Theodore said, "They're hungry. That's all there is to it. Bodies so large need tremendous amounts of food to keep them going. On shore they eat everything that's edible—trees, shrubs, animals, human beings if they can catch them. That first morning they broke open a row of houses and found them full of food. Can you blame them for continuing to smash into houses, even though they've been evacuated?"

"But how long will this go on?"

"Until they get tired of coming ashore," Theodore said. "Let's just hope that's soon."

Foster looked at the floor. All he needed was a few dozen atomic grenades; he visualized a bloody scene in which he hurled the grenades into the cluster of monsters just off the shore, and watched them go skyward in a thousand dripping chunks. But there was no way to get grenades. And no more ammunition.

The best they could hope to do was to repeat the blowtorch attack every day, hoping perhaps to discourage the creatures from making further raids on shore.

SHORTLY after sundown that night, word came excitedly from the beach. The monsters were leaving the sea again! For the second time that day, they were coming ashore.

Foster hurried to the beach. The man in command of the patrol was Deputy Leader Hollis, who said, "They came out a little while ago. But they don't seem to be attacking this time. They're settling down near the shore."

"Rig up floodlights," Foster ordered. "I want to see what they're doing."

Floodlights were placed along the boardwalk. Foster stared down at the beach.

The great creatures from the sea were remaining within a twenty-yard strip adjoining the edge of the beach. They were squatting down on the moist sand, making booming sounds and flapping their flippers agitatedly.

"Should we get the blowtorches?" Hollis asked.

Foster shook his head. "I don't think we'll need them this time."

"You don't expect an attack?"

"No," Foster said. "Let's just sit here and wait. I think the monsters are laying eggs."

"Laying eggs!"

"It certainly looks that way, doesn't it?"

The creatures remained squatting in the sand for more

than an hour. They lined the entire shore for as far as a mile in each direction, squatting at a distance from each other as if depositing something in the wet sand just at the edge of the water.

Foster waited. The creatures had a silvery gleam under the floodlights and the partially full moon. Their booming sounds echoed and re-echoed from the sea.

"Look," Charley Leeton cried. suddenly. "One of them's going back into the water.'"

"More are doing it over there," Hollis said.

Foster nodded, biding his time. One by one, the monsters were finishing their egg-laying and returning to the sea. Apparently they were finished with their short cycles as air-breathing land animals. Only a few days, Foster thought, and they were gone. He sighed, thinking of his dead loved ones, feeling the bitter pain in his heart, as he watched the immense creatures waddle one by one into the sea.

This time they did not cluster in the shallow water. As each completed its egg-laying it swam away into the distance until it could be seen no more.

It was nearly midnight before the last of the creatures had enterd the water.

"Let's go down to the shore and take a look," Foster said.

The foul stench of the creatures was everywhere, but not one was visible. Either they were hiding submerged, or, what was much more likely, they had simply gone back to their deep-sea haunts.

The sand was greatly disturbed. Enormous flapper-marks showed signs of where each of the monsters had been squatting.

"Get that flashlight over here," Foster called. When the light came, he poked in the matted-down sand with a driftwood stick until he struck something solid. Kneeling, he clawed away the sand while the others gathered round him curiously.

A foot below the surface of the sand, he found what he had expected to find.

"Eggs. The stupid beasts laid their eggs and went away. Here, take a look."

He scooped into the sand and pulled out something evil-smelling and leathery-looking, about a foot in diameter. The grey skin of the egg was covered with coarse, ugly knobs and projections.

"Hand that knife here," Foster said.

He jabbed it into the huge egg. Greenish fluid gushed out. Steadying the egg with one hand, he hacked at the tough outer layer of it with the knife, until he was able to peel the skin of the egg back.

"Pretty, isn't it?" he asked, looking up at the others.

A miniature monster lay curled within the egg, its eyes closed, its flappers coiled together.

Smiling coldly, Foster straightened up and brought his booted foot down on the embryo. It squished beneath his foot, and fluid trickled off into the sand.

Foster cupped his hands. "Listen to me, everyone! Go back to town—get everyone you, know! I want the whole settlement out here. We're going to prowl the shore and dig up every one of these filthy eggs, and stamp the life out of them!"

Hollis said quietly, "Mark, it's after midnight. Why not wait till morning, when we'll be able to see better—"

Foster turned on him fiercely. "We don't know how fast these things hatch. Maybe by morning they'll be crawling around alive. I want to find them now—tonight—everyone of them." He gestured to the watchers. "Get everyone!"

The patrol dispersed. Foster looked out to sea, and there was a smile of triumph on his face. The monsters had lost, after all, and the weak, pitiful human beings would be victorious. No grenades from Earth would be needed, after all. If the monsters had to come to shore to lay their eggs, and if after every egg-laying the colonists dug up every single egg—why, very shortly there would be no monsters at all. Just as mammals the size of rats had destroyed the race of dinosaurs by gnawing at their eggs, Foster thought, so, too, will we vanquish the beasts that plague us.

No victory, though, would be sweet enough to wipe out the pain of his great loss. But Tom was alive, at least. Perhaps by the time Tom was a man, Foster thought, the monsters would be extinct and the shores of the colony would be safe for all.

He looked seaward and shook his fist bitterly at the giant dumb creatures that had shattered his life. Then, turning, he began fiercely to dig for eggs, with a cold, vindictive smile of victory on his face.

THE END

ACKNOWLEDGMENTS

"Introduction" by Robert Silverberg, copyright © 2012 by Agberg, Ltd.

"Catch 'Em All Alive" by Robert Silverberg, copyright © 1956 by Headline Publications, Inc., copyright © 1984 by Agberg, Ltd. Reprinted by permission of the author and Agberg, Ltd.

"Who Am I?" by Henry Slesar, copyright © 1956 by Headline Publications, Inc., copyright © 1984 by Henry Slesar. Reprinted by permission of Manuela Slesar on behalf of the Estate of Henry Slesar.

"Every Day is Christmas" by James E. Gunn, copyright © 1957 by Headline Publications, Inc., copyright © 1984 by James E. Gunn. Reprinted by permission of the author.

"I'll Take Over" by A. Bertram Chandler, copyright © 1957 by A. Bertram Chandler, renewed 1985. Reprinted by permission of the Estate of A. Bertram Chandler and the Estate's agents, Jabberwocky Literary Agency, Inc., P.O. Box 4558, Sunnyside, NY 11104-0558.

"A Place Beyond the Stars" by Tom Godwin, copyright © 1959 by Headline Publications, Inc., copyright © 1987 by the Estate of Tom Godwin. Reprinted by permission of Barry N. Malzberg.

"The Loathsome Beasts" by Dan Malcolm, copyright © 1959 by Headline Publications, Inc., copyright © 1987 by Agberg, Ltd. Reprinted by permission of Robert Silverberg, the author, and Agberg, Ltd.

Interior artwork by Frank Kelly Freas, copyright © 1956 by Headline Publications, Inc., copyright © 2012 by Laura Brodian Freas. Reproduced by permission of Laura Brodian Freas.

Interior artwork by Ed Emshwiller, copyright © 1956, 1957, 1958, 1959 by Headline Publications, Inc., copyright © 2012 by Carol Emshwiller. Reproduced by permission of Carol Emshwiller.

Interior artwork by Paul Orban, copyright © 1957, 1958 by Headline Publications, Inc.

Interior artwork by William Bowman, copyright © 1959 by Headline Publications, Inc.

FIRST EDITION
2012

TALES FROM SUPER-SCIENCE FICTION was published by Haffner Press, 5005 Crooks Road, Suite 35, Royal Oak, Michigan 48073-1239.

One thousand trade copies have been printed on 55# Booktext Natural from Adobe Bembo and Gill Sans. The printing was done by Edwards Brothers of Ann Arbor, Michigan. The binding cloth is Ecological Fibers Brillianta 4086.